THE TORTOISE

Emma Williams

Prosimian Press

FOR JASPER

Praise for The Tortoise

Impressive. I loved the eccentric but believable characters; it made me want to move to Marlow.

Funny....... poignant....... unexpected.

A fabulous mix of dark humour, engaging characters and a twisty plot.

1

It was a bright cold night in January and the clocks were striking twelve, smiled Clara to herself. The book she had been reading, Nineteen-eighty-four, had slipped from her lap to be replaced by George, her Bengal cat, whose motorbike purr idled on her chest. What a delightful way to see in the New Year, no obligations, no effort, no stress; start as you mean to go on old girl.

As a rule, she did not drink and the bottle of Tullamore Dew on the side table, a present for her sixtieth in June, had remained relatively intact. At nine o'clock she had raised a glass to Phineas to mark the arrival of 2019 in Madagascar, later a swig to toast Padraig, then another to forget him. She was feeling the effects. Well, why not; she refilled her glass and listened to the last chime give way to silence. How many people were appreciating the stillness of the brand new year? Something about the depth of this tranquillity reminded her of the minutes following a death. A sense of being fully present, something she felt it her duty to be when she shared those moments. God, now she remembered why she didn't drink; it made her maudlin.

She established a gentle rhythm of the rocking chair, an ironic retirement gift from her colleagues, and rested her eyes. As the dust started to settle on her long days of nothingness something malevolent had stirred. Here it was again, creeping in unbidden, fleeting but disconcerting. She allowed herself to face the accompanying thought that wormed up from deep within her medial prefrontal cortex. It spoke directly to her, schizophrenia style.

You have wasted your life.

A hammering on the door.

'Jesus, what the hell?' She tilted forward with a start sending George skittering across the polished oak floorboards.

She struggled to her feet, flicked on the hall light and opened the door.

'Happy New Year Doc!' The man blew a party horn in her face. 'Care to join us?'

Tim, her next-door neighbour - dressed in a ridiculous elf outfit complete with pointed ears – gestured to the straggle of neighbours now gathering in the close. She could just make out the fur-clad figure of his wife, never could remember her name, knocking on the door opposite. Fortunately for them they appeared to be out or had had the presence of mind to pretend. Unable to concoct a reasonable excuse Clara managed a weak smile. 'Certainly, I'll just get my coat.'

Well I won't be long, she reassured herself as she wrapped a scarf around her neck and buttoned her old woollen coat. George appeared from behind the settee and protested loudly.

'I know, I'm sorry old thing,' she bent to stroke him, 'bloody tiresome humans.'

From his basket in front of the wood-burner Blue opened one eye and closed it, being a whippet of a certain age, he generally chose comfort over exercise.

A dozen or so people milled around the recently tarmacked frontage of number five upon which a trestle table had been erected. Over the years Clara had observed the shielding privets of Penns Lane give way to low box hedging to be succeeded, following a virulent infestation of blight, by the American-style picket fencing that now demarcated the boundaries. She mourned the gradual loss of the cheerful flower beds as they were replaced first by squares of lawn and then by sterile paving to accommodate the proliferation of cars. Her medley of flowering shrubs and hardy perennials was the only surviving front garden.

The annoying couple from number one, adorned in garlands of flashing Christmas lights, ladled hot mulled wine from the Le Creuset on the rickety table; it was a health and safety nightmare. She really did not want to be attending to burn injuries at this time of night. Children, who appeared to Clara to be far too young to be awake, ran up and down the pavement wielding sparklers, giddy with the excitement of transgression.

She listened to the wailing of an ambulance speeding to its first call of the year. Clara weighed the odds in favour of a suicide. Sadly, she had been in general practice long enough to have noticed the pattern for herself. Those who thought themselves burdensome, socially isolated, disconnected, found that they felt the same on the first day of the year as they had on the three-hundred-and-sixty-fifth. As the clock ticked round, they still hated their job, their partner had not returned, they remained broken. She supposed that the realisation that the arbitrary marking of time made no difference was sufficient to load the dice.

Tim's wife, Sally was it? handed her a glass of mulled wine. A drink that she thoroughly disliked although the rising aroma of orange, ginger and cloves was strangely comforting.

'How was your Christmas?' with years of practice Clara managed to make her inquiry ring with genuine interest.

'Chaotic as usual, Tim's folks came over, and his sister and her family, and my brother; six adults, five children for Christmas day.'

Clara inhaled the scent of the hot wine and attempted a smile. The raucous intrusion through the shared wall of their Victorian townhouses had been the deciding factor in her three-hour drive to the nursing home, although she knew she would not be recognised or acknowledged.

'Did you go away? We didn't see you at all?' chirped Sally.

'Just for a couple of days, to see my mother.' She noticed a flicker of surprise cross Sally's face before endeavouring to conceal it, she evidently thought Clara far too old to have a living ancestor. She couldn't think what else to say so added, 'she likes jigsaw puzzles.'

A strained silence ensued. They listened to the muffled banging of fireworks. At least none of those gathered had thought to launch a display of their own, small mercies.

'Are you enjoying your retirement doctor?'

God, how many times would people revert to this topic?

'Oh yes, people told me I'd be bored but I rather like being idle.'

She didn't add that it was a joy to no longer have to care for the sick, the slightly sick and the not sick at all.

'Do you have any plans?' asked Sally, apparently warming to the topic.

'I made a list of all the things I could do when I retired. Actually, I haven't even looked at the list.' In a rare moment of self-disclosure - likely brought on by the whiskey - she added, 'I'm cultivating solitude, thinking about breaks in isolated cottages, going on silent retreats, that sort of thing. I need an antidote.'

Clara lurched violently forward, her mulled wine tracing a slow-motion trajectory onto Sally's fur-coat. A small child, now lying prostrate at her feet, looked up in astonishment before releasing a high-pitched wail. Clara registered a deep gash on his forehead and instinctively bent to stem the flow, as she applied pressure the wound came away; it was a cinnamon stick. She checked the small limbs for breaks and sprains.

'Just a grazed hand,' she told a woman wearing reindeer antlers who was now hoisting the child roughly to his feet.

'I told you not to run, what did I tell you?'

Clara clenched her jaw, she was not a fan of rhetorical questions, especially when aimed at young children.

Sally pressed a paper napkin to her mink and bemoaned the cost of specialist dry cleaning, a diatribe that appeared to be lost on the antlered mother. The commotion was now attracting the attention of the others.

'No harm done,' announced Clara, a verdict that drew a scowl from both women.

'Just wine and whine,' she muttered to herself as she turned towards her house.

Tim grabbed her arm. 'Don't disappear just yet Doc, we're about to sing Auld Lang Syne.'

Despite her protestations he manoeuvred her into the throng that was now attempting to form a circle; the effects of alcohol, combined with sudden fresh air, was rendering the task a challenge. The reluctant relinquishing of wine glasses was followed by general confusion regarding the crossing of arms and which hand to hold. Clara found herself sandwiched between Tim and an older man who apparently lived at number twelve and had a three-legged terrier called Jack.

At last the circle was complete and they began to sing, some starting at the first verse, others at the chorus. A blaring police siren supplied an incongruous soundtrack. Several people were intent on moving their arms up and down, while a minority tried to guide the circle in and out Hokey-Cokey style. Adolescent boys kicked their legs, regardless of their neighbours' shins. Thankfully no-one could get beyond the second verse and Clara was not going to prolong the fiasco.

Amidst the hugging, cheering and happy new yearing, she

made her escape. Blue came to greet her, wagging his skinny tail. She breathed a long sigh of relief as she closed her front door.

The blue-light urgency turned out to be needless, the woman was beyond medical assistance; she had been dead since Christmas Day.

2

Jo was enjoying the party despite Andrea's no-show. She crossed her legs to display her new high-heels to best effect and numbed the pain in her feet with another glass of champagne. They usually worked as a team but she was garnering plenty of male attention flying solo. Mission accomplished she moved away from the man with halitosis who had refilled her glass whilst looking down her dress. By the time Big Ben rang out from the radio and the music was turned back up, Jo had forgiven Andrea for not replying to any of her texts, calls, WhatsApp or Facebook messages and for not bloody turning up. She recalled last New Year and the optimism with which they had both vowed to make 2018 their best year ever. As it turned out it was pretty much one of their worst. It was good to see the back of this cursed year.

Jo tottered outside with her drink and lit a cigarette; New Year resolutions could start tomorrow. She rooted through her fake-snake handbag for her iPhone and called Andrea again. She let it ring out. Jesus, she could be dead in a bloody ditch. She shut it off and listened out for distant sounds; a technique championed by Dr Aaron Bayliss-Cooper MD in *Get Out Of Your Mind*. She registered a volley of fireworks and the wail of an ambulance.

Not helpful.

She sat on the wall, swallowed her champagne and stubbed out her cigarette. She told herself that she was being silly; Andrea must have had a better offer. Wait 'til I see her. Her thoughts turned to James, an estate agent with a Range Rover and a roguish smile, who would be ready to hit the dance floor. She checked her hair in her diamante compact; switching shades to ultra-platinum blonde had been an excellent call. She pinged the gold rim of her champagne flute, it gave a pleasing ring, she wrapped it in her silk scarf, put it in the bottom of her handbag and went back to join the festivities.

Jo awoke to the sound of sawing wood; who the hell was doing DIY on New Year's Day? Her head was an anvil, she turned over, pressed her finger to her ear and slept again. The noise of an argument in the street finally spurred her to disentangle herself from the duvet and crawl numbly from her bed. She was annoyed at herself for wasting the first day of 2019. The morning had passed in a blur of headaches, nausea, and semi-consciousness. She was not going to drink champagne ever again. She could not recall what had happened to James but at least he wasn't here. She peeped through the curtain with aching eyes; a neighbour was scraping ice from his car as a woman in a mint-green tracksuit screamed at him. She checked her phone, Christ, still nothing from Andrea. Her head was pounding. She made it to the kitchen and scanned the fridge: half a pot of natural yoghurt, a slimy bag of spinach, an egg. No milk. She felt too weak to get dressed, or to make toast, or to decide what to do next. She stood by the fridge for a while. The doorbell pierced the silence. She stood by the door and hesitated, vaguely aware of her dishevelled appearance. A loud rapping made her fling the door wide to reveal a delivery man, his arm raised mid-knock.

'Special delivery, sign here,' he handed her a box and an electronic machine.

She took both and stood helpless.

'Perhaps you could put the box down?'

She put it down. She looked at the machine. She signed her name. She stood at the open door and breathed cold air. He drove away. She watched the exhaust cloud hanging in the air. Her scrawny birch was crisp with frost; the only survivor of the gaggle of saplings planted in the development. The skinny Indian woman opposite waved cheerfully. Jo closed the door and carried the box into the living room. Her name and address were written in Andrea's unmistakable cursive.

How odd.

She grabbed a nail file and slit the tape to reveal a jumble of parcels, each wrapped in tissue paper. She picked out the red cashmere scarf and inhaled Andrea's scent. She rummaged further;

no envelope, no card, no note. She checked the outside, nothing. She unwrapped the other packages: Andrea's Tiffany bracelet, her salmon-pink handbag, her fake Rolex, her leather-bound *British Trust for Ornithology Guide to the Birds of Britain and Ireland.* She flicked through the book, some of the birds had been highlighted with orange marker.

What on earth could this mean? She lit a cigarette and poured herself a stiff hair of the dog. It bristled, she downed another. She recalled a conversation they had had about the things that they would save if their house was on fire. She of course had chosen her Prada handbag and sable jacket; both gifts from generous but hapless boyfriends. Andrea had chosen her bird books and Darwin, her beloved tortoise, she was so silly.

Jesus Christ. She dressed hurriedly and grabbed her car keys.

Frozen swirls encrusted the windscreen of her 2008 Fiat Punto, she scratched out a porthole with her credit card. The car had formed part of her divorce settlement, she remained wedded to it despite its capricious nature. She ratcheted up the heater, the prematurely applied wipers screeching across the glass. From the radio high-octane presenters seemed inexplicably hyped about the New Year's honours list. Jarrod Soames-Grayling, that Pro-Brexit guy that Andrea hated, had received one. The chat segued into *I Predict A Riot.* She turned it off and sped down the deserted streets, beneath a darkening sky. She screeched into the nineteen-seventies estate and parked next to Andrea's battered Clio. At least she was in. But that feeling again. Dread. Even from the road Andrea's flat gave off an air of neglect, she had stopped inviting Jo over, preferring to meet in town or to invite herself for lunch. She scanned the second-floor windows, third from the left, it was wide open, the curtains billowing in the icy wind. What the hell? She took the concrete steps two at a time arriving breathless outside 22A and held her finger on the doorbell.

A stocky officer with pigeon eyes opened the door.

'She's dead, isn't she?'

'And you are Madam?'

'Jo Burns-Whyte, Andrea's best friend,' she pushed past him into the hallway where an older, dark-suited man appeared from the kitchen.

'I'll see to it Constable Beech.' He had a kind tone that made her feel that she was going to cry. 'Please come through to the living room.'

She followed him in a daze and sat on her usual armchair by the window. The table lamp cast a mournful glow. It was freezing.

He took the seat closest to her and cleared his throat. 'I'm Detective Inspector John Appleton, I'm afraid I have some distressing news. Your friend was found last night. I'm afraid she had been dead for some time.'

'I knew something was wrong, I've been phoning, I knew something bad had happened,' she trailed off. 'Was she attacked?'

'Why do you say that?'

'Because you're here.'

'I'm the investigating officer, we don't yet know if a crime has been committed.'

The twinkling Christmas tree lights were an affront. 'Jesus, can't you turn those things off?'

DI Appleton rose calmly and disconnected the plug.

'What are you actually doing here? Where's Andrea? What the hell happened?' She wished she wasn't hung over, it was all so surreal, she thought she might faint. The medicinal shots of bourbon were backfiring.

'I'm the investigating officer,' he repeated. 'Andrea is in the hospital mortuary, I'm afraid we will have to wait for a post-mortem to determine the cause of death.'

'Oh my God. Oh my God. I can't believe it. How did she die?'

'I'm afraid I'm not at liberty to give any details at the moment. We're conducting preliminary inquiries, nothing has been ruled in or out just yet,' he smoothed his trouser leg. 'May I ask you a few questions?'

'Yes, I suppose so,' her voice a hundred miles away. She wondered where Andrea died. She imagined her sprawled on the carpet in a crime scene pose, white chalk marking her outline.

'Would you like a drink or anything?'

'A brandy please.'

'Sorry, I meant a cup of tea or coffee, although I'm sure we could all do with a brandy.'

She looked at his shoes, soft Italian leather, expensive. 'Oh, of course, no I'm fine.'

'Jo, when was the last time you had any contact with Ms Gibbons?'

Andrea, a glass in hand, laughing in her living room, wearing the jumper with the little dancing robins and that red velvet skirt.

'Christmas Eve, she came over, brought cup-cakes, we exchanged presents.'

'Did she appear to be worried about anything or say anything unusual?'

Jo was aware of her hands shaking. She looked at the side of his face, he radiated a sense of quiet confidence. It calmed her. She watched him write in his notebook, he was serious and attentive. Instinctively she looked for a wedding ring. Sometimes she appalled herself.

'Ms Burns-Whyte? Anything out of the usual?'

'No. She was going to spend Christmas day with her brother in Wales. Ed.' She had been disappointed that she had not been asked, despite all her hints. 'Oh my God, does Ed know?'

'Ms Gibbons' brother has been informed, yes. He had been worried when she didn't turn up or answer his calls. Unfortunately, he didn't think to call the police.'

Bloody hell, what an idiot. Mind you she hadn't either, all those unanswered calls.

'Did they get on well?'

'Well, he struggles with company; she was just staying overnight.'

'Had you any plans?'

'No, I spent Christmas alone.'

'Sorry, I meant to see Andrea.'

'We were going to meet up at a New Year's Eve party, but she didn't turn up. Obviously,' she paused. The room felt empty, needles dropped from the Christmas tree, joining the ones she imagined Andrea had watched fall.

'Did she have any other close relatives that you know of?'

'I don't think so; her parents are dead. Natural causes,' she added and then felt foolish. She could smell his sandalwood aftershave. Perhaps he could detect the alcohol on her breath. She was still clutching her car keys, she slid them into her coat pocket and pulled up her collar against the draught.

He rose and closed the window, then opened it one notch. 'Did she have any plans for a holiday?'

'No, we were thinking about Greece but not until the summer. Why are you asking me about holidays?' He was getting a bit irritating.

'Just trying to get a full picture.'

She registered the empty space where the tortoise-house had stood. Where the hell was Darwin?

'She's been burgled. She had a tortoise, in a big cage thing,' she waved her finger at the gap. She watched him look at the rectangular impression on the carpet.

'Do you know if it was here on Christmas Eve?'

'Yes, definitely, she'd brought him a little present. She is hilarious.' She was aware of using the present tense and did not correct herself.

'I see.'

There was a long pause, they listened to a baby crying upstairs. 'Are you alright to continue?'

'Yes.' The nausea was returning but somehow she didn't mind.

'I'm sorry to have to ask this but can you think of any reason Andrea might have had to take her own life?'

'Absolutely not. No way. She just wasn't that sort of person.'

'All sorts of people do I'm afraid.'

'No, not Andrea, she was very positive.'

The toilet flushed. The thought of that rookie officer peeing into her bowl suddenly made her furious.

'Did Ms Gibbons have a partner? Boyfriend? Girlfriend?'

'What?' she snapped.

'We can leave this for another time if you prefer, I know this has been a huge shock.'

His look of genuine concern brought a tear.

'No. She has had in the past, boyfriends I mean, but not recently.'

'Can you think of anyone who might have wanted to harm her?'

'No, not a single person. She was divorced. Leon Maynard. You can rule him out as a suspect on account of him being dead.'

DI Appleton scribbled something that seemed to end with an exclamation mark and closed his notebook. The room was freezing but she did not want to leave. The owl shaped clock ticked from the mantelpiece, she had bought it for Andrea's birthday,

Andrea's last birthday.

'I understand she was a school teacher?'

'She used to be; she lost her job. It was all ridiculous, a Facebook post about a worm or something,' she trailed off.

'Thank you, Ms Burns-Whyte, you've been very helpful. Could I take your details in case we need to contact you?'

She recited her phone number and watched him tap it into his phone, he passed her his card. She felt Andrea's absence, a little part of her had died. The best bit.

'If there's anything else that comes to mind please do call me. Would you like Constable Beech to take you home?'

'No, I have my car, I'll be alright,' reluctantly she stood to leave, she felt unsteady.

She glanced into the kitchen; the rookie was standing by the boiling kettle eating a chocolate digestive. One of Andrea's.

She closed the front-door behind her and burst into tears.

3

Detective Inspector John Appleton had not slept well. Potential murders always raked up the dormant embers of his first case. The five words the accused whispered to him as he walked free Bad girls make good victims. Would he ever be free of them? Tracey Taylor, a young woman with a string of willing-to-testify gormless exes, a neck tattoo and cocaine in her system. Strangled in her own bed. The jury needed little persuasion that her death was accidental, a sex-game gone wrong. He had almost quit his career before it had started.

He was late for his meeting with DCI Wallace. He felt her watching him from her first-floor window as he stepped into the onslaught. He imagined her smirking as he bolted across the tarmac, hail ricocheting from the briefcase he held above his head. He took a moment outside her door, knocked and entered bringing with him the chill of the day. She sat impassive behind the neatly arranged desk. A straight-backed officer handed her a set of files and awaited instruction like an eager puppy.

'Two coffees, milk, no sugar, biscuits if you can find any.'

'Ma'am.' He turned on his heel and left to his task with unaccountable pride.

The coat hooks taken, John draped his wet coat on the back of his chair and sat in front of the desk. The date block made him wince; it had not been updated since Monday.

'How is Matt?' She examined the files not looking up.

'Good thank you Ma'am.'

He always felt uneasy at her apparently friendly enquiries, treading the shifting sands of their relationship ran the risk of falling into a sinkhole. They had never socialised, it seemed too formal to ask after Mr Wallace, too casual to use his first name. He decided to say nothing.

'And the boys?' She raised an eyebrow.

It was not the content but the intonation that was offensive, the suggestion of concern for their moral welfare. She was shrewd, staying just the right side of overt homophobia for any tribunal to find no case to answer and to brand him as over-sensitive. Well, what can you expect with his type?

'The boys are good, thank you Ma'am.' He opened his notebook.

'What would you like to start with?' Her mouth a draw-string purse.

'The death in Marlow. Andrea Gibbons, female late-thirties, found by a neighbour at 11.45 pm New Year's Eve. She had been dead for six days. Fortunately, the boiler was broken so the body was not deteriorated.'

The phone rang, she picked up the receiver and replaced it. 'What did the coroner find?'

'Post-mortem ruled out natural causes, she was fit and healthy. No evidence of trauma except bruising to the back of the head consistent with a fall.' He rifled through the papers and took out a yellow form. 'Toxicology report, blood alcohol concentration 0.16. Benzodiazepine level equivalent to ingesting 700 mg. So basically, a lethal dose.'

'Smells like suicide. CCTV?

'Out of order, had been for months.'

'Medical records?'

He scanned the badly photocopied notes. 'Her history is fairly unremarkable, an abortion in late twenties, no significant illnesses, prescribed temazepam for insomnia and anxiety in September. She attended in November with concerns that she had contracted Creutzfeldt–Jakob disease from eating budget burgers. The G.P. diagnosed health anxiety.'

'I remember the original scare, it was years ago, mad cow disease, politicians feeding their children burgers live on T.V. Beef became very cheap until people forgot about it. I suspect you're a vegetarian, aren't you?'

'Yes Ma'am.'

The special envoy returned carrying a melamine tray with two stained mugs and two buttered crumpets.

'Found a little treat,' he announced triumphantly, 'anything else Ma'am?'

'That will be all.'

'Ma'am.' He clicked his heels gestapo style and gave a single nod. She seemed to hand-select the most sycophantic officers for her team. He himself had never been keen, even as a rookie.

'So, the woman is neurotic, stressed and thinks she's going to die, might be enough to prompt a self-check-out,' she tore off a piece of crumpet and popped it into her mouth.

'Perhaps.' He could stand it no longer; he forwarded the date block to sixteenth January as discreetly as possible.

'Really?'

'Sorry Ma'am.'

'Anything of interest at the scene?'

'The body was found face down in the hallway. No sign of forced entry or struggle but the paramedics kicked the door in so the scene was compromised. There were a few anomalies; Andrea's mobile phone is missing. So too her tortoise and its cage.'

'So too?'

'Yes, that's how you say it.'

'Um. So, a burglar with a key who wanted a second-hand phone and a scabby tortoise. Hardly.'

He could feel the dampness of his coat seeping through his jacket. Was it the reawakened sense of injustice, Wallace's officiousness or the scene anomalies that were unsettling him? He ploughed on. 'Also, she had packed her suitcase and her passport was on the bedside table.'

'Marbella or death? I know what I'd choose,' she let out a thin laugh.

'She had New Year's resolutions pinned to a corkboard. The place looked neglected, not dusted for some time.'

'Well, we don't all have your high standards.' A hint of mockery in her voice. 'What were her resolutions?'

'Give up smoking, stop eating meat and sadly, get a life.'

'Well, she managed the first two.'

Her glibness was grating but he managed a weak smile.

'Anything else?' She started on the second crumpet.

He was regretting missing breakfast. He had wanted to ensure that he presented the case as worthy of investigation, no stone unturned, not on his watch.

'Social circumstances: she was fired from her teaching job. A post of her nature group went viral; they were holding an amphibian that resembles a penis.'

He noted her raised eyebrow.

'Okay, so phone records, check her financials, if they don't throw anything up mark it NFA pending inquest.' DCI Wallace made a note in her file. 'And find the bloody tortoise.'

'The coroner has released the body, her brother is keen to arrange the funeral.'

'That's that then,' she looked at her watch.

'Oh, there was one other thing. Her friend, a Ms Burns-Whyte has phoned several times, she's convinced that Andrea was killed. She received a parcel of her belongings, things she had admired but also a bird book and Ms Burns-Whyte has no interest in birds. She thinks Andrea was trying to tell her something.'

'She was probably trying to tell her to stop watching crime dramas and develop an interest. Giving away possessions is clear support for suicide.'

'That's what I told her just before she hung up on me.' He watched Wallace finish the crumpet, melted butter dropping onto the notes.

'If it's shaped like a duck and sits on a pond it's a duck. It's strange how people would prefer their loved ones to have been murdered than to have topped themselves, mitigates the guilt I suppose.'

'Lots of wild fowl sit on ponds Ma'am.'

'Yes, but they don't all go quack. I have to admit to a slight disappointment, we haven't had a murder inquiry for months.'

'Be careful what you wish for Ma'am.'

A burst of hail clattered against the window.

4

C lara opened her laptop and typed in: How to care for a tortoise. *WikiHow* suggested the reason for its malaise was likely vitamin deficiency, also a larger heat lamp seemed advisable. It transpired that tortoises sleep when cold and that hibernation was best prevented as it reduces life expectancy. Perhaps there lay a lesson for herself.

She viewed a short series on tortoise diet, enrichment and general health. Another site invited questions to an expert: Do I need to oil my tortoise? How do I clip her nails? Should I soak my tortoise? And other such vagaries. She learnt that they can live up to one hundred years in captivity. Good grief. She switched to *Amazon* and spent an hour ordering tortoise paraphernalia.

Radio Four announced the arrival of NASA images from four billion miles away. She must tell Phineas that the craft had set off in 2006, he would have been doing his GCSEs. She imagined his response: Wow, mind blown. Perhaps he would not say that now he was a married man. Probably not. Her eyes were drawn to the wedding photograph on the bookshelf, four faces grinning under a cherry tree, Phineas's head tilted to hers, Peter's hand on his mother's arm.

NASA sounded like an interesting place to work. Perhaps she could have been an astronaut? No, she didn't like confined spaces or prolonged proximity to other people, not to mention that girls did not go to the cinema on their own in the nineteen-eighties, never mind into space.

You have wasted your life.

She imagined the worm lodged in a cerebral fissure, it had spread its bulk, made itself comfortable. A pallid creature, blanched through lack of sunlight, content to taunt.

Squandered.

Sometimes she blamed her father. He had worked in General Practice with a conscientiousness that boarded on obsession and had passed the madness onto her. Mostly she blamed herself. She had grabbed the baton without question. Taken the paved road without examining the map. She had inherited his 'bedside manner', his ability to portray the perfect blend of empathy, gravity and interest. Except that after the first few years she knew that she was faking it. Mid-career landed like a stone with the abrupt realisation that it was too late to specialise; there was nowhere else to go. She could listen, diagnose and prescribe. She was good at it, she had done it forty times a day, five days a week. For thirty-five years. She had only survived the last eighteen months by thinking about her final salary pension and checking her countdown App to watch the minutes tick away.

The doorbell. Sally from next door wanting to borrow baking parchment. Good grief, as if she were the sort of woman to stock random baking accoutrements, although come to think of it she did have some. Since she had allowed her hair to grey, she was starting to draw benign smiles from shop assistants, beatific nods from passing clergy and now this. The triumvirate of pearl-earrings, varifocals and pixie-cut seemed to announce her as a type. She told Sally to keep the roll; she rarely baked. As she returned to the living room it struck her that perhaps Sally had wanted to talk. She had hovered unnecessarily in the doorway holding the parchment, she had had to practically close the door on the woman. Oh well, the last thing she needed was to be a confidante.

She opened *Animal Farm* at chapter four and recapped for Blue as he nestled in for their regular reading session. Suddenly it was lunch time. She heated a carton of tomato and lentil soup and flicked through the local paper as she ate. She scanned the obituaries for ex-patients. Mrs Ann Greenway, seventy-nine, ah yes sweet lady, most likely her heart. The others did not ring a bell. Oh Lord! What's this?

A service in celebration of the life of Andrea Gibbons, Wednesday 23rd January, 11.00 am, Marlow Town Hall, no flowers, retiring collection RSPB.

She sat in stunned silence. Why the hell didn't I pick that up? Damn.

She peeped through the lid of the cardboard box where Darwin was nibbling a stalk of lamb's lettuce and placed it on the sofa next to Blue who was determinedly asleep with a paw across his eyes. She could see that Phineas was already online, his profile picture of a mouse lemur staring straight at the camera with tiny round eyes. He called at exactly two.

'Hi Mum.' He appeared smiling in front of the Madagascan flag draped across a flaking wall.

'Hi sweetie, where are you?' He looked thin, she noted a constellation of bites on his arms.

'A store in Betioky, the guy lets me use his back room. It's about twenty miles from the field site. So, how are you?'

'Well, I've just heard some terrible news. You remember Miss Gibbons?'

'Of course.'

'Well, sadly she passed away.'

'Oh my God, that's terrible, she must have only been in her thirties. What happened?'

Bless him, he looked genuinely upset. 'It seems that she killed herself.'

'Bloody hell.'

'The thing is she brought her tortoise over on Christmas Eve, she wanted you to have him, "Teacher's pet for the teacher's pet" she said. She seemed quite jovial.'

'Blimey.'

'I told her that you were in Madagascar, but she was very insistent, said she was going away and couldn't take him with her. She must have been planning it. I feel terrible that I didn't question her more.'

You are a disgrace to the profession.

'It's not exactly something you would suspect though is it?'

Dear Phineas, he always knew the right thing to say.

'She made it sound as if she was emigrating, I really should have pursued it.'

She saw his eyes brim with tears.

'Don't beat yourself up, it's not your doing.' His voice cracked, the ceiling fan whirred, he whisked away a fly.

Blue stood up and circled before throwing himself back down.

'Oh, I can see Blue's legs. Move the laptop so I can see him.'

Clara tried to find the right angle. Blue sniffed the screen.

'Hi, how're you doing boy? You looking after Mum? Aww miss you.'

'He misses you too, he's always sniffing around in your room.'

'So, how was your first Christmas as a free woman?'

'Lovely not to have to worry about off-duty rotas. I went to visit Gwam.' It was what Phineas called his grandmother when he was a toddler and somehow it had stuck. 'She was very confused, didn't have a clue who I was, but she was happy to come out to lunch with me. She has that photo of you as Theseus in the school play next to her bed.'

'Blimey, no wonder she's confused.'

'How did you celebrate Christmas and New Year?'

'We made a nice meal on Christmas day and sang a few carols. It was just me and my tracker Armand over New Year, the thing with nocturnal primates is they don't take the night off. We had a break at three am to raise a flask of coconut milk to you.

'How's the research going?'

'Very well. We've got radio-collars now, we're getting great data on torpor patterns.'

She could sense his excitement but it seemed forced somehow. 'That's fabulous, what's it showing?'

'Early days but we're hoping to extend the study to look at potential dormancy factors over a full year.'

'Oh, does that mean you're going to stay longer?' She tried to sound upbeat.

'It depends on funding and whether I can extend my visa.' There was a hesitancy in his voice. She glanced at her image in the corner of the screen, she looked like a knackered mouse lemur.

'Well, I'd better go Mum, I don't want to hog the Wi-Fi.'

'Okay sweetie, look after yourself, love you.'

'Love you too.'

Clara stared at his profile picture for a while. She had forgotten to tell him about the NASA voyage. Oh well. She went through to the kitchen, turned the cover of her empty 2019 calendar and marked the twenty-third.

It was lovely to see him, but the experience left her unsettled and with a sense of foreboding that she knew she would carry for days.

5

Jo clutched a posy of lilies positioned to avoid the pollen staining her black silk dress whilst drawing attention to her décolletage. The crematorium was nearly full, she strode to the front and took the seat next to Ed. He looked up red-eyed and embraced her, he smelt faintly of sheep.

'So sad,' she managed.

He took her hand and squeezed it, his skin unpleasantly rough, she must recommend a good moisturiser. Her attention turned to the woman in pink framed glasses who was placing additional cushioned chairs at the end of each row. They looked considerably more comfortable but it was too late to change seats. She surveyed the woman; dark purple skirt-suit flecked with silver, very nineteen-eighties, hair chopped in that straight bob so favoured by female MPs. Jo imagined that she could be quite pretty if she made more of herself. The woman checked her watch and stood beside the wicker coffin, threaded with winter jasmine, where Andrea beamed incongruously from a silver frame. Blimey, she must be the vicar. The woman clipped over to a CD player from which Robbie Williams's *Angels* erupted, startling the mourners from their reflections. She adjusted the volume to a dignified level and lowered her head. As the final bars faded, she returned solemnly to the coffin and addressed the room.

'A warm welcome dear relatives and friends of Andrea Gibbons. I am Josie Jones, your celebrant, and I'm honoured to have been asked by Andrea's brother to conduct this ceremony. Ed and I have met to create a fitting tribute. Indeed, the music was chosen by Andrea herself, who had the foresight to write down her wishes. I feel that through our discussions I have come to know Andrea, her hopes, her dreams, her values, and I believe that we would have been great friends.'

Jo decided that neither herself nor Andrea would have been friends with this tubby humanitarian. And God she could talk, they were going to be here all day. She herself had prepared a short speech although Ed had neglected to ask her.

'We are here to celebrate Andrea's life and to reflect on the impact she has made upon ours.'

A shuffling of chairs at the back signalled late arrivals, how rude.

'It is clear from the impressive turn-out that she was a much-loved woman.'

Jo glanced around; she barely knew anyone. Look at them all just sitting there accepting Andrea's death as if it were nothing. Where was the anger? Where was the disbelief? Where was the bloody outrage?

'For those of you who have not attended a Humanist funeral before, nothing untoward is going to happen! One does not have to identify as Humanist to have such a service, I understand that Andrea described herself as "very spiritual". I would firstly like to invite Ed to read a poem that he has selected.'

Coughing and muffled whispers filled the pause as Ed rose to his feet, retrieved a sheet of A4 from his inside pocket and slowly unfolded it. He might at least have ironed his shirt and found a decent tie, it had parrots on it for goodness sake.

'The Summer Day by Mary Oliver,' Ed read with suppressed emotion, his voice cracking on the final line: '*Tell me, what is it you plan to do with your one wild and precious life?*'

His choice seemed hugely inappropriate, she would have gone for something about the sanctity of life, a nod to Andrea's terrible fate.

'That was beautiful Ed, thank you. The children of Marlow Academy Chamber Choir will now sing one of Andrea's favourite songs.'

A gaggle of girls and a boy, smart in black and white, assembled themselves into a crescent. The choir leader hummed the starting note and conducted them in an a cappella version of *Wind Beneath My Wings*. As the teenagers shuffled back to their seats someone initiated a hearty clapping.

Josie stood and joined in. 'Yes, please feel free to express your appreciation.'

Oh, for God's sake, where were we, the London Palladium?

The applause grew louder, tailed off and came to a self-conscious halt. Josie retrieved a roving microphone from behind a floral display. She tapped it several times eliciting dull thuds and a high-pitched squeal, adjusted the knob and tapped again. Jo was finding her increasingly irritating, honestly, where did Ed find this amateur?

'Now, in place of a scripted eulogy, I would like to invite you all to share your memories of Andrea. Do not feel obliged to speak, if you prefer not to please just pass the microphone along.' She nodded encouragement at the rows of mourners, Jo noted several exchange worried glances. Finally, her big opportunity.

The room seemed to hold its breath as the clip-clop of Josie's heels stopped at Ed. He cleared his throat and ran his hand through his straggle of hair. 'Andrea was my sister,' he paused, 'I was always the shy one, she looked out for me. She persuaded Mum and Dad to buy me a guinea pig when I was ten. We didn't always get on. She was the kindest person I knew. Our parents were so proud of her when she became a teacher and so was I. Sorry, this is a bit disjointed. When I sprained my ankle last year, she took a week off and drove up to help look after my sheep, even though she was trying to be a vegetarian.' A ripple of laughter ran through the room. 'I'll miss her.'

He passed the microphone to Jo, she felt the brief touch of his hand. 'Andrea was my best friend, she was my rock and I was hers.' Her voice sounded shrill, she tried to modulate it. 'We met at primary school and our lives have run in parallel ever since. There are so many memories, I'll choose just one. The night we designed our own tattoos. We were celebrating the end of a particularly difficult year. We decided to mark our new beginnings with something transformative. Andrea was very artistic, I asked for a phoenix rising from a flame. I know that Harry Potter has made them quite commonplace but at the time it was very unique. She drew a beautiful design for me, I have it on my thigh. Anyway, I popped to the corner shop to buy another bottle of Blue Nun,' she paused for laughter, none came, 'by the time I returned she had finished her own design. I laughed and laughed. It was a pigeon pecking grain! Not a dove, or a graceful swan, no, a common-or-garden pigeon. That summed Andrea up, she was silly and quirky and exceptional.'

Several people smiled and nodded. Jo girded herself. Now was her chance to bloody stir them from their stupor.

'I will get justice for you Andrea, I know that you would not take your own life.' She was vaguely aware of people shuffling in their seats. 'The police have dismissed my concerns, but I will fight on.' Josie reappeared and tried to gently prise the microphone from her clenched fist. 'I love you Andrea,' she shouted, tears now flowing. 'I'll get it, I will bloody get it. Justice at any price.'

She relinquished the microphone, causing Josie to hit herself on the forehead with a resonant thud. Josie passed it quickly to the next row. She sat trembling, Ed's arm around her. In a moment of insight, she realised that she had found her purpose, her mission, her True North. She had sanctified her promise to Andrea in the presence of God, well in front of humanitarians. She had made a public pronouncement and she would not let Andrea down. Yes, everything happens for a reason, if the police were not going to act then it was up to her. She imagined her triumph, standing tall as the perpetrator was led away, his eyes narrowed in menace, she staring back undaunted. She graciously accepts a nod of admiration from the judge. The press hail her as a heroine. Her appearances on *Good Morning Britain, Justice by any Means,* and *Loose Women* are dazzling. Her reverie was interrupted by Josie's return from shepherding the microphone.

'Thank you all so much for your contributions. We now have an opportunity for private reflection, accompanied by another of Andrea's favourite songs.'

She changed the CD as people bowed their heads. A chinking piano and melodic humming introduced Barbra Streisand's plaintive voice as *The Way We Were* filled the room. Jo, unable to summon further contemplation, sang along in her head.

As the song ended, Josie placed her hand tenderly on the photograph. 'And now we bid farewell to our beloved Andrea, we thank you for your friendship and the enrichment that you brought to our lives.' She pulled a gold cord, velvet curtains closed around the coffin. She left a long pause and smiled. 'Please do join us for light refreshments in the garden room.'

Jo scanned the guests: a dispiriting ragbag of dowdy teachers, mundane middle-aged couples and a few old dears. Andrea had possessed the art of acceptance and non-judgement that she herself had never mastered - despite completing an online Mindfulness course and a disastrous silent retreat. A handsome man in a Paul Smith suit caught her eye and held it as he wove his way through the mourners. He stood directly in front of her, took her shoulders, and kissed her gently on both cheeks. The intimacy of the gesture, from a man she had never met before, took her breath away.

'Jo, how lovely to meet you at last, but in such tragic circumstances.'

She smiled coquettishly and took a steadying swig of Prosecco. He continued to hold her gaze, his ice-blue eyes hypnotic. She found herself unable to respond.

'I'm sorry, Ludo Mansfield, I realise that perhaps you don't know who I am. I knew Andrea from T and C; did she never mention me?'

Jo was confused, exhausted and had already finished two glasses on an empty stomach. 'Terms and Conditions?' she asked.

Ludo's laugh was charming. 'Turks and Caicos. I manage offshore assets, I often popped over to T and C for some R and R. Andrea and I frequented the same bars.'

They turned their heads in synchrony towards an incongruous burst of laughter before resuming their connection.

'That one I do know, Rest and Recuperation. I can't believe Andrea kept you a secret.' She felt a stab of betrayal, they had shared everything.

'Well, we weren't, you know, intimate, but we did get along very well. She told me about you, her best friend, she said that you were very close.'

'Yes, we were. You must have known her husband Leon. What did you make of him? I'm sure I would have seen straight through him; Andrea was always too trusting.'

'Actually, I never met him, he was away a lot but yes poor Andrea persistently backed the wrong horse.'

'When it came to men, well most things actually, she had very little will power. She tried so hard to be vegetarian, bless her, she'd constantly beat herself up about the occasional Burger King.' His eyes were ridiculously blue. 'Did you contribute to the eulogy?' She stumbled over the last word and registered that she was a little drunk, 'I'm afraid I zoned out.'

'Just a few words, the least I could do. I hope you don't mind me asking what you meant when you said that you wanted justice for Andrea?'

Jo stepped closer, she recognised his aftershave, Hugo Boss. 'She was murdered,' she hissed, 'the police said it was an overdose, perhaps it was, but who administered it?'

'Oh no, I can't believe it, who on earth would want to murder Andrea?'

'That's exactly what I'm going to find out.'

'Do you have any leads?' Ludo reached for the Prosecco and smoothly refilled her glass.

'I'm compiling a list of possible suspects,' she dropped her voice to a whisper and leant in conspiratorially. 'Some of them are here, the woman with the eyepatch has just been added.'

They glanced over at a large woman who was folding a napkin and passing it to a woman in a grey woollen suit, who tucked it into her handbag.

'Why is she a suspect? Is it the eyepatch?'

'No, she's in the RSPB. Andrea left me some clues, one of them was a big arrow pointing to a birdwatcher. I don't know her or the woman she's in cahoots with, but they have been acting strangely. And laughing like drains at a funeral, disgraceful.' She cast an outraged eye in their direction.

'I'd be happy to help, I'll go and introduce myself, I'll let you know what I discover,' he gave her a surreptitious wink and made his way towards the food table.

She saw Ed extricate himself from a group of Andrea's ex-colleagues and head over. They hugged; he was painfully thin.

'A lovely service, very Andrea,' she watched Ludo chatting to the suspects over Ed's shoulder, he had lovely posture, like a matador.

'Her will included her funeral requests. She wrote it a few years back, just after Mum and Dad died.'

'And she hadn't updated it? She was so organised, that's very suspicious, don't you think?'

Ed looked confused. 'Is it?'

She ploughed on as if explaining to a small child. 'If she was planning to commit suicide, she would have updated her will.'

'Suicide is not a rational act Jo. I've known a few unfortunately. Who knows what she was thinking? Besides, she had nothing left to bequeath. Still, let's not dwell on that.'

'That weasel Leon took the lot?' Jo flushed, 'then he goes and snuffs it, well he bloody well deserved it.'

The buzz of background voices fell silent and Jo realised that she had been shouting. A pause gripped the room before polite conversations gradually resumed.

Jo knew better than most that suicide needed to be planned. When Ben left her, she impulsively decided to drive off a cliff, *Thelma and Louise* style. Unable to find vehicular access to Beachy Head she had cruised around crying before making the long journey home. It had cost her further damage to her tattered self-esteem and a whole tank full of petrol.

She drained her glass and fixed Ed with a knowing stare. 'But what about the funeral songs? She would have added her new favourite, it was our anthem.'

'I'm sure that would have been the last thing on her mind. What was it?'

'*This is Me*, from The Greatest Showman,' Jo started to hum the song and sang the chorus in full mezzo-soprano, she was attracting attention but didn't care.

Ed cast his eyes down and wrung his skinny hands. 'Yes, it would have been perfect.'

What was it that the detective inspector had said? It's best to keep an open mind at this stage; code for everyone is a suspect.

'Andrea said she was going to spend Christmas with you.'

'I was looking forward to seeing her, she phoned on Christmas Eve to cancel, said she had the flu. I was just making the nut roast. Spent the next four days eating it.'

'What did you do with the money?' A technique she had seen on those daytime cop shows: don't give them time to think.

'The money?'

'Your inheritance, from your parents, you got the same as Andrea?' She was rising to her role as interrogator. It was rather fun.

'Umm, yes,' Ed shuffled awkwardly. A flush travelled to his white cheeks.

'What did you do with it?'

Ed appeared to be lost again, he was evidently not used to

crowds or questions or conversation. He pulled at his earlobe. 'I bought the dilapidated sheep farm with the dilapidated sheep. You know, you came to visit that time with Andrea.'

'Oh yes, how are you doing? Is it making money?' She eyed the parrots on his tie suspiciously.

'Well, I make enough to get by, I've never needed much, Carmarthenshire is a pretty cheap place to live. It's quiet, it suits me.'

There was a pause. He evidently knew that Leon had squandered Andrea's inheritance. She could conjure no other motive. 'You must be a bit lonely up there on your own?'

'A little. My nearest neighbours are a mile away and they don't talk to me since I called the RSPCA about their puppy farm.'

'Poor you.'

She evidently needed more intel on him. She moved him onto the suspect list, excused herself and headed to the ladies. She examined her reflection in the harsh light; grief was ruinous to one's complexion. She reapplied her foundation, scarlet lipstick and a further layer of volumizing mascara. She took a deep breath and returned to the fray. To her dismay Ludo had disappeared. She sighed and gave herself permission to pause her 'no carbs' resolution. Ed approached as she took a large bite of chocolate éclair. A globule of cream landed on the bodice of her silk dress, they both looked at it, he lifted a napkin then lowered it helplessly.

'The man you were talking to sends his apologies, he asked me to give you this.' He passed her a thick embossed card, *Ludovic Mansfield, BA, MBA, CFA, Private Asset Management.*

Jo felt a quiver of excitement, well now, it looks like I've found my investigation buddy.

6

C lara noted, with slight consternation, that she was looking forward to the funeral. It was something to do. She decided on her grey woollen suit, off-set with her black rose brooch. She stroked Blue who trembled by her side having picked up a deviation from her usual routine of retiring to the study with tea, toast and a good book.

The weather was fitting, a steady rain under a mournful sky. The radio warned that an accident on the A404 was causing tailbacks so she took the back roads, splashing through potholes, regardless of the sanctity of her new car.

Thankfully she was not the only late-comer, a large woman in a grey velvet cape was peering through a crack in the door waiting for an opportune moment.

'It's just started,' she hissed. 'I can spy two seats at the back, should we advance?'

She had a roseate complexion and a velvet eye-patch that perfectly matched her cloak, her good eye twinkled. Clara liked her immediately. 'Yes, let's.'

They settled into their seats as the celebrant closed her introductory address and invited Andrea's brother to read. His pain was tangible, even from the back Clara could detect the loss that shrouded the recently bereaved. The poem was a perfect choice: the questioning of creation, the detailed description of an overlooked insect, the recipe for a life well lived. Poignant. She liked Mary Oliver, she made a mental note to reread her.

The Chamber Choir took her back to Phineas's school days. She recognised the choir mistress, Miss Everett, nice woman, although perhaps a little too keen on *The Lion King*, songs from which had littered every school performance. Clara disliked *Wind Beneath My Wings*, but the arrangement was excellent and the three-part harmony quite moving. Her neighbour, wiping her eye on her cloak, initiated a hearty applause which she took up.

Now it appeared that they were expected to speak. Andrea's

brother again both touching and germane. A woman in a black cocktail dress spoke, seemingly more about herself than Andrea, before becoming a little over-wrought. The tension dissipated as the microphone travelled on. The celebrant was doing an excellent job. Clara felt the need to say a few words, primarily because the microphone relay had become a veritable pass the parcel.

'Hello, I'm Clara Astrell, I did not have the pleasure of knowing Andrea very well but she taught my son and nurtured his interest in zoology. I always found her to be friendly and to go out of her way to help pupils. She ran a popular nature club and encouraged the children to become involved in conservation and to care for the environment. It is a great shame that she died so young and at her own hand, she had so much more to contribute.'

She was adept at patting the elephant in the room. With the exception of the histrionic friend no-one had mentioned Andrea's untimely death, Clara felt that a measured comment had been required to restore balance. She passed the microphone to her neighbour.

'Henrietta Cuvier. I too didn't know Andrea terribly well but we met many times at RSPB events. She was excellent at spotting and was generous in helping those with compromised visual acuity. She had an extensive sightings list, really very impressive; 275 of the 285 listed in the British Trust for Ornithology Handbook. She also helped a great deal with the Tawny owl calling survey. I found her to be a thoroughly decent human.'

The microphone made its way to a man standing by the door. He drew attention to his tie - navy accented with light blue stripes - smoothing it as he spoke. His voice was confident, unemotional. Clara felt that his tribute had the quality of a condolence card.

'Andrea and I were great friends; I was shocked and saddened to learn of her passing. She was an inspiration to her pupils, some of whom sang so beautifully this morning. We always spoke of doing more together, somehow life gets in the way and before one knows,' he gestured theatrically towards the coffin. 'Andrea was a great teacher, what I have learnt from this tragedy is to make the most of every opportunity life brings. She will be very sorely missed by us all.'

Clara would have preferred to make a hasty exit but could not leave without giving her condolences. A small group had already commandeered Ed; she guessed from their physiognomy that they were relatives. She waited by the buffet, amused by the retro cheese and pineapple hedgehog. Josie Jones removed the cling-film from the platters and took a cheese straw to signal permission to eat.

'Lovely service,' Clara detached a spine and chewed the cheese cube. A little waxy.

'Thank you, your words about Andrea were lovely too. If you are interested in Humanist services may I recommend the excellent guide *Funerals Without God*,' Josie swallowed a tiny vol-au-vent.

'Have you been a celebrant long?'

'Twelve years. I like getting to know someone after they have died. Relatives often share very private memories and somehow distil the most pertinent things. It seems to help, closure after disclosure as it were.'

'I'm more familiar with rapid divulgence in ten-minute slots.'

'Ah, G.P? That must be emotionally challenging.'

'Retired. Yes, I found one had to keep one's feelings on a short leash, measure one's words and demeanour. No-one wants a demonstrative doctor.' She felt the worm stirring in its burrow, fat with accumulated emotion.

'Our roles have a lot in common doctor, we are both used to the mundanity of death, even of suicides.' Clara noted that she had mastered the knack of being able to eat and speak simultaneously.

'A long-term solution to a short-term problem I used to say. Believing in your inner voice can be deadly.' She ate a comforting pineapple chunk.

They exchanged knowing nods.

Clara's new acquaintance lumbered towards them throwing off her cape to reveal a grey velvet dress, the high neckline and sleeves trimmed with black lace. It looked home-made.

'Hello there, what a lovely send-off, mother will be sad to have missed it.' She deftly stacked a pyramid of sandwiches onto a tiny plate.

'Yes, very moving, I'm Clara, nice to formally meet you,' she extended her hand, it was firmly shaken.

'Henrietta but do call me Hen.'

Josie was called away to attend to a car-parking issue.

'Well done dear for mentioning her untimely death, I'm so glad someone did,' she fitted a crustless triangle into her mouth and swallowed. 'The headmaster didn't contribute, he who sacked her, one hopes he feels some regret.'

'Indeed. Do you know the reason she lost her job?'

'Oh, ridiculous fuss about a model of *Dermophis donaldtrumpi.* An interesting caecilian, buries its head in the sand, named to highlight Trump's climate-change denial. Apparently, it attracted rather lewd comments and photographs illustrating its penile resemblance. Parents complained, got up a petition, Andrea was dismissed. Tragic.'

'Actually, I did see that photograph in the local paper, I cut it out for my son, he was an occasional guest speaker at Andrea's nature club. I had no idea she was fired, totally disproportionate. Of course, that might not have been the final trigger; one can be plagued by many worms.'

'Very true, very true.'

'Your tribute was a nice snapshot of her life. Do you work for the RSPB?'

'No, it's a hobby, I used to train race-horses, now I breed ornamental ducks.'

'How interesting, what species do you have?' Clara took a sandwich, suddenly she was ravenous.

'Mostly the ancient breeds, various teal, a number of Fulvous whistling ducks and an ever-expanding flock of Indian runners. They are so adorable I find it hard to part with them, not much of a businesswoman I'm afraid!' She roared with laughter causing heads to turn.

'I imagine you can become quite attached, I would too. Grebes are my favourite. There are quite a few ornate ducks on the Thames, apparently escapees from the bird park at Pangbourne.'

'Likely some of mine too, fickle little buggers! You must come and visit, I have a pair of mergansers that I'm sure you would appreciate; they are not dissimilar to the grebe.' She had somehow managed to finish the sandwich stack and was now wrapping a piece of cake in a paper napkin. 'For mother!'

'I'd love to see them, thank you.'

'Excellent!' Hen wrote her contact details on a napkin.

'Hello ladies. Anyone care for a top-up?'

A man in a sharp suit, with a poor grasp of interpersonal space, waved a wine bottle perilously close to their faces. They both declined.

'Ludo Mansfield,' he extended his hand. 'And you lovely ladies are?'

'Clara Astrell.'

'Henrietta Cuvier.'

Clara noted with a wave of affection that she had not invited him to call her Hen.

'Ladies, just a heads up. Woman in the black silk,' he nodded in Jo's direction, 'allegedly Andrea's best friend. Convinced she was murdered.'

'Poor lamb. Grief is a mire.'

Clara was grateful that Hen took up the conversation, despite his passing resemblance to Clint Eastwood she somehow found the man repellent. Like most handsome men he evidently adored himself.

'You two are on the suspect list. Might be best to steer clear.'

She noted that Ed was finally free. He was very pale for a farmer; his eyes had the glazed look of the over medicated. 'I must go and give my condolences. Would you like to join me Hen?'

Ludo handed them both his business card and moved on.

'What an unpleasant creature, I caught the distinct aroma of rodent.'

'Me too,' said Clara.

7

John bit the inside of his lip. The drone of conversation, tapping of keyboards and occasional bursts of laughter sapped his concentration. There had been a memo reminding those fortunate enough to have their own side-room to keep their door open. It was meant to foster inclusion and teamwork, no matter that it made it impossible to think. He retrieved his earplugs from his desk drawer and returned to the list of dates and figures.

Unlike his fellow officers he liked analysing the financials. A life condensed, choices and personality revealed, a secret vault wherein lay a person's hopes and dreams. Opening it felt like a trespass, a privileged intrusion into the most private of chambers. Matt always said he was too sensitive to be a copper.

He highlighted the key transactions in green marker. It appeared that following a considerable period of stability - in which her teaching job had paid just enough to cover the mortgage, provide nights out, spa-breaks and regular donations to the RSPB - Andrea Gibbons had met with both triumphs and disasters.

In September 2015 she received a parental inheritance of one-hundred and thirty thousand pounds.

Three months later her salary stops. Brave or foolhardy? Would he do the same? Probably not but he would love to.

Early the following year her house sale nets four-hundred and fifty thousand. Wow, she really burnt her bridges.

A new Turks and Caicos account receives a regular income from the education department, paid in US dollars. Okay, not so crazy, she got herself a nice job in the Caribbean, good for her.

There followed a frugal lifestyle with occasional expenditure in cocktail bars. He was rather warming to her.

Then a joint account, Mr and Mrs Leon Maynard. Substantial outgoings joined her previous careful purchases: boat refurbishments, fishing gear, golf course membership. The healthy balance steadily depleted. To zero.

One return flight to the UK. Poor thing.

He trusted Matt implicitly but they still kept separate accounts. If there was one thing the job had taught him it was never say never.

Monthly rental payments to Marlow housing association. God, she was back on the first rung.

The salary from St Birinus school recommences. At least they took her back but how depressing. In April 2018 the salary stops.

A windfall of fifty thousand pounds, with no identifier; the opening balance of a Cayman Islands account. Closed three days later. Very odd.

Her last purchase was a one-way ticket to Venezuela mid-December 2018. Unused.

He removed his earplugs, made a cup of tea and brought it back to his desk. That was another 'perk' that seemed to have been eroded; the tea break. He would take ten minutes anyway. He opened *Pets for Homes* and searched for dalmatian puppies. The boys were nearly old enough to look after a dog and their persistence had finally worn him and Matt down. There was a nice-looking litter in Reading.

'Got a minute gov?' Constable Beech tapped on the open door and entered.

John closed the tab. 'Sure.'

'Update on the Gibbons case.'

'Ah, what news?'

'Complete blank I'm afraid. We searched her flat and her car, contacted her known associates and her brother. No sign of the tortoise or the mobile phone, it's not been used since Christmas day.'

'Disappointing. Keep a trace on the number in case of any activity, we might just get lucky.'

The phone records had revealed a number of missed calls from Turks and Caicos, all traced to public phones. Only one call from her brother late on Christmas Day.

He sent an email to Wallace with the findings to date and asked for more time. Her response: *Sometimes people just give up* loaded with double meaning.

Andrea did not strike him as the sort to just give up. What was it that Tony Hancock wrote in his suicide note? 'Things seemed to go wrong too many times.' But she struck him as resilient, she had friends, she had interests, she had taken leaps of faith. She was fearless. Of course, one needed to be fearless to kill oneself, it was certainly not a coward's way out. But why plan to go to Venezuela? Her bags packed.

He needed to find the phone, and the missing fifty grand. Also the tortoise.

8

Jo cracked open the living room window and lit another Dunhill fine-cut. She had watched enough true crime series to know that victims nearly always knew their killer. She had her suspicions but she needed to be methodical; where to start?

Oh my God, the Book of Condolences that Ed had sent might just contain the name of Andrea's murderer. It was a shame that he had not given her the original, the photocopy with its red plastic spine lacked gravitas, without leather-bound solemnity the words of condolence seemed trite. She opened an Excel spreadsheet which she entitled 'Persons of Interest' and began to enter the names in alphabetical order. Whether to include Josie Jones? That frumpy lady vicar was a long-shot but in Midsomer Murders the perpetrator was always the most unlikely suspect. Rule no-one out. She felt a frisson of pleasure at seeing Ludo's signature. In a surprisingly child-like hand he had written Dearest Andrea, you are gone to soon too a better place, rest in peace my angel. Andrea had been such a pedant when it came to the English language, perhaps the to-too errors were ironic, a private joke that they had shared. The thought made her sad. Her finger hesitated over the keyboard; with a slight thrill of betrayal she added his name for the sake of completeness. Thirty-two names, impressive.

She created three columns: Means, Motive, Opportunity and after a moment's thought, a final column labelled Evidence. She conceded that this was a weak spot but she did have a missing tortoise, Andrea's box of parcels signalling a link to the RSPB, the note-passing behaviour between Clara Astrell and Henrietta Cuvier and their outrageous laughter at the funeral. It turned out that Clara was a G.P. so she had access to lethal medication, Henrietta was a birder; those two were at the top of the list literally and figuratively. And then there was Ed Gibbons, he was definitely evasive when she asked him about the money. And let's face it he had always been odd. She sat and thought for a while, nothing else came to mind. She needed caffeine.

She listened to the spatter and hiss of the coffee machine and tore the page from her Zen quotation one-day-at-a-time calendar. A Christmas present from Andrea that now served as a daily reminder of her absence. *Thousands of candles can be lighted from a single candle.* She imagined Andrea questioning the grammar. The date a sudden slap in the face. February fourteenth. Not one bloody card. Valentine's day always unsettled her, set hares running: what is, what was, what might have been. Their wedding day. She wondered what Ben was doing now. She wanted to feel nothing but hatred for him, the same loathing that she felt towards the second Mrs Burns. Crazy as it was, even now it upset her not to receive a card. Somehow, they were still connected. She had never grieved for him maybe that was it. She remembered the Five Stages of Grief from nurse training, perhaps she had got stuck on anger. Of course, he had not actually died, he had moved to Slough. The pregnant secretary was such a cliché, she deserved better than that. She had sought an acrimonious divorce, a blow-by-blow fight to make him bloody suffer, but he had acquiesced to all her demands. It had left her with no release. Anger hung like a wasps' nest within her shredded heart. She had stalled the house sale, putting off potential buyers with casual mentions of damp and subsidence: just a few centimetres a year, it's really not a problem. Ha! Ha! Ha! Yes, let the bastard keep paying the mortgage, see how his bitch likes that. In truth the house had always been too big, three redundant bedrooms mocking her as they awaited children that never came. The oaks that gave the house its name blocked the sunlight and mired the house year-round in a gloomy air. When it finally sold, and she moved into the modern maisonette, she felt lighter and regretted delaying her new start.

But still.

She imagined him out for dinner with bubbly Carly, bloody bitch. Their child would be ten, they would have had to get a baby-sitter. Right now, he would be ordering his favourite meal: pepper-steak and chips, a side of mangetout. How smug he always was knowing how to pronounce it, a covert reminder of her stupidity. Carly was the Caesar salad and granary bread type, probably a bloody vegetarian. The queen wasp stirred in her chamber, a buzzing of waking drones. Jo scrolled through her phone, where had she saved that site? Ah! Valentine's Day Special. El Paso Zoo will name a cockroach after your ex and feed it to meerkats, live streamed via webcam. She bought one. The voracious meerkats were already fully booked and could eat no more, so Ben was fed to a black-tufted marmoset. Watch it chew, mouth open, eyes tight, crunch, crunch, crunch.

She felt a little better.

The phone trilled. Ludo calling. Oh my God. She sat up straight, smoothed her hair and answered in what she hoped was a carefree voice.

'Hi, Jo speaking.'

'Hello there, Ludo Mansfield. Sorry I missed your call, I was in the Caribbean.'

Oh Christ, that night she had drunk one too many martini spritzers, thankfully he had not picked up.

'Ludo? From the funeral? I must have called you by mistake.' She realised too late that she was contradicting her attempted ignorance.

'You left me a charming message,' he sounded as if he was smiling.

Jo's heart sank, she had no recollection of what she had said. There was a long pause whilst she thought how to rectify the situation. Ludo continued, his voice was deep, intimate, she liked it.

'I wondered whether you would care to meet for lunch? I know a lovely little place by the river. I've gathered some intelligence about the suspects that might be of interest.'

Jo pretended to check her busy schedule and proposed they meet in three days' time – a technique she had learnt from *Hook Line and Sinker: How to land your man*. Perfect.

Within an hour her exhilaration had been supplanted by self-doubt. Why would a man like Ludovic Mansfield, *BA, MBA, CFA, Private Asset Management* be interested in a middle-aged, laid-off, divorcee? No, no, no, that is not the way to think. She rooted frantically through the Formica bureau; there it was, she retrieved a set of dog-eared index cards fastened by a faded treasury tag. *Promoting Self-Esteem. Tools to take home: Positive self-statements.* Her ward-manager had suggested that she attend the workshop at her 2014 Personal Development Review. A recommendation that had reduced her self-esteem sufficiently to deem the referral appropriate. She flicked through the pack:

I am a strong independent woman. I am physically attractive. I have a nursing degree. I hold a position of responsibility. I have good friends who love me. I care about myself. I have my own maisonette. I enjoy socialising. I go to the gym. I am fit and healthy.

She removed the four that no longer applied, struck her Power Pose, as practiced at the seminar, and reread the cards aloud. Yes, of course a man like Ludo would be drawn to me, we are just the perfect match.

Ludo was sitting at the best table in the orangery, a private alcove overlooking the river. He blended into his territory with a pale pink shirt, tailored navy blazer, sunglasses stylishly positioned in his hair. She walked the full length of the room under his gaze, an opportunity to exhibit the sleeveless dress that had cost far more than she could afford, still 'speculate to accumulate,' as Ben used to say.

Ludo stood, kissed her lightly on both cheeks and drew back her chair. She felt as if she had not breathed for several minutes.

'You look delightful, new dress?' A flash of white teeth.

'Oh, this old thing,' she tilted her head Princess Di style and raised demure eyes.

The waiter appeared with a bottle of Prosecco, a platter of fresh oysters and the menus. He seemed to know Ludo.

'I took the liberty of ordering hors d'oeuvres and drinks, I remembered you like Prosecco.'

Another woman might have been affronted by his presumption but she loved a man who took control. She forced down an oyster, they were really quite revolting, what was all the fuss about? It was thoughtful of him to tuck in without pressing her to have another; he must have noticed she was not a fan. He seemed to delight in them, he swallowed several with unconcealed abandon. She took a cursory glance at the menu.

'What would you recommend?' She appeared to have developed an upper-class accent.

'The Onglet steak is good, or perhaps the fish.' He held her gaze as he drank another oyster.

She would have preferred the steak but opted for salmon, it was more lady-like.

'So, this is all very cloak and dagger, it's so sweet of you to help with my investigations. What is it you've discovered?'

Ludo glanced overtly to his left and right like a pantomime villain, a part he appeared to relish. 'Clara Astrell, aged 60, retired G.P., never married, one son, lives in Marlow, drives a Nissan Leaf. Andrea taught her son at St Birinus, he was the first in the school to go to Cambridge.'

Jo felt a little disappointed in the information, basic facts, most of which she already knew or could have gleaned from LinkedIn. Nonetheless she smiled encouragingly as he continued.

'I checked out her registration plate; it's a brand-new car, quite decadent for a retired lady.'

Actually, that was a good point, she would add 'profligate spending' to Clara's evidence column. 'Do go on.'

'Henrietta Cuvier, although an unusual suspect, is definitely a person of interest.' He took a sip of wine and leaned forward conspiratorially. 'Old money but must have fallen on hard times, lives with her elderly parents.'

He finished the last oyster, his napkin leaving a glistening trail across his cheek.

A passing strawberry-blonde glanced at him; Jo glared to reinforce ownership until she looked away.

'As far as motive,' he continued, 'there are generally only three reasons to commit murder: love, money, or both,' he paused to hold her gaze. She loved his eyes. 'Money is the more plausible in this case. They were acquainted through the RSPB; Henrietta might well have known about Andrea's inheritance but not that it was spent. Alternatively, Andrea had something on her and was blackmailing her or vice versa.'

Jo nodded although this seemed like a long shot. 'Did you find anything to indicate an interest in tortoises?'

The waiter reappeared. During the pause in conversation she was hit by a terrible realisation; if he had researched Clara and Henrietta online it was also likely that he had Googled her. Did he know about the Serious Incident Review? Her suspension from

Goredale? She took a deep breath, get a grip, whatever he knew he was here, and he was being charming.

'Tortoises? No, is that something I should add to my line of inquiry?' He looked quizzical.

'It's a possible lead. Andrea's tortoise is missing, presumed stolen, it is clearly linked to the murder.' She could not read Ludo's Mona Lisa smile.

'I understand there is a lucrative market in trafficking such things but I suspect one needs more than one.'

'That sounds as if it has legs,' she released her girlish giggle.

'You are quite the wit Detective Inspector Burns-Whyte.'

'Well perhaps we might make a good duo, I'll be the side-kick,' she tucked a tendril of hair behind her ear.

'You could be the pretty one from Line of Duty, I'll be H.' He sliced his steak, it was shockingly rare. 'But seriously, I know you'll get to the truth and I'm always here to help.'

She watched him eat, he reminded her of a tiger devouring its krill on a David Attenborough documentary. Powerful, majestic, fearsome. It was time to switch up a gear.

'So, where is it that you live?' She guessed that it would not be her side of town.

'I have a house in South Kensington, but I stay over on my boat when I have business in Berkshire.'

Jo was unable to conceal her delight, this man had it all, he was definite husband material. 'How lovely, I adore boating.' In truth she had only ever ventured out in a swan-pedalo as a child, but she had enjoyed it.

'You must come over one evening,' Ludo chewed his steak and eyed her as if she were a gazelle.

'Thank you, I'd love that. It means a great deal that you believe in me, the police seem to be dragging their feet.'

'Well let's keep digging, justice will prevail,' he held her gaze.

There was a moment's silence.

'Life is a balance of holding on and letting go,' she hoped that she had remembered today's Zen quotation correctly.

Ludo looked impressed. 'That's very true. I propose a toast. To holding on and letting go.'

They clinked glasses.

9

C lara lifted the heavy brass wolf and knocked twice. The studded oak door demanded a horror film squeak but opened silently to reveal Hen in moleskin trousers, crocheted waistcoat over an orange-flecked jumper and matching eye-patch.

'How lovely to see you, dear heart, do come in and meet the parents.'

'It's so kind of you to invite me.' Clara handed her a large spider-plant resplendent with offshoots.

As she stepped into the hallway the hint of winter honeysuckle was replaced by the smell of beeswax and wet fur. A dachshund danced a jack-in-the-box greeting from the open lid of a monk's bench. It produced a howl that harmonised with the plaintive cello coming from a distant room. Clara guessed at Vaughn Williams or Elgar; she had always found the two indistinguishable.

'Did you not bring your whippet?' Hen adjusted her patch as if this might clarify the matter.

'He's in the car, I worried he would upset the ducks.'

'Nonsense, do bring him in, he'll be no trouble.'

Blue was sniffing the air through the gap in the car window, he slinked out and followed her into the house, his tail between his legs.

The wood-panelled hallway gave a choice of four doors each ajar. She followed Hen and the heady tang of marmalade into a huge but chaotic kitchen. Battered pots adorned the walls, onions dangled from brackets, washing hung from slats above the stove. A thin-haired woman in a scarlet pashmina looked up from her easel and peered through thick glasses.

'*Chlorophytum comosum*, did you propagate it yourself?'

'Yes, they are unfashionable but I'm a big fan.'

'My mother Dolly, my father Charles,' Hen gestured as if revealing unexpected delights.

A tall man in a herring-bone jacket rose, propped his cello against the fridge and took her hand.

'Delighted to meet you. What a splendid dog, whippet is he?' His voice was surprisingly strong, it put her in mind of John Mills in *In Which We Serve*.

'Yes, this is Blue, he is a little nervous I'm afraid.'

'He'll soon settle. Betty was the same, rescue dog, wouldn't come from under her blanket for the first week, now there's no stopping her, part terrier, part mountain hare. Morris is a standard poodle, we don't clip him so he looks feral. And this is Nosferatu, miniature dachshund, occupies a world of his own.'

Apparently having provided Clara with all the information she required Charles returned to his chair. Hen handed her a cup of coffee. She appreciated that she was welcomed without fuss or expectation. Sweeping brush strokes rasped across the large canvas.

'What is it that you are painting Mrs Cuvier?'

'Dolly, please. It's a landscape, the Namib desert at sunset. Abstract. My eyesight is not what it was, I like colour contrasts.'

'May I?' Clara examined the canvas, a riot of red and gold. 'Why, it's beautiful, you have a real talent. Have you always painted?'

'Only the last twenty years, I started when I was seventy. Perhaps Hen will point out some of my portraits.'

'I'd love to see them.'

'Dolly went to art school for a while, but she found it too corporate. She's done a lovely set of satirical paintings of our twenty-first century Prime Ministers,' said Charles with evident pride.

'I don't recall painting a cormorant,' Dolly looked doubtful.

'No dear, corporate, the art school.'

'Oh yes, I should have gone in the sixties, well no matter I've developed my own style.'

Clara loved her.

Hen retrieved a pair of leather boots drying by the Aga. 'Should we see the ducks while the rain holds off?' The indication of imminent activity unleashed a contagion of barking that negated any further discussion. 'Father would you be a lamb and make a start on the sandwiches? Clara might like to join us for afternoon tea.'

Clara, usually forearmed with an excuse to avoid prolonged social interaction, found herself genuinely delighted to accept.

The two women and four dogs set off along the overgrown path.

Hen wore a horse blanket fashioned into a make-shift shawl. They walked in companionable silence, Clara admiring the skeletons of elm and oak silhouetted against the mauve sky.

'Oh, I must tell you, that awful man we met at the funeral, Hugo was it? no Ludo, telephoned me. He said he'd looked up my number in the directory, Cuvier being an unusual surname. Wanted to know if I was interested in having my antiques valued.'

'That's very presumptuous. How odd, his card said he was a financial advisor. What did you tell him?'

'I said they might be antiques to you chum but to me they are furniture. I had the distinct impression that he was up to no good.' She held back a bramble with her stick to allow Clara to pass.

'Yes, his attempted charm was a tad heavy-handed.' Clara trusted her ability to deduce character, a skill that she had honed over decades of ten-minute appointments. She ascribed to Ludo a core of malevolence.

'Oh yes an inveterate charmer, quite the puff-adder. And wearing an old Etonian tie of all things, sadly, I've been acquainted with enough public-school boys to know he is not one. As bent as a dog's hind leg.'

'He followed me out to my car, noted it was electric and said he was "interested in all things eco", then asked about my pension.'

'Fellow is a scoundrel.'

Clara loved her candour. 'I did like Ed, Andrea's brother, he seemed to be still in shock, poor thing.'

'Interesting gait and complexion; put me in mind of the Eurasian wigeon, so avian one felt he had hollow bones. Very knowledgeable, he certainly knew a great deal about sheep.' Hen directed the dogs to sit, only Betty obeyed.

'Very edifying you might say,' Clara slipped a lead around Blue's neck as they approached Round Pond.

'Edifying, oh you are a hoot!'

Clara stopped in her tracks. An army of slender-necked ducks hurtled towards them in a cacophony of calls.

'Indian runners,' Hen announced proudly, 'they have a lovely temperament, rather exuberant.'

The runners jockeyed for position as she opened the grain hoppers.

'Their carriage is endearing.'

'The morphology is somewhat of a compromise between walking and swimming.'

Clara watched as Morris flung himself into the pond and Nosferatu rolled enthusiastically on duck droppings, Blue seemed overwhelmed by the sensory load.

'Such a beautiful place to live, you must be very happy here.'

'Oh yes, I've been here all my life. I shan't move. The old farmhouse was getting a bit much for the parents so I converted the pigsties for them: all super-insulated, ground source heating, single storey, easy to manage. Of course, when it came time to move, the old dinosaurs decided they would prefer to stay in the draughty homestead. Each to their own nest I suppose. So now I live in the piggery, it's marvellous.'

Clara was unprepared for the hail of birds that greeted them as Hen recklessly launched fists full of scraps from her satchel.

'The merganser,' she pointed out two thin-beaked birds with spiky head crests.

'You were right, I do love them!'

'Eat fish, nest in holes in trees, great fun.'

'You seem to be having a happy retirement. Why ducks?'

'I stumbled across them quite by accident. I was visiting a vineyard in Stellenbosch; chap had a huge flock of runners to keep the snails down. I was hooked, came back home and bought my first dozen, never looked back.'

'I do envy your passion. I haven't done anything since I retired.'

'Quite right to. First twelve months do nothing, let your dreams percolate and meet up with them later.'

'That's very sound advice. People will keep asking what I'm doing, now I can tell them that.'

They stood absorbing the scene, the water alive with the pale winter sun. Clara gradually discriminated quacks, whistles, honks and chatters from the wall of sound.

'Can you identify them by their calls?'

'Oh yes, most of them have a characteristic that one can recognise, that high-pitched whistle is Monty the Fulvous.'

'Gosh, I meant identify by species, not individual birds, that's very impressive.'

Hen appeared delighted by the compliment. Clara helped to fill the hoppers and they headed back for afternoon tea.

They entered through a side door into a dimly lit utility room. Clara ducked to avoid the coils of glue paper that hung from the ceiling heavy with flies. Motes of dog hair danced in the air.

'Welcome to the decontamination chamber, the trick is to catch them unawares.'

In a practised scoop, Hen grabbed the guano covered dachshund by the scruff of the neck and held him under a warm tap. A scrawny black cat lay draped along the coat rack observing proceedings through suspicious eyes.

'That's Aunt Jobiska, our oldest cat, best give her a wide-berth until she gets to know you.'

Clara examined a portrait of a man with beady eyes and a receding hair-line, sheltering beneath a tattered American flag. Bombs rained down, on each WMD was written as if in blood, alongside his name: Tony Blair.

'Gosh that's quite a statement.'

'Wait until you see David Cameron, we've put him in the downstairs loo, the porcine likeness is marvellous; of him and the pig.'

The disembodied voices of Charles and Dolly echoed from the counter. Fortunately, the conversation was not about her but Jarrod Soames-Grayling, the local MP and his record expense claims.

'Two-way baby monitor in case assistance is required,' said Hen. She swaddled Nosferatu in an old towel and carried him through to the kitchen.

Dolly sat in her blue velvet Bath chair at the head of the table upon which were arranged plates of finger sandwiches and a tiered cake-stand laden with petit-fours.

'Perfect timing, I was just about to pour the tea,' said Charles.

'Are you still using that old teapot? What happened to the new one I bought you for Christmas?'

'It's so nice, I'm saving it for special occasions.'

'Father, you're ninety-seven, how many more special occasions are there going to be?'

'Well you can inherit it.'

'It's so nice having young people around,' said Dolly, patting the chair for Clara to sit beside her.

'That's nice of you to say, but I'm sixty!'

'It's all relative dear. Do you have your parents?'

'My father died about fifteen years ago, cancer, he was a G.P., recently retired.'

She hadn't been asked about her father for years, her mother had forgotten his existence. Sixty-five, robbed of his hard-earned pension, an age that seemed younger every year. The image of herself as a skinny girl singing along with him in his beige Morris Minor *Ain't Nobody Here But Us Chickens*. Her mother laughing.

'My mother has Alzheimer's; she lives in a nursing home in Shrewsbury.'

Dolly nodded sympathetically and negotiated a mouthful of egg and cress sandwich. 'Old age ain't no place for sissies. Bette Davies.'

Clara was glad she did not pursue the topic.

'I see you follow George Orwell's rules for a good cup of tea: strong, Indian, and poured before the milk,' said Clara.

'Pure coincidence, I don't know them,' said Charles with interest.

'He wrote an essay on the subject in 1945, setting out eleven golden rules. He maintained that one feels wiser, braver and more optimistic after a nice cup of tea.'

'Well, I would have to agree with him,' smiled Charles.

'Oh, my favourite, petit fours, *je ne me dérange pas si je le fais!*' said Hen in an exaggerated accent helping herself to a pink fondant cube.

'I love your satirical portraits Dolly.'

'Thank you dear, well it keeps me off the streets, although I do miss public protests.'

'Mother has been a lifelong activist: CND, Greenham Common, Occupy London, she's been arrested several times. It is perhaps time she retired.' Hen's mock censure failed to disguise her evident delight.

'Clara dear, might I ask your opinion on laser eye surgery? Hen is as blind as a bat.'

Hen made the sound of a cracking whip, 'Oh, what was that? I do believe someone is flogging a dead horse! I can see perfectly well.'

'Charles, remind me where did we read about monocles being pretentious?'

'Tatler.'

'You see, you should go under the laser, hardly any risk, what do you think Clara?' Clara decided to sit this one out, she tilted her head as if in consideration.

'Monocles are only pretentious if you have two eyes mother. And where on earth were you reading Tatler?'

'Your father read it to me in the dentist's waiting room, he had just started a very interesting article on the rise of the far-right in Westminster and Washington, I was rather sorry to be called in.'

'And what are you planning to do with your retirement?' asked Hen mischievously.

Clara took up her lead, 'I've booked onto an alpaca husbandry course. I'd like to spend some time outside after thirty-odd years behind the stethoscope.'

'Patsy Clifton,' said Dolly decisively.

Clara considered early-stage dementia. She looked to Hen to handle the situation.

'Manor Alpacas at Pangbourne. The owner is Patsy Clifton,' Hen clarified.

'Oh, you know her? Does she have a good reputation?' Clara wondered whether her impulse to diagnose would ever dissipate. Dolly's senses might be failing but she was fully cognisant.

'Yes, nice woman, talks mainly about alpacas, total fanatic, I think you will learn a lot.'

'She even looks like an alpaca,' said Charles, selecting a fondant fancy. He protruded his lips, *Alpaca-lypes Now* I call her.'

His laughter turned to coughing then to choking. He grasped his throat, he looked scared.

'Stand up!' shouted Clara.

She ran behind him, dragged him to his feet and thumped his back with the heel of her hand. Nothing. His face was ashen, a terrible rasping came from his chest. She tightened her arms around his abdomen and heaved upwards with her fists. A piece of fondant icing shot from his mouth and he breathed again. Clara checked his airways, took his pulse and calmly resumed her seat. Despite protestations that he felt fine, she insisted that Hen call for an ambulance.

'Thank God you were here. Charles, I do keep telling you not to speak with your mouth full, and you will bolt your food,' Dolly held Charles's hand whilst she reprimanded him.

'The paramedics are on their way,' said Hen returning from the hallway. 'They agreed it is best that he is checked out.'

'Thirty-plus years of mandatory life-support training finally paid off, that was my very first Heimlich manoeuvre.'

'Thank you for saving father's life, we would have missed the old stick.'

Clara told the worm to take note.

10

I t felt to Jo as if the universe was conspiring to keep her from
her detective work. The letter bearing its NHS logo was om-
inously thick. She steadied her nerves with a menthol cigarette.
Today's quotation seemed snide, Relax, nothing is under control.
Bloody Buddhists. She inhaled the cool smoke and tore open the
envelope as if removing an aberrant hair.

Dear Miss Burns-Whyte,
We write to inform you that further to your suspension from the
post of ward manager, Kingfisher Ward, a disciplinary hearing
has now been arranged.
The hearing will consider the facts, hear from witnesses and rule
on outcomes up to and including summary dismissal.
We strongly advise that you are formally represented.
Although not a legal requirement it is important that you appear
in person to provide the opportunity to question witnesses and
to present any evidence in your defence.
Please be advised that there are serious matters calling for explanation. The Panel are likely to draw adverse inferences from
your non-attendance.
The hearing will take place at Goredale Hospital, Marlow, Berkshire
9.00 am Thursday 30th May 2019
S.F. Forbes
Head of Human Resources

Bastards.
She had made one silly error and was being disproportionately
punished. Poor Andrea had slunk from the job she loved, had not
asked for a tribunal or demanded a hearing. Look what that got
her: a place in the bloody dole queue. Well, she was not going to
go quietly. She was going to make a bloody racket.
Of course, she felt terrible for the bereaved family. She thought

of his widow, Mabel, she was very sweet. But really who was to blame, the administrator of the medication or the prescriber? One decimal place the distance between life and death. She had been lined up and took the bullet, it's never the doctors' fault, they cost too much to train, and to bloody get rid of. In truth she was on her final warning, twice before she had taken the blame rather than point the finger. God knows why. She recognised that this behaviour was not entirely altruistic, those she had saved had reciprocated; overlooking her smoking in the hospital grounds, her poor time keeping, the occasional hangover. And she derived a pleasure from self-sacrifice. The martyr trait inherited from her long-suffering mother, who had spent a lifetime doing the right thing whilst building up a backlog of resentment.

She imagined life without her career. She had had no calling, no vocation. She had chosen nursing with the sole aim of marrying a handsome doctor; before she had found one, she met Ben. She sighed at the irony of being flung from the top of a ladder that she had never wanted to climb; she would have happily left that to Ben. She had planned to work until their first baby arrived, take maternity leave and not return. Career progression was of little interest, she showed up, did her job, she went home. Whilst she had never actively sought promotion the nursing shortage in older-adult wards assured her unremitting rise through the ranks. Repeatedly asked to 'act up' when others left for better jobs, she eventually found herself Ward Manager. 'Everyone rises to their own level of incompetence' - Ben had heard the saying on an aspirational management course and liked to present it as his own witticism - he meant everyone except himself. He meant Jo in particular.

But as a divorcee her job had become important; it meant night's out, spa breaks and shopping sprees. She could not live without it.

She lit another cigarette and reviewed her position: her best friend murdered, her investigation faltering, single, broke and now she had to fight for her job. Of all the maelstrom years, twenty-nineteen was turning out to be an über-shitstorm. Ludo her only lifeline.

As if by telekinesis, or was it telemetry? her phone pinged, a text from Ludo: *How's your day?* She tapped in *really shite*, deleted it and wrote *All good here, fancy meeting for drinks?* She added a cocktail emoji and three kisses. Send. It was bold, but she felt it suited her new persona. He believed in her. The minutes ticked by, she began to regret her forwardness, had she got this horribly wrong? She scrolled back through their texts, he had definitely been the first to add a kiss, and to instigate the double. She lit another cigarette and checked her phone, nothing. The ringtone made her jump.

'Hi, it's me,' he Barry-Whited.

Slightly presumptuous, although he knew that she had his contact in her phone. He didn't know that she had added a special tune to his number; the James Bond theme.

'How nice to hear from you.'

'Listen, I'm just going into a meeting, when are you free for those cocktails?'

'How about tomorrow?' Her enthusiasm overrode the play-it-cool strategy, in truth she had never really mastered it.

'The Golden Frog at Henley, after work?'

'Oh yes, it's lovely there, one of my favourite haunts.' She had no idea where it was, but she could Google it.

'Great, see you there.'

Another of Ben's phrases came to mind: 'Fortune favours the brave' too damn right. She noted that the thought of him did not ignite any anger today, perhaps watching the reruns of Ben the cockroach being heartily chewed had done the trick. She peeked at tomorrow's Zen wisdom: *Life begins where fear ends.* Yes, her stars were aligning.

She spent an hour trying on outfits before deciding on a red cocktail dress, suitable for the occasion if slightly tight; she hadn't worn it since that disastrous night with Jonny the polo player who had had one too many Pinots and been sick on her carpet before passing out. She checked her phone, a text from Ludo apologising, something's come up, he'd have to work late, would rearrange soon. Three kisses. The same vague excuse that Ben had used when he was seeing Carly. No, Ludo wasn't like that. The three kisses absolved him of everything.

Rays of sunlight illuminated the mosaic of finger marks on the high-gloss cabinets. She put a Frappuccino pod into the coffee-maker, stared out of the window and imagined herself into the role of detective Burns-Whyte. Beyond her scrubby patch of lawn, the squirrel-proof bird feeder - a gift from Andrea - swung empty in the wind. She sighed. What would *Vera* do? Or that one from *Line of Duty*? Build a picture of the suspects. Yes, she needed background. She tried to imagine ways of casually bumping into Clara or Henrietta, she doubted that they would frequent Pizza Express or Greggs. And she needed more time with Ed. Oh my God; a party!

She knew that she had been avoiding her birthday party planning. She and Andrea had promised to have a joint celebration for their fortieths and to invite forty people. Now, as she trawled her address book, she had to admit that she had very few friends, most of the names were male; the majority crossed out. Even widening the net with Andrea's acquaintances, she mustered only thirty potential invitees. Still, it was a perfect opportunity to gather intelligence and to seal her relationship with Ludo. Two birds with one stone. Win-win.

She smiled to herself, she was so cunning. Like a badger.

11

John stared out of the window at the brick wall that threw its blank shadow across his desk. He had had a bad day. After six hours in the cold investigating a suspected arson at Kwik-fit tyres, the fire officer had contacted him with news of a faulty fuse box. Meanwhile, there had been another petrol station robbery to add to the spate of car-jackings and cash machine ram-raids on his patch. The Gibbons investigation was almost light relief.

Constable Beech had been thorough with the background checks: Andrea kept squeaky clean company. The only greyish sheep was her brother Ed who had acquired an assault conviction in 2001.

Cayman National Bank had finally responded. Their attachments included a colour copy of her photo ID. She looked fun. Dark wavy hair, chinchilla eyes, the hint of a mischievous smile. Happy. In her prime. The information they released was not exactly illuminating, the little light it did cast was dim and fell squarely on the bank's meagre money laundering safeguards. Mystery solved; Andrea had received the lump sum from Berkshire Education Authority. The money had been deposited in Cayman National Bank and swiftly transferred to Trident Holdings Incorporated, the company was immediately liquidated and its CEO Harold Grousemoor no longer appeared to exist.

There were three possible explanations: Andrea Gibbons - secondary school teacher with not so much as a parking ticket - had been involved in international money laundering; she had executed an audacious tax scam; or she had been conned.

The headmaster had lied. He closed his door and dialled St Birinus. He had not warmed to Mr Geoffrey Taylor during their first conversation, the man had damned Ms Gibbons with faint praise, 'a popular teacher who will be mourned by pupils and staff' insipid and meaningless. That's what you get for a life in public service. Half a life. He wondered what DCI Wallace would say about him. "Not too bad for a homosexual." At least he could laugh about it.

'Mr Taylor this is DI John Appleton, Thames Valley Police, we spoke in January.'

'Yes, I remember officer, poor Miss Gibbons.' He had one of those watery voices to which one wanted to add spirit.

'I'd appreciate the truth this time. You can tell me over the phone or down at the station.'

'The truth in what regard?'

'You led me to believe that Andrea had been dismissed from her post and had not pursued the case. So why did the education authority pay out a substantial sum in July last year?

A long silence.

'I'm afraid that I'm not at liberty to say,' his voice further diluted.

'Any concerns regarding confidentiality do not apply when helping police with their enquiries. Obstructing such an investigation can however have serious consequences.' John had spoken these words many times, they sounded best as bullet points with an undertone of threat.

'Very well officer. I was perhaps frugal with the truth. It was in Miss Gibbons' best interests and in the interests of the school not to endure a long-drawn-out disciplinary procedure and employment tribunal. These things can be very stressful, especially when working relationships have broken down irretrievably.' He paused.

John imagined that he had said this to Andrea, likely with a hint of pleasure. The man was very irritating.

'Please, if you could get to the point.'

'Miss Gibbons waived her right to contest the termination of her employment in return for a settlement.'

'Fifty thousand pounds?'

'Yes, thirty thousand of which is tax-free.'

'With a gagging clause?' He was losing patience, had he known this weeks ago Wallace might not have been breathing down his neck to close the investigation. People had been killed for a lot less than fifty grand.

'As is customary, we signed a non-disclosure agreement.'

'And the limits of the agreement?'

'She was unable to disclose the settlement and its terms to any-

one except her representative and her immediate family.'
Bloody hell.
John hung up.
So, Ed knew.

12

Clara could not recall a Jo Burns-Whyte or imagine why on earth she had invited her to her birthday party. It was only as she was adding another layer of topsoil to Darwin's enclosure that she remembered the histrionic woman from Andrea Gibbons' funeral.

A dilemma. Generally, she disliked parties but she had decided to try to be more sociable; it was not healthy to hibernate. It might be refreshing to meet people who would not ask about their son's acne, or migraine treatments, or how to influence their position on the hip replacement list. Also, it was to be held at Radingley Abbey, a lovely venue; Ms Burns-Whyte was certainly pushing the boat out. Likely a post-bereavement revel, those frantic affirmations of life that people launched into, desperate attempts to live everyday as if it were their last. It generally petered out within a couple of weeks. Another problem with parties was the men. She had never considered herself attractive, it was baffling that men flirted with her, an interaction that she found both amusing and tiresome.

She settled into her rocking chair and opened chapter three of *Keep The Aspidistra Flying*. Blue crawl onto her lap for the reading. A persistent thudding broke her concentration. Why a three-year-old was up at nine o'clock she had no idea, he appeared to be marching up and down the uncarpeted living room of number five like the Grand Old Duke of York. It was very annoying. She reached for the TV remote control to mask the noise of the elephantine child. A French maître d' was welcoming a woman in dangerously high-heels to the *First Dates* restaurant. At the bar a tattooed man, holding an incongruous mojito, turns to examine his date. He is not disappointed. She imagined Phineas asking why she was watching such a low-budget hetero-normative programme; she asked herself the same question.

She poured herself a glass of Tullamore Dew and took it out into the back garden and down to the orchard. She felt close to him here, the only man she had ever loved. The clever, outrageous, mesmerising, Padraig Devlin. No other man ever came close. The key-note speaker at a conference on alcohol-related neurological dysfunction, she had found him utterly beguiling. Durham University, 3rd - 6th October 1990, the best four days of her life. She still had the programme. She had approached him after his talk to ask about the clinical management of Wernicke-Korsakoff syndrome and did not hear a single word of his reply. They went for dinner; they ordered poached pears, he cut a heart into hers, a liver into his. They cried with laughter. They spent the next 72 hours together. It passed in a whirlwind of conversation, drinking and careless sex. She returned to Marlow, he to Dublin.

She stood beneath the pear tree that she had planted that year; a conference pear, it would have made him laugh. Tim was smoking in the back garden, he waved over the fence; it seemed that he too was escaping from the demon child. She wondered what he thought of her standing in her overgrown orchard drinking whiskey; she decided that she didn't much care. She examined the tree's new buds, it was thriving. She raised her glass to Padraig.

Oh well, perhaps she had idealised the whole relationship. Would she have tired of him? His jokes become hackneyed? His bodhran playing clichéd? At least her memory held those days as unspoiled, precious, without compare.

The worm spat out the single word: *Spinster*.

She did not regret her choices; never having had a husband meant she was at least spared the pain of losing one. Her mother's deterioration following her father's death had been difficult to witness. Of course, it later transpired that the apathy, social withdrawal and confusion were early signs of dementia. It was not until the topographical disorientation kicked in that the diagnosis became apparent. She was found two miles from Tesco, her intended destination, having turned left instead of right out of the house she had lived in for forty years.

She returned to the living room; silence. The boy must finally have gone to bed. She sighed, stroked Blue and reopened her book. As for the party she would check whether Hen was going and then decide.

A drone of voices punctuated by raucous laughter emanated from the Sunbury Room. Clara was not quite ready to join them. She strolled through the abbey admiring the mullioned windows, stone hearths, ornate ceilings. Being in an eight-hundred-year-old building, even one that had reinvented itself as a corporate venue, soothed the soul. The continuity of history stretching forwards and back a reminder of one's insignificance, a mere snapshot in time. She found herself in the Great Hall. She imagined it was 1600; from the minstrels' gallery three slender trumpets announced the arrival of a procession of regal guests. A string quartet resonated around the vaulted ceiling. The dancing began.

'If it isn't the lovely Dr Clara, how nice to see you again.'

The smarmy man grabbed her, his embrace and cheek kisses wholly inappropriate to their casual acquaintance. She managed a perfunctory smile.

'We meet again, Ludo Mansfield at your service,' he affected a deep bow.

Everything about this man was annoying. 'How are you Mr Mansfield?'

'Do call me Ludo. I was hoping I would hear from you, perhaps you mislaid my number?' He produced his business card like a magic trick.

'As I said, I have no need for financial advice.'

'Everyone can benefit from my impartial tips. Perhaps you would care to meet up to discuss pension plans? Or anything else that might be of interest.'

His wink made Clara feel distinctly uneasy. 'Shall we join the others?' She turned for the door.

He stepped in front of her, she could smell his aftershave, alcohol on his breath.

'I'm so glad I bumped into you. I'm a little worried about our mutual friend.'

Clara wondered who he was talking about. She said nothing.

'Jo. I thought perhaps you might be able to help her, you being a doctor.'

'I'm retired.' She didn't like the way his eyes scanned her figure.

'The thing is doctor,' he leaned in unnecessarily closely and lowered his voice, 'she is not dealing well with dear Andrea's suicide and entre nous, she has a little cocaine habit.'

'I really don't know her well,' she tried to step past him.

He caught her elbow. 'Must you rush off? I'd love to get to know you properly.'

His tone was lewd, an image of Harvey Weinstein came to mind.

'Ah! There you are,' Hen blustered into the hall. 'Come along dear-heart, they are serving the canapes,' ignoring Ludo she took Clara's arm and they walked out together.

The Sunbury room was smaller than she had envisioned, two waiters circulated with rapidly diminishing platters, voices rose above the ricochet of heels on the wooden floor. She recognised several people from Andrea's funeral.

Hen handed her a glass of red and popped a square of toasted pâte into her mouth. 'Oh, dear Lord,' she spat the chewed remnants into her hand, 'Duck!'

Clara fished a tissue from her bag.

'Thank you dear-heart, I really must check, I assumed mushroom.'

'Ermintrude!' cried Clara.

'A friend?' Hen scanned the room.

'The cow, from The Magic Roundabout. That expression, 'dear-heart', I've been trying to recall why it's so familiar, it's what Ermintrude called Dougal.'

'You are quite correct. Delightful programme, Brian the snail was my favourite. Who was yours?'

'Ermintrude the cow, she still is.'

'Why thank you dear-heart,' Hen mimicked the character's voice perfectly.

'How is your father? I received his lovely thank-you bouquet and card addressed to Dr Clara 'Crusher' Astrell.'

'It transpired that he sustained a broken rib from the back blows but he's absolutely fine.'

'Oh no, I'm so sorry.'

'He thrives on soldiering on, he is in his element.'

'Hello girls, so glad you could come.' Jo Burns-Whyte appeared like an Oscar statuette in a gold silk dress, her hair snaked on her bare shoulders, she was unrecognisable from the funeral.

'Thank you so much for inviting us,' Clara struck an affectionate tone to mitigate the fact that she hardly knew the woman.

'Ed gave me your contact details, he has Andrea's address book. I wanted to invite all of Andrea's close friends. I'm sure she's here in spirit.'

Clara winced; Andrea would only have had her address because she occasionally dropped Phineas home. She felt that she should tell Jo about their last meeting, the slight tremor in Andrea's hand as she stroked Darwin goodbye. Now was not the time. 'Is Ed here? I thought his tribute to his sister was beautiful.'

'No, he couldn't come, it's lambing season apparently,' Jo appeared hugely displeased.

'Yes, he must be terribly busy.'

'You are an expert on lambs are you?' Jo snorted.

'Ah, Ed. Such a gentle soul.' Bless her, Hen had the knack of sailing through hostile atmospheres undaunted.

'Yes indeed,' Clara agreed.

'Apart from when he lamped that chap with a milk bottle.'

'Ed attacked someone?' Jo seemed aghast.

'Well one expects he deserved it. Happy birthday dear.' Hen produced a crumpled paper parcel from her jacket pocket, 'do open it.'

Jo removed the brown wrapping with some disdain. A book of postcards, each showing an exotic variety of waterfowl. She looked at it uncertainly.

'They are detachable,' said Hen by way of explanation.

Jo stuffed the book into her clutch bag without comment. 'Andrea was very keen on bird-watching as you know.'

'Yes, she was rather fond of owls. Bagged sightings of all five British species and a good number of Caribbean ones I believe.'

'If you were to recommend one bird book what would it be?' Jo appeared to be struggling to retain a cheery manner.

'The British Trust for Ornithology Guide to the Birds of Britain and Ireland is a marvellous reference, I would start with that.'

'Would you now.'

'Yes, I have an old copy if you would like it, my sightings are marked but otherwise it's pristine.'

Jo ignored the offer and turned to Clara. 'And are you interested in such things?' The question appeared almost accusatory.

'I do like wildlife documentaries, but my son is the expert. Phineas was always one of Andrea's favourites.'

'I'm sure she didn't have favourites; she was very professional.'

'Of course, I meant that she went out of her way to encourage him, let him look after the stick insects, that sort of thing.' God this woman was hard work.

'What is the lethal dose of Temazepam?'

'I don't follow,' Clara wondered whether Jo had an atypical thought disorder. Knight's-move thinking was rare outside of psychosis.

'Caught you off guard doctor?' Her eyes widened.

Perhaps Ludo was right and she was under the influence of a stimulant. Clara resorted to her professional stance; she had always found it useful to point out discontinuities without comment. 'I was talking about stick insects; you asked me about Temazepam.'

'Andrea is alleged to have taken her own life. I was merely asking if you knew the required dose.'

Clara had somehow found herself in a disjointed court-room drama. 'I understand that you're a nurse, perhaps you could look it up in the BNF?' she said calmly.

'Are you insinuating that I have a problem administering medication?' her left eye twitched.

If you gave this woman a stick, she would take the wrong end.

'Well, well, if it isn't the birthday girl,' Ludo grabbed Jo by the waist and kissed her neck.

Clara cringed.

'Ludo darling, I'm so glad you could come,' Jo transformed back into an exemplary hostess.

'Apologies again that you couldn't use my boat, if someone went overboard you know, better safe than sorry.'

'Oh, not to worry this was my original venue, I just thought it might have been fun.'

'Where do you moor?' asked Hen.

Ludo flashed his teeth. 'Henley, just up-stream from The Leander Club.'

'Oh yes, I know it. I used to row for Reading, women's coxless fours, going back half a century of course.'

Clara looked at her friend in admiration, she was a source of constant surprise.

'I prefer my boats horse-powered. You ladies must come out with me now that the weather is improving.'

'I'd love to,' Jo turned her back on Clara and Hen.

Hen took the opportunity to wink at her.

'Did you not row at Eton Mr Mansfield?' Hen raised her monocle.

'No, rugger was more my thing. Looks like you need a refill my sweet,' he took Jo's glass and disappeared into the crowd.

Clara seized two cheese straws from the passing waiter and handed one to Hen. 'I hope you don't mind me saying Jo, but it might be wise to tread carefully with that one.'

'Whatever do you mean?' Jo looked indignant.

'He seems a little untrustworthy. Lecherous. I'm not sure he has your best interests at heart.'

'A philanderer if ever I saw one,' added Hen.

'That is my boyfriend you are talking about.'

'I'm sorry, he made me feel uncomfortable earlier.'

'I have to agree dear, a wolf in wolf's clothing.'

'As if he would be interested in two old crones, you're deluding yourselves,' Jo turned on her heel and strode off towards the drinks table.

'Enjoying the party dear-heart?' Hen's eye twinkled.

'Further confirmation that parties are not my thing.'

'Do not give up, you have not been to one of mine yet.'

13

Jo was seething. Furious at herself and at those old hags. And the party had cost a bloody fortune.

Her scheme to compile suspect profiles had yielded little on Clara or her one-eyed side-kick. Ludo had said she should try to rattle them; that's when they make mistakes but she really must learn to rein in her emotions. Oh well, as Buddha would say look on the bright side, she did glean some new information; Ed had "previous". Weedy Ed was capable of violence. Also, Phineas the smart-arse son was a definite lead. Taunting her with 'he was Andrea's favourite.' What the hell did that mean? Was she insinuating a relationship? Love or money, that's what Ludo said. Whatever she meant there was something very unpleasant about Dr Clara Astrell. She loathed mothers, always banging on about their children's accomplishments, didn't they know that the childless couldn't give a damn?

And how dare they slander Ludo like that? Envy was not an attractive quality, especially in the over sixties. Although another positive, she and Ludo had shared 'a moment' after the party; he had made his feelings clear and they were X-rated. Several texting flurries later he had requested a topless photo! As encouragement he had sent one of himself. The tattoo had been a surprise. She uploaded the image onto her laptop to study in detail. An eagle, its wings spread across his muscular chest, intricate feathers in gold and black, quite beautiful. The eyes were intense but the bird was almost smiling. It held something in its beak, perhaps a twig, her fingers gently traced its outline, she recoiled. A scorpion. Shiny black, its tail arched over its contorted back. The eagles' legs were sturdy, the thighs covered in downy feathers that made her feel better. The scaled talons held a scroll that unfurled down his abdomen revealing a list of names in blood red. She read each one out loud: David, Paul, Jimmy, Abi, Tracey, Andi, Hannah. She guessed that they were people who were special in his life, family and friends. How lovely. The overall impression was of a centred confident man. And evidently he worked out. His photographic request was flattering, a cementing of their relationship. She would have to be careful of the camera angle, she didn't want him to see the scars. She might as well show them off, they had cost enough, another post-Ben recovery treat.

The clatter of the letterbox, a thud on the laminate flooring. Discarding the pizza offers and double-glazing leaflets she examined a heavy envelope; return address Thames Valley Police. Yes, finally some action! She tore it open. What-the-actual? She sifted through the sheets: Act now. Your rights explained. How to appeal. Your penalty options. A blurred photograph of her car. Bloody speeding fine. Thirty-four miles an hour in a thirty-mile limit, unbelievable.

Jo opted for the speed awareness course and took a cancellation although it meant driving to bloody Reading. Right, if she was a lawbreaker, she would act like one, get her money's worth. She glanced at the thirty-mile per hour sign and put her foot down, thirty-five, forty, forty-five. It was fun. Twenty years of sticking to the speed limit, cut up by boy-racers, tailgated by suits in BMWs. Now she was being sent off to be re-educated, where were we living, bloody Russia? Oh, I'll change my behaviour alright. She braked heavily and sat at the lights revving the engine. The Punto juddered in protest. As the lights turned to green a hooded youth stepped into the road transfixed by his mobile and ambled on oblivious, she lent on the horn and swept passed in a cloud of fumes. In the rear-view mirror she watched him stoop to pick up his phone from the zebra crossing, the shock on his face, he couldn't be more than twelve.

Okay, I have to calm down. She fumbled in the glove compartment for her CD, veering perilously across the centre line. The familiar pan pipes and New England accent were an immediate tonic:

'Welcome to growth and resilience, your ten steps to inner contentment. By buying this programme you have taken the first step in shaping your own future; you are in the driving seat.' She

swung into the carpark. *'Whatever might be wrong in your life you are ready to befriend it, only you have the power to change, what are you waiting for?'* At the moment a bloody parking space. She drummed her fingers on the steering wheel. Maybe life was different in Boston, or Massachusetts, or wherever Dr Jonas Woodrow-Emerson M.D. was fortunate enough to live. She imagined him recording his audiobooks in a fashionable beach house, his pretty wife whittling sculptured driftwood and fixing healthy meals. Of course, they would have a clutch of tanned children, Zac and Jim who played baseball, and beautiful long-limbed daughters with perfect teeth. In some worlds it was easy to be good. Fat raindrops dotted the windscreen, she pulled the car under a tree and waited for a space. A bird with black and white stripes and an orange crest called in alarm. Andrea would know its name. It fled from its perch splattering the Punto. She flicked on the wipers smearing the thick droppings across the windscreen. This day just gets better.

Giving up on the car park she drove past miserable office blocks and abandoned her car in a side street. She searched in vain for her umbrella and, as best she could in kitten heels, made a dash for it. She marched into the hall, removed her polka-dot Alice band, as worn by Catherine Duchess of Cambridge, and shook her hair like the L'Occitane advert. A harsh light buzzed in the featureless room. She scanned the unlikely assortment of people: a tiny Asian man in his sixties was making polite conversation with a smartly dressed Caribbean woman her hair piled in a tower, a pregnant Millennial scrolled through her phone, a range of corporate types, builder types, women who might be teachers or secretaries, a young man with dreadlocks and a vacant expression. They hovered around the metal urns and took in turn to titrate strong tea or weak coffee into flimsy cups. A few uninspiring custard creams lay unclaimed on a paper plate. No-one was yet to take a seat; each shared the unhappy knowledge that they would be sitting on those hard plastic chairs for the next four hours. Oh God.

A man Jo recognised caught her eye, he too was evidently trying to place her. He wore jeans and a bottle-green fleece, he was unshaven but yes, it was Detective Inspector John Appleton. Unbelievable. She strode over and fixed him with her harshest scowl.

'So this is why my friend's murder gets shelved, so that you can teach a bloody speed awareness course. Outrageous,' she saw recognition emerge.

'Ah, Miss Burns-Whyte. Hello, actually it's my day off. The course isn't run by police, they get trainers in, generally driving instructors. I'm a participant.'

Jo struggled to adjust to the new information.

'Surely police officers don't get done for speeding?'

'No-one is above the law.'

His smile was warm and friendly, she regretted her attack.

A stout bald man entered from a side-door. He reminded Jo of the two old men from *The Muppet Show* who heckled from the balcony. He clapped his hands headmaster style, the room quietened.

'Alright Ladies and Gents, please turn off your phones and find yourselves a seat.'

They acquiesced, shuffling like a chain-gang. Jo sat in the back row, put her phone on silent and scrolled through her naughty texts from Ludo. The muppet was attempting to create a 'we're all in this together' vibe by getting them to repeat some kindergarten rhymes about stopping distances.

'Only a fool breaks the two second rule,' he pronounced.

'Only a fool breaks the two second rule,' they repeated in a singsong.

'When it's pouring with rain you say it again.'

'When it's pouring with rain you say it again,' they said in unison.

'Miss, Miss, excuse me Miss.'

'Miss, Miss, excuse me Miss,' she echoed before realising that no-one was joining in.

'Miss, perhaps you would like to share what you are reading with the group?'

Jo dropped the phone into her bag. 'I'm on-call, I was just checking in with the hospital.'

'If you could ensure that it is turned off, you will be able to check at tea-break,' he said with a faux smile.

Jo listened to the clock ticking and attempted to amuse herself by placing the participants in order of attractiveness. She studied

DI Appleton's strong jaw line and the definition of his shoulders; he was certainly in the top three. She wrote her shopping list, earning herself a nod of approval from the muppet who evidently assumed she was taking notes. The slight flicker of reprieve at the promise of 'some light-hearted fun,' was quickly extinguished as sets of road-traffic-sign cards were distributed. The game was to be played in pairs; she caught DI Appleton's eye and they retreated to the far corner.

'Don't worry it gets better, they show a video of car crashes after the break.'

He really was sweet. 'Have you done this course before Inspector?'

'Yes, I have. I'm off-duty remember, please call me John.'

'It obviously didn't work then; you should ask for your money back.' They exchanged conspiratorial smiles. Bonnie and Clyde.

'Listen, I really am sorry about your friend, we are investigating, it is being treated as an unexplained death.'

'I believe she knew her killer and that he, or she, made it look like suicide.'

'We are carrying out some background enquiries, but at the moment it's not a murder investigation,' he shuffled the pack and turned over a card.

'Uneven road ahead. I'm not giving up that easily, I'm conducting my own enquiries. I have a list of over thirty suspects,' she imagined that she sounded smart and decisive. She liked her new vivaciousness; Ludo was obviously good for her. The thought of Ludo bought a ripple of guilt.

'Suspects are one thing; evidence is quite another. By the way, when did you last speak to her by phone?' He fanned out the cards.

She chose one and studied it. 'Road narrows in both directions. Trying to catch me out? You must have her phone records.'

'Yes, we have, but not the phone.'

'Christmas eve, it was turned off after that, I left so many messages. So, the murderer has it.'

'We are yet to locate it.'

'Or her tortoise,' she held up a card.

'Slippery road.'

'By the way, is it true that most murders are committed by

spouses or family?'

'Sadly yes.'

'Alright, Ladies and Gents, I hope you all enjoyed that, if you could please return to the group, we will look at defensive driving before tea break.'

She took the seat next to John, ignoring a tut as she removed a mousy woman's mauve cardigan from the back of the chair and dropped it behind her. John and Jo had quite a ring to it. She tried to listen to the principles of road safety, but John's words were clomping around in her head. Spouse could be ruled out; Leon was dead. Family members might be a wide pool for some but Andrea only had Ed.

'Ed has a criminal record for violence,' she whispered into his ear.

'I know, I'm a police officer,' he whispered back.

'No talking please,' called the muppet.

He had ample opportunity; she imagined him phoning Andrea, saying he would come to Marlow and would bring the Christmas dinner, save her driving on those treacherous Carmarthenshire roads. He had no verifiable alibi; alone in a remote Welsh farmhouse, how convenient. Of course, there would be no evidence in Andrea's flat, no forced entry, no struggle, not if it's your brother. He had means; he would be the one plating up, he could easily have crushed tablets into her food or drink. The problem was that he had no motive. That weirdo Clara seemed very enamoured of him, perhaps they were in cahoots.

She decided to make the most of the tea-break, strike while the iron is hot. She took her weak coffee into the carpark and called Ed.

'Hi there, it's Jo, just wondering how you're doing?'

'Lovely to hear from you, I'm ok, it's a busy time with lambing and everything so that's good. Keeps me focussed, you know.'

'I can hear baaing; they sound like cartoon sheep.'

'I'm in the lambing shed. Hold on, sorry, just checking on Mable.' A rustling sound, more bleating. 'She's fine, she's had triplets. Anyway, how are you?'

'Getting there. I'm keeping busy too. Just wanted to talk to someone, you know how it is, someone who's going through the same. I was thinking about the flat clearance, I suspect you'll need some help.'

'I'm happy to do it on my own. These things can be very upsetting.'

'I'd like to. The police seem to have drawn a blank. I'll be more thorough.' She smiled at her cunning; keep them rattled.

'Jo don't take this the wrong way, but I wonder if, the thing is, the police said it was an overdose. Maybe it's best to, you know, try to come to terms with it,' his voice raised above the bleating.

God another bloody amateur psychologist, or was he trying to throw her off the scent? Wasps stirred. 'Yes, sure I'll just come to terms with it, brilliant idea.'

'Sorry Jo, I didn't mean to patronise. It's just that I'm a bit worried about you.'

'One more thing. Where did you spend Christmas Day?' She had learnt this tactic from *Columbo;* drop in the killer question when the suspect thinks they are home and dry, catches them off-guard.

'At home, well I did go to the pub to be honest, just for some company.'

'Which pub?' Don't give them time to think.

'The Hanged Man, it's a good thirty-minutes' drive but it's my local.'

'Okay Ed, I have to go; we're being rounded up, I'll text you about the flat clearance.' She didn't wait for his reply.

The lights had been switched off, she stumbled back to her seat as the muppet fiddled with a temperamental DVD player. John gave a welcoming smile. She sprayed herself liberally with Chanel Number Five. They sat together watching images of people being cut from cars, lorries jack-knifing, motorbikes careering down embankments. She felt his muscular arm against hers. It was turning out to be a simply lovely day.

14

C lara paced the living room as Blue watched from the kitchen, ears down, eyes wide, sensing unease and hoping he was not the cause.

The phone call had been a surprise, Phineas was on a tight budget and international charges were usually prohibitive. She had been looking forward to telling him about her Heimlich manoeuvre on their next video-call, instead she had listened in silence as her only son, voice wavering, had asked her to come to Madagascar. He said only that he needed to tell her something face to face; he would arrange a hotel and collect her from the airport. He offered the most commonly bestowed and least heeded of all advice - not to worry.

She tried to recall her tropical medicine; a specialism seldom required in West Berkshire. Bubonic plague? A re-emerging disease in Madagascar, but how would he have contracted it? From lemurs? Exposure from handling infected animal tissue was possible but unlikely. Yellow fever? Malaria? Viral haemorrhagic fever? He was not in hospital. Aside from serious illness, why would one need to speak to one's mother face to face? To ask for help with drug addiction, to divulge a calamitous event, to confess a crime; she found it hard to imagine Phineas in any such scenario.

She had enjoyed being a single mother and had seldom wished to share the worries of parenthood but she could not help wondering what Padraig would say. It would have been supportive. Seven months into her pregnancy she had attempted to contact him but learnt that he had become engaged to his childhood sweetheart. She followed his career from a distance, enjoyed reading his journal articles, bought his engaging book, Advances in the Treatment of Wernicke's Encephalopathy; the dedication was to his wife and three sons. She hoped that he was happy.

Phineas had been named in recognition of his Irish heritage but she had kept his paternity to herself. He inherited his father's intelligence along with his dove-grey eyes and curly hair. When, at age four, he had asked about his daddy she told him that he was the best man in the world. 'Like a superhero?' he had asked. She framed the one photograph she had taken of Padraig - laughing in a sea of late-flowering golden daisies at the university botanic gardens. She put it on Phineas' bedside table where it stayed for fourteen years; he took it with him when he went to Cambridge. That was the day she told him that his dad was a Professor at University College Dublin and that he would have been so proud of his son.

Right, concentrate. She ran through the things she had to do: buy plane tickets, get vaccinations, inform mum's nursing home, renew travel insurance, find someone to look after Blue, George and Darwin. She opened her laptop. The next available flight was via South Africa on 27th March, five days should be long enough to organise everything. She booked the flights within ten minutes. There followed an hour of peripheral choices that eroded the initial efficiency: seat selection for each of the four flights; an array of airport parking options; priority boarding or additional baggage allowance. So much decision making was exhausting. How on earth had she processed forty patients a day, where every potential misdiagnosis was a matter of life or death? She was grateful that she had never dwelt on such matters.

What about Mrs Jenner's perforated gallbladder?

Retirement must have freed the worm from its chamber, it rose from its dormancy carrying thirty-five years of unasked questions.

George heaved up a fur-ball, his convulsing body a chilling augury as she wrote 'Madagascar' on the kitchen calendar and drew a line through to mid-April. She was disappointed to cross out the long-anticipated alpaca husbandry course and her red kite day with Hen. She phoned to cancel, offering no explanation; she could not trust her emotions. Hen's response was delightful, 'No matter dear-heart, it was an arbitrary date, let us go tomorrow!'

It somehow made her feel that whatever Phineas had to tell her she would be able to cope.

Clara liked being up early, but now she had a couple of hours to kill before Hen was due; she needed to be busy to keep thoughts of Phineas at bay. The new deluxe tortoise enclosure had arrived. She washed and prepared it with a mix of loam and soft play sand, added a smattering of hemp and sphagnum moss, wooden arches and caves. She placed him carefully under the new heat lamp. His old housing was not worth salvaging, she would have to dismantle it. Under the layers of substrate Andrea had wedged a rolled-up sheet of paper presumably to stop the soil leaching through the gap. She unfurled it to reveal a handwritten list of countries. She read through them, from Afghanistan to Yemen; they were certainly not holiday destinations. Interestingly Madagascar was on the list. She saw no evident link between the thirty-three countries. She liked a cryptic challenge, she put it in the bureau drawer to consider later.

She turned on the news as she prepared a picnic of cheese and pickle sandwiches, Lebanese spinach triangles and a large bag of marmite crisps. She had hoped to find an analysis of the latest failed Brexit deal, instead she was treated to a *vox pop* of a market trader in Walsall espousing his opinion that 'leave means leave.' She turned it off.

A car horn sounded, she waved from the living room window. Nosferatu bounced on his hind legs in the passenger seat, scanning the scene like a crazed meerkat. She attached Blue's lead as he rose reluctantly to his feet.

'Lovely to see you, I'm happy to drive if you prefer.' Clara had been repeatedly astonished at the cavalier issuing of licences to patients whom she would not have trusted with an egg whisk.

'Oh, not necessary, I know all the shortcuts, hop in dear-heart.' Hen launched Nosferatu into the back to join Betty and Morris and made a cursory attempt to remove the dog hair from the passenger seat. 'Don't worry dear thing, my eyesight is not A-one but it is good enough.' She breathed on her monocle, rubbed it with her handkerchief and fixed it firmly to her eye. 'Is Blue happy in the footwell?'

'Yes, he'll just curl up down there.' Clara fastened her seatbelt and stroked Blue to reassure them both.

With one sweeping motion Hen reversed recklessly from the drive.

Clara noted that the side mirror was missing. 'Did they save the eye or enucleate? Sorry, that was intrusive; an occupational hazard I've yet to conquer.'

'Once a G.P. always a G.P. I suspect. Not at all, I have the rind of a rhino. The eye is gone. I did flirt with a glass replacement but we really did not get along. I prefer the statement eye-patch.'

Today she wore a waterproof olive-green one that perfectly matched her birding gilet, all six-pockets of which bulged with lumpy contents.

'I do like your patch coordination.'

'Thank you, I have a draw full: casual, formal, waterproof. Specially made, bespoke! Lady in the village, she makes teddy bears and such-like for charity, she is rather a good seamstress, she donates my payment to the RNIB.'

'The lifeboats?'

'Royal National Institute for Blind people.'

'Only teasing.'

Hen let out a bark, 'Oh, you are a hoot!' She slammed on the brakes and took a sharp turn into a country lane, a tractor waving her through. 'Another advantage of the eyepatch, one never has to wait at junctions. And the dents on the Landy help, they are mainly courtesy of father, he really should not be driving at ninety-seven, but he says if it's alright for Prince Philip then it's alright for him.'

'Well that argument is wearing a little thin.'

'True enough, father loves bumping around, mainly off-road thankfully. He calls it his Disco-Very.'

'Excellent.' The car scraped along a hawthorn hedgerow. 'How did you lose your eye?'

'My one and only skiing holiday, I fell down the steps disembarking the 737, ski pole straight in the socket, jolly bad luck.'

'Gosh that sounds traumatic.'

'Absolute disaster; didn't even make it to the slopes.'

Clara breathed a sigh of relief as they juddered to a halt in Watling Hill car park. The air crisp, the hillside empty.

'Release the hounds,' cried Hen as she opened the doors.

They made their way along the muddy path, the four dogs chasing each other up the hill in a cacophony of excitement. A score of red kites wheeled high in the cloudless sky.

'They're amazing birds, I've never seen so many together.'

'Wait until we get over the ridge,' Hen winked her pale blue eye and patted her shoulder bag.

Struggling against the wind, they made their way up the slope, Hen leaning heavily on her cane. They stopped to catch their breath and watched the kites rising on the thermals.

'I've bought my old bins for you; I use a monocular now.' Hen thrust an enormous pair of binoculars into her hand.

She followed the flight of one bird as it dived at another then veered away. 'They seem to be enjoying themselves, they're quite mischievous.'

'My thoughts exactly, mother always tells me I am being an-thropomorphic, but they are just like children playing tag.' Hen shook her inhaler and took several shots. 'Right one last push for the summit.'

The wind dropped as they passed onto the leeward side, the whistling of kites growing louder.

'Here is a perfect spot.' Hen unrolled a tartan blanket and pro-duced a cooked chicken from her bag.

'Oh Hen, I said I'd bring the picnic.'

'Jolly good that you did, this is for the kites. Are you ready?' She hurled the chicken down the slope with the proficiency of a dis-cus thrower and located it through her monocular.

Kites appeared from nowhere, circling the carcass in gradual descent as more and more joined the aerial merry-go-round. On a seemingly covert signal they swooped in turn picking out chunks of meat and soaring away. Within minutes the bones were clean and the kites dispersed.

'Wow, that was a real treat, for them and for me. I'm glad we made it after all.'

'You didn't say where you were going, last minute holiday?' Hen settled herself on the rug as Clara laid out the picnic.

'Actually, I have to go to Madagascar, my son doesn't sound too good, he's asked me to come.'

'Poor thing, is he unwell?' Hen removed a bottle of homemade elderflower cordial and two bamboo cups from her gilet.

'He didn't say. He looks terribly pale, he's lost a lot of weight. He was always such a robust child but there are so many tropical diseases that he won't have been exposed to. Plague for example.'

'Goodness, what a worry. So, you are off soon? What are you doing with the animals?' Hen munched through a spinach triangle, 'these are delicious dear-heart.'

'Thank you. On Wednesday, the animals are still on my 'to do' list.'

'Well, you must bring them to me, one more dog is neither here nor there. George can room with me if there are any territorial issues. Aunt Jobiska stays in the annex so she will be fine.'

Clara recalled the moth-eaten cat on the coat rack. 'Why did you name her Aunt Jobiska?'

'Edward Lear. The Pobble Who Has No Toes.'

'Yes, I do remember that poem, he swam across the Bristol channel and something stole his toes. I don't recall an Aunt Jobiska. Are you sure it's not too much of an imposition?'

'I'd be delighted. She was the Pobble's delightfully eccentric aunt,' Hen clarified through a mouthful of sandwich.

'Oh, there is another pet. I inherited a tortoise from Andrea Gibbons.'

'How lovely, well that is hardly going to be demanding.'

'That's really kind of you.'

'I almost forgot,' Hen fished out a crumpled piece of paper from an inner pocket. 'Father won second prize in a poetry competition. He wanted me to thank you for the inspiration,' she read it aloud accompanied by the piping of kites.

'Poems,
Haiku, whatever.
Really quite hard
to read or write.
Often not worth the effort,
until one that takes your breath,
A Heimlich manoeuvre on your suffocated soul.'

'Gosh that's lovely, he is a dark horse.'

'Where are the gang of four?' Hen surveyed the landscape with her monocular.

On cue they crested the hill and hurtled down to join the picnic; for an older dog Blue seemed to be enjoying his new adventures.

Clara resolved to emulate his recent embracing of unchartered territory.

15

Jo sat hunched in the Punto, a copy of *OK! Magazine* obscuring her face. Heartened by the words of adorable DI John, she had returned to her investigations with renewed vigour. She had three promising avenues of enquiry: learn more about Clara Astrell including Andrea's relationship with her son; verify Ed's whereabouts on Christmas day; solve the mystery of Darwin's disappearance. Today's Zen wisdom boded well, Find the truth, speak the truth, live the truth.

From her vantage point at the top of the road she could see all vehicles that entered and exited Penns Lane. The driveway of number three was empty; the suspect was not home. She surveyed the scene, an old man with a three-legged terrier stooped to pick up a crisp packet, pulled a weed from the tarmac and went into number twelve. Nothing happened for the next hour. The reality of a stake out was nowhere near as exciting as she had imagined.

She tapped 'The Hanged Man Carmarthenshire' into her phone. Well, it existed; although it looked closer than thirty minutes from Ed's farm. She closed her eyes and imagined herself into the role of Detective Inspector Dai Jones, a well-respected local copper, salt of the earth. She called the pub.

'Hanged Man, bore da.'

'Good morning, to who is it I'm speaking?' She wished she had practiced a Welsh accent; it had sounded so convincing in her head.

'Are you taking the piss?'

'No, I'm not madam, I'm calling from the police station in Carmarthen. DI Dai Jones. I want to speak to the proprietor,' she was quite pleased with the lilt on 'proprietor' although her introduction sounded suspiciously Australian.

'Well you've found her, what do you want?'

'I need to ascertain the whereabouts of one of your regulars, a Mr Ed Gibbons, on Christmas Day.'

'English Ed? He's hardly a regular. Once a month for a pint and a packet of salt and vinegar more like.'

'Was he in your establishment on Christmas Day?'

'Police matter is it? He's a ceffyl tywyll, seems such a quiet lad.'

'Can you just tell me if he was there?' Oh God she had forgotten the accent.

'Is that you Carrie?

'DI Jones, Dyfed-Powys police, please can you answer the question?' That sounded more convincing, she felt she was rising to the challenge.

'Well yes he was here, I recall because he was knocking them back, not like him.'

'How did he seem?' Short sentences helped the accent.

'Well, a bit upset actually. He got quite meddwi, felt sorry for him being on his own at Christmas. Not killed anyone has he?'

'Why would you say that?'

'On the way home I mean. After all the double whiskeys.'

'You allowed him to drive home whilst intoxicated?' She was really getting into role.

'That's you, isn't it Carrie? You the bloody alcohol police now is it?' The woman laughed like a screech owl.

'I'll overlook your infringement on this occasion. I just want to know what time he arrived.'

'Not 'til after two, stayed 'til closing time. Come to think of it, he was on his new tractor so he would have been off-road. Wouldn't want to get the chappie into trouble, he's alright is English Ed.'

'Thanks, that's very helpful.'

'Funny your folks giving you a boys' name.'

'They thought it was a girls' name.'

A small van emblazoned with *Enterprise Rental*, drew into number three. Jo hung up. She made a note of the make and registration number. She regretted having that second cup of coffee; investigators always had a flask in TV dramas, they never wanted the toilet. She watched Clara hurry into the house. She reappeared twenty minutes later dragging a large box and spent a good ten minutes heaving it into the back of the van. The behaviour could hardly be more suspicious. Clara returned to the house, come on woman, get a bloody move on. Finally, she was back, this time with a hold-all, a whippet and a cat box. She started the engine, Jo started hers.

Tailing a vehicle was harder than portrayed, there were right turns to negotiate, traffic lights to synchronise, roundabouts to gauge. By the time they turned off the bypass she was practically tailgating the woman. The van slowed and took a sharp left down a rough farm track. Jo made a note of the location: Coney Field Farm, Marlow Bottom. The address was familiar from her party invitation list, the home of one Henrietta Cuvier. The limits of her bladder control about to be breached she raced home.

Jo could not settle. Ed's alibi did not quite stack up. She drummed her shellac nails on the kitchen table; he would have had plenty of time to kill Andrea and then drive back to Carmarthenshire to show his face in the pub. Clever. So, he had opportunity. He had means. What possible motive could there be to murder your own sister? She needed to search the apartment before he came to clear it. She rifled in the pot for Andrea's spare key, the keyring a little blue penguin with a missing flipper made her sad. The thought of walking into her flat, the place where she drew her last breath, was appalling. Smelling her scent, hearing the echo of her laugh, remembering all those nights in the living room putting the world to rights. The contents of the fridge would be putrid, the houseplants dead, the Christmas tree naked.

Come on girl. Bite the bullet.

The Punto coughed back into life, to keep her mind from what lay ahead she thought again about yesterday afternoon, her rescheduled cocktail date with Ludo. With hindsight she should not have allowed him to order; three Long Island iced teas had made her reckless. It was a little embarrassing his studying her intimate photographs in the middle of the crowded wine-bar, although that lean-back pose shot from above in half-light, did look stunning on his high-definition iPhone. He had been the perfect gentleman, paying for her taxi, well at least to the station, and calling to see that she was home safe. It had been fun, he had such anecdotes: his time as head boy at Eton, his army deployments in Belize and Iraq, his stint as a Lear jet pilot, his beach home in Turks and Caicos. He had certainly crammed a lot into his forty-five years. Perhaps it had been too early to talk about wanting to remarry, had she detected a flash of panic in his eyes?

She pulled into the potholed carpark. Andrea's car had gone, surely no-one would steal a battered Clio, even around here. She located the living room window, even from the street the flat seemed different, dead. She wondered momentarily if she would be disturbing a crime scene. Hardly, the police seemed to be doing the bare minimum, the case was clearly at the bottom of the bloody pending tray. She kept her driving gloves on just in case.

Two hooded youths were sitting in the ammonia rich stairwell, their legs extended across the concrete steps. The white one looked her up and down and smirked to his friend. She wished she had not brought her Prada bag.

'Problem lady?'

'May I pass?'

'What's the magic word?' he grinned. He was missing a front tooth.

'I don't have time for silly games, I'm investigating a murder.' God what was she saying.

'Which one?' The other one laughed.

'My friend Andrea Gibbons.'

'Andrea was killed?' The boy looked shocked.

'Yes, so if you don't mind, I need to get on with my inquiries.'

The boys got to their feet. 'Sorry lady, if you need any help, let us know.'

'You knew Andrea?'

'Yes, she was dope. Good luck Mrs.'

'Thank you,' she stepped past them.

Her heart pounding, she slowly climbed the steps, she wanted to turn back, have a cigarette with the stairwell boys, go home. She steadied herself outside number 22A, inserted the key, exhaled deeply and opened the door.

The smell of disinfectant. Her feet echoed on the uncarpeted floor. The flat was completely empty.

16

J ohn carried a mug of Earl Grey back to his desk and stared at his flashing answerphone. He took a sip and pressed play. God, he regretted giving his contact details to Jo Burns-Whyte. He listened to the rambling messages about tortoises, sheep farms and dodgy doctors. He really did not have time to decipher the disjointed babble, geez that woman could talk.

He hit delete all.

He scanned his emails and sighed, several bore the subject line *Andrea Gibbons Urgent* and were marked with a red exclamation mark. Sender 'foxyloxy123'. Good God. He opened the most recent. She had attached a spreadsheet of her investigation to date. It was endearingly hopeless. She appeared to have cast her net wide; the list included pretty much everyone who had attended Andrea's funeral, even the humanist: *claims to have never met Andrea but knew all about her/very friendly with Clara Astrell.* She had homed in on two prime suspects whom she had highlighted in orange: Ed Gibbons and Clara Astrell. Gosh, she really had it in for Dr Astrell. He scanned her evidence column, it read more like a character assassination.

Ed's evidence was more convincing; he had cleared Andrea's flat although they had apparently agreed to do it together, had a big hole in his alibi and had allegedly bought a new tractor. *Where did he get the money???* Was written in the evidence column.

Andrea had clearly abided by the confidentiality clause; Jo did not know about the fifty grand, nor that it was missing.

True, Ed was a bit of a strange one, he had put it down to having lost his sister, but he had been very cagey on the phone. He had shown no interest in Andrea's missing phone and had not mentioned the absent tortoise. Even though the official status of the death remained 'unexplained' Ed had not questioned him, had not offered any information or even sounded surprised. The only question he had asked was when could he bury her.

He reread the pathology notes. The head injury was apparently consistent with a fall, but could she have been hit? In his experience most overdoses were found in bed or on the sofa, not in the hallway.

'John. Hard at work I see.'

'DCI Wallace, I wasn't expecting you,' he swung his legs from his desk.

'Clearly.'

'Please take a seat Ma'am.' He removed the stack of files from the chair.

DCI Wallace closed the door and cast a critical eye around his sparse office. 'How is Matt?'

'Good thanks.'

'The boys?'

He bristled at the note of concern. 'They are fine.' Had he imagined the smirk?

'Where are we with the car jackings? I understand the latest victim is Jarrod Soames-Grayling, his new Range Rover Evoque was nicked and he wants action.'

'We have located the vehicle; it was used in a ram-raid so it's not in the best of health.'

He handed her a photograph of the crumpled vehicle next to a large hole in the ESSO petrol station on Little Marlow road.

DCI Wallace examined and returned it. 'We would not wish to lose his considerable support.'

'We are doing everything we can Ma'am, the gang left no DNA, or prints and disabled the CCTV.'

'All efforts. Get them caught.'

'Yes Ma'am. We also have a stabbing in Flackwell Heath, the Bovington Green robberies and the Andrea Gibbons case is ongoing.'

She stood up. 'All efforts.' She left the door open.

John closed the file and finished his tea. Constable Beech entered looking unusually pleased with himself. He waved a sheet of paper and grinned.

'Just got a signal on Andrea Gibbons' phone. It pinged in Carmarthenshire.'

17

Clara made her way down the aisle checking the overhead luggage compartments, they were all full. She now understood why people paid an additional twenty pounds for priority boarding although they would occupy the same seat. She waited as a family blustered past trailing an unpleasant tang of garlic and sweat. A stewardess, bristling with efficiency, told her to sit down and to place her bag under the seat in front of her. The mountainous man in 37B looked up from his newspaper with yellow eyes and an apologetic smile. He made an ineffectual attempt to free-up the meagre square footage allocated to 37A by shifting his bulk slightly to the left. The young man in the window seat was fast asleep unaware of the intrusion. She guessed from his colourful tunic that he was returning home; she was glad that he had been born into a post-apartheid South Africa. She stowed her bag as requested and placed her feet uncomfortably on either side.

'I'm sorry I'm encroaching into your space,' wheezed the man, stuffing his newspaper into the seat-net. South African accent.

'Hardly your fault, these seats appear to have been designed for elves.'

'Ted, nice to meet you,' he extended a doughy hand.

'Clara,' she allowed the moist digits to engulf hers and cursed the security jobsworth who had confiscated her antiseptic hand-gel.

'It's hellishly hot in here,' sweat beaded on his bald head and pooled in the creases of his neck. He attempted to adjust the air supply above his head, inadvertently brushing Clara's face with a nylon shirt sleeve.

'Well that's made no difference, perhaps it's not working,' he puffed.

'Hopefully it will cool down once we're airborne.' Clara rummaged in her bag for her book, *The Road To Wigan Pier*, psychological preparation for the poverty of Madagascar, and tried to focus on the annoyingly small font.

'Have you been to South Africa before?' The man was evidently immune to the message implied by the opening of a book.

'No.'

'Then you're in for a treat, it's a beautiful country.'

His breath was laboured, she just knew he was going to be a snorer.

'Sadly, I won't get to see it, I'll be in transit.'

'In transit? Where on earth are you going?' His aftershave was not unpleasant but over applied.

'Madagascar.' Clara hoped that resorting to one-word answers might curtail the conversation, she didn't trust herself to talk about Phineas.

'What will you be doing there?'

Here we go. 'Just sightseeing.'

'I'd never have thought to visit. I assumed it was just jungle.'

Clara weighed up her options: educate him about the topography and wildlife of Madagascar, ask him about his own plans, feign illness, pretend to nod off or perhaps to suffer temporary deafness. Her decision was thankfully postponed by the announcement of the safety demonstration, to which she made clear she was to give her full attention. With relief she remembered her noise-cancelling headphones. Never too early to put them on, even if not attached to the entertainment system headsets were a universal sanctity that no-one could fail to observe.

Clara closed her eyes to savour the roller-coaster experience of rapidly increasing speed and incline. A tapping on her arm interrupted the moment. Ted waved a bag of boiled sweets in her face, he appeared to have placed several in his cheek pouch. She raised her palm to signal her decline and shut her eyes. As the plane levelled a more urgent tap; the young man had woken and seemed to want the toilet. She had selected the aisle seat to ensure easy access for her anti-DVT walks but the compromise was intermittent disturbance. Ted heaved himself to his shoeless feet, sweating profusely. She pondered the possible causes of his hyperhidrosis, most likely high blood pressure or medication side-effect, perhaps diabetes - the sweets should help with low blood sugar - possible hypothyroidism and of course cancer could not be ruled out. Maybe he was just hot, man-made fabric was not a good choice for international travel. The boy returned, he put both hands over his heart and gave an almost imperceptible bow of gratitude, it was such a beautiful and unexpected gesture that it made her eyes rim with tears.

Clara scanned the film list for something light and escapist, *Finding Dory,* perfect. She relaxed into the simple distraction. She decided that Hank the octopus was her favourite, perhaps because he had attitude and was missing a tentacle. She knew Phineas would like Dory, he always rooted for the underdog. She imagined Hen roaring with laughter over Becky the common loon. The film was a tonic and it killed one hour and forty minutes. The smell of cabbage and tomato sauce effused the cabin. Clara watched the dispensing of plastic trays and listened to the stewardess's repetitive 'chicken, pork or pasta?' as the trolley inched down the aisle. Ted chose pork, the boy declined and went back to sleep.

'Mac and cheese? Interesting choice,' Ted eyed her food critically.

'I'm vegetarian, there was no choice.'

'Ah well, fills a hole,' he commiserated.

He ate surprisingly delicately, seeming to savour each mouthful. The pasta was cloying and bland, she added the condiment sachets to little effect. A rectangle of cheese sweated in a plastic casing. She examined the crackers and decided against.

'So much plastic packaging,' she shook her head.

'I'll have it if you're not going to eat it, waste not want not,' Ted dabbed his face with the tiny paper napkin.

She handed over the snacks.

Two and a half hours down, nine to go. She envied the boy for his ability to sleep, his head against the glass, a peaceful expression. She remembered Daniel. She was flying to Havana for a three-month sabbatical prescribing the out-of-date medications that the US government had somehow off-loaded with impunity. If there was a doctor on board could he please make himself known to cabin crew. He? Really in 2011? She had impulsively pressed her call button in dissent of the sexist assumption. Daniel turned out to be a master of the monologue. She supposed from his demeanour that he had finished his stash of skunk before proceeding through airport security. Not much older than Phineas, with a mop of hair that had formed itself into dense clumps, he talked at her with a startling intensity. He described the planet's imminent demise due to various *force majeure* events: asteroids, invasion of deadly life-forms, ionising radiation. He was particularly upset by pressure waves from metal devices - including the plane in which they were travelling - that were reputedly 'upsetting God's babies.' It transpired that this was particularly germane as he had swallowed one of said babies whilst swimming off Eastbourne. They apparently took the form of cuttlefish hatchlings. Hence, he had become a saviour, his role was yet to be clarified but was likely to entail destroying the world in order for it to be reset and begin again. People do bad things with the best of intentions. She wondered what had become of him, she hoped he had negotiated his way through the psychiatric system and had found companionship. Her four and a half hours with Daniel had taught her two important lessons. Firstly, that the ten-minute snapshot presented to a G.P. is empty, listening for longer one can move from diagnosis, in this case paranoid schizophrenia with drug-induced manic episodes, to real understanding. His beliefs served a function, they gave him power and purpose and meaning. The consequences of relinquishing these beliefs would be to leave him just another poor, oppressed black man. The second lesson was never to make your medical qualification known to cabin crew.

The meal cleared away Clara repositioned her headphones, pulled the SAA blanket over her head and reclined her seat a respectful two notches. Oh, she had not done her anti-DVT walk, never mind. She closed her eyes. Thoughts of Phineas invaded, taking her into a labyrinth down which she did not wish to travel. A vision of him lying on a hospital bed, pale and sick, blood engorged buboes erupting from his lymph nodes. Bubonic plague bacilli swarmed in front of her eyes.

He was dying.

For goodness sake get a grip. She shifted position. Up crept the blasted worm, carrying with it a bulging saddlebag of unexpected deaths. It reclined in her frontal lobe and unpacked its dark cargo one by one. Sweet Miss Bircher hit by a roof-tile whilst walking her cairn terrier. Jolly Mr Sheridan a brain haemorrhage at Sainsburys' checkout. Mr Woolley crushed when he got out to see why the carwash had not started. Mrs Sulby's heart attack at her grand-daughters christening. Little Freddy who fell into the Thames the day before his sixth birthday, went down like a stone, his tiny body recovered the following day miles downstream. Andrea Gibbons, alone in her flat on Christmas day. She thought deeply of each one until they loosened their grip and were gone.

She switched on her iPod: *Leonard Cohen Live in London*, her favourite album, the last concert she had attended, she made a mental note to get out more. She set it to repeat, Ted's elephant-ine arm was radiating heat, his snoring competed with Rafael Bernardo Gayol's astonishing percussion.

A gentle shaking roused her from an unexpected sleep. Her neck twisted and stiff, pins and needles in her left foot. The boy, leaning across Ted's bulk, looked pleadingly at her.

'Sorry to disturb you Madam but I need to use the bathroom. I can't wake your husband.' His voice soft and melodic.

Clara took a moment to register the situation, she shook Ted tentatively, he felt cold. She took his wrist; no pulse, she leaned in close; no breath. She turned on the overhead lamp. He was grey, he had probably been dead for several hours. An announcement competed for her attention.

'We are starting our descent into O. R. Tambo International airport please will all passengers return to your seats and fasten your seat belts. It is 9.05 am local time and 25 degrees. We are sorry for the lateness of our arrival; we will ensure that those passengers with connecting flights will be first to disembark.'

Clara pressed the call button. Cabin crew distributing landing cards remained steadfastly oblivious to any extraneous needs. She pressed again. A curt stewardess appeared and switched off the call light.

'We'll be with you shortly,' she said over her shoulder. Suddenly she was five rows down.

'Excuse me, the gentleman in 37B has died,' Clara shouted.

'Oh Lord,' the boy crossed himself.

The stewardess cycloned back, passengers craning to see. She leant over and stared accusingly at Ted. 'Are you sure that he is dead?'

'Be my guest,' Clara stood up. It was a good opportunity to use the bathroom.

Where is your compassion Dr Astrell? hissed the worm.

Buried under thirty-five years of tragedy.

On her return Ted's face had been covered by a blanket, the boy was silently crying, due to grief or the need to empty his bladder she did not know.

Fortunately, the onward flight to Antananarivo was uneventful. She walked past the crush of tourists waiting anxiously at Lost Luggage. And suddenly there was Phineas amiable and smiling in a creased linen suit. Their embrace was tender, she felt his thinness, his fragility and his strength.

'So great to see you Mum, how was your flight?'

'Great to see you too, well I survived.' She scanned for illness, he was pale but not anaemic, bore insect bites but no buboes, his eyes clear but haunted.

'I can't believe you're here.'

He was fighting back tears.

18

Jo exhaled a jet of minty smoke and narrowed her eyes. She would not drive to Carmarthen and scream at Ed. She would not confront Clara and tell her she knew she was in on it. She would keep her powder dry, slowly build her case, get to know her suspects. Slow and steady wins the race.

She had to get inside Clara's house. That witch must think she's beyond suspicion, a G.P. in her sixties, bloody pillar of the community, doubtless loved by her patients, well yes so was Harold Shipman. The thing with doctors was they thought they were Gods but they were just the same as everyone else, with access to a prescription pad. She knew what a dangerous instrument that could be.

Two pm, Clara was definitely not home. There was a landing light on, not fooling anyone. Jo opened the side gate and peered through the kitchen window. Clean, tidy, no evidence of occupation. She pulled on her driving gloves, tried the garage door, back door, patio door; all locked.

'Can I help you?'

'Jesus Christ!' Jo stepped back in alarm.

The man was clean shaven with the eyes of a small mammal.

'Oh, my goodness you made me jump,' she steadied herself and got into role.

'Are you looking for someone?' His tone obliging.

'Yes, sorry I'm Abi, Clara's friend, she appears to be out.' She searched for a reason why she needed to get into the house, nothing came to mind.

He held out his hand. 'Tim Forth, next door neighbour, I'm keeping an eye on the house while she's away.' His handshake was firm and warm.

'Well you're doing an excellent job, lucky for me I'm not a burglar,' her laugh a little too enthusiastic. 'How long is she away?'

'Ten days. She's gone to Madagascar.'

'Oh dear, she borrowed something of mine, I need back,' she

peered through the kitchen window for inspiration. 'Tap shoes.'

'Tap shoes? Gosh, I didn't have Clara down as a tap dancer.'

'It's a broad church tap dancing, that's how we met,' she toyed with a strand of hair and treated Tim to a wetting of her lips.

'Well, I have a key in case of emergency. This could count.' A slight tremble in his voice.

'I don't want to put you to any trouble, but I'd be ever so grateful,' she breathed, Marilyn Monroe style.

Tim fumbled in his pocket. He was attractive in a 'man-next-door' sort of way, his tight-fitting M&S roll neck hinted at hidden delights. He opened the door solicitously. The house held the stillness of absence.

'I won't be long, just a quick scoot around.'

She kept her gloves on. She felt Tim study her as she opened cupboards, scanned shelves, looked in boxes. Violating Clara's territory as a man watched was strangely exhilarating. She took note of dog toys, cat food, fur on the sofa.

'What did she do about the animals?'

'She took them to a friend's house, I would have offered to look after the tortoise but to be honest they freak me out a little, it's the retractable neck and those stubby little legs.'

'Tortoise?' Jo steadied her voice, 'I didn't know she had a tortoise.'

'It's quite a recent acquisition I think.'

'Surprising purchase for an older lady.'

'Should I make us a cup of coffee while you're looking? My wife's away with the children this week, half-term. I could do with the company.'

'Lovely, black no sugar,' she held his gaze and watched his pupils dilate.

Jo rifled through the bureau drawers; utility bills, cheque book stubs, instruction manuals. She unfolded a sheet of paper; Andrea's unmistakable handwriting. It was a list of countries, no explanation. She stuffed it into her pocket.

'The shoes don't seem to be down here,' she called, 'I'll just have a check upstairs if that's okay with you?'

She paused at the top of the stairs. There were four rooms, the first a large bathroom with traditional roll-top bath, adhesive ducks in the shower cubicle, turtle shaped mirror, tropical frogs on the curtains; the woman was a nutcase. The second was sparsely furnished, housing a leather wing-chair, a desk and a reading lamp, each wall lined with books; a library, how pretentious. The next was decorated with bizarre wallpaper; singing monkeys and dancing anteaters, a single bed, beanbags, presumably the room of the elusive Phineas. She scanned a cork-board pinned with photographs, most of which were of a black man in various foreign looking locations - perhaps he was a rap artist - and a series of tiny monkeys in a forest. There was a newspaper cutting showing Andrea and her nature group holding that revolting worm thing. She put it into her pocket.

The master bedroom was undeniably elegant, the dusky-pink throw smoothed flat on the queen-sized bed. She had only one wardrobe hung with drab suits and cardigans, God that woman needed to lighten up. The dressing table held perfume, a collection of fine bone-china whippets and a jewellery box. Jo selected a black rose brooch and absently slipped it into her handbag. She smiled at Tim's footsteps on the stairs, he was defenceless against her charms. Her dalliance with Ludo was making her feel wanton; she was a magnet, men were her filings. She was the irresistible star of one of those movies Ben used to keep under the bed.

Jo stood motionless under the shower. She might never feel clean again. She focussed on the sensation of the skin on the soles of her feet. She turned up the temperature, the scalding water lashed her back and burnt her shoulders.

What the hell had she been thinking?

She sat at her kitchen table in her Champneys's bathrobe and poured herself another glass of cheap red. She hated herself. She had not seen it until it was too late, when Tim was reinstating his greying Y-fronts. The burgundy birthmark on his left buttock like he had sat in something unpleasant. It could only be him. The one-night stand that Andrea had told her about, the fumbling disaster. He was that alright. At least it was over quickly. The thought that he had been with Andrea made her sick. What was wrong with her? Ludo, John, Tim, all that male attention had been intoxicating, had spun her off balance. She was lost with only herself to talk to, she didn't know the answers, she hardly knew the bloody questions. She had been worrying about sleeping with Ludo. That was it. He was so sophisticated, used to city girls, skinny models, debutantes, his expectations would be high. Tim was a dress rehearsal, preparation for the opening night. Pun intended. Andrea would have laughed.

Perhaps promiscuity was a grief reaction, didn't Freud say something about sex and death? One thing she did know, she could never go back to Clara's. The wine was tart, she poured another regardless. She needed to move her relationship with Ludo to the next level, if only to get the horrible Tim out of her pores. She shuddered and drained her glass. Plus, she was running out of money. She sent a suitably ambiguous text: *Love to see more of you (and your boat) xxx*

19

T ana was an assault. Pandemonium. The jeep bumped its way over outrageous potholes, the noise of the engine and the crowded streets making conversation fruitless.

Clara stared through the rolled-down window trying to decipher the mayhem. Mopeds, broadcasting fumes and dust, wove around obstacles in the road, dwarfed by trucks piled high with bananas, spiky fruits, sacks of dirty carrots. The smell of raw meat, putrefying rubbish and diesel hung heavy in the air. There were people everywhere, people sitting, people walking, people shouting and laughing. They passed perilously close to ramshackle stalls strung with garlands of peanuts, bright coloured popcorn, mobile phones. A pack of mangy dogs marked their territory on crates of bottled water stacked sweating in the sun. Schoolchildren, proud in their white uniforms, overtook dusty boys leading zebu. Further out people sat by the roadside selling handmade bricks still steaming from the furnace. Barefoot children pulled overloaded hand carts. Every thirty metres they passed an armed police guard, stone-faced, weapon drawn, waiting in the heat for dignitaries to speed past in limousines. Clang, clang, click. Tana was an assault rifle.

The hotel was a relief, pleasant, clean and deserted. They had a choice of rooms, Phineas selected two that overlooked the tangled back gardens as there was a chance of spotting lemurs. Clara emptied her suitcase of gifts onto his bed: Earl Grey tea, Pom bears, liquorice allsorts, hiking socks, Marks and Spencer underpants, insect repellent, a comprehensive medical kit, a bottle of Tullamore Dew.

'I did buy Marmite as well, but it was confiscated by Heathrow security. The woman insisted it was a liquid, my exposition on the properties of a semi-solid was met with some hostility.'

It was a joy to see him laugh. Clara returned to her own room, laid out her toiletries, showered and changed. She took her anti-malarial tablet, brushed her hair and sat for a moment absorbing the cantata of frogs and cicadas. She readied herself to hear whatever it was that Phineas had bought her six thousand miles to tell her.

She found Phineas on a barstool in the *Bamboo Bistro*, talking to a young woman with a poinciana flower in her hair. She was mixing rum cocktails, she emanated the same quiet dignity that she had sensed in the receptionist and in the woman who had shown them to their rooms. He was handsome in his white shirt and pale linen trousers, a young Ernest Hemingway.

'I was going to have coffee,' she kissed him and hoisted herself onto the barstool.

'That's why I ordered for you, we're on holiday, let's go crazy.'

'You don't have to work while I'm here?'

'No, I've left detailed instructions, besides Armand knows what he's doing. I thought you might like to see the field-site but we'll leave it to the end.'

They clinked glasses and sipped the El Floridita. His eyes were sad, his smile non-Duchenne. Clara recognised the acting 'as-if', he was very accomplished, a skill he had learned as a boy. Acting as if he wasn't worried about the school play, as if he was looking forward to the French exchange and later, when the acting was evident only to her, as if he was straight. She never reassured him that everything would be fine, gave no false hope, she disapproved of the trite guarantees that people trotted out as if they knew what the future held. She had generally found that things either got better, or worse, or stayed the same. That had become their shared mantra, she and Phineas united in facing whatever would be. She focussed on his eyes and asked the question that had been festering since his telephone call.

'Phineas, are you dying?'

'No Mum. I'm not dying,' his voice an affronted teenager's.

'Well then, whatever you have to tell me will be better than I had imagined.'

'Geez mum, I'm sorry, you must have been worried sick,' he drew his fingers through his hair. It looked as though he had cut it himself.

'Are you unwell?'

'To my knowledge I'm not housing any viruses, bacteria or parasites.'

'Good, so I can cross that off my list.'

The waitress appeared with a menu and placed another two drinks on the bar.

'You chose.' She was not hungry although she had not eaten since she was over North Africa.

Phineas ordered two vegetable curries with coconut rice.

'How are you mum? You look really well.'

'I think retirement suits me; it's been nice shifting down a few gears.'

'And Gwam?'

'They have stopped wheeling her out for meal-times so she spends all day in her room. She doesn't seem to mind.'

'Poor thing.'

The waitress disappeared through swing-doors.

'Do you remember that dog you used to carry with you all the time? It had been through the washing machine so many times it had faded to white and lost most of its fur.'

'Pupper.'

'Yes, I found him in a box in the garage. I've kept him just in case.'

'What I have to tell you is pretty bad,' he stopped.

She allowed him to take his time but he did not speak. She took his hand.

'Have you killed someone?'

He looked at his hand in hers. 'Not directly, but I am responsible for someone's death,' his voice caught.

'Phin, just tell me.' She felt herself detach; whatever he had done she would accept it.

'I don't quite know where to start. I'll just say it,' he withdrew his hand. 'It's dad. I should have told you, I'm really sorry but I'm afraid he's dead.'

'Padraig,' she had not spoken his name for years.

'He was killed last summer. He was on his way to see me in Cambridge, except he didn't make it,' he paused, perhaps allowing the news to register and to find the strength to continue.

Clara became aware of soft jazz crackling from the speaker;

Ain't No Sunshine.

'We had been in touch for a few months, I found him through the Dublin University website. Like you said, he didn't know about me, I was a huge shock to him,' he looked at the row of rum bottles.

Clara felt her heart-rate slow; she was barely breathing.

'Anyway, we spoke on the phone, we talked for hours. Then we Skyped a few times and arranged to meet up in London. He had booked the hotel rooms and everything. Then I got cold feet, I worried we might not get on so well in person, or I might be a disappointment, I don't know. Anyway, I bottled it and cancelled.'

Clara watched a fly crawl across the bar, fuss at a small crumb and walk on.

'He told me to take my time and he would be there when I was ready. Ironic really, the one thing we didn't have was time and I wasted it.' He finished his rum with shaking fingers.

'Anyway, we started talking again and I invited him to Cambridge. I thought I'd feel more confident on my home turf. He was driving to Dublin airport for the early morning flight, it had been stormy, raining all night,' he stopped. 'A tree fell on his car.'

She pictured a car crushed by a giant oak. 'Oh God.'

The waitress arrived with their meals, she took a CD from her pocket and waved it enthusiastically, it had a Union Jack on the cover. She loaded the CD and hurried back to the kitchen. Tom Jones crooned from the speaker, *Green Green Grass Of Home.*

'You must have been devastated.' She thought she should feel sad or upset but all she felt was numb. And a strange relief.

'His obituary was in the BMJ, I hid it from you when I was home for your birthday. It said he left four children, Conor, Noah, Oisin and Phineas. I didn't want you to know that I had betrayed you.'

'You haven't betrayed me, I'm pleased that you got to know him, I should have encouraged you to contact him.' She stared into the space between them and at the food steaming in front of them.

'He told me there was something special that he wanted me to have. It must have been in the car. I imagine him giving it to me, watching my reaction. Sometimes I dream about it, I'm unwrapping it but there's always another layer, like pass the parcel.'

'It's a huge thing to come to terms with.' She knew whatever she said would sound trite. There really was nothing she could say.

Tom Jones moved on to *Delilah.* She wondered about turning it off but Phineas didn't seem to notice.

'The thing is, it's not about losing a father because I never really had one, it's losing the idea of a father, you know the promise that one day we would meet up. Our imagined future, I've had that since I was little, the possibility was enough, like a comfort blanket.'

'Oh Phin, I wish you had told me how you felt. We never really talked much about him.'

You are a bad mother.

'I didn't want to ask, sometimes reality doesn't match the fantasy.'

'You were always so self-contained.' She remembered the little boy drawing superheroes and humming to himself. 'You are not responsible for his death.'

'If I hadn't contacted him, or cancelled the London trip, or invited him to Cambridge,' his voice tailed off.

'If you were responsible then so was the tree.'

Phineas rubbed the back of his neck. 'The thing is, I've been getting a bit obsessed with how he died. I go over and over it. The odds, the what ifs. The millimetres of rainfall the previous night, porosity of the soil, wind direction, velocity, angle of fall, speed of the car, volume of traffic, exact time of departure. If he had stopped at a red light. If he had stayed to finish his coffee. It's driving me crazy.'

'But you asked me to come here. If the plane had crashed would you have been culpable of my death?'

'Jesus Mum, what a thing to say,' he paused. 'Actually, that does help a bit,' his smile was genuine.

She raised her glass, 'Here's to Padraig, a lovely father, a lovely man.'

They drained their rum. They picked up their cutlery and ate in silence, Tom Jones the incongruous soundtrack to their private thoughts. Clara recalled Padraig reading poems aloud in their room in Durham, *The Lake Isle of Innisfree, On Raglan Road, The Wayfarer.* Poems she had reread a hundred times but knew she would read no more.

What's New Pussycat? Reached its climax as Clara set down her fork. 'The BMJ don't state the cause of death, they tend to stick to the common euphemisms - unexpected death is an accident, after a long illness is cancer, suddenly at home is a heart attack, tragic death is suicide.'

Phineas cast his eyes down, the little boy who had eaten the chocolate cake.

'Thing is, I've been in touch with Oisin, the youngest son. Dad. Padraig told them about me, the oldest are twins. Well, I guess I'm the oldest.'

'It must be strange suddenly having half-brothers.'

'Only Oisin made contact. We messaged on Facebook. He seemed really lovely. That's something else I have to live with, taking their father. After the accident he sent me a long message explaining what had happened, the tree and everything. I never wrote back.'

'After the accident,' Clara emphasised, psychotherapist style.

'Yes, I get it, I know that's what it was, the inquest verdict was accidental death. But that's not the small print. I'm the small print and I read it every day.'

The waitress appeared with coffee and Grand Marnier. 'Digestif, on the house.' She was gone before they could object.

'Thanks for keeping Pupper.'

Clara took his hand. 'I'm so glad that you told me and that you invited me over. I'd like to promise that things will get better,' she smiled.

'They might get worse,' he replied with a grin.

'Or stay the same,' they said together.

20

Ludo had taken the bait and had invited her for cocktails on board his boat tomorrow evening. She seemed to have hooked herself a goldfish, all she had to do now was to reel him in. She felt skittish with nerves.

She tried to focus on a productive task, a technique recommended in her current bible, Isaac P. Henderson's New Life: New You. She unfolded the newspaper cutting taken from Phineas' bedroom and studied the list of names under the photograph, Phineas Astrell wasn't featured, of course he must have left several years before the worm fiasco. So why on earth would he have this on his wall? The picture showed Andrea grinning, proudly surrounded by her geeky nature group. She looked radiant. Had he fallen in love with her? Became obsessed, the way young men develop fixations on older women. Maybe he had been stalking her. She recalled that he had moved to Cambridge and was now in Madagascar. Ah! He came back home for Christmas, went to declare his love to Andrea; she spurned him, he killed her in a jealous rage and fled abroad. Except administering an overdose is not the act of an impulsive young man. She unfolded Andrea's list of countries. Madagascar. As DI John would say, it's all conjecture, you need evidence.

The tortoise seemed to hold possibilities. From information provided by the revolting Tim it was clear that Clara Astrell had taken Darwin to the Cuviers's farmhouse. She entered the address into Google Earth and zoomed in. A sprawling stone house, two stories, an annex, an octagonal conservatory; the image was practically a floor plan. A path snaked to the back door studded with strangely shaped bushes, she expanded the image until the pixels gave up, the hedges seemed to be cut into the shape of giant chickens; bloody weirdos. A few scattered outbuildings, ponds, no near neighbours. Perfect. She printed a screenshot.

Motive was trickier, she Googled 'Why would someone steal a tortoise?' The first result provided the answer. A Daily Telegraph article: *Stolen tortoises fetch up to £6,000 on the black market as strict environmental protection laws make them harder to buy legally.* The piece stated that the British police dealt with forty-four cases last year, owners were encouraged to protect their pets by micro-chipping, photographing their shell for identification and installing CCTV. She clicked on a link to a National Geographic article *10,000 poached tortoises found in house in Madagascar.* At first, she thought that they were cooked, but no, they had been stolen and were destined to be smuggled out of the country. She scrolled down; the radiated tortoise was particularly prized due to the intricate yellow-star pattern on its shell. The illegal wildlife trade was worth billions. Madagascar. Oh my God, she's trafficking them! That's what Ludo had suggested. Perhaps Andrea had found out somehow and threatened to go to the police. She had been up on all that environmental nonsense. Clara could have gone to silence her. Stealing Darwin was just a fortuitous opportunity not to be missed. She printed off the article. She was definitely onto something; all she needed now was evidence that the tortoise was in the Cuviers's possession and she could hand this case to John on a plate. Ludo would help, he was full of excellent advice. The thought of their date intruded. The reconnaissance of Coney Field Farm would have to wait, she had an outfit to buy. She deserved a little reward.

A doughy marshmallow in a dark suit stood in her path.

'Excuse me Madam, I think there may be some items in your bag that you haven't paid for.'

'Oh, I don't think so, there must be some misunderstanding,' Jo tried to walk around him.

'If you could just accompany me back into the shop,' his face impassive.

'I really think you are mistaken,' Jo clutched her bag tightly.

'Madam, please come with me and we'll sort this out.'

She weighed up the likelihood of successful escape, her spike heels stacked the odds against. She flicked back her hair and stalked into the shop with all the indignation she could muster. The back room was dismal, the smell of stale roll-ups emanated from a plastic bin. Not very Waitrose. The marshmallow emptied her bag unceremoniously onto the table, compared her purchases with the receipt and replaced the listed items. A box of gourmet chocolates, a tub of honeysuckle moisturising hand-cream and a bottle of Bollinger Special Cuvée remained on the desk. She admired the products; she was evidently a woman of class and distinction.

'Explanation?' The marshmallow narrowed his already minimal eyes.

'I must have missed these. I did a self-scan check out, I'm terribly sorry I'll put them through now,' she affected her best Henley accent.

'It's not that easy I'm afraid Madam this is a chargeable offence, I have to notify the police.'

'Surely that won't be necessary. It was a simple mistake, just three little items.'

The room was airless, the marshmallow stabbed numbers into a calculator with his disgusting sausage fingers.

'Those three little items amount to seventy-five pounds Madam,' he sounded pleased with himself.

'That's extortionate, I would never have bought the hand-cream if I'd known it was that much.'

'You didn't buy it I'm afraid Madam.'

The smug bastard was enjoying it. 'Silly old me, here let me pay,' she produced a clutch of notes and put them meaningfully into his hand. No matter it was her council tax money.

'I've already told you Madam,' he put the money on the table, 'it's too late to pay, you left the shop.'

'I came back though,' her little girls' voice. She toyed with a curl of hair.

'The police have been alerted; they'll be here shortly.'

Jo wondered whether she should call DI John. No, she didn't want to sully their relationship just when she was making progress. She clutched her chest, her breath came in short bursts, 'I don't feel well, I think I'm having a heart attack.'

The marshmallow was unfazed, he filled a stained mug from the tap and plonked it on the table, tepid water sloshing onto her manicured hand. They sat in silence. The clock ticked. She folded the money back into her purse. Finally, two uniformed police officers swaggered through the door, all belts and radios.

'Community Support Officer Malone and this is my colleague CSO Briggs.'

Two women, bloody typical.

'Can we take your name please Madam?'

Jo hesitated, 'Abi Addis. I've never been in trouble with the police.'

'You're reading that off the bin Madam,' the officers exchange eye rolls. 'That's got to be one of the worst aliases of the year.'

Patronising cows.

'Proof of identity please,' clipped the stout one through chapped lips.

Jo rummaged in her handbag and produced her driving license.

'Joanne Burns-Whyte, 32 Lester Piggot Way, Marlow,' the officer read aloud, as if her details alone were incriminating evidence.

Her collaborator wrote it down, her tongue exploring the inside of her cheek.

'Do you have an explanation for the non-payment Miss Burns-Whyte?'

'It was just an oversight, they failed to scan properly, I think the machine was faulty.'

'We can have the till checked okay, but in the meantime I'm afraid it's Waitrose policy to prosecute all thefts.' She looked at the marshmallow who managed to nod without the benefit of a neck.

'Three items, it's hardly the crime of the century.'

'You said there was no crime at all, are you now acknowledging the theft Madam?'

'No, it was a turn of phrase for God's sake. Jesus, what is wrong with you?'

'There's no need to be hostile Madam, we're only doing our job.'

'That's just what the Nazis' said.'

'Miss Burns-Whyte, you really need to calm down okay? You are just going to make this worse for yourself, okay?'

The officer bought herself up to her full height - Jo estimated it to be five-foot-two – before delivering her verdict.

'As the value of the goods is less than £200, as long as you have no previous convictions this can be dealt with as a summary offence. Okay? That means you will receive a charge under Section 176 of the Anti-Social Behaviour, Crime and Policing act. You won't have to attend court, you can enter a guilty plea by post, okay? You'll get a fine.'

'What about innocent until proven guilty? Where are we living, bloody Kurdistan?' Her head was throbbing, she needed a drink.

'If you prefer, I can arrest you. You have the right to elect to be tried by a judge and jury in the Crown Court, okay.'

Jo sat for a moment. The police radios crackled. The marshmallow emitted an unpleasant smell.

'I'll take the fine.'

Jo was seething. It wasn't her fault, they made it too damn easy. It had not even been her idea; she had read an article in *The Mail on Sunday* exposing the new 'middle class offence' that had rocketed since the introduction of self-checkout. Shoppers scanned one item and took three, pressed the onion button instead of asparagus, potato instead of wasabi root. More carrots were sold in Waitrose last year than were ever harvested. She had started small, substituting pink grapefruits for oranges, oolong tea for PG Tips, errors she could explain away. It gave her a feeling of pure excitement, a sensual pleasure. Who dares wins. Stealing became a drug and she grew tolerant, the value of the goods steadily grew: caviar, truffles, salmon. Stuff she didn't even like. Besides, she spent most of her disposable income in that bloody shop, she deserved the occasional freebie. A victimless crime. She suspected that far more people were caught stealing tea bags from Morrisons than Champagne from Waitrose. Those gilet-wearing yummy mummies loading Burberry shopping bags into their Range Rovers were bloody untouchable. She vowed to stop now, she no longer needed excitement or consolation, finally she was a winner. She had Ludo.

Jo felt alluring in her new outfit; nautical striped top and Versace jeans. To hell with the budget, her finances were so depleted that a small rise in credit card debt was hardly here or there. She strolled past the moorings scanning each boat, there she was, *Ariadne*, a lovely sleek thing. Expensive.

'Hello, anyone home?' her sophisticate accent.

Ludo appeared from below deck, navy blazer, joke captain's cap. 'Come aboard first mate,' his grin a white line.

She clambered over the rail as gracefully as her heels allowed. Ludo had advised deck shoes but she couldn't possibly wear flats for a date, what was he thinking? He took her hand and guided her into the cockpit.

'She is fabulous, you're so lucky to have such a splendiful boat,' damn she was going for splendid but switched to beautiful too late.

'I bought it from a client actually, I made him a good return, so he returned the return.'

Jo released her practised laugh, girlish but sexy.

'Let me show you around,' he slipped his arm around her waist.

The cabin was extravagantly furnished: kidney-shaped red leather sofa, mahogany table, flat screen television. The white carpeted berth exuded luxury, she took in the mirrored ceiling, circular bed, polished brass portholes. Elegant and delightful.

'Make yourself comfortable, I'll prepare us a little something,' he winked.

As Ludo busied himself in the galley Jo sat up on deck, she was in a Hollywood film, a warm breeze rippled the shimmering river, she could almost hear the rising violins. A vague memory stirred; running across an echoey sports hall, the squeak of plimsolls on polished floorboards as Brown Owl shouted out exotic nautical terms: *port, starboard, bow, stern*. She had loved that game, there must have been more to it than changing direction, oh yes, *hit the deck* they all had to lie down, *climb the rigging*, they effected an exaggerated sailors' ascent, and something to do with a shark. How thrilling it was but lurking within the fun was the sickening fear of ridicule, of being last to reach port or the horror of erroneously running to starboard. She imagined organising such an activity for her own children's parties, she would provide a little prize for each eliminated player to mitigate potential humiliation. Back then parents did not consider whether they were sowing the seeds of failure and self-loathing.

Ludo emerged beaming with a tray of canapés as if expecting a round of applause. Jo obliged.

'Champagne or cocktails?' He slid open a mahogany panel to reveal a well-stocked drinks cabinet.

'Oh, you're spoiling me. I'll have a Kir Royale.' She had heard it described as 'unashamedly classy' on a recent food programme.

'Do remind me of the ingredients.'

'Crème de cassis and champagne.'

He looked a little blank.

She retrieved the blackcurrant liqueur from the cabinet. 'This goes in first,' she cooed. She was a little disappointed at this gap in his knowledge but it was a ladies' drink after all.

He took the champagne from the ice bucket and mixed two. Jo resisted the urge to take a selfie, she reminded herself that for her new persona this was normal for a Thursday evening.

'So, how's Ludo?' She leaned forward like an attentive wife.

'Good, the usual fast lane, work, work, work, you know. Networking dinners, functions, schmoozing clients. It's nice to escape to the river for some down time,' he downed his Kir Royale as if it were a pint of lager.

'Do you come here often? Sorry that's such a cliché,' Jo purred.

'As often as work allows. Of course, there's always space for you in my schedule. So, what have you been up to?'

'Gosh, the usual, shopping, lunching. I've been doing some detective work too. I'm following up leads on Andrea's brother Ed and on Clara Astrell, remember that frumpy G.P.?' The repulsive memory of Tim squirmed in her gut. 'But let's not talk about that just yet. I'm dying to hear about your time with Andrea in T and C.'

'There's not much to tell really. She was a spirited thing, lively, funny, loved a drink, she really enjoyed herself. I don't want to upset you talking about her.'

What a thoughtful man he was. 'Oh, not at all, we need to keep her memory alive. Tell me about what you did together.'

'Well, mainly we just bumped into each other in bars. One time she came out fishing with me, we had great fun.'

'How odd, Andrea loathed any harm to animals, she was trying to be a vegetarian years before it became fashionable.'

'Yes, of course she made me throw it back, waste of a good pollock if you ask me.' He laughed, she joined in.

A thin cry from the towpath. They turned to watch a young couple, the man stroking his baby's head swaddled in its mother's kangaroo pouch. Two slender black birds perched high in a tree exchanged guttural grunts, wings open towards the last rays of sun. Ludo refilled their champagne flutes.

'It's getting chilly, should we take this below deck?'

21

As Phineas topped up the jeep's water Clara positioned a dusty cushion behind her back, put on her sunglasses and sprayed herself with DEET.

The previous seventy-two hours had passed in a riot of forests, lemurs, rice fields, markets and rum. It was the first time that Phineas had allowed himself time off and he had indulged her in the whirlwind sightseeing tour with all the proprietorial pride of a local. They had agreed to shelve any further talk of Padraig's death for a while and just enjoy their time together. She sensed that he needed to allow his invasive thoughts to percolate and settle, no amount of restating would help. The carefree manner with which he checked his reflection in the broken wing mirror suggested that he was starting to shed his burden. Another good sign was that he had sent a message to Oisin confessing that his lack of contact was not due to Madagascan Wi-Fi but to his guilt and grief. She had found that coming to terms with death was like befriending an unpredictable animal, you had to allow it to come to you, offer your hand, pat its head, whilst always knowing that it could turn and claw and bite. Today at least would be light-hearted and fun. Phineas' tracker had invited them to a family fiesta, it was just what they needed.

They drove through the bleak lowlands, smiling children - the colour of the red earth - sat beside bundles of charcoal like tiny Buddhas. Clara noted the tell-tale signs of malnourishment and retinal disease. Although they had no use for cooking material they stopped and bought every tiny bale, leaving gifts of fruit and water.

The jeep's suspension was reigniting her old back problem and she was pleased when Phineas finally pulled into an array of erratically parked vehicles on the hillside. She was hit by an oasis of colour and sound. Tethered zebu grazed on sparse shoots, children danced to make-shift drums, women stirred blackened pots over small fires, people lazed under the shade of wizened trees while others moved like colourful fish through the patchwork of blankets. It gradually dawned on her that this was not a village; this was the family gathering.

A man in a raffia fedora, his shoulders draped in a striped blanket, greeted Phineas with a warm hug, stood back and respectfully took her hand. Armand was a delight. Skinny as a stick with lively eyes, his head a toothy skull. His shirt suggested that he had lost a significant amount of weight or possibly it had never fitted.

'Welcome to our Famidihana, doctor Phineas, doctor Clara. We are very honoured that you are joining us, please come and have some food and beverages.' He led them to the cooking area and ladled huge lumps of meat and watery stock into coconut-shell bowls. 'Traditional, freshly slaughtered zebu, please enjoy,' he grinned.

Clara and Phineas exchanged panicked glances.

'I don't want to appear rude but remember I don't eat meat, nor does Mum, we've brought cheese and bread, we are happy to eat that.'

'My sincerest apologies. I thought that you do not eat meat because of the expense. It is part of your tradition?'

'Well Mum made me vegetarian so I guess you could say that.'

'Then please drink,' he poured a line of pungent liquid from a stained bottle.

Unable to refuse Armand's hospitality twice they drank the harsh liquor, allowing it to froth on the tongue and burn the back of the throat. Clara reassured herself that the high alcohol content would mitigate any bacterial growth.

'Delicious, thank you,' she surveyed the chaotic festivities. 'This is quite a gathering; you have an enormous family.'

'Yes, some we only meet here every few years, so it is always a very joyous occasion. They come from all over the country, some have travelled for days,' he nodded at the bodies lying under woven blankets. 'Today we will meet my daughter and my cousin and my father, tell them our news and introduce new family members.'

'How lovely, when will they arrive?' She would struggle to remember so many names.

'Oh, they are already here, they are lying in the tombs,' Armand gestured to the white-washed blocks dotted up the scrubby hill-side. 'This is a 'turning of the bones', we are here to honour our relatives.'

'They are deceased? I'm so sorry,' she found herself slipping into compassionate G.P. mode.

'Meeting our loved ones is a time of celebration. Sadness is not allowed, this is a party.' He finished his drink and re-filled their glasses.

'You've experienced a lot of loss Armand, I didn't know,' Phineas paled.

'They are not dead my friend, they remain in the land of the living until their bodies and bones are completely decomposed. Only then does their spirit move on to the next life.'

Clara leant in to ask Phineas whether he wanted to leave but a burst of energetic drumming drowned out any further conversation. It signalled the start of the procession. People assembled, chatting and laughing as they made their way towards the tombs, toddlers dragging sticks through the dust.

'Come, bring your drinks, let us go and meet my family.' Armand led the way, his shoeless feet seemingly impervious to the stony ground.

The tombs were decorated with naively painted figures, Clara could make out birds, vases, zebu, yellow suns rising behind nimbus clouds. The crowd encircled the nearest tomb, some clambering onto its flat roof others leaning against the walls. She stood with Phineas at the periphery not wishing to intrude. She took her son's hand as Armand removed the rusted padlock. Several people followed him inside and reappeared with a body wrapped in silk as if it were a roll-end carpet. They hoisted it on raised arms and paraded to a levelled area where others were waiting to attend. Another body was bought out, and another. She pictured news footage of national disasters; dust-covered bodies retrieved from the rubble. From a respectful distance they watched family members kneel to remove the discoloured shrouds and wrap them in fresh silks. She found the corporeal intimacy both shocking and moving. At last, to a lively musical accompaniment, the redressed bodies were raised on a huddle of shoulders and danced between the empty tombs. The deceased were passed like crowd-surfers through the throng as people related their family news and children stroked their silken relatives.

Phineas clutched her arm. 'I'm feeling slightly sick, not sure if it's the dressing of the corpses or the dog alcohol but I'm just going to sit down under the trees for a bit.'

A cacophony of whistles, guitars, and wheezy accordions filled the afternoon air. Crocodiles of young men and women moved to the rhythm, the bodies high on their shoulders turning and rotating in time to the music. The assembly on the crypt roof were dancing as one, laughing and swigging from bottles. It had become a crazy fiesta. The air of release and celebration was infectious, Clara found herself dancing with a group of women, many with babies strapped to their chests. She mirrored their movements, stepping as if on hot coals, lifting her arms, palms open to the sky. Her back pain dissipated, she felt lithe and timeless. Phineas brushed the red earth from his trousers and came to join them. He took her hands and twirled her round in an Irish jig. They danced for Armand's relatives, they danced for Padraig and for living-but-gone Gwam and for all that they had lost and all that they had found.

The singing, laughing and dancing went on into the evening, she had never enjoyed herself more. Armand insisted that they stay; it was too far, too late and they had been drinking for eight hours. He led them into a sparsely furnished room, the function of which was not apparent and rolled two thin mattresses into settles.

'Please sit to avoid the unfurling.'

A graceful woman dressed in a highly patterned lamba and matching hair wrap, smiled shyly. Armand introduced his wife with solemn formality although Clara had been dancing with her for several hours. She brought hot sweet tea and home-made biscuits. The four of them sat and listened to the music outside.

'Thanks so much for inviting us today, it was amazing. To be honest I was a bit freaked out when your relatives came out of the tomb but I have to say I was a little sad to see them returned,' Phineas slurred but Armand seemed to understand.

'As the sun sets the bodies must be kept safe from evil spirits and negative energies. They are taken in feet first and laid upside down to close the cycle of life and death.'

'So, what happens to them now?' A drumbeat punctuated his

questions. 'Do they go to heaven?'

'We have a mixture of beliefs, taken from Christianity, from the natural world, others from the specific tradition of our tribes. It is like the sweets that you told me about, Pick and Mix!' Armand sipped his tea. 'We will eventually go to a second life, it is similar to our first life, that is why we put in clothes, suitcases, photographs.'

Clara could see that he was enjoying teaching Phineas, an evident role reversal, but perhaps all this talk of death was too much.

'But you believe in spirits?' asked Phineas.

'The spirit lives on through death. Our ancestors are now between the living and God. They have the power to intervene in our lives.'

Phineas ran his hands through his hair and stared at the ceiling fan, apparently having difficulty assimilating this information.

'It's certainly very different from our culture,' said Clara, hoping to draw the topic to a close. 'We tend to see death as final and just hope there might be an afterlife; most people don't count on it.'

Armand laughed, he seemed to find Western values highly amusing. 'There is a close bond between the living and the not living. We honour them like this every three, five and seven years. Always an odd number to show that it is unfinished.'

She saw tears in her son's eyes. 'The dancing was fabulous, really great fun.'

'Armand,' Phineas extricated himself from the rolled mattress, stood and cleared his throat, 'tonight I have seen you as head of your family. You have always had my utmost respect as a tracker and field assistant. Now I have respect for you as a man and a human being.'

Armand rose to his feet, 'Doctor Phineas, I too respect you and am very honoured to be working with you in the protection of our lemurs.'

Phineas returned to the unfurled mattress and leant back against the wall. Clara sensed that he had made some peace with himself, perhaps he had realised that the thoughts that had been plaguing him were socially constructed, that emotional responses were culturally determined, that beliefs were not facts. Or perhaps he was just drunk.

'Mum, there was something else I wanted to tell you,' he slurred, 'it's about Andrea Gibbons,' he closed his eyes. 'What she said the last time we met.'

Clara leant forward and waited. She listened to him breathing. He was fast asleep.

22

L udo had been more than she had hoped for. He took charge, directed her like Quentin Tarantino, she willingly played his leading lady, she had been a triumph. And later he had listened attentively while she told him about Ed and the flat clearance and Clara and the tortoise and her plan to watch the Cuviers' farmhouse. He had suggested that she stepped up the investigation before they destroyed any evidence, he knew his stuff, apparently a photograph of Darwin would be inadmissible, she needed exhibit A itself. Drawing on his extensive army experience he helped her to formulate a plan of operation. Okay, he had declined to join her but he had had a better idea, he would be her alibi in the unlikely event that she needed one; a respectable businessman willing to vouch for her whereabouts would be a watertight defence. He was such a star.

Ludo possessed detailed knowledge of the professional execution of night-raids; one needed stealth, silence and strategy. She needed to wait until all the lights were out, then another twenty minutes to ensure that the residents were asleep. He gave her his army combat jacket, it swamped her but this was ideal to hide her figure and to confound any eye-witness reports. He seemed to relish helping her with her disguise, he even applied face camo, a souvenir from his deployment in Afghanistan. Her war hero. Ludo had found the dress rehearsal unaccountably provocative, he dragged her back to bed, called her his little law-breaker, took photos on his phone. It was all very exciting. What a shame that he had had to rush off, she hoped he had made his early morning meeting. She would have liked to have learnt more about the names on his chest, he had merely said that they had all played a part in making him the man he was today. They included fallen comrades from Iraq and Afghanistan and of course his beautiful mother. She imagined one day he would add her own name.

Back home she checked her kit list. The living room floor was strewn with equipment; torch, hoodie, balaclava, Google Earth map, swag-bag for Darwin. She could not find the type of jemmy tool that Ludo had suggested but she substituted a pizza cutter. She retrieved a pair of walking boots from the jumble under the stairs. They had never been worn. She had bought them on impulse to impress a gorgeous new doctor on Kingfisher Ward who had mentioned that he was a keen hiker. The day the boots were delivered she discovered that he had a fiancé; she did not have the heart to return them.

D-day. Operation Darwin was green for go. Jo consulted the day's Zen wisdom *To seek is to suffer.* Yes, she was willing to suffer for the truth. Lady Justice meet Field Commander Burns-Whyte. In the practice run Ludo had applied two black lines over each cheek bone but she did not really care for the apache effect. She had found a more subtle 'desert storm' style that seemed to lend itself to spray-tan application. The professional tanning kit that she had stolen from *Boots* had been reassuringly expensive. Okay, so she had promised herself to stop shoplifting but she was broke; the end justifies the means. She scanned the information sheet, the lotion contained botanical plant extracts and vitamin complexes. And it was alcohol free; too bad, ha-ha-ha. She did not bother with the small print instructions. She twisted a hand-towel into a turban and applied a generous layer to her face.

Jo set the timer for thirty minutes and turned on Judge Judy. Some creepy guy with enormous hands had shot a neighbours' cat with an air gun. There was a mock-up picture of the back-yard layout and the trajectory of the pellets. After much argument the man was ordered to pay the vet bills; the owner was vindicated, the man unrepentant. The cat had died. Jo touched her face, little pimples were erupting, it was as itchy as hell, she rushed to the bathroom. A hideous sight, her face was a huge strawberry, complete with surface seeds. She scrubbed at her inflamed cheeks with soap and water but the stain had leached deep into her pores. She applied a layer of foundation that only served to exacerbate her resemblance to a soft-fruit. Now it was burning, her face was swelling up. Jesus Christ. She poured herself a whiskey and took a double dose of antihistamine. Her next visual check revealed a bloated proboscis monkey, she phoned NHS one-one-one. The call handler sounded bored, Jo just knew he had her on loudspeaker, she imagined that he was chewing gum and doing a crossword. He read out a series of questions from his crib sheet, Jo was aware that she was answering all in the affirmative. Now the operative stopped chewing, with an undisguised urgency in his voice he told her to go directly to the out-of-hours surgery. He would telephone to alert the doctor to her imminent arrival.

Fortunately, the need for urgent medical attention in Marlow at eleven-thirty on a Sunday night was low. The woman at the reception desk glanced up from her phone, took a sharp intake of breath and waved her through. The doctor was hard-boiled and Scottish. A squat woman, thin-lipped, unsympathetic, probably a lesbian. She adjusted the angle-poise desk lamp, shone it directly into her face and tutted. She lectured her on the dangers of parabens and dihydroxyacetone, the woman was evidently a stranger to beauty products, although Lord knows she could have benefitted. The doctor proposed a belt and braces approach; she left with a course of prophylactic antibiotics and her face smothered in corticosteroid lotion. The recommendation was to go home, monitor the reaction over-night and return should the condition worsened.

No, she had come this far; the mission would go ahead.

Jo cruised past the farmhouse driveway, parked in a lay-by and pulled the balaclava over her head. She realised she had not needed to camouflage her face after all. Bloody hell. The row of domestic-fowl topiary provided excellent cover, she crept from chicken to duck enjoying the excitement of the advance. A light rain started to fall, she scanned the torch across the rutted terrain, it would be easy to turn an ankle. She made a dash for the farmhouse, arms flailing for balance. Damn, she should have carried out a full reconnaissance, things looked very different in the moonless night. Pausing beside a stone outbuilding she tried to establish the best access point. She rotated the Google image several times before deciding on the door which seemed to lead into an annex connected to the main house. On the count of three she bolted across the gravel path and pressed herself against the door. Suddenly it was pouring, the wool of her balaclava clung soaked and heavy on her head. She rummaged in the kit bag and retrieved the pizza wheel to jemmy the door. Sustained leverage bent the wheel and trapped it in the frame, she jerked it forwards and back until a crisp snap left her holding the broken handle. Oh God, no plan B. Her face was itching again, perhaps the lotion was washing off. She twisted the door handle in exasperation, it opened.

She froze.

A firing squad of men stood against the wall, as her eyes accommodated to the dark the shadowy figures transformed into a bank of coats. Jesus. The beating of her heart accompanied her across the tiled floor, she could just make out a sink, cabinets, an orange lamp glowed in the corner. The stench of diarrhoea. Breathing through her mouth she flashed the torch into the darkness. A large glass tank stood on the wooden counter. My God, it must be Darwin, what a stroke of luck. She inched forward, hardly daring to breathe. Closer inspection revealed a large clutch of eggs set neatly under a heat lamp. A tortoise farm; she had hit the jackpot! A crash echoed through a speaker on the counter, she spun around and made a dash for the door. A sticky coil of flies hit her in the face. Her feet slipped from under her and she landed with a thud, her burning cheek squished against something disgusting, the smell made her retch. She dared not move. A dim light flicked on, a large figure loomed over her and stuffed something hard and tangy into her mouth. Barking erupted into her ear, she could smell its breath, a firm wet object prodded her eye.

'Nosferatu, Nosferatu, enough now.' A woman's voice.

A rough sack was thrown over her head, would she never wake from this nightmare? Two sets of arms firmly grabbed her elbows and hoisted her into a chair. As they tied her wrists and feet, the man and woman spoke happily to each other as if they were preparing an evening meal. The voices were muffled by her balaclava, her hoodie and the sack, but her captors were hatching a plan. One set of footsteps receded. She peered through the mesh, beyond the close-up of a dead fly she watched an ancient fossil of a man pull up a chair. A piercing falsetto yowled in her ear as something flung itself into her lap, gripping with needle claws. The fetid stench again, a warm liquid seeped through onto her cold thighs. Her nose now being the only source of oxygen she had no choice but to breathe it in. She was in hell.

A crackle from the speaker, the woman's voice.

'Hello dear, Henrietta Cuvier here. Coney Field Farm, Marlow Bottom. I know it's terribly late but I wonder if you might send an officer?'

'What seems to be the problem Madam?'

She must have the phone on loudspeaker, Jo held her breath and strained to hear.

'We've had a break-in. Well not strictly a break-in, we tend to leave the door unlocked, it's generally such a safe area.'

'Has anything been taken?'

'Nothing of which I am aware. I don't think they got very far before they were disturbed. Fortunately, I was just getting up to turn the duck eggs and I heard something in the annex. Father was up because he was fretting about Aunt Jobiska, she has not been too well, poor thing, dodgy tummy, scoffing from the bins no doubt. We keep her confined to the annex, she keeps messing on the floor, poor lamb.'

What the hell was the woman talking about?

'Does Aunt Jobiska often eat from bins?' The voice sounded concerned.

'Unfortunately, yes, silly old coot, no consequential learning. It is her age I'm afraid. Father keeps threatening to have her put down but she knows we love her really.'

'Have Social Services ever been involved with your family?'

'Goodness no, we are quite self-sufficient.'

Jo struggled in vain to eject the object from her mouth.

'I see. Your local station isn't manned at night, I think under the circumstances we'll send someone out to check on you all in the morning.'

'What's that dear?' An even older voice.

'He is saying that the station isn't manned mother.'

'Well tell them to send a woman.'

'Is everything alright there Madam?'

'Yes, mother is a little hard of hearing. In the morning you say, so in the meantime what should we do with the intruder?'

'The intruder is still in the house?'

'Yes, he no longer poses a threat, he has been immobilised, he is tied to a chair.'

'Tied to a chair?'

Jo tried to rock in confirmation, she didn't want to be with these lunatics all bloody night.

'Yes, father was in the Royal Navy during the war, so he knows his knots. Ninety-seven but as tough as an old rhino.'

'Don't worry Mrs Cuvier, a car has been dispatched; it will be with you very soon.'

'It's Ms.'

'Tell them he's tied to a chair,' called the feeble voice.

'Yes, mother they know, they are sending a car.'

Jo tried to make a guttural sound but it seemed to lodge the object more firmly in her mouth.

'Okay Mrs Cuvier, I'm just going to keep you on the line until the officers arrive. Can you tell me anything else about the intruder?'

'It's Ms. Not really, the lights down there are quite dim, low wattage, father insists, frugal old goat. The intruder is wearing a camouflage jacket, balaclava helmet and training trousers, you know the type that young people wear for sports. I put a satsuma in his mouth to prevent biting.'

'A satsuma?'

'Yes, or possibly a tangerine. On reflection, I think a tangerine because I had one yesterday and they were rather hard to peel.'

'Is the man able to breathe?'

'Oh yes, Father put a potato-sack over his head but it is hessian so it's quite safe.'

'And have any injuries been sustained?'

'I think not, well nothing worse than a solid muzzle in the eye.'

'He has a gun?'

'No no, the muzzle belongs to a dachshund not an AK47, the little sausage was just being friendly, he tends to go straight for the eye.'

'I see. Anything else that you can tell me, age? ethnic origin?'

'Hard to tell. We have yet to look under the balaclava. Mother is just going through to do a sketch. Oh, I can hear sirens, looks like they have blue-lighted it over here, thank you dear, I'll go and let them in, cheerio.'

It was not how she had planned it but at least the police would now see that the Cuviers were nutters and that they had possession of Andrea's stolen tortoise. And she could play her trump card; she was on first name terms with a detective inspector.

Thank god for the boys in blue.

23

White mesh, the smell of mosquito repellent, a cacophony of calls. Clara took a moment to gather where she was; a wooden hut with a concrete floor in an isolated corner of Madagascar. Phineas' field-camp. With the primary aim of keeping out spiders she had tucked the mosquito net tightly around the mattress and now, in her sleep weakened state, she struggled to release it. Giving up she lay back to appreciate the eccentric morning choir. The riot of frogs had quietened with the dawn, the few fanatics who sustained a back-beat of grunts were joined by cackles and gabbles and a whooping lemur descant.

It seemed to have stopped raining, the patter on the tin roof had been a comfort at four in the morning; a point of familiarity in an alien world. Phineas had taken her on a nocturnal survey. They had seen an aye-aye - supposed harbinger of death - clinging to a branch, it fixed her with its amber stare and pointed directly at her; it was utterly beguiling. The strange creature cocked its head and twitched its bat-like ears before resuming its tapping of the bark with its elongated finger. It was searching for grubs using percussive foraging; the things Phineas knew were a delight. Bless him, he had been so thrilled when she finally caught a glimpse of a mouse lemur before it bounded away into the darkness. It had struck her that of all the species he might have studied he had chosen a tiny, fast-moving, nocturnal lemur. He had certainly made it hard for himself, but he had always been drawn to the cryptic, sought out the under-dog. Something had shifted between them; without words or effort a new bond had formed seamlessly around the old. An unspoken respect that perhaps only seeing the other in a new environment can bring.

And they now shared a new guilt, borne of regret. He had finally told her about Andrea. What she had said. He had dismissed it at the time, she was prone to catastrophising - she had been devastated when Iggy, the nature club hamster had died – the words had barely registered. But with hindsight he should have pressed her, encouraged her to explain, maybe he could have helped. She had said it in a whisper. Five words that might hold the clue to her death. 'I have done something terrible.' There was nothing to be done about it, no one to tell, just another burden. She imagined that he was feeding his own worm. Her specimen had been relatively quiet over the past week.

A scraping of chairs on the veranda, chopping sounds, humming, a song from years ago *Wake Me Up Before You Go-Go*. Phineas preparing breakfast. The thought compelled her to prise the mosquito net free, she did not want to miss a minute of her last day with him.

Phineas was wearing the T-shirt she had bought him at Vorondolo market, moss green with a motif of a smiling chameleon draped over one shoulder. She noted with pleasure that he had put on a little weight; she need not worry that he had a tapeworm. He had prepared an indulgent breakfast of mango, pineapple and Mofo Gasy; a sweet egg-shaped pancake that she had grown to like. A jam jar of poinciana flowers stood beside a pot of strong coffee.

'This is lovely, thanks for looking after me so well,' she kissed him good morning.

'It's been great having you here, thanks for travelling six thousand miles to see your daft son.' He poured the coffee, adding raw sugar to both.

'The time has flown, I can't believe it's been ten days, I'm really going to miss Madagascar, and you of course.'

'Actually, I have some news. You know Peter's program in Montreal has pretty much finished, well they've just offered him a project in Exeter.'

'Oh gosh, still so far from you.' She lit a citronella candle; the day-insects were waking up.

'Yes, but I discovered something being away from the field-site: I'm not indispensable,' he put down his coffee. He was evidently leading up to something. 'Armand is quite capable of running the field site,' he cleared his throat, 'he said he would be delighted to accept the role of lead researcher. He cried actually. Thing is I don't need to be here. I could start writing up the results, do an occasional site visit and we can Skype any issues. Long story short, Peter has accepted the Exeter job and I'm coming back in

May!' He grinned triumphantly.

'That is fantastic news!' They stood and hugged. 'When will Peter be starting?'

'Not until the end of the year but I thought I could find us an apartment, get settled in,' his eyes shone.

'Well I'm delighted. You can finally take all the stuff you've been hoarding in your bedroom and the piles of wedding presents in the garage. Oh, and I can hand-over Darwin, he's actually very sweet, but I'm getting too fond of him.'

'I'll give you visiting rights,' he gave her the last pancake. 'Talking of which I had an idea for how to spend your last day, how do you fancy visiting a top-secret tortoise sanctuary?'

'Sounds perfect.'

They pulled up to an ordinary looking brick house on the outskirts of Antananarivo. Ordinary except for the huge rolls of barbed wire encompassing the boundary that Clara imagined was a potential give-away for a 'top-secret' facility. A small wrinkled man in a battered straw hat came to the door.

'Mum, this is Gabriel, the founder of the sanctuary. Gabriel, my mum, visiting from England.'

He fixed her with his tiny eyes and gave a toothless grin. 'Please come through.'

He moved slowly with a lumbering gait, she did not need to ask what drew him to tortoises, she had never seen anyone quite so chelonian. The house was full of tortoises.

'These are all in quarantine or require special attention,' he gestured to the cages stacked on every available surface. He led them out of the back door to the enclosures where numerous patterned carapaces dotted the sand. 'We house tortoises according to their size.' He seemed immensely proud of his wards. 'We have over five hundred. Most have been rescued from traffickers smuggling them out of the country for the pet trade. As you can see, they are the most beautiful of all tortoises.'

She admired the black and yellow stars on their shells and could see their attraction as pets. 'Ah yes, their beauty appears to be their downfall.'

Gabriel nodded, he picked one up and handed it to her, it was no bigger than a ten pence piece. 'Sadly, they are critically endangered. We will keep these until their shells are strong enough to protect them from wild dogs, then release them back to the dry-thorn forest. It takes five years.' He offered the tortoise a piece of cucumber. It opened and closed its beak in obvious enjoyment, it was surprisingly voracious for such a tiny animal.

'Seems hungry,' said Phineas stroking its shell.

'They often come here in a poor state, some have been hidden in baggage without food or water for days. Many die. We are swamped. Last year we took in over three thousand seized by the authorities. We release them and often they are poached and return again.'

The poor man seemed jaded, resigned to walking an endless treadmill.

'This must cost a fortune. Do you get any government funding?' Clara felt overwhelmed by the scale of the problem. She wondered how Darwin was getting on, whether Hen had remembered to mist him.

'A little but it is not sufficient, we would like to focus on education and reducing habitat loss, but we have become a rescue centre. We are barely coping with demand.'

'You are doing a great job.' Phineas put his hand on Gabriel's shoulder, a warm and natural gesture.

'We hope that things will get better,' Gabriel replaced the tiny tortoise.

'They might get worse,' said Phineas.

'Or stay the same,' said Clara.

Gabriel released a delighted laugh. 'You two are, what is that phrase you told me? A breath of fresh air!

'What you're doing here is astonishing,' said Clara, 'If there is anything I can do.'

Phineas had chosen the perfect location for their last night; a traditional Malagasy hotel with lush tropical gardens and a stylish restaurant known for its vegetarian cuisine. Clara wore her favourite midnight blue dress, a last-minute packing decision.

Phineas looked very handsome in his Ernest Hemmingway suit.

He ordered the 'plant-eater banquet' for two. He had certainly got his appetite back.

'I feel sad to be going home, this has been such an unexpected tonic.' She sipped a physalis rum, her new favourite drink. 'Despite the news about Padraig.'

'I have to admit it's still a burden but it seems a little lighter. The nightmares have stopped. That reminds me, I got a lovely message from Oisin earlier.' He searched through his phone and read it aloud.

Greetings from Stoneybatter

Hey Phineas, so great to hear from you. Oh man sounds like you are beating yourself up pretty bad. He was your dad too, at least we had him for a couple of decades, I'm sad you never got to meet him. Do you ever get to visit home? I guess even lemur botherers take a holiday. Can you come to Dublin? I have something for you from dad. You can stay with me. Brexit is approaching, bring your passport and plenty of euros! Take it easy brother. Oisin x

'He sounds delightful. Well there's another bonus of coming home, you can take him up on his offer.'

The waiter filled the table with an array of bowls of colourful vegetables, assorted leaves, rice and pulses. It resembled the tortoise kitchen.

'Yes, I'll definitely go over, maybe take Peter. Perhaps the thing he has for me was retrieved from the car. I'll have to wait and see, it's not really something I can ask.'

'Has he mentioned his mother? How does she feel about all this?' She had wanted to ask since the first night but had desisted.

'Oh, sadly she died a couple of years ago. Dad. Padraig told me. Breast cancer. They are orphans now. Bloody tragic.'

Phineas took out a small box from his jacket pocket and handed it to her.

'A little thank you for coming, a memento of your trip.'

She opened the lid to reveal a delicate porcelain brooch, smooth red enamel on silver. 'A poinciana, I love it.'

He pinned it to her dress, it looked stunning. 'It's the national flower. They call it flame of the forest.'

'Thoughtful gifts are definitely another bonus of having a gay son.'

They smiled and clicked glasses.

'To us.'

24

Voices outside. The clunk of the hatch sliding open. Jo lifted her head from the vinyl mattress like a wounded animal.

'Brought in last night covered in cat shit ranting about Darwin. Definitely one for you lot. We've removed possible ligatures. She put up quite a fight when we tried to get her boots off.'

Silver-lidded eyes stared at her through the door.

'Why is she in a paper suit?'

'Her clothes were heavily soiled but she refused to select anything from our garments box. Said she would rather be seen dead than wearing Primark. She's calmed down a bit but she's still refusing to cooperate, she declined the duty solicitor and breakfast. Good luck.'

'What's her name?'

'Jo double-barrelled something. I'll put an officer outside.'

'Thanks.'

The clang of keys, a tall woman in a red jacket entered, the door banged shut. Jo swung her legs onto the floor and fixed her with a cold stare.

'Hello, I'm Precious Ollennu, Community Psychiatric Nurse. The officers who brought you in were a little worried about you. I just want to ask you a few questions and see if I can help you.'

'I need to get Darwin and I urgently need to find the person who murdered my best friend. If you can't help with either of those you can just fuck off.'

'Is it alright if I call you Jo?'

'Please don't.' God, she had met her type in Goredale; nurses who thought they were bloody social workers. The more they said they wanted to help the less they actually did.

'Perhaps I could contact your next-of-kin?'

Case in point.

'The only help I need is to find the perpetrator. Also, I have been attacked and held hostage and fricken tortured and no one seems the least bit bloody interested.'

'Who has been torturing you?' The woman could have been asking the contents of a sandwich.

'The people who have the tortoise; Henrietta and her ammonite parents. Then I was savaged by Nosferatu, jumped on me, went for the neck, stuck his disgusting wet nose straight into my eye, they took the hood off, an old sack of spuds in a kimono was wheeled in and started painting my portrait with an orange in my mouth. Bloody sadists.'

'Do you think that you might have dreamt all of this?'

'No, I did not bloody dream it. I have the scars to prove it,' Jo held out her wrists to reveal red marks. 'See, I was tied to a chair by the fossils.'

'Were you handcuffed by officers?' Her face a poker player's.

'Yes, outrageous.'

'I see. Could you tell me why you think that these people would want to do you harm?'

'Your guess is as good as mine love. They're bloody nuts the lot of them. Talking to Aunt Jobiska all the time when she doesn't even bloody exist.'

'What has happened to your face?'

'What do you mean?' Jo put her hand to her cheeks, they felt bloated and pimpled.

'It is not really the colour of skin.'

'You obviously skipped diversity training.'

The woman opened her mouth and closed it. She adjusted her cuffs.

'What can you tell me about the tortoise?'

'It was stolen from my friend after she was poisoned. That is why she was murdered. Yes, she was killed for a tortoise!'

'Killed by a tortoise?' The woman sounded doubtful.

'No, for a tortoise. Christ, pay attention this is important. Andrea must have found out. Clara is a trafficker, she's also a G.P., that's her cover. As we speak, she's in Madagascar organising another consignment. Six thousand pounds per tortoise.'

'I see. Jo, have you ever heard voices when no one else was in the room?'

'Yes, I heard them talking through a speaker, a little indistinct but I could hear them alright.'

'And what about since you have been here?'

'Yes, all last night, they won't bloody shut up.'

'What do they say?'

'Mainly just rubbish; insults, demands, yada yada yada.'

'Have you ever been given medication to help you with these ideas?'

'Are you kidding me? I don't want medication, I want justice. Oh, I get it, you think I'm nuts. Well you can just fuck off.' Jo pressed the alarm bell. 'Conversation over. Don't come back.'

Jo sat motionless on the plastic chair, her back against the flaking magnolia wall. The woollen roll-neck jumper was starting to itch, she regretted choosing it over the grandad-shirt but it was considerably more flattering. Four staff sat huddled in the nurses' station glued to computer screens. She reread the summary sheet she had stolen from under the eyes of the muskox officer as she was escorted past the front desk and into the unmarked police car.

Caucasian woman, mid-to-late thirties, unkempt, hostile, verbally aggressive. Appears to have self-harmed by application of a noxious substance to her face. Injury to her wrists likely self-inflicted or caused by handcuffs. Clear evidence of self-neglect, detained wearing soiled army combat clothing, highly pungent.

Overt psychiatric symptoms include: pressure of speech, thought disorder; tangential thinking, flight of ideas and paranoid ideation. Complex delusional system appears to centre on vampires, beliefs about evolution, Charles Darwin and a special tortoise. Persecutory ideation: believes she has been kidnapped, tortured and her friend murdered. Disclosed current auditory hallucinations and described an urgent personal mission.

Lacks insight.

Recommendation: Continued detention under Section 136 MHA, Place of Safety. Request urgent transfer to hospital under Section Two. Provisional diagnosis late onset paranoid schizophrenia. To contact Acute services, Saint Mangabey's Hospital.

P.Ollennu. Community Psychiatric Nurse.

Stitched up like a bloody kipper.

A large West Indian man leant against the window rolling a cigarette, his stained T-shirt riding up to reveal dirt encrusted scabs. A crew-cut nurse cracked open the door.

'Daniel, how many times? Move away from the window and do not light that in here or we'll confiscate your tobacco.'

Daniel wedged the cigarette behind his ear and raised his middle finger as he sauntered off. An elderly woman in a pink nightie paced the length of the corridor, her grubby mules slapping every step, the stench of stale urine that accompanied her competed with a harsh disinfectant. Despite the choice of empty chairs, a gaunt youth with a neck-brace and a large welt on his forehead took the seat beside her. He smelled strongly of cannabis.

'What you in for love?'

His accent was hard to locate, Birmingham meets Glasgow via Newcastle.

'Because the police are bastards and the psychiatric system is run by incompetents.'

'Amen to that sister,' he raised his hand to high five her.

She let him hang.

'I'm Terry by the way people call me Bang Bang you wanna go to my room for some base?' He spoke without drawing breath.

Jo gave him a dismissive look. 'Do I look as if I enjoy club music?'

'No you know whizz speed pure base,' his speech rapid fire.

'Oh, I don't take drugs. Besides, I have an appointment with the psychiatrist. I'll be home by tonight.'

'Good luck with that lady your first day right? They'll have you doped up to the eyeballs and hopping down their fricken rabbit hole by this evening what doctor you got?'

'Eppendorf.'

'Oh geez she's a piece of work,' his enthusiasm escalated into a hail of words. 'Tweak we call her forever putting your meds up 'til you lose the will to live you can tell her patients they're the ones who spend all day in bed NMPs they call them No Management Problem by the way....'

'Who have you got?'

'Devonshire he's alright takes a special interest in us druggies he's doing a study on drug-induced psychosis he's nice to us so we'll fill in his questionnaires brings chocolate cake to the CTM and everything only he....'

'CTM?'

Bang Bang warmed to the question; he was seemingly unused to being cast as the expert. 'Clinical Team Meeting once a week nurse doctor occupational therapist psychologist sit in a room and talk about you then you get hauled in and get told off for the things you've done wrong like taking your tablets in the computer room when no one even told you that you can't....'

'No tablets? That's what we're here for, isn't it, to receive treatment?' Jo wondered whether he was a reliable source of information.

'Computer tablets not meds.' He roared with laughter attracting the attention of a nurse who scribbled something on his clipboard and walked on.

'If you're in Eppendorf's team you get your meds increased if you're in Devonshire's you get told you're doing really well won't be long before we get you home have a piece of cake fill in this questionnaire see you next week.'

'God, I thought this was an acute admissions ward, how long have you been here?'

The putrid old woman slapped passed again.

'Alright Eileen? Alright love? Six months I caused a ruckus on the rehab ward so I'd get moved back here I don't want to be discharged just yet I lost my hostel place so I've got nowhere to go I'm holding out for a flat the other place was full of druggies and I kept getting beaten up and then....'

'Is that what happened to your neck?'

'No I jumped head first off a wall on the shopping trip last week for the tramadol you know only got two days-worth this time then bloody paracetamol I bang my head as well that works if it's a duty doctor or a locum best is Friday night get a whole weekend then Devonshire comes in Monday morning and shouts at them down the phone and I'm back on paracetamol.....'

He was exhausting.

Jo tapped on the office window, a bespectacled nurse closed down the *Patience* tab and opened the door.

'What is it?'

'How much longer do I have to wait for the doctor?'

'Dr Eppendorf telephoned, she's running late, she'll see you tomorrow.'

The door shut.

'Are you fricken kidding me?' Jo banged on the glass; a nurse motioned for her to move away.

She banged again.

Crew-cut stepped out. 'Move away from the window or you will be moved away.'

'I'm a nurse actually, I know my rights, I demand to see a doctor.'

'You need to go back to your room and calm down.'

'You need to do your bloody job and get me a doctor, I need to go home,' she kicked the door.

Crew-cut motioned to the other nurses, they all stood up. Jo armed herself with a plastic chair.

Jo struggled to open her eyes, her lids metal shutters, her left buttock ached. She slowly registered the location of her limbs; the recovery position. A dim glow penetrated the flimsy curtain; the sun? The moon? A line of light marked the base of the door. She moved her desert dry tongue. The canned laughter of a sitcom seeped through the wall. Gingerly she drew her body from the mattress and manoeuvred her feet onto the floor. She sat hunched on the side of the bed, her head swimming.

A harsh light flicked on as the door opened. 'Ah, you're up are you? Do you want food? We left some out for you.'

Jo's tongue squatted in her mouth like a toad, she nodded tentatively, the nurse disappeared. Ten minutes passed, maybe twenty, had the nurse registered her nod, or she was meant to go to the dining area? Currently an impossibility. She stared at her toes growing cold on the linoleum floor, they did not appear to belong to her.

A tapping on the door, a garishly dressed woman appeared holding a tray. 'Hello, I'm Maz, can I come in?' A floral headwrap, an outlandish rainbow dress, blue fluffy slippers with rabbit ears.

'Yes,' Jo's voice a witch's rasp.

'Nurse Tut said I could bring this in for you, saves her the bother of walking twenty meters, the lazy cow.'

Jo contorted her aching face into a grimace.

'Don't worry, I know what it's like when you've been zapped. You put up a grand fight by the way, they floored you and jabbed a good dose in your arse.'

Jo tried to articulate the words *rapid tranquillisation?* but found it was not possible.

Maz set the tray down on the side table and peeled off the cling-film to reveal a slice of wet ham and a wilted salad. She poured water from the jug, Jo drained it in one go and held out the beaker for more.

'Dry mouth, that'll be the sedation, it's a bitch.' She refilled Jo's mug.

'Thanks so much.'

'Don't mention it,' Maz perched on the bottom of the bed. 'So, what the hell happened to your face?'

'Fake tan. Allergic reaction. Need lotion.'

'It looks pretty bad. I've got some Nivea Hand and Body you can borrow. It's best to bring your own kit and caboodle, by the time the request form is discussed, ordered and supplied you'll have been discharged.'

'How long have you been here?' Jo managed.

'This time, six days. I've got it down to a fine art. I generally don't stay longer than a fortnight, but I'm in and out like a fiddler's elbow, bipolar is a bitch.'

'How do you get out?' rasped Jo.

'Acquiesce.'

'What?' Jo chewed a piece of flaccid cucumber.

'Agree with everything, yes sir, no sir, you are absolutely right sir. Especially agree with your diagnosis, if they think you have no insight you're screwed.'

'But I'm not mentally ill, no offence, but really I'm not.'

The fog was clearing to reveal a bleak outlook.

'None taken, but that's the kind of attitude that will keep you locked up.'

'I really need to get out of here; I've got a murder to solve.'

'Oh, yes you were ranting about an Andrea Gibbons as they walked you down the corridor; that will be all over your notes.'

'It is true.'

'Actually, I knew a guy called Ed Gibbons, he was in my first out-patient group, painfully shy, we all reckoned he was the sort to top himself. I wonder what happened to him.'

'Well, he might have killed his sister. I don't know yet.'

'Best keep those surmisings to yourself in here. Also don't keep saying you're a nurse, it makes you sound crazy. Ironically, crazy is not good in here, not good anywhere really.'

'But I am a nurse, I was a ward manager at Goredale,' Jo stuffed the plastic ham into her mouth. Oh God, her disciplinary hearing was next week. She still hadn't prepared.

'Yeah, like I say, it makes you sound crazy.'

'Isn't anyone interested in the truth?' Jo felt a rising hysteria, she pushed it down.

'The truth is a loose thread; you start pulling it in here the whole damn thing will unravel.'

The door flew open, a nurse with a black eye appeared. 'I said you can take her the meal, not read her a bedtime story. Go on, back to your room.'

Maz stood up.

'So sorry nurse, we just got chatting. My bad,' she winked at Jo and skipped out.

Jo needed a new best friend; it seemed that she might just have found one.

25

C lara had anticipated the joy of lying on her Egyptian-cotton sheets snug under her fifteen-tog duvet. The reality was not as she had imagined, something was amiss. She had registered a vague unease last night before she fell into an exhausted sleep, only now did she put her finger on it; her bedding had been recently laundered using a detergent with which she was not familiar. How could that be possible? She put the notion down to an olfactory anomaly bought on by the air pressure changes of a long-haul flight.

It was a delight to realise that she had no idea what the time was and nor did she care. She decided on a leisurely breakfast of vegetarian sausage, scrambled eggs and toast with fine-cut Oxford marmalade. Tim had left a small vase of violets and a welcome home card, there was fresh milk, eggs and butter in the fridge, how very kind - she had underestimated him. Radio four commentators were discussing the latest Brexit debacle, Teresa May appeared to have thrown what she imagined to be the hand-grenade of her imminent resignation and retreated to assess the effect, no-one had seemed to notice. She turned it off.

She retrieved her cafetière from the back of the cupboard and the bag of ground Madagascan arabica from her suitcase. Freshly brewed coffee beans were another simple delight which she had had to travel six thousand miles to rediscover. She poured it into her favourite mug, the one with the dancing aardvarks that Phineas had bought her last Christmas. As she took it to her lips she flinched, a faded but obvious lipstick print adorned the rim. It was scarlet, a shade she had never worn.

The answerphone was flashing. Six messages: Cow Lane dental practice; she had incurred a fee of twenty pounds for a missed appointment, Magnolia Court; her mother was unwell could she phone back asap, Long Mead veterinary group reminding her that Blue was due his annual booster, her friend Josie calling for a catch-up, Donald from the practice asking her to dinner last Friday, Magnolia Court again; her mother had taken a turn for the worse please phone back urgently.

For goodness sake she muttered dialling the number, 'Daughter away please use mobile-phone for all contact' was hardly an ambiguous message.

'Hello, Clara Astrell here, I'm calling about my mother Veronica Astrell. I understand that she is unwell.'

'Ah, Doctor Astrell, we have been trying to contact you. Yes, I'm afraid your mother had a nasty chest infection. Our visiting G.P. Dr Solomon-Mailings prescribed antibiotics but she has deteriorated. She is very weak. Perhaps you should come.'

Clara abandoned her intention to make a fuss about the mobile contact request and told her that she was on her way. She finished her coffee from the other side of the mug and grabbed her car keys.

Magnolia Court loomed into view; the weathered façade stolid in the dying rays of the afternoon sun. Clumps of bluebells struggled under the gnarled oaks. Lithe squirrels chased each other through the branches as if to mock the ancient eyes that peered from the mullioned windows. The twin magnolias, for which the nursing home had been named, were trying valiantly to bloom but over-pruning had taken its toll, there were signs of stress and die-back, Clara feared that without remedial action they would lose them. She rang the bell and waited impatiently under the spidery portico. As she was about to ring again Mrs Pinfold, a dry leaf of a woman with a pronounced stoop suggestive of Scheuermann's kyphosis, opened the door and ushered her into the foyer.

'Dr Astrell, do come in, Mrs Bostock is expecting you.' She retreated along the corridor as if she were following the colour-coded arrows back to her room.

Clara waited by the reception desk where a sucked-and-spat-out woman in a yellow cardigan embroidered with tiny flowers, avoided her gaze. The tap-tap of Mrs Bostock's sensible heels advanced down the corridor her hand prematurely extended. Her handshake was unpleasantly limp.

'Dr Astrell please come through,' she opened an ornate door

that led into the wood-panelled drawing room.

Clara had not been invited into this room since her reconnaissance visit in the autumn of 2012, an occasion in which she had been served hot tea and buttered muffins as if she had stepped into a 1930s film set. The room was unchanged. Mrs Bostock needlessly patted her hair which was drawn into a neat bun. A faint smell of stale whiskey and cigarettes seemed to permeate the heavy curtains.

'How is mother?' Clara was anxious not to prolong the conversation.

Mrs Bostock turned to gaze out of the window and spoke in an ephemeral voice. 'Please do take a seat,' she gestured to a faded floral chair by the bay window.

'Is something wrong?'

'I'm afraid your mother has passed.'

'Passed?'

'Away.'

'Dead?' said Clara.

'Please do take a seat.' Mrs Bostock busied herself pouring tea from a china service that had been arranged on the mahogany side-table. 'It was very peaceful; I can assure you that she was in no pain.' Her voice resumed its usual tone of efficiency. 'May I offer our deepest condolences.'

'When did she die?'

'About an hour ago.'

Clara stood with her arms by her sides. She would have been on the northbound M6 just passing junction ten. 'I would like to see her,' she did not phrase it as a question.

'Of course,' Mrs Bostock seemed a little taken aback, 'I'm afraid Dr Solomon-Mailings has yet to arrive to erm, pronounce. Officially I mean.'

'Well when he arrives, send him in,' said Clara as she turned to the door.

'I'll ask our senior manager Mrs Pinfold to accompany you.'

'No need, I would prefer to see her alone,' she did not wait for Mrs Bostock's reply.

Her mother lay flat on her back, staring glass-eyed at the featureless ceiling. Clara gently closed her eyelids with her fingertip. The ease with which they shut indicated the time of death to have been within the last hour. She knew that the tranquil bedside passing with the exchange of treasured last words was rare except in sentimental dramas, but still she felt cheated. Well at least she had not died next to strangers on an airplane, or alone in her living room as she imagined had poor Andrea Gibbons. She breathed in the scent of disinfectant and lavender soap. She scanned the medication chart: amoxycillin was started last week, dose increased and augmented with erythromycin, all perfectly reasonable. There was nothing more she could do. With tenderness she laid her mother's arms by her sides, straightened the sheet and drew it gently over her face. A memory of the Malagasy corpse wrapping intruded. At least she looked peaceful, more so than she had done in the past years as her confusion rendered life perplexing and turned friends and family into strangers. She was eighty-nine. A good innings.

Clara sat on the bench overlooking the duck pond. Their bench. She had spent the majority of her visits here, her mother slumped in her wheelchair clutching a few slices of white. She had had to redirect her to feed it to the ducks, more recently she had just let her eat it. The ducks gathered and demanded food before waddling off happily enough when none was forthcoming. She identified a few teal and a wigeon dabbling at the water's edge; she wondered if Hen was down at her ponds. Oh Lord, she was meant to be collecting the animals today. She did not feel up to conversation, she sent a text.

Dear Hen, mother passed away, I'm up in Shropshire, back tonight. So sorry, can I collect tomorrow?

A swift reply.

Terribly sad news. We all send our heart-felt condolences. Of course dear thing, take as long as you need. Animals all well. Take good care of yourself.

Although in electronic form, Hen's condolences touched her in a way that Mrs Bostock's face to face offering had not.

Clara's memories of her mother were of her aproned and busy in the kitchen, where she seemed to spend a disproportionate share of her life. Given the limitations imposed by her gender in the mid-twentieth century she had been successful. She had achieved the goals of the aspirational housewife: a good marriage, a clever, not unattractive daughter, sufficient allowance to enable her to follow the latest fashion trends and to benefit from advances in domestic appliances. Her life had been an undemanding one, as the wife of the local G.P. she had only to attend the village fete, host fund-raising coffee mornings and offer cake and solace to the newly bereaved. She had played the role impeccably, a conformist through choice. Two holidays per year, Cornwall or Devon, monthly whist drives, sherry parties, a London theatre on her birthday, the surprise of flowers or chocolates. She had not seemed to want any more. Or less. Had her mother ever been troubled by thoughts of what might have been? Ever been beset by writhing worms of reproach?

Clara realised she was crying, she rooted in her handbag for a tissue. Amongst the paraphernalia was a cellophane wrapped CD *Malagasy Celebration,* bought with her last Ariary at Ivato International. She dabbed her eyes and headed back to the home. Mrs Bostock stood in the entrance hall talking in hushed tones with Mrs Pinfold, she turned and addressed Clara with a condescension that she seemed to think passed as sympathy.

'There you are dear, Dr Solomon-Mailings has just left, he asked me to pass on his condolences. He will prepare the certificate and organise her transfer to the mortuary.'

She seemed anxious for Clara to be on her way. Her mother's belongings had been packed and left discreetly behind the reception desk. One medium-sized cardboard box and a bin bag. All her worldly goods. Clara took a red A4 folder from the top of the box: *All About Me* in comic sans. The pages were slotted into individual plastic wallets, the first a large photograph of her mother, a puzzled expression on her face; her first day at Magnolia Court, Clara recognised the drop pearl earrings that Mrs Bostock suggested she remove pending a health and safety assessment. She never wore them again. The second page contained a printed series of statements, the gaps completed in an unfamiliar hand.

My preferred name is *Veronica*

I was born in *1930*

I worked as a *housewife*

I had *one* child/children

I lived in *Uffington near Shrewsbury*

I was/was not married to *Hector*

The third page was optimistically entitled 'Things that make me happy'. It was a short list: *knitting, singing, jigsaw puzzles, watching television*; knitting had been crossed out. The last page held a montage of pictures, her mother sporting a variety of hairstyles and fashions, her father in a bow-tie, Phineas wearing a pirate outfit, herself at various family celebrations, a nice one of Rupert, her old spaniel who was hit by a car in 2001. She closed it with a sigh. All about me. Not even close.

'Is there anything else we can do?' asked Mrs Bostock with a simpering smile.

'Yes, I would like to have some time in the day room.'

'Certainly Dr Astrell, although most of our residents will be in there at present. Perhaps you might be more comfortable in the visitor's lounge, it is generally unoccupied.'

'No, thank you, the day room would be perfect.'

She strode into the cavernous room where twenty or so residents sat in the large wipe-clean chairs marking the outer perimeter of the room. Others were planted in straight rows in front of a television blaring out an advertisement for funeral plans. Formica tables were strewn with blue plastic mugs, artificial flowers and out-of-date copies of the *TV Times* and *People's Friend*. An assortment of bored looking care assistants in blue tabards hovered around doing nothing in particular. Clara turned off the television causing a few blank faces to periscope in her direction, the majority continued to doze. She inserted the CD into the music centre, adjusted the volume to acceptably loud and began to dance. She moved anti-clockwise around the room inviting others to join her, eliciting toothless smiles and arthritic foot-tapping. A dapper man in a Panama hat rose unsteadily with the aid of his frame and hopped from foot to foot. Frail hands started to mark out the beat, wizened arms raised up to mirror Clara's gestures. The carers took up the initiative and encouraged those sufficiently able to stand and to dance. More and more residents shuffled to their feet, a dozen now migrated to the centre of the room swaying and moving to the simple rhythms. Whoops, laughter and an occasional incongruous 'yee-haw' rang out.

Mrs Bostock and Mrs Pinfold appeared at the door, twin looks of disapproval on their faces. A portly gentleman with ruddy cheeks took Mrs Pinfold by the waist and manoeuvred her onto the dancefloor. Despite herself she acquiesced and proved to be an excellent dancer. Mrs Bostock, not wanting to appear a killjoy, danced self-consciously in the corner until grabbed by a good-looking carer with several facial piercings. He led her to the centre of the room, his gyrations causing several pencilled-on eyebrows to raise. The celebration continued to the end of the CD, forty-five minutes of revelry. For the first time in as long as any-one could remember - for most of the residents less than a day - afternoon tea was not served on time. No one seemed to mind.

Mrs Bostock hugged Clara goodbye and promised that a musical soiree would be added to the weekly timetable. She said that the pierced carer 'knew about YouTube and such like' and had volunteered to compile playlists of world music. Clara donated her Malagasy CD to 'Veronica Thursdays'. Mrs Bostock assured her that she would be most welcome to drop by whenever she wished. Clara said she would love to return, every three, five and seven years.

26

John hated lying to Matt, his invention of a sudden middle-ear infection was shameful, but it was best that he did not know of his plan. He would have talked him out of it. They would get to have some family time together and, if the weather held, perhaps a walk on the coastal path, a cream tea at St David's.

He had desperately needed a break. A long weekend in Carmarthenshire would be just sufficient to stop him from reversing repeatedly into Wallace's car. He dropped Matt and the boys at the theme park and sped back down the A485 to Gwyddgrug. He tried not to think about the cases languishing in his pending tray, about Wallace and the absurd exclusive focus on the ram-raiders. It was ridiculous anyway; who would steal a fifty grand motor and smash it into a wall to steal twenty grand from a cash machine? It seemed that Soames-Grayling had enemies in low places as well as friends in high ones.

The sky was clouding over by the time he passed through the tiny village and turned down a single-track road that wound between patchwork fields. A hand-carved wooden sign prematurely announced his arrival at Defaid Tenau Farm, he took the sharp left and continued down the rutted track for another mile. God it was bleak. A hedgerow of bent trees took the brunt whilst offering scant shelter from dogged northerly winds. The farmhouse slumped in an untarmacked yard as if waiting to die. The once terracotta stucco had faded to a dull rust, large areas had given up and jumped leaving patches of pitted grey brick. The uneven roof tiles told of unstoppable draughts and an interior of carefully positioned buckets. Two wet border collies sat forlornly outside the front door. There was no other sign of life. As he stepped from the car the dogs perked up and dashed over, bounding up to leave muddy streaks on his Barbour jacket.

He rang the bell and waited. Perhaps he should have phoned ahead but he did not want Ed to go to ground. He walked around the farmhouse, the dogs trailing him as if he were an errant sheep. He knocked on the flaking back door instigating a round of excited barking from the collies. No one home. He wandered past a dismal outbuilding, its corrugated iron roof raised like a half opened can. He peered through the open window of the filthy Land Rover parked beside the barn. It was unclear whether this was Ed's car or an abandoned vehicle; there was a chicken nesting on the passenger seat. The barn smelt strongly of wet sheep. It housed an old tractor, a heap of corroded metal partitions and piles of sacks containing something lumpy. The dogs stopped and waited outside.

John allowed his eyes to accommodate and made his way through to the back of the barn. Despite the overwhelming feeling of desertion, he sensed that he was not alone. A rustle from the shadows. Christ, not rats. He tiptoed gingerly back towards the entrance and stopped in his tracks; a pair of muddy boots poked from behind the sacks; one of them definitely moved. A weak ray of sunlight threw the lengthened silhouette of a man against the dark wall.

He had one arm raised.

It was holding a gun.

John froze. No one knew his whereabouts, he could not radio for assistance, he had no weapon. Shit. Three options: run for it, confront him, pretend the man had gone unnoticed. He decided on the latter. He walked towards the figure keeping his eyes on the floor. A blur of fur and wagging tails ran to greet him, they stopped, sniffed the air and hurtled towards the figure. They circled in a confusion of excited yelping. In one balletic move John grabbed the gun, flung the man to the ground and held the weapon to his head.

'Don't shoot. I'm sorry.'

John could not shoot; he had no idea what he was holding. 'Put your hands behind your head and get to your feet. Slowly.'

He did as instructed. He looked terrified.

'Hands against the tractor and spread your legs.'

John patted him down; he found only a ball of twine and a bag of wine gums.

'DI John Appleton, Thames Valley Police.'

Ed dropped his hands and turned around, 'Jesus, I thought you were someone else.'

'What the hell were you thinking?'

'I could ask you the same. You don't look like a copper.'

'I'm off-duty.' He examined the weapon, still none the wiser he dropped it behind the sacks. 'I've come to ask you a few questions about Andrea.'

'Well, you'd better come in. I'll put the kettle on.'

John sipped his Earl Grey tea and replaced it on the saucer. The tap dripped onto a stack of dishes.

'Sorry for surprising you, you looked pretty shaken-up back there.'

'I've had a bit of trouble with the neighbours.'

'Ah. What was your weapon by the way?'

'A sheep gun. For worm drenches. It wasn't even loaded.'

John looked through the cracked windowpane, beyond the yard bright green fields were dotted with grazing sheep. 'Not quite the rural idyll?'

'No, I've had a few threats; entrails left on the doorstep, that kind of thing.'

'Blimey. Not nice.'

'Been trouble ever since I reported their puppy farm to the RSPCA.'

'What actions are the police taking?'

'I haven't told them. I'd rather leave it to be honest.'

Ed looked ill. Impossibly pale. His chequered shirt fraying at the collar. He had an air of bafflement. The naked light bulb cast a sallow glow on the table. He thought about Matt and the boys enjoying the roller coasters.

Ed glanced at the carved wall clock and pulled at his earlobe. 'You had some questions?'

'I wondered why you lied about not having Andrea's phone.'

Ed's face accommodated another layer of confusion. 'How do you know I do have it?'

'Well, thanks for confirming it. The phone pinged off a mast in Carmarthen when you turned it on.'

Ed fumbled with an egg-stain on the table cloth. 'I was going to tell you. It's just. Well, I thought you would confiscate it, I wanted to keep her photos and the funny messages she sent to friends.'

'You would have got it back.'

'Sorry,' Ed wrang his skeletal hands. 'I was thinking maybe I should, then I learnt I was a murder suspect. I thought concealing the phone would make me look even more suspicious.'

'You were right.

'The thing is officer, I've got a previous offence.'

'I know, we pulled your record, just routine. What was that about?' He glanced at the mouse droppings on the floor and put his feet on the rung of the wooden chair.

'I hit a guy who I knew from school. He wasn't a nice person.'

'Bullied?'

'Yes.'

'Me too.'

A strange tang hung in the air, perhaps it was the smell of poverty. Or wet wool. Or both. 'By the way, who told you that you were a murder suspect?'

'Elin.'

'Elin?'

'The landlady of The Hanged Man, said the police at Carmarthen had been asking questions. A female officer with a funny accent and a boy's name apparently.'

John pictured Jo Burns-Whyte and rolled his eyes. 'We haven't been formally investigating you. Just trying to piece a few things together.'

'I don't go to the pub much. They think I'm a bit odd as it is, and that's saying something around here.'

'You don't feel you fit in here?'

'I don't fit in anywhere to be honest. I'm okay, I like the quiet, I like my sheep.'

The cuckoo clock whirred above the table. They watched the door snap open and the wooden bird appear and disappear eleven times.

'Nice clock.'

'Thanks.'

'Do you know what happened to Andrea's pay-out?'

'Oh, you know about that? It was all meant to be hush-hush. She said that she invested it but I can't find it anywhere. I'm trying to sort out her estate, there's no trace.'

John scanned the kitchen; from the piles of unopened letters on the butcher's block it appeared that Ed was not on top of his own paperwork let alone able to mastermind a tax evasion fraud. It was also clear that he had not spent any money recently, perhaps ever. He remembered Jo's spreadsheet. 'I understand that you have a new tractor.'

'It's in the barn, you frisked me on it.'

'Sorry about that. Okay, so it's new to you but second hand.'

'Got it at the farmers' auction, fifth hand actually.'

John noted Ed's tremor as he replaced his cup on the saucer.

'Is there anything else you need to know? I've got a few sick lambs need feeding.'

'Did Andrea keep in touch with anyone from Turks and Caicos?'

'Not that I know of. She didn't like talking about it so I never asked.'

'We pulled Andrea's phone records. There were a number of calls from public phones on Providenciales. Any ideas?'

'Well, her husband had a sister. Lucy or Lilly or something. She kinda blamed Andrea for his death. He fell off his boat.'

'The senselessness of some deaths is hard to bear. Don't take this the wrong way but you seemed to accept that Andrea killed herself without question.'

'That's what you are meant to do,' he said emphatically.

'I don't follow.'

'Accept the most obvious explanation and do not search for malevolent intent.' He recited it like a mantra.

'I can see the advantages but it's not such a good philosophy if you're a copper.'

'My therapist told me. It does help.'

'You have a therapist?'

'Did have. I have paranoia. The pills help too. The entrails are real though.'

'I'm sure they are.'

Ed furrowed his brow, a position with which his face was evidently accustomed. 'So, are you saying that Andrea was killed?'

'We don't know. There are some things that don't quite add up. She had a suitcase packed and a ticket to Venezuela.'

'Yes, that is pretty weird. I try not to think about that.'

The weak bleating of lambs came from the living room.

'One more thing; I heard that you cleared Andrea's flat without letting her friend Jo know.'

Ed dislodged a splatter of dried mud from his trousers. 'Thing is, I'm a bit scared of her.'

John smiled and rose to leave. 'Mate, I think we all are.'

27

A persistent banging roused Jo from her grogginess. The dead-fly littered fluorescent light flickered to life as calls of 'wakey-wakey campers' echoed down the corridor.

She imagined that she was falling slowly down a bottomless well. Her first morning on Primrose Ward. How sardonic; this hellhole could not be less reminiscent of the jaunty English flower. A new nursing shift had appeared, at least she was to be spared a face-off with her previous evening's attackers. The nurses stared at her, their backs against the wall, a report of her 'violent outburst' had clearly been handed over. She could see the fear in their eyes; she liked it. Radio One competed raucously with day-time television; for a place of supposed asylum it was bloody noisy.

Maz sat at one of the Formica tables, she waved her piece of toast and gestured to the empty seat beside her. She was practically unrecognisable; the head wrap was gone revealing a neatly combed auburn bob, she wore a soft lavender blouse and a string of pearls. Jo joined the queue at the food hatch and cast her eye over her fellow inmates: she registered Daniel, Terry and the dried husk still wearing that putrid pink nightie. A motley crew of dishevelment, defeat and podginess was shovelling down toast and cereal before heading back to bed. Several sat alone and looked directly ahead. Daniel was arguing with a nurse, it seemed that he was being denied extra sugar to feed God's babies. She collected her bowl of Rice Krispies softening in warm milk and slipped her allotted two sugar sachets into her pocket.

Maz looked up with shining eyes. 'Morning mate, how are you doing?' She sounded very chirpy for seven-thirty.

'I feel grim but I slept like a bloody log.'

'Haloperidol is a bitch, it takes a while to wear off. Your face is looking a bit better though.'

'Thanks, it feels less puffy. There's no mirror in my room.'

'No mirrors anywhere, someone must have cut themselves with

broken glass in about 1970. Once things are verboten they are never returned.'

'Geez. And I'm desperate for a cigarette, where's the smoking room?'

'No smoking on hospital grounds, you'll have to go cold turkey.'

'Oh my God.' Jo swallowed her cereal to stop herself from screaming.

She reviewed her situation: it seemed that the disciplinary hearing allowed a rescheduling if there was legitimate reason for non-attendance, but on second thoughts compulsory detention in a psychiatric hospital would not be helpful to her case. For the sake of her sanity and of her future career she urgently needed to get out of this cesspit.

'I hate to ask but do you have any clothes I could borrow? I've got a meeting with the psychiatrist, this top is filthy from being floored yesterday,' she threw a narrowed eye at the nearest nurse.

'Sure.'

They finished their breakfast assailed by the twin soundtracks of traffic updates and a shouty reality-show. Maz scanned the nurses and selected the flushed one with acne who stood like a flamingo, one foot against the wall. She padded over and requested permission for Jo to come to her room. The flamingo cast a long critical eye over Jo, they took his monotone, 'Your funeral love,' as permission granted. Several sets of eyes followed them across the dining room and down the long corridor.

Jo admired the posters of sunflowers and starry skies as Maz tipped the contents of her chest of draws onto the bed. 'You're in luck. Norm, my husband, brought my 'week two' wardrobe in yesterday, I leave it in a bag in the spare room so he just has to pick it up. My day-seven transformation has begun; I'm moving to my muted colour palette. You have to be totally obvious in demonstrating change or they don't notice.'

Jo picked out a baby-blue cashmere jumper and navy trousers.

'Oh yes, great choice for a session with Tweak, it simply screams conservative stability. Always good to wear something that she might have in her own wardrobe. I have a lilac twin set ready for my pre-discharge meeting.'

'So, you don't normally wear those clashing colours?'

'Good God no, I might be bipolar but I'm not bloody nuts. It's all part of the formula for accelerated discharge. Ridiculously out-landish is week one. They've got to see that their treatment is working, gives them something positive to write about.'

Jo changed into the outfit as Maz struggled to replace the draws.

'So how the hell do I get out of here?'

'Well firstly don't 'dis' the nurses, you need them on-side, the doctors make the decisions, but they haven't got a scooby with-out the Carenotes record. So suck up. Apologise for your behav-iour, use key phrases they can write in your notes: 'Had time to reflect', 'totally uncharacteristic behaviour', 'deeply regret', blah, blah, blah, if you can tear up go for it, think Puss-in-Boots from *Shrek*.'

'That sounds tricky when I just want to bloody strangle them.'

'Oh, that looks great on you, perfect, want a bit of eye shadow?'

'Please.'

Maz applied a subtle blue to Jo's lids. 'Second thing is don't ask for anything, sit quietly, eyes down. Paradoxically the less you do the faster you progress. They'll try to enhance your motivation by forcing you to do stuff, you'll be out on a rehab trip before you can say "lack of volition."'

'I hear Tweak is heavy on the medication, how do I manage that?'

Maz looked through the reinforced glass window and scanned the corridor for spies. 'The main thing is, don't swallow it. Well I do, I'm generally okay as long as I take my salts. Lithium carbon-ate, dampens me down to ordinary. My problem is I settle back into normal life and it's so bloody boring. When I can't stand the monotony any longer I discontinue and enjoy my life for a while. Nothing beats that feeling when you're buzzing with en-ergy, hypomania is wicked. Everything is ier'.

'Eeyore? What do you mean?'

'No ier. Livelier, funnier, sexier. The occasional fortnight in here is a small price to pay. Sometimes I get too high and the next thing I know I'm eating cat food and booking myself onto sky-diving courses. I don't even like heights.'

'Is that what happened this time?'

'Well that and I was found in the street at two in the morning posting boil-in-the-bag haddock through my neighbours' letter-boxes.'

'Oh my God, why did you do that?'

'Because I was fricken bonkers,' Maz let out a peel of laughter. 'A couple of doses of salts and I'm back to hum-drum normality. Thing is, if you don't need meds you'll have to box clever. Take the first dose because they'll test your levels. Tweak, aka the zombie maker, will up the dose, after that just hold it under your tongue, scuttle back to your room and spit it down the sink.'

'It's as easy as that?'

'Well, you'll have to be convincing, complain of side-effects: palpitations, tachycardia. She won't want any of her patients keeling over, doesn't want to end up in front of an inquest. Not again. Take a bit of Bang Bang's speed before the ECG, get the old spikes going, that'll press halt on the medication escalator.'

Jo was wide-eyed with reverence; this woman was the sanest person she had ever met. They paused as a nurse stared at them through the safety glass, her footsteps punctuated by brief stops outside each door.

'It's really nice of you to help me.'

'You remind me a lot of myself, I used to be a chair wielder too. I like your spirit. The thing is the longer you stay here the more you go under. I had a job and a lovely allotment before my first admission, three bloody months in Bluebell Ward, until I didn't recognise myself. You could say I lost the plot literally and metaphorically,' she let out a donkey haw. 'Anyway, it doesn't help to dwell, come on let's do your hair.'

They sat together on the bed as Maz combed Jo's hay bale and fashioned it into a stylish French plait.

'I was a hairdresser before I went all Edward Scissorhands on a couple of regulars. That was years before the asymmetrical look became fashionable, I'd probably be the toast of the salon now!' She stood back and admired her handiwork. 'There you go, very National Trust volunteer.'

'Thanks Maz, I owe you. By the way, could you give these to Daniel?' she slipped the sachets into Maz's hand, 'I don't take sugar.'

On cue the flamingo stuck his head around the door to announce the arrival of Dr Eppendorf.

A spiritless rain mottled the window overlooking a flowerless patio. Dr Eppendorf already occupied one of the two stolid chairs. They were evidently chosen for safety not comfort; they were too heavy to be used as weapons. She gestured unnecessarily to the empty chair directly in front of her. She was an insubstantial woman who exuded cold authority, late fifties, no jewellery, she wore her blue-framed glasses on a silver cord and her greying hair in a tight chignon. She did not return Jo's smile. Jo stared back at the doctor, she listened to the ticking of the clock, it was an hour behind. The muted sounds of a game of table-tennis and The Jeremy Kyle Show emanated from the day area. She would have been happy to continue the Mexican stand-off but recalled Maz's last words of advice; to treat the interview like a first date: *look nice, be nice, goodnight and go home.* She adopted a pleasant tone and smiled again. 'Good morning doctor, thank you for coming to see me.'

Dr Eppendorf flicked open a thin file. There was a long silence as she read the referral letter and a photocopy of Precious Ollennu's summary. Finally, she removed her glasses letting them dangle on her Marks and Spencer's twin set.

'Tell me, why do you think you are in a psychiatric hospital?' Her tone accusatory.

'Well doctor, unfortunately I made the mistake of investigating a suspected crime myself instead of handing my intelligence over to the police. A decision that I deeply regret.'

'And why would that result in psychiatric hospitalisation?'

'I was taken to the police station because they thought I had broken into the property, actually the door was open. By the time the police arrived I was a little upset.'

Dr Eppendorf held her glasses to her eyes and read from the police notes:

Whilst being cautioned the suspect repeatedly shouted obscenities at the arresting officers. It became clear that despite the attempt to conceal her gender the suspect was a woman.

'Do you experience gender dysphoria?'

'I'm perfectly happy being a woman,' she crossed her legs hoping to emphasise her femininity. She lamented choosing trousers instead of a skirt, she had gone for sensible and demure. And bloody annoying that she had no mascara or heels, those markers of a real woman.

'Where did you get those clothes, they look very familiar?'

'Perhaps we both shop at the same stores,' Jo smiled in attempted sistership.

'No, I meant that I have seen that outfit on another patient. Have you not been availed of the hospital rules? Trading of belongings is expressly forbidden. Are you deliberately transgressing them?'

Jo considered informing on the nurse but didn't want to risk a backlash.

'I'm sorry,' she offered a placating smile.

Dr Eppendorf scribbled an illegible note.

A long pause ensued during which she felt the doctor's eyes scrutinise her with a distinctly negative bias. She decided to move to the front foot.

'It was just a terrible mistake; the police have blown it out of all proportion.'

Dr Eppendorf returned to the file. 'You appear to have been charged with breaking and entering, going equipped, possession of an offensive weapon, resisting arrest, and use of threatening words and behaviour.'

'There you see, going equipped, possession of an offensive weapon, honestly, I had a pizza cutter.'

'The charge sheet states that you had a folding hunting knife in your combat jacket, are you saying that the police are lying?'

Jo thought for a moment, perhaps the police had set her up, she could not say that it sounded paranoid. Oh, Ludo. He must have left the knife in his pocket by mistake.

'I didn't know that I had the knife,' she said lamely.

'I see,' another scribbled note. Jo made out the word 'dissembling'; she must look it up.

'I do regret my behaviour. I was a little distressed, police officers can be intimidating, it was so out of character.'

'It appears that you used threatening words to nurse Ollennu. Did you also find her intimidating?'

'She said that she wanted to help and then seemed to deliberately misinterpret everything I said. I found her a little frustrating,' Jo felt her hackles rising at the memory.

She noticed the doctor's jaw clench and reminded herself to stay focussed on her release.

'The thing is doctor, I've never been in trouble with the police so it was all very upsetting.'

'That is not actually true is it?' She stabbed a bony finger into the notes. 'You received a section 176 in relation to a shoplifting offence only a matter of weeks ago.'

Jo practised her pant-breathing as suggested by Dr Ryzen-Jones M.D.

'Do you think that you have a mental illness?'

'Well.' The clock ticked. 'I understand that my diagnosis is Schizophrenia.'

'And what are the symptoms upon which that diagnosis is based?'

Jo dredged up her final year nurse training, took a deep breath and prepared to dive down their rabbit hole. 'Hearing voices, paranoid thoughts, unusual beliefs, hostility.'

Dr Eppendorf nodded almost imperceptibly. Jo supposed that this was as animated as she became.

'I think we will start you on Olanzapine ten milligrams and we'll tweak it from there.'

'When can I go home doctor?'

Dr Eppendorf closed the file and rose to her feet, the interview apparently over. She stopped at the door and affected a warning tone. 'I understand that you have been attempting to pass yourself off as a nurse. I have told staff to exercise increased vigilance particularly with regard to the medication trolley. Please desist from this pretence.'

Wasps flew from their nest and assembled in attack formation. 'I really need to go home. I have to attend an extremely important meeting. The most important meeting of my career.'

'As I said. Please desist. I will see you at the CTM.'

Jo clenched her fist. Wait. What would Dr Jonas Woodrow-Emerson say? 'Stay calm. Accept what you cannot change.'

She nodded her head.

Maz recommended that they attend the art group, a perfect opportunity to demonstrate compliance, sociability and recovery. The participants shuffled in and took their seats in silence, less a group more a coalition of the alienated. Sheets of paper were spread across the paint splattered tables, jars stuffed with fat brushes stood in the centre. A reedy voice punctured the air, it belonged to a woman with a disarmingly thin beak of a nose, a turkey neck lurking beneath a butterflied scarf.

'Welcome everyone, it is nice to see two new faces, would you like to introduce yourselves to the group?'

'Hi, I'm Jo, I have schizophrenia, I came in yesterday but I'm already settling in and....' Maz kicked her under the table and she tailed off.

'Lovely,' said the turkey, turning to the thin youth with glazed eyes, 'would you like to introduce yourself?'

'Craig,' he said.

'Thank you and welcome to the group Jo and Craig, my name is Alice Sims, I'm an art therapist.' She appeared to be unaccountably proud of this dubious accolade. 'Please feel free to express yourselves in any medium, be it paint, crayon, felt-tip, pencil or collage.'

Having exhausted herself with the instructions she sat on a paint encrusted stool and observed the group in silence. Under the cover of scraping chairs Maz hissed in Jo's ear. 'Make the symbolism as obvious as possible, banishing the demons that kind of thing.'

By the time Jo settled to the task most of the decent paints had been taken, she was left with red and black. She had not painted since primary school and found the experience strangely comforting. As she mixed the poster paints a long-forgotten memory surfaced. She was cutting her friend's fringe with blunt paper-scissors, the tiny strands falling like dandelion fluff. She was sent home with a post-it note stuck on her V-neck jumper: *I was naughty in art today*. The memory made her laugh out loud.

Creativity was not her forte, she glanced around for inspiration. Craig was drawing stick figures of what appeared to be a boxing match. She cast her mind back to her only art gallery visit, not long after her divorce, her first foray into on-line dating. The man suggested that they meet at the Tate's Michelangelo exhibition beneath the suggestively titled *Temptation of St Anthony*. In the event he was a no-show but she had sat in front of that hideous picture for a good half-hour. St Anthony, a grim looking man with a long white beard, was being ambushed mid-air by a variety of grotesque demons. He evidently resisted their temptations. A perfect message to convey. The sizable brushes lent themselves to a simplified abstract version. She started with the haunted figure of St Anthony, his flowing black robes taking up the centre of the paper, a red halo around his bald head. She added the demons, a riot of red mouths sporting fishes' tails and flapping bat-wings. They wielded black clubs as they tore at his robes. She was pleased with it.

The turkey asked if anyone would like to talk about their work. After an uncomfortable silence Maz held up her crayon sketch of birds and spring flowers, the sun emerging from behind a dark cloud. 'The title is *Redemption*. It feels hopeful and full of anticipated joy.'

'Very nice Maz, I love your use of light and shade and the pretty dancing daffodils, very Wordsworth, lovely. Anyone else?'

Jo held up her painting to a stifled gasp from the turkey. 'This is my representation of where I am just now, flying high, banishing my demons from whence they came.'

A long pause followed; the turkey cleared her throat.

'Thank you Jo, may I keep this?' Her voice struck a particularly high note on the reediness scale.

'Be my guest.'

'Anyone else?'

The silence announced the end of the session. Her fellow artistes binned their efforts and filed out.

28

'**C**ome in, come in dear heart.'

Blue rubbed his flank against Clara's legs. A dynamo of wriggling energy he sprang up with unexpected gusto and caught her in the eye. 'Thank you so much for looking after the animals, I hope they haven't been too much trouble.' The flat of her consoling hand mirrored Hen's eyepatch.

'Oh, hardly noticed they were here, much better behaved than our lot. We inherited another three moggies from the sanctuary while you were away. Poor things had been there forever, Bee knows I can't say no to a sob story, they have to be housed together, inseparable, she said. Turns out they loathe each other. No mind, they are terribly sweet.'

The kitchen table had been covered with a clean chequered tablecloth set with four places.

'I do hope you can stay for a bite to eat, we are all dying to hear about your travels. Oh sorry, dreadfully insensitive. We were very sad to learn of your mother's passing. How are you holding up?'

'Well it wasn't unexpected of course but still a shock. She didn't recognise me in the last couple of years, so I feel I have already grieved to some extent. But yes, thank you, I'd love to stay.'

Clara scanned the chairs; each held a central cat curled like a designer cushion.

'Where's George?'

'Oh, he's taken rather a liking to Aunt Jobiska, he tends to sneak off to the annex for play time, given the old girl quite a new lease of life.' Hen ejected the nearest cat that complained loudly before settling in a dog basket.

Clara took the warmed chair, Blue resting his chin on her knee. 'How have you all been? Has Charles recovered from the cracked ribs?'

Hen mixed a large pot of soup and threw in an alarming quantity of salt. 'Oh yes, he is a tough old goat, regales everyone with the story. A new one to add to his the-day-I-nearly-died collection. We had a bit of a to-do here actually,' she slid a tray of bread rolls into the Aga. 'Jo Burns-Whyte, queen of the canapé and the disdainful look, broke in.'

'Good Lord!'

'Astonishing isn't it? The nice officer who came to 'give an update' - Bobby he was called; you could not make it up - said she had developed the notion that we were harbouring trafficked tortoises of all things and that we were implicated in Andrea Gibbons' death. The poor dear has ended up in St Mangabey's.'

Hen rang the old school handbell. 'Just hailing the parents from their afternoon nap.'

'Tortoise trafficking? How odd. Was this something to do with Darwin?'

'One assumes so, oh he was a delight by the way, quite a character isn't he? Bobby was non-committal viz-à-viz the details, confidentiality and all that. He did seem rather pleased with himself having spotted a tortoise. One would have thought he were David Attenborough discovering a rare stick-insect when in fact Darwin was sitting centre-stage on the kitchen table nibbling a lettuce leaf. He also eyed the duck eggs rather suspiciously. Occupational hazard I suppose.' Hen embarked on a rapid peeling and chopping of windfall apples.

Clara noticed that she was cavalier regarding the worm holes and likely let through the occasional maggot. 'Late onset psychosis is tricky but can respond quite well with the right treatment.'

'How do you imagine one becomes deluded about a tortoise?' Hen added a hearty quantity of sugar to the apples.

'Psychotic episodes often have some basis in reality. If one has a certain predisposition under extreme stress one can become convinced that two and two make twenty-two. And of course, grief can disturb critical thinking.'

'Indeed, the poor thing is as mad as a bucket of frogs.'

Charles appeared in a velvet dressing gown pushing Dolly in her Bath chair. 'Ah! My dear Clara, mind the old ribs now,' he hugged her warmly.

'Lovely to see you both,' Clara kissed Dolly's papery cheek, the slow craning of her neck reminded her of Darwin.

Dolly took her hand. 'So sorry to hear about your mother, I do hope it was a peaceful departure.'

'It seems so, she would have known little about it. She developed a chest infection, possibly progressed to pneumonia, antibiotic resistant.'

How many death certificates had she signed? Maybe ten per year, say a career total of three hundred. About two hundred fewer than that psychopath Shipman. Most people died in hospital now, in her experience no one died at home sitting in a chair with their sleeve rolled up, what a bastard. Certificate completion was an unpalatable task, one she had always undertaken with the solemnity it deserved, she used her specifically designated fountain pen, stylish black with gold trim.

'You look miles away.'

It took a moment to realise that Charles was addressing her. 'Oh, I do apologise, I was thinking about my fountain pen.'

A peel of laughter rang out, Hen's hyena cackle making Clara laugh too.

'You are a card,' said Hen.

'I've just been hearing about your unwanted visitor,' said Clara.

'Yes, the twelve-year-old who turned up demanding to see a Mrs Jobiska!'

'No father, she meant our intruder, but do go on I can see you are itching to tell the tale.'

'So, this social services chappie arrives uninvited, he's hopping up and down in the hall restless as a wren. Seems he had been unsettled by Dolly's portrait of Teresa May, did not find the image of her hanging from a European flag after falling off a 'strong and stable' table in the least amusing.' Charles proudly patted his wife's shoulder.

'Where is Mrs Jobiska? He asks, I inform him that it is actually Aunt Jobiska. He demands to know Mrs Jobiska's first name, apparently she doesn't appear on the electoral register for this address! Hilarious. I say her first name is Aunt, that got him riled, he insisted that he see her straight away,' Charles grinned as he built to the story's denouement. 'Off he strode to the annex in high dudgeon. Cue yowling, screaming, general caterwauling, Aunt Jobiska streaks into the kitchen followed moments later by mister SS holding up a bloodied finger and demanding a tetanus jab.'

Clara burst out laughing. Charles ejected a cat from his chair and basked in post-anecdote glory. She placed a decorated paper bag on the table, 'a thank you for being my temporary animal sanctuary.'

Hen reprimanded her generosity but was evidently delighted, she loudly described each in turn allowing her mother to be seamlessly included.

'Vacuum packed vanilla pods, gosh they are huge, perfect for custards. Pink peppercorns, how delightful, Madagascan chocolate seventy percent cocoa, just divine. Oh, and what is this? Photographic guide to the birds of Madagascar, goodness what a beautiful book.'

'Very kind of you old bean, you must go away more often,' said Charles examining the chocolate.

'And how was your boy?' asked Hen.

'He was struggling with a family issue, but he seems considerably better thank you. The fabulous news is that he's returning to England soon.'

'How marvellous I look forward to meeting him. Righto, let us eat.' Hen ladled the soup into large earthenware bowls and dropped a plate of hot rolls onto the table. 'Entirely homemade to my own recipe. All dietary requirements have been catered for: vegetarian, gluten-free and able to be processed by nearly century-old digestive tracts.'

The soup was a muddy brown, Clara identified beetroot, sweet potato, parsnip and lentil; it was absolutely delicious. Despite the likelihood of traces of animal protein, she was looking forward to the apple crumble.

George had been reluctant to leave Coney Field farm both he and Blue seemed delighted to be home. Clara felt less so. A listlessness crept over her.

You have wasted your life. The worm appeared to have developed a slavering lisp, it was no longer moving, it merely lay prostrate in its fissure and mocked her. She buttoned up her cardigan and put the kettle on.

I know about Ted. Sleeping as he died. Negligent.

A fine rain misted the windows, a car cruised past with shining headlights although it was still early afternoon. Glorious May in England. She settled into her rocking chair and sipped her Earl Grey. George jumped onto her lap and affected a position of immovability. Alright, let's face the demon worm, what else could I have done? She ruled out any form of creativity; she was a rational thinker. A physical endeavour? No, she preferred to challenge her mind not her body. Anything corporate bored her. She discounted the armed forces; she could not take orders and they would likely have rejected a pacifist. Academia might have suited, but she had treated enough stressed and dysphoric lecturers to know that that was a pit of vipers. As a teenager she had imagined being part of the Monty Python team but by the time she got to Cambridge the Footlights were full of public-school bores. Her musings seemed to temporarily rebuff the worm, it turned and slumbered.

She adjusted Darwin's heat lamp and rearranged the architectural layout of his cabinet. He was looking a little dusty, she had not wanted to bother Hen with his complex bathing regimen. She filled his baby bath and sprinkled in the required quantity of *Reptoboost,* an isotonic probiotic 'for tortoises in need of a pick me up'.

'Ready for your spa day?'

Darwin seemed to nod in affirmation. She placed him into the lukewarm water and stroked a soft toothbrush under his chin. He floated peacefully, stretched out his legs and closed his eyes. She took a photo to send to Phineas. She set him on a towel and sprayed him lightly with his dehumidifier, he elongated his neck with pleasure. His horny beak leant his face the distinguished look of an ancient prophet, she filed it gently to reduce the overhang. She placed him back and watched him sift through his salad leaves seeking out the lamb's lettuce. It was very satisfying looking after a tortoise. She thought of Gabriel and his five hundred, she envied him; a person with a true vocation.

She checked her *Justgiving* page, wow over ten thousand pounds already, sufficient to employ an outreach worker for the education programme. She sent Gabriel an update and attached the photograph of Darwin in his bath.

She checked her post: two quick-off-the-mark condolence cards, both from Magnolia Court. She had yet to tell Phineas about his grandmother, it was proving more difficult than she had thought. She had certainly left him less fragile than she had found him but he was still grieving for his father and had been close to Gwam. She had broken bad news many times, she had even had to role-play it on one of those interminable 'professional development' days. The problem was the form of communication; breaking bad news from home to a relative in a remote Madagascan forest had not been covered. Such announcements should not be received via text, email or God forbid, Facebook. They were not due to Skype for another week, a letter would take two. Did telegrams, those traditional harbingers of bad news, still exist? Unlikely. She sent a text asking him to telephone her when he had the opportunity. She added not to worry and then deleted it, that would have the opposite effect.

Clara was finding it hard to settle back into her usual routine, what on earth did she do all day? Reading, walking Blue, a spot of gardening, bi-weekly trip to the supermarket. She looked at the calendar, the remainder of May was clear apart from next Tuesday; the re-scheduled alpaca husbandry course. She re-booked her dental appointment and Blue's inoculation. She hoovered. Then she remembered the list of countries that Andrea Gibbons had written. How odd. It had definitely been in the top of the bureau drawer; the contents of which appeared to have been rifled. Either she was developing early-stage dementia or someone had been rooting through her belongings.

Not wishing to dwell on the differential probabilities, she turned to the twenty-first century panacea for boredom: *Google Scholar*. She typed in *Medieval marginalia* and read the first article. In a world of information proliferation not nearly enough had been written on the marginal depictions of animals. She studied the lepidopteran images in European medieval manuscripts; the butterfly symbolised the human soul, its metamorphosis representing transcendence after death. God, mortality seemed to be stalking her.

With some relief, Clara remembered that she still had some unpacking to do, that would kill an hour. She carefully unwrapped Phineas' poinciana brooch and placed it in her jewellery box. How strange, there was an empty compartment, she examined each piece; her black pearl brooch was missing. She checked the lapels of her jackets. No, it was definitely gone. It had been her favourite piece, a delicate arrangement of tiny pearls, unusual and understated. She had worn it to work a dozen times before a colleague pointed out that a black rose was traditionally a portend of death. Not ideal on a doctor's lapel. She thought back, the last time she had worn it was for Andrea's funeral. She distinctly remembered replacing it in the box wondering when she would next have cause to wear it.

The laundered bedsheets, the lipstick on her cup, the ransacked drawer, the missing brooch; someone had definitely been in her house.

The only person with a key was Tim.

29

Jo assumed a convivial air as she entered the room, she offered her hand to Dr Eppendorf, who failed to reciprocate, before perching expectantly on the vacant chair. A circle of faces surrounded her; some alert, some not. Her consultant peered at her through lowered glasses and spoke without intonation.

'Tell us about your week.'

'It's gone very well, I've been feeling much better, I've been to art therapy,' Jo nodded towards the turkey who sat with a rictus smile clutching a rolled painting.

Dr Eppendorf sighed. 'Ms Sims, if you could be brief.'

She cleared her throat apologetically. 'Jo exhibited some over disclosure and incongruent laughing but was otherwise appropriate and orientated in time, place and person.' She unfurled Jo's painting and held it up to the group. Wide-eyed glances were exchanged.

Dr Eppendorf raised her palm to signal that Ms Sims need not elaborate. She adjusted her glasses before gifting her opinion to the room. 'A brutal portrayal of the interminable battle of man versus woman. The large phalluses speak of the terrible power wielded by men. The patient evidently feels attacked and violated. There is likely childhood trauma, where is the psychologist?' She paused briefly, the question apparently rhetorical. 'Tell him to put her on his waiting list.'

A nurse scribbled a post-it note as Dr Eppendorf continued.

'To survive this male oppression, she imagines herself as a man.'

'If you can't beat 'em join 'em right?' grinned the CPN.

Dr Eppendorf swung her icy gaze in his direction ensuring his silence for the remainder of the meeting. 'Yet even with such self-identification she feels threatened, desperate, tormented. Her demons pursue her. I suggest that we adjust the medication accordingly.'

'But I feel absolutely fine, that's a Michelangelo.'

'Does anyone else have anything to add?' Dr Eppendorf scanned the room. The Charge nurse, a thick-necked man with the air of a wounded bear, read from his notes. 'Since her assault on staff nurses MN, LS and BG she has presented as withdrawn and self-isolating. Minimal engagement, seldom present in the day area, observed playing dominoes with Maz Nankivell, frequently seen laughing together. Adequate intake of food and fluids. No further management problem,' he closed the file.

'I want the nurses to organise a trip to Sainsbury's for budget shopping.' Dr Eppendorf addressed her comment to the bear who nodded without enthusiasm.

Jo recalled a quote from Stephen Fry and grasped the opportunity to follow Maz's advice to be engaging and light-hearted. 'The great thing about Sainsbury's is it keeps the scum out of Waitrose,' she affected a jolly chuckle.

The social worker and CPN exchanged amused smiles but no one laughed.

Dr Eppendorf critically surveyed Jo's outfit. Not wanting to risk borrowing from Maz she had reverted to the nylon pullover, now provocatively tightened following an unsuccessful hot-wash. To mitigate any suspicion of gender dysphoria she had fashioned a wrap-around skirt from the back panel of Ludo's camouflage jacket. She had found a cheap pair of tights in the communal drier, a snag now causing a noticeable ladder to run the length of her leg. Dr Eppendorf turned her attention to the medication chart.

'We are going to tweak your medication,' she scribbled on the chart, 'we will review you next week.'

The Charge nurse rose to escort Jo from the room. Jo remained seated.

'What? Is that it? But I feel fine, I'm ready to go home, I don't need another week,' a note of panic rose in her throat.

'Do you have a qualification in psychiatry Miss Burns-Whyte?'

'No but I am an expert on myself, I know that I'm fine and I will be better convalescing at home.' She was aware of an escalating forcefulness but could not stop herself. 'I have important matters to attend to.' No one seemed to be taking any notice. She stood up, her skirt had become unwrapped and remained on the chair. 'I'm conducting a murder inquiry,' she shouted.

Dr Eppendorf addressed the minute taker. 'Please summarise the CTM opinion as follows: Patient exhibits residual hostility, grandiosity, self-neglect, and compensatory over-sexualization. Olanzapine doubled, review next week.' She turned to Jo, 'I think you have just demonstrated why you should leave the timing of your discharge to the experts. That will be all.'

Jo sat fuming in the day area and waited for Maz who had been called directly into the meeting.

In under five minutes Maz reappeared and discreetly returned Jo's skirt. 'Budget shopping on Thursday, home by the weekend, how about you?'

'Increased meds, budget shopping, review next week. I don't fricken believe it.'

'Sorry mate that's a bitch, I guess it's because you're a first timer, when they don't have much history they feel they need to make some.'

Jo put her head in her hands, 'I'm pleased for you, honestly, but I won't be able to cope in here without you,' she lowered her voice. 'I'm going to do a runner from Sainsbury's.'

Maz's eyes widened, she leant in, thankfully the blaring television game show drowned out their conversation. 'Are you fricken crazy? No offence. The cops will haul you back here and you'll be on Close Obs for bloody weeks. Ask Bang Bang, he did a runner from a cinema trip, it cost him three months with no vitamin D. You're going to have to get a grip.'

'Honestly, I can't hack it. You're the only thing that's keeping me sane.'

'Mate, whatever you do, don't tell them that.'

Bang Bang was proving to be a star. He had heard about her thwarted murder investigation and had slipped his tablet under her door. She retreated under her lank duvet and Googled her suspects.

Henrietta Cuvier yielded nothing except a photograph of her holding a weird duck, a rosette and a silver cup.

Dr Clara Astrell had more hits; she appeared to have been involved in various committees, had written some papers about

G.P. stuff, campaigned against Brexit, the privatisation of hospital services and the closure of the local library. Boring, boring, boring. Clever though, what was that saying? 'The best place to hide a tree is in a forest.' She had made herself so bland that she was unnoticeable.

Edward Gibbons had little social media presence; his Instagram photos were of, mainly of scrawny sheep, some of new born lambs and one with Andrea. Well, that showed his priorities.

Just for fun she tapped in Ludo Mansfield. He had a website, financial services blah, blah, blah. A lovely photograph of him in his Paul Smith suit. Gorgeous. Interesting, he had no social media presence, but of course you had to protect your privacy if you were a high-flyer.

Who else? As an ex-boyfriend, horrible Tim Forth had links to Andrea. She braced herself and searched for him. Lots of photographs of his wife and children smiling at school events, waterparks, birthday parties. Bloody hypocrite. He was all over Facebook, he evidently had far too much time on his hands. Look at his weaselly face, how had she ever found him attractive? He seemed to have a huge number of followers. She bought up his most popular posts. Her blood ran cold. St Birinus Parents Action Group; Campaign to dismiss Andrea Gibbons. Photographs of the worm thing with endless comments about impropriety, misconduct, bringing the school into disrepute, even suggestions of her risk to boys. He had lobbied the head master. He had organised a petition. Oh my God.

She shut the tablet and stuffed it under her pillow with shaking hands.

Jo prowled the frozen food aisle with Maz, Daniel and Terry, she felt a strange sense of belonging, of moving with the herd. They were escorted by the flamingo and an agency nurse who had not introduced himself. She had been issued with eleven pounds fifty pence from the Occupational Therapy cooking fund. She had been instructed to buy enough food to prepare two healthy meals encompassing the main food groups and to keep the receipts. Her basket contained three bananas, chives, a small cauliflower, a lump of cheese, new potatoes, frozen peas and a carton of yogurt. She selected a plump salmon fillet, calculated that she only had two pounds forty pence remaining and mournfully returned it. She noticed that Daniel was causing several well-shaped eyebrows to be raised, a large West Indian man with matted dreadlocks and an exposed midriff apparently being an unacceptable sight in suburban Berkshire. The trolley he shared with Terry was piled high with budget burgers, white bread and an array of neon fizzy drinks. She donated two of her bananas to help them pass the 'food group' police. She grinned at Maz, who with only one cooking session before her discharge, had opted for steak, chips and chocolate.

Jo sighed as she tossed a packet of reduced fish fingers into her basket. The thought of Maz's imminent departure weighed heavy, another long week of incarceration felt unbearable. Her Tim intel required urgent action. Her career hung by a thread that she needed to gather. The flamingo was engrossed in his mobile phone, the anonymous nurse absently studied a packet of potato waffles. This was her chance. She placed her basket in the chest-freezer and calculated the shortest route to the exit. As she took a steadying breath Terry sped past her and hurtled towards the door. The agency nurse, previously the epitome of indifference, sprang into action. He launched a flying double-leg tackle; Terry struck his head against the edge of an abandoned trolley as he crashed to the ground.

The flamingo yelled and flapped his arms. 'You don't chase them you pillock, that one's always running off, he gets wasted and comes back in the morning.'

Jo and Maz tended to Terry who lay motionless, a rivulet of blood seeping from his temple. The flamingo phoned the ward to request back-up.

'Call an ambulance you moron,' screamed Jo. She checked Terry's airways. His pulse was weak and irregular. She rolled him into the recovery position and staunched the blood with her sleeve. Maz stroked his back. Daniel was pacing up and down telling people to stand back, there was nothing to see, although no one had shown any interest.

Finally, the sound of an ambulance siren. Terry's eyes flickered, he spat out a globule of phlegm followed by a tirade of expletives, the full gist of which was fortunately masked by his accent.

Jo patted his hand. 'Just lie still mate the paramedics are here, they'll take you to hospital.'

Terry gave a broad smile. 'Severe pain, need tramadol 400 mg,' he rasped.

Jo was the sole guest at Maz's 'last supper'. It was her first time in the Activities of Daily Living kitchenette, a restricted area for those rostered to prepare their own food. The cook was encouraged to invite a guest to promote 'appropriate social interaction'. A buzzing fridge and a dripping tap provided the ambience. Jo wiped the sticky table as Maz plated up the medium-rare steaks with Bearnaise sauce, French beans and oven chips. After two weeks of cook-chill meals it looked and smelled delicious.

Jo winked as she presented a bottle of Ribena, sommelier style. 'A fruity red to compliment the steak, Madam.'

'Why thank you, how very kind,' Maz affected a Knightsbridge accent.

'I hope Terry will be alright, what a nightmare,' Jo glanced through the reinforced window into the corridor before pouring a rich Malbec into plastic beakers.

Maz inhaled the heady aroma. 'Wow, it's a bloody miracle, turning Ribena into wine.'

'I made the most of the distraction when Terry was being carted off and swiped a bottle. I thought we deserved a treat, I decanted it in my room, so it's had time to breathe.'

'Here's to us,' Maz raised her beaker, 'and to the time to breathe.'

They tapped their cups together.

'You were going to do a runner today weren't you?'

'Well yes, I spied an opportunity; you have to trust your inner voice.'

'And to know when it's talking crap. Just as well Bang Bang beat you to it or you'd currently be tucked up in Emergency Ward Ten. Promise you'll box clever when I'm gone.'

'You're right. I'm going to up my game, I've got my ECG tomorrow. Luckily Terry delivered a little arrhythmia powder for me this morning.' Jo sawed into her steak with a blunt knife.

'That's good, take it easy though, just enough to get the heart racing. Also, I'll leave you a novel so you can sit and read in the day area. Something cerebral to show your concentration has improved, you don't have to read it just turn the pages. God these knives are crap, next time we eat together we'll be using proper steak knives.'

'I'll definitely drink to that.'

They raised their beakers.

'I've got a Dostoyevsky, a Shakespeare and a Samuel Beckett, which do you fancy?'

'I haven't read any of them, I'll go with Beckett, sounds more straightforward.'

'Good choice *Waiting for Godot*, it's good actually, although spoiler alert - he doesn't turn up.'

'Well that sounds like the story of my life.'

A face she had not seen before poked through the door and flashed a warm smile.

'Hi, how's the meal going? You must be Jo Burns-Whyte, I'm Niki Sookun, Charge nurse. I'm your key worker, it seems you were admitted on my first day of leave.'

She appeared to be disconcertingly friendly and lacked the hallmark air of disaffected apathy perfected by the Primrose ward nurses. Jo eyed her suspiciously then remembered to be polite. 'Nice to meet you Nurse Sookun.'

'Call me Niki,' with a theatrical flourish she produced two plastic bowls from behind her back. 'They've just finished supper out there, I saved you jelly and ice cream if you'd like some.'

'Ooh, lovely thanks,' they said together.

Niki flicked on the air-conditioning to dispel the smell of alcohol that hung in the air.

It was turning out to be a very fortunate day.

30

C lara prepared to go next door with an open mind. Judge not that ye be not judged; she had memorised Mathew seven verses 1-10 when she was forced to attend Sunday school aged eight and could still recite every line. She had illustrated her reading to the Easter congregation with an anatomically detailed crayon drawing of human eyeballs floating in a moat, cast out the mote out of thy brother's eye. Her mother had been asked not to bring her again; mission accomplished.

Despite her intention to remain objective she registered that Tim looked uncomfortable as he showed her into the living room. More than uncomfortable, shifty. She had yet to mention the reason for her visit, her mere presence appeared sufficient to elicit a shame response. He cleared his throat unnecessarily, his eye contact alternating between staring and avoidance. Sally, who had appeared from the kitchen like a startled roedeer, seemed to notice too, she looked questioningly at her husband as she struggled to open a packet of fig rolls.

'Do take a seat doctor,' she trilled. 'Would you care for a cup of tea?'

'Please call me Clara. Not for me, thank you.' She felt disquieted by the familiarity of the room. The layout was a mirror image of her own, her slate-grey William Morris wallpaper substituted for a chintzy Laura Ashley. A living-flame gas fire stood in place of her wood-burner; that explains the whirring sound she could hear all winter.

She gathered herself. 'It was very nice of you to keep an eye on my house. I hope it didn't cause too much inconvenience.' She perched on the plush armchair and inhaled the smell of floral air-freshener.

'I was away with the children for a fortnight so I can't accept any gratitude.' Sally transferred the fig rolls to a china plate and offered them to Clara.

She took one out of politeness. They both turned to Tim who

was studying his fingernails.

'Was everything alright? No problems with the house?' Clara raised an inquiring eyebrow.

'Oh yes, no problems everything was just fine and dandy,' his tone inappropriately jolly.

'No need to go inside at all?' Clara persisted.

'Um, no, no need. So how was your trip doc? Good weather? You don't have much of a suntan.'

'We were mainly in the forest. I try to avoid the sun as much as possible.' The fig roll was as dry as a bone.

'Very wise. I heard on the radio about a rise in skin cancer, it seems it mainly affects indoor workers who spend two weeks a year frying by a pool.'

'Honestly Tim, I'm sure Clara knows all about skin cancer.'

Tim looked chastened.

'It was very thoughtful of you to leave the provisions and flowers.'

'Oh, don't mention it.'

'So, you did go in.'

'Yes, yes indeed, I went in, then came straight out.'

Clara looked from a bemused Sally to Tim whose neck was fashioning red blotches. A long pause followed. She knew that once a person was on their guard they would continue in denial, it was best to allow them to relax before presenting the evidence. 'How was your holiday with the children?'

'Good, thank you, Issy went pony trekking every day and William was off quad-biking, I curled up with a Jackie Collins and a Prosecco, absolute bliss.' A volley of high-pitched laughter erupted and died.

'You didn't fancy a break yourself Tim?'

'Oh, I used the time to catch up on my accounts.'

They really were the dullest of couples. 'Well, thank you again for keeping an eye on the house,' Clara rose to leave.

'Not at all, any time. Are you sure you won't stay for a cup of tea?' asked Sally. Tim was already up and showing her to the door.

'I won't thank you. Oh, just the strangest thing,' Clara stopped in the hallway and addressed Tim Colombo style. 'A list made by Andrea Gibbons is missing from my bureau.'

'Andrea Gibbons?' Tim opened his mouth and closed it.

'Yes, did you know her?'

'Andrea Gibbons? No, no I don't think so.' He opened the door.

'Oh, of course you do, the teacher from St Birinus, honestly Tim we were talking about her only last week. The children were so upset. They were going to be in her set next year.'

'I never met her.' From the sudden sheen on his forehead, this was evidently not the case.

'One more thing. I noticed that my bed clothes had been freshly laundered, there was a scarlet lipstick print on a coffee cup and a brooch missing from my bedroom.'

Both women turned to Tim who looked at the floor. Clara became aware of the muffled sound of children's voices and electronic machinegun fire from upstairs.

'Tim? Explanation?' Sally bristled.

'I'm sorry, I really have no clue.'

It was clear that there was only one explanation. Clara closed the door and left them to discuss his adultery.

The conversation with Phineas had gone better than anticipated, he had taken the news about Gwam stoically, expressed the appropriate sentiments, asked her how she was doing. But talking on a weak phone line was unsettling, the geographical distance spun out between them. She made a cheese and pickle sandwich and sat on the sofa with Blue and George. *Danny Boy*, some minor celebrity's choice on Desert Island Discs, came on and she was crying. The tears took her by surprise, she let them fall, there was a cleansing in the release of trapped sorrow.

She turned on the television.

'Krishnan Guru-Murthy's report contains images that some viewers might find disturbing.' Heavily armed Hong Kong police in a stand-off with civilian protestors. At least our police state is fairly benign, she thought. She flicked through the channels to find something diversionary. She settled on a repeat of *The Big Bang Theory*, the one in which Amy and Sheldon split up and he adopts a clowder of compensatory cats. She remembered it in sufficient detail to find it a little dull.

The worm stirred. It seemed to be feeding on her recently excavated memories. She felt it digesting her childhood, growing fat on its litter. It inched closer to her inner ear.

You have wasted your life. She let it squirm, perhaps it would wear itself out. *So much potential, so much privilege, such an unglittering career.*

As it shifted its bulk a happy memory made a run for it; she was sitting cross-legged on the pale green carpet of her bedroom examining Maisie's cloth head. Evenly spaced cardboard boxes circled her, each housing a prostrate doll. They were swaddled in bandages like a collection of miniature Egyptian mummies, glass-eyes staring through the gaps. She listened for Maisie's heart-beat with the plastic stethoscope. With fierce concern she rummaged in her satchel and brought out a disposable syringe, plasters, cotton-wool swabs, a thermometer. She was in her element; she was eight years old. She dealt calmly with a range of serious medical emergencies, tending to her critically ill patients until her mother called her down for dinner. A happy casualty ward where no-one ever died.

Clara sighed and turned on her laptop, she needed new slippers. She decided on a nice pair in pure wool with a firm sole for putting the bins out. She needed to spend another fifty-nine pence to qualify for free shipping. Amazon informed her that people who bought a reptile heat-lamp had also bought a deluxe egg incubator. It boasted digital temperature control and automatic 360-degree rotation, no need to get up at night. It had excellent reviews. A little pricey, but Hen would love it; she added it to her basket. *The Big Bang Theory* had given way to a programme about farming in East Anglia.

Pitiful.

Perhaps the worm was right. Maybe it was time to change her life.

31

Jo sat up in bed. Oh my God, Tuesday. The hearing was tomorrow; she had to get out of here. She retched, fortunately her toilet was located next to her bed. Could two weeks on the wagon lower one's alcohol tolerance to zero? Unlikely. Must be the bloody Olanzapine, she kept forgetting to spit it out, although anything that took the edge off this hellhole was a bonus. She forced herself to get dressed, attendance for toast and Rice Krispies seemed to be taken as an indicator of mental health or at least of compliance.

A bright yellow envelope was wedged under the door, she pulled it loose. A glossy card of Van Gough's Sunflowers, she recognised Maz's flamboyant hand: Shine on you crazy diamond. She smiled and placed the card on the windowsill, a welcome oasis of colour in a beige desert. She checked her watch, bloody hell ten-fifteen, three hours late for breakfast. And she had missed morning meds, shit, a strategic disaster.

Her ECG was scheduled for 'the morning', she felt under the bed frame for Terry's wrap and examined the white powder with some trepidation. Well, it cannot be worse than antipsychotics. Unfortunately, he had not left any administration instructions, she poked at it with her finger and hesitantly dabbed it on her tongue, it tasted horrible. She racked her brain for inspiration and recalled Leonardo DiCaprio in *The Wolf of Wall Street* snorting lines of amphetamine from a mirror via rolled up bank notes. Or was that cocaine? Either way, it seemed like a reasonable method of ingestion. Of course, she did not have a mirror, or a bank note. She poured the powder onto the back of Maz's card and searched for a suitable applicator. Niki had kindly provided a mini ball-point pen to mark her menu choice, she removed the ink reservoir, covered one nostril and inhaled deeply.

Nothing.

She repeated with the other nostril.

Nothing.

She snorted up the rest of the powder. A feeling of euphoria emanated through her body. It grew like a rampant sunflower filling every cell with golden rays. She hungrily hoovered up the remaining flecks. She stared at the card but somehow could not recall the name of the flowers, were they euphorbia?

'I'm filled with euphorbia!' she laughed out loud.

Her heart was pounding, beating out an urgent message, she should be doing something important but she could not remember what. A three-letter acronym. BBC? LOL? DIY? FAQ? It was something to do with a machine, OMG! ECG! She flung open the door and hurtled into the corridor narrowly missing a decrepit old man with a long white beard.

'Jesus Christ,' she said.

'Yes, 'tis I,' he replied.

He held up his hands for inspection, Jo looked at the black dot in the centre of each palm.

'It's just marker-pen, soak it in soapy water, it'll come off no problem,' she said.

'Heathen. Doubter. Non-believer be gone,' he screamed.

Jo watched him stagger backwards away from her, shielding his eyes theatrically. His penis protruded at an obtuse angle from a large hole in his trousers. 'Jesus Christ.'

'Yes, 'tis I,' he replied and held up his palms.

Jo's heart thudded through her jumper reminding her of the task in hand. She skidded into the nurses' station yelling 'ECG!'

A startled nurse ushered her out of the door. 'Can you please wait outside, the doctor is not here yet.'

She felt a wave of confusion as several emotions competed for her attention. Daniel was leaning nonchalantly against the glass, observing the nurses observing him. She felt him gently take her elbow and steer her away.

'Simmer down girl, you going to blow it.'

'But I feel awesome now I see what all the fuss is about I get it I really do this is just bloody amazing the power the fricken glory it's amazing I'm....'

'Listen girl, go back to your room. Let me take you down; you need to chill out a little bit.'

'Let me take you down 'coz I'm going to Strawberry fields nothing is real and nothing to get hung about Strawberry fields forever,' she sang in a warbling soprano.

She felt Daniel tighten his grip and manoeuvre her back down the corridor, she was going to sing forever; it was her new vocation.

'You got pigeon-eyes girl, you better lie down.' He pushed her into her room and closed the door.

Alone in her twelve-foot cubicle Jo experienced a flash of insight: it was May, time for her New Year's exercise regime to begin in earnest. Star jumps, sit-ups, air-swim, lunge, repeat. Star jumps, sit-ups, air-swim, lunge, repeat. Star jumps, sit-ups, air-swim, lunge, repeat. She collapsed onto her bed laughing. She felt fantastic.

She had never felt so alert, so energised, so excited; not since she was a teenager, that halcyon time when everything seemed possible. And yet she had settled for a podgy suburban life with a dodgy plastics-salesman from stodgy Slough. The thought made her scream with laughter. She had to dance. Daniel had lent her his iPod in return for cleaning his room, a task that had turned out to be far more onerous than she had anticipated. She pressed 'shuffle' and turned up the volume - Soul II Soul, *Get a Life*. The beat and the lyrics were perfect, they electrified her: *elevate your mind, free your soul* she sang as she gyrated around the tiny room. She could do anything, she could be anything, it was amazing to be alive.

Jo sat on the edge of her bed with a weight of melancholy so heavy that she felt she might never move again. She had not eaten all day, no one had been to see her or to call her for her ECG, or for lunch, or to check that she was still alive, no one would care if she had died. The words Schrodinger's cat formed in her head but she did not recall what it meant. Her life was meaningless, she wished she was dead. Another hour passed. And another.

Finally, a tap on the door; Niki Sookun looking concerned. 'Hi Jo, I've just come from handover, they said you've been hiding in your room all day. Is everything okay?'

It was asked with such genuine warmth that Jo burst into tears. She buried her face into her hands and sobbed.

'Good Lord, whatever's wrong?' Niki sat beside her and allowed her to cry.

She tried to articulate through heaving sobs. 'My best friend Andrea died, the police won't believe she was murdered, my new best friend has been discharged, my boyfriend will think I'm ignoring his calls and will have moved on, I miss my ex-husband even though he's a sad pathetic loser and I hate him, I'm going to miss my tribunal and lose my job, I'm racking up debt, I'm locked up in a bloody loony bin although there's nothing wrong with me and I've missed my ECG.' Somehow it was funny, her tears turned to laughter. 'God, I sound as mad as a hatter, perhaps I'm in the right place after all.'

'Don't lose heart, nothing is insurmountable. Listen, we can reschedule your ECG, Occupational Therapy can help with your money management, you can contact Maz once you're out and you will be discharged eventually, we don't keep people forever, well not many,' she smiled.

'Thanks Niki.' She meant it.

'You're not meant to receive gifts but Maz left this for you,' Niki handed her a small paper bag containing Coco Chanel perfume and an all-body moisturising lotion.

'By the way a police officer phoned, he's on Daisy Ward on another matter, he asked if he could pop in and see you. It's not a formal request so feel free to decline. What would you like me to tell him?'

'What's it about? Do I need a solicitor?' Jo felt her chest tighten, could things get any worse?

'He didn't say much, it's to do with your recent arrest. His name is D.I. John Appleton, he said that you know him.'

Jo sprung from her bed, 'God yes, tell him I'd be delighted to see him.'

By the time she had tidied her hair and applied a liberal dose of Maz's perfume D.I. Appleton had been shown into the interview room. He was sitting in Dr Eppendorf's usual chair by the door, a bored looking nurse stationed outside. Good God, they must think I'm some sort of dangerous maniac. She knocked and entered, registering his stifled shock.

'I'm sorry, I must look an absolute fright. I have no make-up, no mirror and none of my own clothes. The social worker gave me this hideous tracksuit from stores, size fourteen cheeky cow.'

'Relax, you look fine, please take a seat.'

His kindness was a tonic.

'It's so nice to see a friendly face.' It really was.

'Blimey you must be in a bad way if a visit from a copper cheers you up. Is there no one to bring your stuff from home?'

'Well, the social worker offered but there's no need, I'll be out soon.'

The smell of his aftershave took her back to their first meeting at Andrea's flat. Unbelievable that it was five months ago; he had been kind then too. She noted that his question was designed to check out her relationship status, naughty boy. She slowly crossed her legs although the nylon tracksuit mitigated the effect.

'So, what can I do for you John?'

'I have some good news. We've had a response from the CPS, given your mental health disposal and the fact that the Cuviers' do not want to pursue the case, they have advised that the charges be dropped. So, you're a free woman. Well,' he glanced at the walls, 'free from criminal prosecution that is.'

A bingo ball clattered from the dayroom.

'That is good news,' Jo pondered the implications. 'Interesting that the Cuviers don't want to pursue it, suggests that they have something to hide don't you think?'

'That's one way of looking at it. More likely that the victim liaison officer told them you're in here and they are just being nice.'

Jo considered this, being nice did not really fit with putting a sack over her head, tying her to a chair and releasing wild animals on her.

'House!' Someone yelled from the day room, there followed the rumbling of disgruntled voices and scraping of chairs.

'Look I know people think I'm paranoid, unfortunately including my psychiatrist, but I have some new evidence for you. I'm sure Clara Astrell is involved in Andrea's death.' It was hard to read his expression.

'I would have thought Ed Gibbons was your prime suspect.'

'Oh, Ed yes he is certainly up there. It's hard to keep track without my spreadsheet and with a head full of antipsychotics.'

'Well, all I can say is that you can rule him out.'

Jo cocked her head. Interesting; so he was investigating after all.

'Also impersonating a police officer is a criminal offence, especially if it's a terrible impersonation,' he smiled.

'I don't know what you mean officer,' she toyed with a tendril of hair.

'Why do you think Clara Astrell is involved?'

She leant forward and held up her first finger. 'Motive; tortoise trafficking. It turns out that radiated tortoises are mainly sourced from Madagascar and guess where Clara Astrell went recently?' She paused for effect. John remained inscrutable. 'Madagascar! I mean who goes to bloody Madagascar for a holiday, it's hardly the Bahamas?'

'What is the link to Andrea?'

'Andrea must have been on to her; she was very up on those sort of wildlife things. Clara stole Andrea's tortoise and hid it at the Cuviers' that's why I went there, to get the evidence. That weirdo family is in on it. Do you know what I found in their house, take a guess?'

He raised a questioning eyebrow but said nothing.

'An incubator full of eggs. They must be illegally breeding them. Perhaps Darwin is a stud male.'

D.I. Appleton smiled sensitively but she felt his scepticism.

'I understand that you're looking for explanations but to be honest that's not evidence, it's circumstantial conjecture. It all sounds a bit nuts to be honest. No offence.'

A scuffle seemed to have developed in the day room, shouting, a thud and a scattering of bingo balls, an alarm sounded. Jo ploughed on.

'They weren't even friends; Clara and Andrea I mean. Andrea loved that stupid animal; she wouldn't have given him to a woman who was practically a stranger. Clara would only have taken him if she knew that he was worth something, it's not much of a pet.'

'Actually, I believe they are very popular.'

'And another thing; Clara is extremely pally with Tim Forth, her next-door neighbour and he was instrumental in getting Andrea fired. It must at least be worth a follow up? Please John, I don't have all the links yet but I know I'm onto something. It might solve Andrea's murder and be the key to my release. I'm going crazy in here. Ironically.'

He smiled; he was very handsome in his crisp white shirt.

'The best I can do is arrange some background checks, see what comes up.' He glanced through the toughened-glass where three nurses were escorting a distressed looking old lady in a pink nightdress out of the day-room. 'I can see why you want out.'

'Yes, it's supposed to be a place of safety, quite what they are protecting me from I have no idea. Don't worry about me, I'll be tucked up under my own duvet soon enough.'

D.I. Appleton looked doubtful. She told herself she would make this happen. One way or another.

Jo flicked over the pages of *Waiting for Godot* and tried not to think about how many calories were in the Scotch egg with mayonnaise and two portions of roly-poly pudding she had eaten. She decided to take Maz's paradoxical logic to the next level; if she told them that she didn't want to go home perhaps they would discharge her.

She popped her head into the nurses' station to request a one-to-one with Niki.

She was putting down the phone. 'Perfect timing Jo, I was just coming to find you. Let's go through to the reading room, it's always empty.'

They sat next to a shelf of tattered paperbacks, a local newspaper lay open on the table. Jo had not expected a session immediately, she was not prepared. She plunged in with the first sign of institutionalisation.

'I'm really starting to feel at home here.'

'Well, that could be a problem,' said Niki.

'Could it really?' Her eyes were caught by the word Madagascar. She picked up the newspaper. A "grieving widow" was seeking the kind doctor from Marlow who had been sitting next to her husband when he died on a flight to South Africa. Bloody hell.

'The thing is, you've been discharged!'

'What? Why? How?' Jo could not process the information, was this a joke?

'I was just coming to tell you. There was an unannounced visit by the CQC this morning.'

'Did they say that I'm being illegally detained?' She tore out the article and put it in her pocket.

'Are you alright Jo?'

'Yes, yes.'

'Well not exactly,' Niki hesitated, perhaps realising she had said too much. She seemed to be choosing her words more carefully. 'The thing is, the doctor has reviewed her Care Plans, she decided that you would benefit from convalescence in your home environment.'

Jo laughed hysterically.

'Either way you are free to go. The police have released your belongings, we've got them in stores so feel free to phone someone to pick you up.'

'What now? This minute?'

'Sure, whenever you're ready. We've done the Section 117 meeting and Dr Eppendorf has completed all the paperwork, you are good to go.'

'Blimey Niki, I can't quite believe it. I'll have to rely on my Zen calendar for advice from now on.'

'One piece of advice to take home then: Let go or be dragged.'

Jo flicked through her phone, there was really no one she could call. She phoned for a taxi. She might just pay Toxic Tim a little visit on her way home. Then she had a career to salvage and a relationship to save. She texted Ludo, *Operation Tortoise didn't go according to plan! Arrested and released! Took impromptu holiday. Back home now and thinking of you xx.* She hoped it struck the right balance of light-heartedness and enticement.

He messaged back immediately. *Would love to see you. Dinner on Ariadne tomorrow? Xx.*

You bet.

She didn't need a place of safety, she had one, it was in Ludo's muscular arms.

32

Clara answered the front door to a stone-faced police officer who stated rather than asked, 'Dr Clara Astrell.'

Phineas was dead.

'Yes,' she answered, her voice distant.

'Constable Beech, Thames Valley Police, I would like to ask you a few questions if I may?'

She opened the door in a daze. George shot upstairs. Blue hid behind her his tail flicking uncertainly between his legs.

'I trust I'm not interrupting,' he surveyed the living room.

'Is it my son?'

'Your son? No. Just following up on information received.'

Clara noticed his gaze alight on the row of underwear drying on the radiator. 'What is it I can do for you Constable?' She did not offer him a seat.

'A matter has come to our attention, madam, related to possible trading irregularities,' he took out a small notebook and turned to the marked page.

'Trading irregularities? I don't have any shareholdings. I have no interest in the stock market.'

'The pet trade madam. It has come to our attention that you have a tortoise. I wonder whether I could see the animal in question and its documentation?'

'What are you suggesting Constable? Is this something to do with the poor woman who broke into the Cuviers's farmhouse? I understand that she holds delusional beliefs about tortoises. Likely an acute psychotic episode.'

'I'm afraid we are unable to reveal our sources.'

'Good Lord. You honestly think I'm trafficking tortoises? How ridiculous. I have one pet.' She stopped herself from saying 'go and arrest some real criminals', he must hear it ten times a day.

'If I could see the animal in question please madam,' he shut his notebook decisively.

'Very well, if you must, he is in his play pen. Come this way.'

Darwin raised his head and eyed them warily, apparently satisfied he resumed munching a radicchio leaf. He seemed to be proud of his red and green Stegosaurus jacket that fitted snugly around his shell. Charles had worried about draughts and had crocheted the outfit from a pattern he found online. The hexagonal woollen plates standing along his back made Clara smile every time she saw him.

Constable Beech produced a photocopy illustrating basic shell-patterns for tortoise identification and critically surveyed the specimen in front of him.

'If you wouldn't mind removing the animal's vest please madam.'

'What is it that you are trying to determine officer?' Clara was beginning to enjoy this charade.

'The species of tortoise madam. To check whether it is one whose import, sale and trade is internationally prohibited.'

The man seemed to lack all sense of the absurd.

'Oh yes officer, *Testudo hermanni*, *graeca* and *marginata* are listed on Appendix two of CITES. They are also covered by European legislation and require a permit. I assume that as we currently remain in the EU this continues to apply,' she slipped off the jacket and held Darwin up for inspection.

The Constable examined his chart and matched each image against the cycling creature.

'This is not a Madagascan radiated tortoise,' he pronounced.

'Certainly not, that would be illegal officer. I understand that he was taken to the Tortoise Trust as his original owner was unable to guarantee his safety, having unwisely acquired a Rottweiler with a brain injury. He was rehomed by Andrea Gibbons in 2015, she recently entrusted him to me on behalf of my son.

The officer struggled to make verbatim notes.

'Is the lad home?'

'No, he's twenty-seven.'

Clara dressed Darwin and replaced him in his pen, he raised himself on all four limbs and stalked haughtily into his wooden tunnel.

'If I might just see your certificate please madam.'

Clara rummaged in the overcrowded filing cabinet and pulled out a folder labelled 'Pet stuff'. Amongst the insurance statements, vet bills and vaccination cards she found the sheet certifying Darwin's origin.

The constable studied it closely and handed it back. 'Everything seems to be in order madam. Thank you for your time.'

'And to save you another trip to the Cuviers's: tortoise eggs are small, white and round, duck eggs are large, oval and bluish.'

Constable Beech looked crestfallen as he made a note in his book. He cleared his throat, 'I understand that you were recently in Madagascar.'

Evidently an attempt to reassert himself, she was beginning to find him tiresome. She opened the front door without replying.

'Madam, were you or were you not in Madagascar?'

'This is ridiculous, but yes, I was.'

'What was the purpose of your visit?'

'I can't imagine why that is a police matter Constable.'

Blue sensed unease and emitted a low growl from the safety of his basket. Cold air permeated the hallway, she gestured to the open door.

'Is there anything at all that you would like to add Madam?'

'No there is not.'

He stepped onto the mat. The sound of smashing glass and screaming drew his attention to her neighbours; he evidently did not like what he saw. Clara stepped outside; she was pleased that her new slippers had arrived. Someone wearing a balaclava and a camouflage jacket that seemed to have a large section missing, was dismantling her rockery and throwing it through the front window of number five.

'Hey, careful with my saxifrages, they are just coming into bloom.'

Constable Beech radioed for assistance. The front door opened and Tim stalked towards the assailant wielding a rolling pin. He ducked, his shoulder deflecting an airborne rock. The radio crackled a response time of ten minutes.

'Put your weapon down,' yelled Constable Beech.

Clara headed for her rapidly diminishing rockery as the aggressor launched another missile. 'What on earth are you doing?'

'Your creepy bloody bastard neighbour got Andrea fired. He might have even killed her. Or you did. Or you both did,' the voice hysterical.

'Jo, is that you? Shouldn't you be in Saint Mangabeys?'

Jo removed her balaclava to reveal blood-shot eyes under bird's nest hair.

'How dare you? There is absolutely nothing bloody wrong with me.'

Tim had dropped the rolling pin and was now backing away.

'Jo, more police are on their way, you need to get out of here.'

'And I know about you. The dead man on the plane. You're like bloody Harold Shipman,' she screamed.

'Jo, try to breathe. Do you want me to take you back to the hospital?'

Jo glanced at Constable Beech, hurled a last rock at Tim and pelted down the drive into the waiting taxi.

Clara surveyed the rockery. 'Well, there's no serious harm done.'

Tim joined them. 'My wife will be back soon,' he blurted.

'Can I retrieve the rocks from the living room? They are blue granite.'

'Any idea what that was about sir?'

'None at all.' His eyes darted from the empty space formerly occupied by the taxi to the rockery and back to the constable.

'Do you know that woman sir?'

'Erm, well yes, but not in the biblical sense,' he released a ridiculous laugh. 'We only met once. Her name is Abi. I have no idea why she would do this, a case of mistaken identity perhaps.'

Clara tried to make sense of what he was saying. She could not. 'If I may, officer. That was the woman with the tortoise delusion. She was taking allegedly seeking retribution because this gentleman allegedly conspired to get her friend Andrea dismissed. You will be aware that she died recently.'

'Sir?'

'Look, could we just leave this?' He attempted an air of authority. 'My wife is collecting the children from school; I don't want them upset.'

'It would be helpful to get some background to inform her arrest sir.'

'Oh, that won't be necessary. I don't want to press charges.' Tim waved his hand in dismissal.

'That is for us to decide sir. Did you get her friend sacked?'

Tim bounced on his heels and looked at his watch. 'Okay, if I explain will you please go away?'

'Carry on sir.'

'The thing is, I had a brief liaison with Andrea, it was ages ago. An aberration of which I am deeply ashamed. It transpired that my children would be going into her class. It would have been dreadful. Parent's evenings and all that.'

Clara wondered whether the two had met when Andrea used to drop Phineas home.

'Go on sir.'

'I saw the photograph of her nature club with the penis-worm, lots of parents complained. It was my opportunity to get rid of her. From the school I mean. It was a terrible thing to do. I don't blame Abi for this.' He looked at the broken windows. 'Please don't press charges.'

'I have to say I agree with him,' said Clara, 'she does seem to be having a very difficult time.'

Constable Beech seemed to wrestle with the pull of justice and the push of paper-work. He sighed and spoke into his radio, 'Penns Lane disturbance sorted. Cancel back-up.'

33

Detective Inspector Appleton had been at work since seven and was hoping for an early dart; he had theatre tickets. He needed to make amends for the mini-break debacle. Poor Matt was exasperated. He had promised he was going to be a better husband and father from now on. He had promised before. Still, it had been worth dropping in on his old friend in Powys police. He had been more than happy to arrest Ed's neighbour for threats and harassment. It seems that the guy had a long list of outstanding offences, Ed would not even have to testify, they would put him away for a considerable time.

John was ready to turn off his computer when the phone rang. DCI Wallace sounded serious, she dispensed with niceties and addressed him formally.

'DI Appleton, I wonder if you could fill me in on a case? I understand that you sent a Constable Beech to investigate allegations of wildlife trafficking involving Dr Clara Astrell, Penns Lane, Marlow.'

'Evening Ma'am. Yes, the enquiries were preliminary and informal, they related to possible pet trade irregularities and a tenuous link to the unexplained death in Marlow.'

'I thought I had asked you to prioritise the Gibbons case, why has more progress not been made?'

John shook his head in disbelief. 'Ma'am?'

'Anyway, what were Constable Beech's findings?'

'There was no evidence of any misdemeanour. No need for follow up.'

'Really? What were his general observations?'

John was starting to feel uneasy. He scrolled through the electronic notes that Beech had entered in the log. Thankfully he was his most pedantic officer.

'Apparently she was not surprised to see him. She appeared to be financially comfortable, no conspicuous show of wealth apart from a new car. He found her to be detached and a little uncooperative.'

A burst of laughter came from the gaggle of officers gathered around a computer screen. John closed his door.

'Anything else?'

John scanned the additional notes. 'Constable Beech has an 'A' level in psychology, he felt that her pet tortoise acted as a child substitute, apparently it was dressed in some sort of knitted outfit in a play pen.'

'I would like Constable Beech to make a full report of his visit. Also send me the details of the sources of intelligence that you were acting upon. I'll need it by the end of play today.'

'Is there something amiss Ma'am?'

'Could you also prioritise the acquisition of Dr Astrell's bank statements, mobile phone records, list of associates, family and friends.'

God he would have to phone Matt and cancel the theatre.

'Is this in relation to a specific offence Ma'am?'

'Human remains have been unearthed by Thames Water Board. The body was buried in a shallow grave in an orchard belonging to one Clara Astrell.'

'Oh God.'

'I've opened a murder enquiry.'

34

Jo enjoyed twelve hours of uninterrupted sleep; the cumulative effect of her farewell dose of Olanzapine, a very large gin and tonic and the sweet release of enacted revenge. She rose at lunchtime and soaked away the ingrained wretchedness of St Mangabey's with a hot bubble bath. She performed her usual pre-date routine of corporeal and facial depilation, nails and make-up. It was only as she was applying her second layer of varnish that a terrible realisation landed.

Shit!

It was May thirtieth. Her hearing had started five hours ago. Perhaps she could join by video call. She lost precious minutes finding her scribbled notes, practising her power pose and choosing her background; she opted for the spare bedroom where she stood in front of her print of Gustave Klimt's *The Kiss*, very classy. She recited her details to a dull woman who had all the urgency of a sick sloth. There followed an infuriating ten-minute wait listening to the Beach Boys. Finally, the sloth was back. She asked a series of questions to confirm her identity. For God's sake. With some relish the woman told her that the hearing had finished at noon. The full report would be sent by first class post but she had been given permission to convey the outcome by telephone should she wish to know sooner. Yes, of course she would like to bloody know sooner. A silence, a rustling of papers, a clearing of the throat: 'It is the panel's unanimous decision that Miss Burns-Whyte be dismissed from the position of Ward Manager on the grounds of gross misconduct. The termination of contract is to be enacted with immediate effect. The details of the right to appeal will be forwarded.'

Jo hung up. She registered fury tinged with relief. She settled herself with a medicinal brandy. What did her job really mean to her? Early mornings, needy patients, annoying staff. It did provide financial security. A problem that needed to be solved. She cat-walked to her bedroom, applied a liberal dose of Chanel and smiled at her reflection. Another source of life's essentials was the lovely Ludo Mansfield.

Jo ate a small bowl of blueberries with natural yoghurt and made a mental note to mention this healthy diet to Ludo. Ten minutes of silent meditation, well nearer five but she had things to do, a quick review of her positive self-statements and she headed out. The Punto protested its two week abandonment and refused to start. She ran back inside, raided the emergency fund in her underwear drawer and called a taxi. Extravagant but it gave her fifteen minutes to gen up on facts about Sweden on Wikipedia. Recovered from her allergic reaction her skin had returned to its normal pallor and several layers of foundation had been insufficient to simulate a convincing Mediterranean suntan, hence she had opted for a northerly holiday destination. Sweden sounded the most exotic of the Scandinavian countries, sophisticated. The climate chart showed that the May tempera-ture averaged seventeen Celsius, perfect. The taxi driver was eyeing her leerily through the rear-view mirror, he was not un-attractive in a rough and ready kind of way. She stretched out her legs allowing her dress to ride up. She saw him swallow hard; oh yes, she was back.

Ludo looked gorgeous in his rose polo shirt; only muscular men could wear pink with such self-assured masculinity. The choice complemented her scarlet cocktail dress; they were made for each other.

He was delighted to see her, he kissed her on both cheeks and then on her mouth.

'Welcome home. We have a lot of catching up to do. I presume you would like some fizz?' He handed her a crystal flute. 'I think you'll find this cheeky little number the perfect accompaniment to Chinese cuisine.'

They clinked glasses. She had expected pink champagne, but the sharp tang exposed a sparkling Mateus rosé; still he had made an effort.

'It's lovely to be back although the holiday was such a tonic.'

They sat on the upper deck where the warm evening sun lent

a Mediterranean air. A riot of fork-tailed birds darted overhead diving to skim insects from the surface of the water. Jo recalled Andrea explaining the difference between a swift and a swallow but she could not remember; she wished she had paid more attention.

'So, tell me about your adventures,' Ludo leaned back in his chair. 'I'm all ears.'

'Gosh, where to start,' she crossed her legs provocatively. 'It was all such a whirlwind. Stockholm is a fabulous city, there's so much to do, the National Museum, the art galleries, restaurants.'

'You were in Norway?'

Jo froze, she suddenly doubted the Wikipedia page, where the hell was Stockholm?

'Well, I travelled between Norway and Sweden. Sweden was my favourite, it's the sixteenth richest country in the world you know.'

'I've never been, but I am partial to a bit of Abba.'

She felt herself relax. 'And what have you been doing apart from pining for me?'

'Same old, same old,' he linked his hands behind his head. 'Meetings, signing the odd contract, heaving the money to the bank,' he winked.

A young woman holding the hand of a toddler stopped to point at the boats. Jo felt the familiar churn of loss and looked away.

'So, update me on Operation Tortuga, sounds like the Old Bill turned up. Rotten luck.'

'The old codgers called the police. It was all very grim. I was put in a police cell and everything. Anyway, I was released without charge in the morning.'

'Poor baby, sounds dreadful.'

Jo had the impression that he was amused by the idea. 'It was pretty bad; the cells are so smelly and noisy, people shouting, banging doors. Hideous.' The memory tightened her stomach. She took a breath of the evening air; it was lovely to be outside after so long in captivity.

'I have just the remedy for a damsel in distress. Ludo's little helper will make everything better.' He took her hand and led her below deck.

Jo registered her hunger as the aroma of Chinese food wafted from the galley. He led her through to the bedroom, it seemed that food would have to wait. He unlocked the bedside cabinet, opened a lacquered box and laid out its contents like a surgeon's assistant: mirror, air-lock bag, razor blade and a crisp rolled fifty-pound note. Jo sat on the bed and watched as he poured out four piles of fine white powder and fashioned them into tidy lines.

'What you need is a little bit of help from Doctor Snow.' He brought the mirror up to his nose, expertly snorted two lines and handed it to Jo. 'His medicine never fails.'

Jo was thankful for the practise run in St Mangabey's, she felt like a sophisticated woman of the world. She followed his lead, inhaled the lines and threw back her head as Ludo captured the moment on his mobile. He was a rascal.

Cocaine was bloody fantastic. Even better than amphetamine. She could not stop smiling.

'You like?' Ludo grinned.

'I like very much.'

'Take off your dress,' he instructed.

She obliged. He took it from her and put his hand on her stomach. 'Looks like my cherub has had one too many Swedish meatballs.'

True, she had put on weight but she did not care. She was a voluptuous, sensual goddess. 'I can't say no to a Danish pastry,' she laughed.

'Danish? My God, it sounds as if you covered the whole of Scandinavia.'

'It's a veritable smorgasbord and I ate my way round it!'

He was so much fun, her delightful, eligible boyfriend.

Jo had never been truly reckless, she had pretty much played by the rules, perhaps bent them when no one was looking. She had tried so hard to be good. She had trotted steadily on the hamster wheel of life, setting her alarm, paying her taxes. As she lay on the silk sheets with Ludo sweating above her she felt a liberation, an epiphany: sticking to society's expectations gets you nowhere, live by the rules, die by the rules. From now on she was not just going to break the rules she was going to bloody annihilate them.

She laughed as Ludo rolled her over and snorted another line of coke from her back.

'Let's get married,' he whispered into her ear.

Jo craned her neck to check if he was being serious. His eyes were deep wells, his expression resolute. She would follow him anywhere.

'That's not much of a proposal Mr Mansfield, not the sort that I can tweet about, post on Facebook, tell our grandkids.'

She knew that she was rambling, but she didn't care about anything anymore. She was going to do and say whatever she bloody-well liked. Ludo jumped off the bed and rearranged his limbs until he was down on one knee.

'Dear Jo, beautiful plump creature, crazy partner in crime, will you do me the honour of becoming my wife?'

Jo allowed a suitable pause for dramatic effect.

'Why, Mr Mansfield,' she said in her best period-drama accent, 'I do believe I will.'

They sat naked on the carpet and ate the cold takeaway with tiny plastic spatulas straight from the tinfoil. The boat rocked on the wake of a passing dingy. Jo was starting to feel a little sick. She declined the sweet and sour prawn that Ludo dangled in front of her. She watched him scoop up the last of the Sichuan pork balls and Kung pao chicken. He was a man of voracious appetites. He was describing a deal he had struck in Monaco. He had accompanied a client to the Grand prix, all the penthouse suites were occupied and could not be appropriated even for silly money; the client stormed out of the hotel and chartered a private yacht where they spent three days eating oysters, drinking champagne and playing roulette. He flew home with a million-pound investment. She loved his sparkling eyes, his stories, his wealth.

'Jarrod? Jarrod? Hey, S-G old boy are you in there? Permission to come aboard Captain?'

Ludo cursed and leapt to his feet. He pulled on his shirt and trousers. Jo sat like a cornered rabbit surrounded by the debris of their meal. Suddenly she was aware of her nakedness, the sauce he had smeared on her breasts sticky and congealed.

He hopped on one foot and prised on his shoes. 'Stay here and don't make a sound.' He smoothed back his hair and closed the door behind him.

Jo inched along the floor, pulled the sheet from the bed and wrapped it around her. The smell of monosodium glutamate mingled with the sharp odour of spilt wine. She caught a muffled voice from the riverbank then Ludo jovial, upbeat. She strained to hear but could only catch the rise and fall of their voices. The man seemed to be questioning, cross-examining almost, Ludo confident, increasingly assertive. Then raised voices, a challenge that Ludo more than met.

The man wanted to come aboard.

Jo panicked and looked around for her clothes, she caterpillared to retrieve her underwear. Where the hell were her pants? Her arm flailed under the bed locating a hard, flat object, she slid it out. A black attaché case, she sprung the catches to reveal stacks of fifty-pound notes. A shadow moved across the window, oh God the man was looking through the porthole. She gathered the sheet tight around her, she calculated that from his angle he would not be able to see her crouched on the carpet. She kept perfectly still. Minutes passed, she hardly dared to breathe. All was quiet. She skimmed off one of the notes and slid the case back under the bed. The door opened, Ludo looking a little flustered.

'Everything okay?' Jo asked, she felt vulnerable sitting on the floor like a child, her fist tight around the stolen note.

'Silly bugger got the wrong boat.'

'He seemed very persistent.' A headache was starting at her temple and a wave of nausea washed over her. 'Why did you need me to pretend I wasn't here?'

'Why do you think wifey, we're in the company of old Charlie White, I've got a reputation to maintain.'

'I like it when you take charge, it suits you.'

'So, where were we?' He took off his shirt.

Jo felt her stomach rise, she bolted for the bathroom and locked the door. She hunched over the toilet bowl hoping that the sound of her retching was not audible from the bedroom. She washed her face and examined her reflection in the mirror. A wild woman with huge dilated pupils stared back. Her skin was ashen, her smudged scarlet lipstick matched the grip marks on her neck. But there was a freedom in that face, a defiance that she wanted to inhabit.

'Hello,' she said aloud, 'I'm Mrs Jo Mansfield, very pleased to meet you.'

Jo lay on her sofa and reflected on her crazy night with Ludo. She was engaged to be married! She drained the last drop of Prosecco and lit a cigarette, her New Year's resolutions seemed so long ago. She laughed; she had not made herself any promises about her new friend Charlie White. She felt emboldened, excited about her future for the first time since Andrea's death. She would take nurse Niki's advice and let go; she no longer wanted to be dragged.

She was a very positive person, that was the conclusion of the personality quiz in this month's *Cosmopolitan*. She spurned doubt. But there was a niggle about her intended. Not so much a niggle, more the tens of thousands in used fifties under his bed. And damn, now that she had started helping herself, she could not really ask him. No wait, it must be a tax avoidance strategy, top financial people used them all the time. Phew.

She switched on the local news where an earnest reporter was speaking into a fluffy microphone; it seemed that a body had been discovered. Behind him the police had cordoned off a house and stood around waiting for something to happen. A man walked past and laid a cheap bunch of flowers by the crime scene tape. Jo leapt forward, bloody hell it was Toxic Tim. She looked closely at the fuchsia hedges, the red front door, the wrecked rockery.

It was Clara's house.

Oh my God, the murdering bitch had done it again.

35

Detective Inspector Appleton opened his notebook for the briefing, he was pleased to be heading the investigative team but suspected that DCI Wallace would be holding a sharpened knife to his back. He had come dangerously close to spooking their main suspect by sending Beech to check out the spurious trafficking allegations. And the idiot had gone in and harassed the woman without a warrant. He knew he was not on top form; he was working long days, his only break this year had hardly been relaxing and their new dalmatian puppy whimpered all night.

He rubbed his eyes, God, he had not contacted the hospitals in his so far fruitless search for Clara Astrell. Oh well he would just have to wing it. DCI Wallace entered, all conversation stopped, the assembled officers turned their full attention to the small tank of a woman. She certainly knew how to command a room.

'Okay gentlemen, Operation Orchard,' she pinned a photograph of the exhumed remains onto the corkboard. 'I don't need to remind you that the national press are all over this. We need results and we need to keep all intel confidential, please direct any snooping journalists to the press officer.'

She scanned each face as if gauging their trustworthiness, John felt it lingered on his.

'The body was found in a shallow grave in an orchard belonging to Dr Clara Astrell by a contractor. He was digging a trench when his JCB scooped up a human skull. All work on the site was immediately suspended. The foreman informed us. The forensic team excavated the remaining remains.'

A small chuckle ran through the back row. DCI Wallace scanned her audience as a fox would a chicken coup. She waited for absolute silence before she continued.

'We have an initial report from the path lab,' she punctuated each finding by pinning a gruesome close-up of the deceased onto the board. First, the body is that of a young male, late-teens to early-twenties. Second, the remains are entirely skeletal, there was no undecomposed hair or skin indicating that the body was buried at least eight to twelve years ago. Third, the corpse was mutilated. Despite a full search of the site the right forearm and left foot have not been recovered.'

A ripple of intrigue ran through the room, John guessed he was the only one feeling a little sick.

'Due to the condition of the body and the length of time it has been in the ground pathology has yet to determine the cause of death. Initial reports have raised the possibility of poisoning and there is some indication of maceration prior to burial.'

The officers exchanged baffled glances

'The perpetrator made a good job of eliminating DNA, less so of the burial.'

She allowed a full minute of silence before summing up.

'So, there is currently far more we don't know about this case than we do know. As a matter of urgency, we need to ascertain,' she counted off the demands on her fingers, 'One; the identity of the victim, two; the approximate date of death and three; the cause of death.'

The theme tune of *Brooklyn Nine-Nine* rang from someone's pocket. The room froze as a red-faced officer patted his pockets. Wallace held out her hand. He relinquished his phone. Several others switched off their mobiles.

'Until the man's identity is known we have only one potential suspect, that is the owner of the orchard where the body was buried. Dismemberment is very unusual; we might be dealing with organised crime or with a psychopath. DI Appleton I understand that you have been looking into Astrell's background, anything to report at this stage?'

John rose to his feet, ignoring the note of derision in her voice and stuck a large photograph of Clara Astrell next to the grim images. He liked the look of her; she wore a light tweed jacket, a black rose brooch on the lapel, she had a twinkly smile; every inch the psychopathic killer. The picture had been appropriated from the stoat-faced Practice Manager - he had taken an instant dislike to the man - who told him that it had formerly graced the 'Meet the Team' noticeboard. He cleared his throat.

'Dr Clara Astrell has lived at the property for twenty-eight years.

She recently retired having worked as a G.P. locally throughout that time. Unsurprisingly she has no forensic history, not so much as a speeding fine. One son, currently living abroad. We have been unable to contact him but he graduated from Cambridge in 2015 and finished a PhD in 2018 so he is unlikely to be the deceased.'

He tuned out an idiot-voiced 'well duh' from the back of the room.

'The surgery manager described Dr Astrell as "tiresome" he said that her patients seemed to like her but the subtext was that he had no idea why. According to her neighbours she socialised very little, they trotted out the usual "tended to keep herself to herself" response.'

Did anyone actually say anything of any interest?' DCI Wallace puffed out her cheeks.

'I did question her next-door neighbours Tim and Sally Forth. He was disparaging about her, he said that a while ago she had marched over out-of-the-blue and accused him of being in her house, practically insinuated that he had used it as a brothel. He said that she kept dangerous company, although he would not elucidate. He said he had told his wife that there was something mentally wrong with her and that they should try to avoid her in future.'

'And what progress has been made on finding the good doctor?' DCI Wallace's tone was dismissive, she rarely asked a question to which she did not know the answer.

'As yet we have been unable to locate Dr Astrell. The neighbours' said that she has not been seen since the drainage work commenced. I can however confirm that she has not left the country.'

'You can confirm that she has not left the country using her own passport,' Wallace corrected. 'Anything to add? Anybody?'

A young officer with a newly trimmed crewcut jumped to his feet.

'Constable Bobby Beech Ma'am. I attended a call out to a farmhouse owned by the Cuvier family in Marlow Bottom in the early hours of eighteenth April. They had caught and detained an intruder on their premises. The intruder,' he flicked through his notes, 'one Jo Burns-Whyte, was apparently convinced that Dr Clara Astrell had somehow conspired with this family in relation to the illegal pet trade. She was subsequently committed to a psychiatric hospital. Jo Burns-Whyte that is, not Clara Astrell,' he clarified unnecessarily. 'It was noted by officers at Cork Street Station that she believed Dr Astrell had murdered her best friend, the best friend of Jo Burns-Whyte that is, not of Clara Astrell who allegedly did not know her very well; a Miss Andrea Gibbons, who died on Christmas Day 2018.'

He was warming to his theme and looked exceedingly pleased with himself as he delivered his punchline. 'During my discussion with the Cuvier family I further ascertained, and I have of course informed social services Ma'am, that Dr Astrell had broken Mr Cuvier seniors' ribs. He referred to her as "Old Crusher" Astrell.'

'Good work Constable. I understand that you had undertaken some preliminary investigations into the trafficking allegation prior to the discovery of the body. Although it was deemed by your senior officer that no further action was indicated.'

John held her eye as she directed her gaze towards him.

'Yes Ma'am. I do have further information on Dr Astrell.'

'Well let's hear it Constable.'

He straightened himself to his full five feet nine and took a deep breath. 'I visited Dr Astrell at her home, acting on a tip-off in regard to wildlife trafficking, namely Madagascan radiated tortoises. She had one tortoise in her home; I verified that the specimen as owned legally. She was however very reluctant to discuss her connections with Madagascar and attempted to hasten my departure when the topic was raised.'

'Smart lady,' someone mumbled.

'Ma'am, I have ascertained from her bank statements that Dr Astrell booked a return flight to Madagascar with only five days' notice, indicating that this was not a holiday. Whilst there she visited a Madagascan tortoise facility,' he paused to assess his permission to continue.

'Go on Constable, hopefully this will start to make some sense.' DCI Wallace appeared to be tiring of him.

'Ma'am, Dr Astrell has also set up a crowdfunding page; as of nine-hundred-hours this morning the total raised was over eighteen thousand pounds,' he paused, seeming to gird himself before throwing down his ace with full force. 'The money is purportedly for *Sanctuaire des tortues*,' his accent drew titters, 'which is French for *Hiding place of the tortoises*.'

'Interesting Constable, and what conclusions do you draw from this?'

John wondered whether she was setting him up for a humiliating fall but she too appeared to have missed the obvious.

'I understand that the *Sanctuaire* currently houses over five hundred tortoises, at six thousand pounds each, that is,' he checked his notebook, 'three million pounds worth of tortoises Ma'am. It indicates serious organised crime involvement. Perhaps her *Justgiving* site is a cover for laundering payments.'

'Thank you Constable, that was very thorough.'

Bobby flushed with pride and resumed his seat.

'I don't want to tell you how to conduct your inquiry DI Appleton but perhaps you could explore this further. Once you have managed to locate our elusive doctor.'

John winced, his antennae told him that Clara Astrell was too unlikely a perpetrator and for God's sake, were she linked to organised crime she would hardly be setting up links to public forums. Still, he had to find Wallace's prime suspect before he could rule her out. Of course, if she was enjoying a new life in South America he would be lucky to get away with a desk job.

36

Clara was in Argentina.

She was dancing the Argentine tango.

Her partner, chic in black satin, whirled her across the dance-floor as light as a feather. He was extremely accomplished of course, what with so much practice. He had a cruel reputation but she found him charming.

Gracias a la Vida by Mercedes Sosa set a steady mournful beat, he pulled her to him, threw her back, she echoed every move without effort.

An audience of shadowy figures kept the rhythm with crisp handclaps and castanets.

The introduction of a solid bass drum changed the pace, she was quick stepping, her feet impossibly adept, keeping perfect time to *Mi Confesion*.

He allowed her to break away to perform a swirling solo accompanied by a harmonic jazz-funk fusion.

And suddenly he was back, holding her tightly.

'All things move towards their end,' he whispered. Of course, he knew Milton.

She tried to meet his eyes but a deep hood covered his face. She could only see his smile. The reaper was not grim at all. He had surprisingly minty breath, his chest pressing forcefully against hers.

Beep, beep, beep.

'Cardiac arrest, one two three, stand back.'

Her body convulsed and fell, convulsed and fell and he was gone.

Through closed eyelids a brilliant light beckoned. She registered a vague sense of regret that she did not believe in heaven; a likely barrier to entry.

The strangely familiar smell of glutaraldehyde, with undernotes of chlorine, filled her nostrils. She listened to the mechanical rattle of a suction pump over urgent voices. She deduced that she was either in an operating theatre or the ICU, as the anaesthetic was clearly wearing off, she hoped for the latter. Bleeps and peeps formed a strange surround sound. She recalled 'the machine that goes ping' from Monty Python's *The Meaning of Life,* she had the DVD, Phineas loved it too, they watched it every Christmas. She replayed the scene: a hospital administrator strides into the operating theatre where a woman is giving birth encircled by a forest of equipment. 'Amplify the ping machine,' shouts the obstetrician. She laughed out loud. Her chest hurt; it was hard to breathe. She opened her eyes and squinted into a fluorescent beam.

'Hello, wakey wakey.'

Somebody was rubbing her arm.

'You relax, everything is alright, you just fine.'

An accent she could not place, possibly South-East Asian. She attempted to turn her head and felt the vinyl grip of an oxygen mask. The nurse leaned over and adjusted the machine above her head. She was small, middle-aged, she guessed Malaysian.

'Lie still dear, doctor is coming.'

Clara did what she was told, she was unable to do anything else. The nurse vanished. From the corner of her eye she could just make out a concertina of blue curtains; she was in a cubicle in ICU. She listened to the heart monitor's reassuring regularity. The whoosh of an IV pump competed with the muffled wheeze of her own breathing. She moved her attention to her legs, she seemed to be wearing anti-embolism stockings. My God, how long have I been here? A wave of panic accelerated the heart monitor. To slow the beeps she listed the absence of more sinister equipment. No endotracheal tube, that is good. No intracranial pressure monitor, thank goodness. No gastric pipe, a blessing. No ventilator, perfect.

She heard the doors swing open and a young man with minty breath leaned over her.

'Dr Astrell I presume? Back from the jaws of death.' He had an unexpectedly strong Glaswegian accent.

He removed her oxygen mask. She thought that she caught a whiff of whiskey and hoped it was merely by association.

'You've been quite the challenge I can tell ye,' he whisked his penlight from his top pocket, lifted her eyelids and shone it into each pupil.

'Diagnosis?' She rasped.

'*Klebsiella pneumoniae*, led to septicaemia, multi-resistant strain, heavy bad luck.'

'Prognosis?' It was a huge effort to speak.

'You've had enough antibiotics to supply a Norfolk chicken farm. Not out of the woods yet but all the signs are good.'

'How?'

'Apparently you were kicked in the shin by an alpaca.'

Clara's mind reeled back. She was holding Garcia's harness, a sweet pale-brown alpaca with the darkest of eyes. Patsy Clifton was clipping his toenails, the final task of his toilette. He had stood patiently while the host of the husbandry course took his temperature, roughly combed the knots from his fleece and filed his protruding lower teeth. Clara had done her best to reassure him but she could sense that he was becoming distressed. He inched forward protesting; he was literally at the end of his tether. He lunged violently and kicked out hard with his hind leg, his semi-trimmed nails gashing her shin. The pain was shocking but she did not make a fuss. She carried on with the day's programme. She learnt how to weigh the adults and the crias, how to test the quality of the fleece, check for parasites and, ironically, administer antibiotics. By that time the *Klebsiella* would have been swarming through her bloodstream, getting a grip. Back home she had washed the wound, applied antiseptic and had not given it another thought. Instead she had been weighing up alpaca farming as a possible second career: it seems that the universe had spoken.

37

O h, they would listen now.

They would hang on her every word. She would be lauded and applauded oh yes, now that the body count had risen. Jo strode into the police station wrapped in the glory of vindication. She was disappointed to learn that John Appleton was not available. Still, every cloud. This particular silver lining came in the form of roughty-toughty Bobby Beech. He was very thorough, very professional and very cute. Harbouring a wrap of cocaine in her handbag lent an additional frisson to the interview. Since being introduced to her new powdery friend she was cheerful and reckless and bold. Devil-may-care. She looked forward to telling Ludo of her bravado; he loved it when she was naughty.

There was that awkward moment of recognition when the proficient Constable Beech asked if they had met before. Fortunately, her mad-house pallor had since dissipated, her hair had been styled at Vidal's and she was clutching a Prada handbag, not a rock. The darling was kind enough not to ask too many questions about the little misunderstanding at the Cuviers'. He was extremely interested in her trafficking hypothesis, her insider knowledge of the dastardly Dr Clara and the increasingly plausible theory of why she killed Andrea. Okay, she could not shed any light on the identity of the body in the orchard but as the person who revealed the Madagascan connection, she seemed to have earned Bobby's respect. She treated him to a view of her cleavage as she leant forward to confide that there were likely to be more victims to be discovered.

Bobby was a very good listener. He asked for some background on Andrea, it was lovely to be able to talk about her, once she started she could not stop. She gave him chapter and verse; how poor Andrea's well-laid plans had always had a way of ending in disaster. She told him how she and Andrea had supported each other through their respective calamities. True, it was mainly via the medium of Cabernet Sauvignon and constant reiteration of the ways in which they had been wronged, but it had helped. She even divulged their crazy forays into the wine bars of Henley-on-Thames 'trapping' for wealthy men. She herself had bagged a couple, sadly they both turned out to be pre-married. All the old stories poured out, things she had not even told Ludo. The night Andrea had rescued her from a minibus full of rugby players when things started to get out of hand. The time Andrea wrote her a dating profile describing Jo as her best friend who would make a fabulous wife and mother. It was a beautiful biog that strangely did not result in any dates. She described the despicable Leon Maynard, whom Andrea had married in haste before he ploughed his way through her inheritance in under a year. How they had similar taste in men, in fact she had recently become engaged to an old friend of Andrea's, a top-drawer financial advisor.

Bobby wrote it all down. The two hours flew by. He said that he could not promise that Andrea's case would be reopened, but the recent turn of events meant that all leads would be closely examined.

Fuelled by attention and absolution Jo stepped out of the police station into a gaggle of reporters. Fortunately, in anticipation of a meeting with DI John, she had applied full make-up; she was pleased that it would not be wasted.

'Any news on the body in the orchard?'

Jo assumed that this question had been fired at all those exiting the station to be met by a universal 'no comment'. Here was her chance. She stopped and allowed the scrum to close around her. She affected her best Marilyn Monroe.

'I'm afraid that I am unable to give precise details at this moment in time but a primary suspect has been identified: Dr Clara Astrell. Suffice to say that there is far more to come out. Prepare the front pages!' She basked in the explosion of flashing cameras.

A barrage of questions erupted; she raised her hand to silence them. 'All I can say is that the police are currently investigating previous unsolved cases.'

She extricated herself from the throng. With a casual air she collected the contact cards thrust upon her and dropped them into her handbag.

By the time she reached the Punto at the far end of the car-park the excitement of her interview and the press attention had waned. She was exhausted. She shuffled through her bag for the car keys, there lay Dr Snow. A little pick-me-up was just what she needed. She sat in the car and snorted a line from the back of her hand; the quick-fix technique that Ludo had taught her. Suddenly she needed to talk again. She phoned Maz who told her to come straight over.

Driving on cocaine was amazing.

'You're looking good girl,' Maz took her head in both of her hands and planted a Flamenco-red kiss on her forehead.

'You too,' said Jo, a little startled by the intensity of the greeting and of the lime-green tracksuit.

Maz threw herself onto the white leather sofa and propped her bare feet on the leopard-print pouffe. The three-piece suite, adorned with wine stains and cat-scratches, took up most of the living room. The enormous furniture appeared to be one of many hypomanic purchases that had later proven unwise: a long-chained chandelier hung at head-height, a flamingo water feature bubbled in the corner and an ornate grandfather clock restricted access to the kitchen. Nevertheless, it was lovely to see her new friend relaxed in her own home. Maz had prepared two *Bombay Bad Boy* Pot Noodles that now stood steaming in their plastic containers, an ornate silver fork stuck in each.

'So, sit down and tell all. How did you get out of the hellhole?'

'I can't take any credit,' Jo sank in the voluminous chair. 'That place was driving me completely bonkers, no offence.'

'None taken.'

'My unlikely saviours came in the form of the CQC Mafiosi who seem to have inadvertently stumbled across some bad practice. I was discharged the same day.'

'Wow, what a stroke of luck,' Maz scooped a dangerous quantity of noodles into her mouth.

'Yes, the tide is really turning.'

'Ha, I bet they compared the consultants' length-of-stay figures, Tweak's are twice as long as Devonshire's and her medication costs are way above average.'

Jo laughed. 'Thankfully she had me down as an untreatable

long-stayer.'

'So, what did I miss?'

'Things were getting pretty crazy in there. Your replacement was an old nutter who thought he was Jesus Christ. Apparently, he'd been sent back from the rehab ward for fighting with another Jesus. Walked round with his manhood on full display, deeply unpleasant.'

'Oh, that will be Willy Wonka. Left bent but not in the political sense,' Maz released her donkey haw. 'He's quite sweet when you get to know him. Easter is always a stressful time for the Jesuses. God bless 'em.'

'Well, anyway, how have you been? Great to be home I bet.'

'Yes, all good here. My Norm took the first week off to keep me company, we had a nice time: cinema, ten-pin bowling, darts match, pub quiz. He likes to ensure that I'm entertained so I keep taking the tablets. Although things are getting a little dull. I'm so pleased you dropped by.' She drained the liquid from the pot noodle and wiped her mouth on her sleeve. 'What have you been up to?'

'So much has happened. My friend's killer is about to be revealed. It seems she has killed again.'

'Oh, it wasn't her brother then?'

'No, he was always a long shot.'

A high-pitched retching followed by a bittersweet smell emanated from behind Jo's chair.

'Jesus, what is that?'

'It's only Tinky-Winky, silly boy has been eating grass again.'

A haughty orange cat stalked from the room, its tail in the air.

'As in the Teletubbies, God I hated that programme. Creepy little baby in the sun.'

Maz launched into the theme tune; 'Tinky-Winky, Dipsy, Laa Laa, Po, Teletubbies, Teletubbies, say hello, eh oh,' she giggled like the sun-baby. She showed no inclination to clean up the cat sick.

'I have big news,' Jo clasped her hands between her knees like a teenager, 'I'm engaged!'

'What? You didn't even tell me you had a boyfriend. When did this happen?'

'It was very spur of the moment, literally the day after I got released. He asked me to marry him on his yacht, all very romantic, down on one knee, the works.'

'Who is he? How long have you known him?' Her cocked head and sideways glance portrayed a cartoon scepticism.

'His name is Ludo Mansfield. We met at Andrea's funeral. He's a financial advisor, high-end clients.'

'Are you not going to eat your *Bad Boy*?'

'No thanks, I have to lose two stone before the wedding.'

'Pass it over then, waste not want not.'

'Also he's rich AF.'

'Wow, you've landed on your feet girl. Let's see the ring?' She shovelled the noodles into her mouth.

'Well I don't have a ring just yet. It was an impulsive proposal. I suspect he's going to surprise me next time. I've been dropping subliminal hints, humming *Diamonds Are A Girl's Best Friend,* that sort of thing.'

'So, tell me all about this mystery man.'

'He's in his forties, very good looking, pale blue eyes. He has a beautiful boat moored at Henley. We spend most of our time there. He used to be in the army.' She hesitated, she realised that she knew little else about him, nothing about his family or his friends. 'He's great fun,' she added to bolster the information.

'Where does he live, this Ludo?' Maz dropped the empty pot onto the floor.

'Kensington, I haven't been there yet. It's not very convenient from here.'

'Not very convenient for him more like.'

'What are you saying?' said Jo, affronted.

'Mate, I'm the queen of not leaping before I look. It just sounds a bit, you know, fishy.'

'It's not fishy at all, he's a perfectly decent man.'

'All I'm saying is I've met plenty of those types, I seem to attract them when I'm manic. All charm and flowers and candle-lit dinners, then its exit stage left and they're onto the next one.' She lit two cigarettes and handed one to Jo.

'He's not like that honestly, you must meet him, he's a dream come true.'

'Things that are too good to be true generally turn out to be too good to be true. Three questions, if you answer 'no' to any of them you need to tread very carefully.' She held up a finger in turn.

'One, have you met any of his family? Two, have you met any of his friends? Three, do you have his landline number? Four, actually, four things, do you know his home address?'

To Jo's relief the doorbell rang, Maz swung herself off the sofa and rushed to answer it. She returned a few moments later with a uniformed Hermes courier carrying a large parcel.

'Plonk it down anywhere, thanks Danny.'

The courier, finding no space on the floor, placed the box on the letter-strewn sideboard. 'Alright Maz, see you soon.'

She tore off the packaging to reveal a bright robotic lawnmower.

Jo stared in disbelief. 'Are you kidding? Those things cost a bloody fortune.'

'True,' said Maz, lifting out the shiny sphere and grinning at her reflection, 'but it is a quality item, functional and stylish; worth every penny.'

'It's a great lawnmower Maz, but it's only functional if you have a lawn.'

'Well maybe we'll move to a house with a garden, it's good to be prepared.'

'I'm just going to come right out and ask,' she took a long draw on her cigarette for added gravitas, 'have you been taking your medication?'

'Geez, not you as well. I've just cut down to give myself a bit of a lift.'

Jo was aware of her hypocrisy given her own new habit. 'Okay, but just be careful. I don't want to be visiting you in St Mangabey's.'

'Let's make a deal, you slow things down with Game-boy and I won't drop the dose again.'

They shook on it. It felt nice to have a best friend again, even a bat-shit crazy one.

Yes, *Loose Women* she had hit the jackpot. It was such a great programme, one of her regular distractions since joining the terminally unemployed; apparently their target audience. She had contacted the reporters and had ramped up her involvement with the case and her willingness to spill the beans - but only live on TV. She felt as if she already knew the presenters, they were intelligent, sassy, sophisticated women, just like herself. A stroke of luck that *The Jeremy Kyle Show* had fallen through. She had accepted their paltry offer with the promise of a bonus should Clara Astrell also appear. The episode: 'Dr Death killed my best friend' looked set to be a classic but the bloody woman could not be located. Then suddenly the whole series was taken off air following the cuckolded guest scandal. Her new media contacts had hinted at *Piers Morgan* and *Good Morning Britain,* but nothing was firmed up yet. *Loose Women* was the holy grail.

The morning of the show passed in nervous anticipation; a limousine would collect her from her front door. A limousine! She hoped the neighbours would be curtain-twitching. She had decided against telling Maz about her foray into the media spotlight. It might be a burden to her, she seemed a little close to the edge. Besides, she might have wanted to accompany her to the studio and she had her image to consider. She chose the sleeveless peach dress that she had worn for her first date with Ludo and pinned on Clara's black rose brooch with a wicked delight.

38

Clara lay propped against a Jenga of pillows. She had been trundled down in a lift and wheeled through stark corridors by a cheerless porter, who battled noisily with a phlegm-rich buccal cavity, before being unceremoniously deposited in a side room. Nursing staff had yet to make an appearance. At least she had been spared the dormitory where televisions blared from every bed space. A thin blue curtain was drawn tight across the window, she was unable to tell whether it was raining heavily or whether there was a hidden pipe transporting a steady background deluge. Either way it was not helping the urgency with which she needed to use the toilet.

Phineas had brought in her favourite nightie, the one with the sleeping cats. It provided emotional solace, but her arms were cold in the short sleeves and her weakened state rendered her incapable of dislodging the tightly tucked bedding. She remembered lying under the secured mosquito net in Ranomafana; it seemed so long ago. Five hours until visiting time. She reminded herself that boredom was a sign of recovery, although she felt as feeble as a new-born kitten. A reptilian nurse appeared and stuck a thermometer perfunctorily into her ear.

'Ah, good-morning nurse, how are you feeling today? A little better I hope,' said Clara deadpan.

'I'm fine,' she snapped, apparently immune to sarcasm.

'I need to use the bathroom.'

The reptile scribbled on her chart and disappeared. Clara was unsure whether she had gone to fetch a bedpan or whether she had failed to register the request. Ten minutes passed. She pressed the call button. A young nurse with shiny hair rushed in.

'Hello Dr Astrell, are you okay?' She had a soothing Mediterranean accent.

'I'm afraid I need the toilet urgently.'

'Yes, of course, I'll be right back.'

She reappeared with a bedpan, followed moments later by the

reptile similarly equipped; it muttered something malevolent beneath its breath and left the room.

Toileting accomplished she felt considerably better. The nurse reorganised her pillows into a supportive bolster and turned on the television. It was a satire, Boris Johnson was walking into number ten, she did enjoy a political comedy, lord knows we needed some humour to get us through these dark pre-Brexit days. He reappeared with comedic gusto behind a make-shift lectern, super-charged, ready to deliver a speech to assembled reporters. This should be fun.

'You like your new Prime Minister?' asked the nurse.

Clara struggled to accommodate the possibility that this was the news, 'Oh my God, what on earth has happened?'

'Boris won the leadership election, I'm sorry,' she commiserated.

'Please turn it off.'

There was a minute's silence.

'Would you like something to drink Dr Astrell? I'm afraid you have missed the tea-trolley, but perhaps some juice?'

'Thank you, that would be lovely.'

'Your son phoned again for an update; he is very nice. He said he will come this evening.'

'He's just back from Madagascar; spent his first week home sitting outside ICU.'

'So nice.'

'Clara studied her name badge: Pia De Luca, Staff Nurse. 'You are Italian?'

'Yes, this is my second year here. It is very nice, I am learning so much, Nurse Jones you just met her, she is my mentor.'

'Ah, you must be learning what not to do.'

Pia laughed and gave Clara a knowing look. She opened the curtain to reveal a grey day, but no rain.

'What is that noise?'

'That is pipes, I am sorry, it is not so nice but I will bring headphones for your radio.' She closed the door behind her.

The thought of her impending solitary confinement was strangely reassuring. With the exception of Phineas, the Cuviers and three long-term friends, she found prolonged contact with people exhausting. The worm burrowed up from its lair, good grief, even septicaemia had failed to kill it. Now what did it want?

Look what you have become.

Had it been the job that had changed her or had she been predisposed to asociality? Whilst her father, naturally ebullient, grew quietly affable in his later years she had found herself becoming taciturn, overly reserved. Partly it was the need to adhere to ten-minute consultations: no preliminaries, no extraneous questions, certainly no self-disclosure. Increasingly she had felt compelled to self-preservation, if one was too approachable the bi-weekly supermarket trip was invariably punctuated by queries about Mary's acne, little Johnny's stye, and throbbing varicose veins. It was all very tiresome when trying to decide between red or green curry paste. Decades of confidentiality and measured responses had taken their toll, always having to double filter her remarks had eroded her spontaneity. She felt as tightly sutured as a surgical wound. Something to work on as Phineas would say.

Pia returned briefly leaving Clara to consume the drink and custard creams that she placed on her bedside cabinet. The impediment of a saline drip mitigated the hand-eye coordination needed to manoeuvre the unexpected chunkiness of the beaker, resulting in an alarming orange juice spillage.

Spent. Wretched. Invalid.

The worm seemed to have resorted to one-word retorts.

Two hours passed, the only interruption being the lunch trolley that delivered a disappointing Caesar salad that even Darwin would have spurned. She tuned to Radio Four. A discussion about the quality of hospital food, the coincidence made her smile. It turned out to be grim, the presenter announced that five people had died from Listeriosis after eating pre-packed sandwiches and salads in NHS hospitals. A government minister had ordered a full investigation - another scandalous waste of money better spent on patient care. It did not need an investigation to know that contracting out services to the lowest bidder would result in catastrophe. She eyed her limp salad suspiciously and pushed it away.

A knock on the door. The reptile entered with a tall man in a navy-blue suit.

'This is Clara Astrell,' she said impassively. 'This police officer wants to speak to you,' she gave Clara a furtive glance and closed the door.

'Sorry, that wasn't the introduction I had expected, I'm Detective Inspector John Appleton, Thames Valley Police,' he produced an ID card in which he looked considerably younger. 'Your doctor said that you are now fit to be interviewed, it seems you have been unconscious for some time.'

'Yes, a debilitating strain of bacteria; that's what happens when you overuse antibiotics.'

'The interview is entirely voluntary at this point.'

Clara struggled to take in this information. 'What is about? Good grief, not the tortoise again?'

'I wonder if we could have a conversation regarding a recent discovery in your orchard in Penns Lane?'

She became aware of her uncombed hair, sleeping-cat nightie and crumb strewn sheet with its regretful orange stain. 'I'm happy to cooperate DI Appleton but is this an interview or a conversation?'

'It is an informal interview.'

'Could you be more specific regarding the discovery?'

He pulled up a plastic chair and sat next to the bed. He looked very serious. His eyes were tired.

'We are conducting preliminary investigations in relation to a body that has been unearthed on your property. You would just be helping us with our inquiries at this stage.'

'A body?'

'The remains of a young man.'

'I see. Well in that case officer, please go ahead.'

'It is likely that he was buried around twelve years ago,' he paused.

Clara absorbed his quiet scrutiny. Her face automatically assumed the position she used when breaking news of a terminal prognosis. 'I see.'

'Could you confirm whether you owned the property at the time.'

'Yes, I've owned it for nearly thirty years.'

'And have you ever been aware of ground being disturbed?'

'Disturbed?'

'In particular under a pear tree at the top of the orchard?'

'I hope the men have not damaged the tree, it has great sentimental value.'

'I am unaware of the condition of the tree,' he shifted in his seat. 'Can you recall seeing any previous signs of digging?'

'My son and I dug the grave,' Clara gazed into the middle distance and calculated the date, 'less than two years ago. September 2017.'

John Appleton looked shocked, he seemed to have lost his line of questioning. 'September 2017?' He repeated.

'Yes, it was shortly before my son returned to Cambridge to finish his thesis. We buried him together. Well, actually Phineas dug the hole; I told him it wasn't deep enough.'

DI Appleton swallowed hard, he held up his hand.

'Dr Astrell, before you go on, I'm afraid that I need to caution you and to inform you that I will be recording this conversation.' He took a Dictaphone from his jacket and placed it on the tray beside the uneaten salad. He cleared his throat.

'The time is two thirty-five pm. Dr Clara Astrell, you do not have to say anything, but it may harm your defence if you do not mention, when questioned, something which you later rely on in court. Anything you do say may be given in evidence.'

'I see.'

'Could you please repeat, for the tape, what you have just told me,' he spoke clearly, enunciating each word.

'I buried the remains in my orchard in September 2017 with the aid of my son who dug the grave.'

'And who was the young man that you buried?'

'I knew him only by the name that I gave him, Ossy Osman.'

DI Appleton wrote this in his notebook. The sound of cascading water interrupted the silence, Clara leaned forward. 'For the benefit of the tape that is the drainage pipe I think someone must be emptying a bath, sorry officer do carry on.'

'How long had you known the deceased and in what capacity?'

'Since I was at medical school in the early 1980s,' she watched him rub his eyebrow and consider this information.

'We have estimated the deceased to be in his early twenties in which case he would not have been born until the mid-1990s.'

'He was dead when I met him, had been for many years.'

'Dr Astrell, are you currently taking sedatives?'

'I am on co-codamol and a heavy dose of antibiotics but don't worry officer I'm fully compos mentis.'

'Dr Astrell, what was your relationship to the deceased?'

'He was my anatomy skeleton.'

DI Appleton stared at her. She could see the penny dropping.

'You had a real human skeleton?'

'Oh yes, it was common practice. Nowadays they are plastic replicas of course. I had him for nearly forty years, grew quite attached to him.'

'Why did you decide to bury him after all that time?' His manner subtly softened.

'We were decluttering Phineas' old bedroom. Poor Ossy had been sitting neglected on the top of the wardrobe for years. Phin used to hold 'tea-parties' with him when he was little. Time moves on, neither of us really wanted to keep him.'

'So you dug a grave in the garden?'

'He had lost half an arm and a foot over the years so I couldn't donate him to a medical school. Anyway, we wanted to give him a proper send-off, so we decided to bury him.'

'There are strict rules on the disposal of human remains.'

The pipes transported another deluge.

'Oh, I'm well aware of that officer, I asked the MDU for advice. Section 32 of the Human Tissue Act, if I remember correctly,' she watched him re-evaluate her, it was pleasing. 'We chose a nice spot in the old orchard - much better than ending up on some auction site or as a Halloween prop, like so many do. The local vicar performed a blessing. I read a poem, *Miss me but let me go*. Phineas said a few words about friendship. It was lovely.'

DI Appleton turned off the Dictaphone.

'*Latet enim veritas*, truth is hidden.'

'But nothing is more beautiful than the truth,' Clara finished the saying. 'You studied Latin?'

'Yes, so I get Ossy Osman, Bony Boneman, very good.'

'What's going to happen to him now? I don't like the idea of him ending up in a clinical incinerator.'

'Once your account checks out we can return him to you if you like. I'm sorry for my assumptions, I should have been more impartial. Please call me John by the way.'

'*Homines quod volunt credunt,*' do you know that one John?'

'Men believe what they want to,' he smiled.

'If you don't mind me saying you're not a typical police officer. You don't quite fit the bill, pun intended.'

'Well, that's true, it's a long story.'

The reptile entered without knocking and scowled at DI Appleton. 'You said twenty minutes, you've had thirty.'

Clara looked at the wall clock. 'I do believe it is visiting time nurse. John, if you would care to stay that would be lovely.'

He unclipped his tie and put it in his pocket. 'Thank you, I'd like that very much.'

By the time Pia came in with refreshments they were sharing photographs of their dogs on their phones and laughing like drains.

'Sorry to disturb you I just need to check your BP and temperature,' Pia held up a thermometer in evidence.

Tasks accomplished she turned for the door and hesitated. 'I am sorry. There is a programme on TV they are talking about,' she signed inverted commas with her fingers, "doctors who kill", you might want to see.'

DI Appleton turned on the television. Four women, each startlingly coiffured, perched behind a glass desk in a brightly lit studio. Three sat like nodding dogs paying riveted attention to a blond woman with scarlet lipstick. As the camera zoomed in Clara saw with a start that it was Jo Burns-Whyte - and she was wearing her black rose brooch. John turned up the volume.

'I understand that she is still at large although police have launched a man-hunt, or in this case a woman-hunt,' Jo giggled like a tiny child. 'I have been helping the police with their enquiries regarding previous offences the doctor is thought to have committed.'

'Aren't you scared for your own safety?' Blurted a woman with a harsh nasal twang.

'Well, you have to put the public's safety above your own when you hold important information.'

'Can you tell us anything about the other offences? Is it possible that she is a serial killer?' Asked a woman with large hoop earrings as she smiled incongruously at the camera.

'Well, it is too early to know how many crimes she may have committed but I can confirm that the offences are of the most serious nature.'

'Including murder?' Breathed the woman in a pink Burberry jacket.

'Yes, including the murder of my best friend Andrea Gibbons.'

DI Appleton put his head in his hands and groaned.

39

Jo patrolled the living room with the stereotypic pacing of a zoo-crazed tiger.

Bloody bitches, fawning over some C-list game-show host as if he was George bloody Clooney. All he had to talk about was his experience on I'm a celebrity get me out of here whereas she had revealed a serial killer live on air. To add insult to injury she had waited in the green room for two hours for after-show drinks but they had all left without her. The anticipated flurry of TV offers had yet to materialise; perhaps she needed an agent? She added Have I got news for you to her list of shows that she would be willing to consider, although that Ian Hislop was annoying.

She ran for the bathroom for the second time that day. As she vomited into the toilet, she allowed herself cautious optimism. She looked at her body in the full-length mirror, her breasts seemed even more enhanced, she viewed her side profile; her abdomen was distended. Although she had only swallowed half a dozen doses, she had put her expanding waistline down to the Olanzapine side-effects, together with the appallingly calorific hospital food. The giddiness and waves of nausea she had attributed to her current 'lifestyle choices'. But the evidence was mounting. She summoned the courage to count her missed periods. Yes, she was pregnant!

She could hardly dare to believe it. For years she had dreamed of being a mother to Savannah, a delicate flaxen-haired girl, joined eighteen months later by twins Josh and Toby. As time went by and she failed to conceive, the yearning became an obsession. The doctor said to stop fretting, be patient and keep an ovulation chart. They were sent for tests - all normal. Ben repeatedly told her "What will be will be". It drove her crazy how nonchalant he was, jollying her along every month as if she'd lost some eBay auction. He even suggested that they get a puppy, the bastard. His desertion was far more than the loss of a husband, it was the forfeiture of potential motherhood, a pain that smouldered and glowed hot when reminded of her childlessness. Now this wondrous gift, recompense for all that she had endured; her just reward.

She could not wait to tell Ludo. He would be a doting daddy, far better than Ben she was certain. Savannah would be his little princess. He would give her anything she wanted, protect her from harm, vet her boyfriends. If it was a boy, he would play football in the park on Sundays, teach him to ride a bike, take him fishing.

She skipped to the kitchen and made herself an espresso. Oh, perhaps she should not be drinking coffee? She poured it down the sink. A cold horror grabbed her. Alcohol, nicotine, Olanzapine, amphetamine, cocaine, and whatever those bastards had stabbed her with that first day in the hellhole. She grabbed her laptop and Googled the effects of the various toxins on an unborn baby. Tiny Savannah had been exposed to the risk of foetal abnormalities, premature birth, restricted growth, learning and behavioural problems. She was a terrible mother. Her hands were shaking, she needed to calm down; one more espresso on top of that monstrous cocktail would not make much difference. She made a fresh cup and checked her Zen calendar. *We begin to die from the moment we are born.* Not helpful.

Ludo suggested that they meet in Starbucks in Marlow; a disappointing venue for her big reveal. She had imagined making the announcement on Ariadne's fore-deck, complete with champagne and canapés, the sun streaming through the soft willows. He told her that he had a morning meeting but would be available for coffee at eleven-thirty. Obviously, once she had divulged her wonderful news he would cancel his afternoon appointments and whisk her off for a celebratory lunch.

The high street was a chequerboard of chic boutiques and charity shops where one could buy a designer gown for two thousand pounds or its previously worn equivalent for fifty. A rash of coffee shops had proliferated between the clothing stores. She had half an hour to kill before their date and the crisp fifty-pound note, courtesy of Ludo's cache, was trilling its fingers from her purse.

I'll give them budget shopping.

A knot-fronted floaty dress in the window caught her eye, very Meghan Markle; ideal maternity wear. Oh, but it was exorbitant, perhaps she could ask Ludo to buy it. She peered further into the shop, a man at the counter was buying a white tuxedo, he stood like a matador. Her heart stopped as he turned: Ludo. Her bewilderment gave way to anger - business meeting my arse. And how dare he buy his wedding outfit without consulting me? What was he thinking? She took a deep breath and kept walking; she did not want her big news marred by ill-feeling. She power-walked around the block, there must be a perfectly reasonable explanation. She was being irrational, that is what pregnancy does to the brain, she should not jump to conclusions or doubt her fiancé. She concluded that her distrust had been seeded in her hormone-drenched mind by Maz's scepticism and all her bloody stupid questions.

By the time she had completed her second circuit Ludo was drinking a flat white and eating an almond croissant.

'Hello there,' she breathed.

'Hello yourself. I got you a mochaccino that's your favourite isn't it?' He pecked her on the cheek.

'Lovely, thank you. So how was your morning meeting?' She had promised herself she would not ask, but the question tumbled out.

'All good, we finished early, deal sealed.'

A wave of relief passed over her. He really was a darling. She told herself not to mention the tuxedo, that could wait for another, less auspicious occasion.

'So, you said you had something important to tell me. I'm all ears.'

The clattering of cups and the gurgle of the coffee machine provided an uninspiring backdrop to her momentous news.

She played with a strand of hair and affected a coy expression. 'Well yes, it is important, just the most important thing in the entire world.' She had planned to spin it out, tease him, make him guess, but she just could not wait. She blurted it out with jazz hands, 'You are going to be a daddy!'

Ludo slowly replaced his cup on its saucer and looked at her with blank eyes.

'I know it's a lot to take in,' she gushed, 'but it's true, I'm pregnant! It'll be a Christmas baby. It could not be more perfect.'

He stared at her. She could not interpret his body language; his face was motionless, as if his screen had frozen.

The crash of metal as cutlery was shaken into a draw.

'I know it's a lot to take in,' she repeated.

Silence.

'Please say something.'

'Surely you're past all that? Are you sure it's not the menopause?'

She bit her lip, how had he not leapt up and hugged her? It was hardly the response she had anticipated, but at least the news was sinking in. She paused to allow it to permeate further.

'I can assure you that I have a very long way to go before I'm past all that,' she smiled.

Still no response. She ploughed on. 'So, I thought we could bring the wedding forward, I know we haven't set a date but I want to be married in white, I know you do too, and I can't pull that off if I'm obviously showing, so I was thinking next month?'

He finished his coffee. Now she could sense anger, suppressed, seething anger. Her eyes pricked with tears.

'Are you off your head?' He hissed. 'Who said anything about getting married? I bet you are not even pregnant. You're trying to trap me.'

'You asked me, remember? Down on one knee and I said yes.'

They were now attracting glances from neighbouring tables.

'You can't possibly have thought I was being serious. I was jammed. This is an open relationship, you know that. If there is a baby, what makes you think it's mine?'

The café grew quiet, the glances turned to open-mouthed stares. Jo stood up with all the dignity she could muster, slapped him hard across the cheek and walked out to spontaneous applause from four women in the window seat.

Back home Jo registered a sharp burning in her chest, she imagined Ludo stubbing out his cigarette in the ashtray of her heart.

She took two Gaviscon and felt a little better. How could she have been so stupid? No, wait, what did Dr Randy Biarritz, M.D. say in *Learning to Love Yourself*? Reframe those downer questions. The much-visited palace of self-reproach is not a healthy place. Place the blame where it truly belongs. Ask a better question. Ah, yes: How did he fool you? She thought for a while. Because he is an accomplished bloody conman that is how, if he can dupe you, he can dupe anyone. Rise above it, like a phoenix. She took a scoop of Ben and Jerry's and turned her mind to the healing power of revenge. It felt familiar, comforting, like putting on a favourite winter coat. She would make him pay, she totted up the bill: humiliation, deceit, exploitation, the destruction of her dreams. There would be many dishes to her banquet, for the first course she would dob him in to the police. Discovering the stash of cocaine would be a good day's work for John Appleton and one good turn deserves another, win-win.

The wasps were rising and they had a new smarter queen.

40

Clara accepted Pia's help to dress, the loss of independence was unsettling, foreshadowing her future.

De-crep-i-tude. The worm stressed every syllable.

She sat obediently by her bed in a grey wheelchair, ready to be collected. Her mobile rang; Phineas saying hold fire, there had been a change of plan. It appeared that the police cordon had been removed but that the media carnival had yet to leave town. Trailers, catering and production vans had turned Penns Lane into a low-budget film set. Plan B was to stay with the Cuviers, to where he had already decamped. But there would be a delay; Hen had been restocking the bird feeders and tripped over a tub of fat-balls. Phineas would take her to the Minor Injuries Unit and would collect Clara on their way back.

The reptile flashed a watery smile as she informed her that her bed was now formally vacated; she would have to wait in the waiting room.

'It's remarkably well named,' said Clara.

The reptile looked blank. Pia wheeled her through apologising profusely and they hugged goodbye. She would miss her.

The waiting room was bleak. A cavernous space that managed to instil an air of claustrophobia. She had been fortunate in avoiding the need for hospital care for most of her life. Her last admission was Phineas' birth twenty-eight years ago. She recalled being trundled from the labour room down these same corridors, a tiny boy as yet unnamed, swaddled in her arms. Five pounds eleven ounces, nothing but a skinned rabbit the midwife told her. Her beautiful son. It was a Wednesday afternoon, she had wondered what Padraig was doing at that precise moment, perhaps running a neurology clinic, writing a paper, giving a lecture. She imagined transmitting the news across the Irish Sea, perhaps he would feel a shift, somewhere deep within his cells his DNA would be celebrating. Unimaginable that a conspiracy of circumstances on the journey to meet his first-born son would result in his death. She looked around the waiting room at the sick and the lame and the injured; staying alive was a series of near misses. She must tell Phineas.

Orwell's *Coming Up For Air* was in the bottom of her tightly packed bag so she decided against. She scanned the walls hungry for distraction. The stark paint was interrupted by the occasional tattered poster informing one *How to look after your heart* or illustrating the first grim signs of skin cancer. She remembered putting up Labour party posters in her waiting room in a bout of enthusiasm during the 1997 election campaign. The Practice Manager had been incensed, they were meant to be non-partisan, he told her to take them down. She had made the point that without Bevan there would be no NHS, that had shut him up for a while. She looked at the stressed staff, the faces of despondent patients, the running banner announcing a current waiting time of two hours. Despite that wildly optimistic election anthem, things had only got worse, a total betrayal. She was glad she had not been a politician, what a miserable retirement those in Blair's cabinet must be having.

Her eye was caught by a sheet of paper stuck above the empty water dispenser. Initially she thought it was unnecessary instruction on its use but on closer inspection found it was the first verse of William Blake's *Auguries of Innocence.*

To see a world in a grain of sand
And a heaven in a wild flower,
Hold infinity in the palm of your hand,
And eternity in an hour.

Clara imagined an amiable medical student with a rakish sense of humour choosing the verse and she silently thanked them. She tried to recall the poem, something about an owl and a bat, hunted hares and wounded skylarks.

She promised herself she would reread it, perhaps learn it by heart. She was craving mental stimulation. The thought of academic study occurred to her. Maybe the worm was trying to tell her something. Her life was by no means over. Since meeting the Cuviers she had realised that she could easily be in retirement for longer than she had worked. She could finally choose another road and she knew exactly where she wanted to go.

Clara faced her opponent across the card-table. Over Hen's shoulder she could see Dolly applying liberal feasts of colour to a sheet strung across the indoor washing line. The pathos of the scene was not lost on her. She imagined that a naïve onlooker would find them pitiable; three old dears, all similarly incapacitated, two in wheelchairs, one in a velvet Bath chair, quietly passing a wet Monday afternoon together. Yet she felt happy, thankful and utterly at home. She nodded her readiness and Hen dealt another five cards. She glanced at them and moved a stack of chips confidently to the centre of the table.

'What a lovely boy you have, he has been such a delight,' said Hen, matching her bet.

'Thank you, he is nice to have around, I didn't realise how much I missed him until he came back.'

'And he is such a help with the ducks, I do not know how father would have coped without him,' Hen added two chips to the pile. 'I do hope he will stay and he is not too bored out here in the sticks.'

'I'm sure he would love to, this is the height of civilisation for Phineas, for both of us actually. Such bad luck you and me both being debilitated but at least we can recuperate together. I'm out.' Clara revealed three of a kind.

She watched Hen display her two pairs, draw in the winnings and deal another round.

'Quite a feat to get through sixty-seven years without breaking a single bone and then crack three of the blighters in a single bound.'

'Metatarsals are tricky little things. They've done a nice job with the cast.' Clara inspected the neat plaster now adorned with a Spotted Whistling-Duck courtesy of Dolly.

'It is going to drive me a bit doolally not being able to tend to the ducks,' said Hen.

'You are looking at upwards of six weeks to heal, nearer twelve until you are fully weight bearing.'

'You'll have to lose some weight dear,' called Dolly, adding a large skull to her design.

Hen raised her one visible eyebrow in mock exasperation.

Clara looked at her new cards: nine, ten, Jack and King of spades, she exchanged the diamond. Hen matched her five-chip stake. Clara threw down her Straight Flush. Hen had one pair. She had never met anyone who could hold their nerve like Hen, she was an inspiration.

'By the way, the inspector called. Good news,' said Clara.

'"An" dear, not "The". An Inspector Calls, J.B. Priestley,' said Dolly.

'No mother, in real life. It sounds like Clara might finally be off the most wanted list.'

'He said they have confirmed my account. They'll be issuing a full apology and a press statement shortly.'

'I should jolly well think so. Outrageous the whole shenanigans,' said Hen wheeling herself over to examine her mother's artwork. Clara could make out a large encircled egg-timer, a skull and the words TELL THE TRUTH.

'Very nice mother.'

'Thank you dear, I'm also working on a design for Boris's portrait. I was thinking of him on a soap box berating single mothers, the crowd made up of his illegitimate children.'

'Sounds excellent,' Hen sifted through the drinks cabinet. 'How is Darwin? Still off his food?'

'Yes, I'm getting a little worried about him, he's been listless, stalking around his enclosure, constant digging, he's become quite agitated poor thing.'

'I have seen that in broody ducks.'

'By the way did a parcel arrive for you?' Clara had noted that the Cuviers tended to neglect their mailbox.

'Not that I'm aware dear-heart.'

Clara went to check and returned with a small package. 'Just a little thank you for putting up with Phineas and myself, I couldn't resist the title.'

Hen unwrapped the leather-bound first edition of *Ducks and How to Make Them Pay*.

'Oh, my word, that is simply marvellous I've always wanted a copy, look mother.' Dolly brought it close to her face. 'I assume it's about duck husbandry rather than exacting retribution,' she said.

Clara smiled. 'It's so great to have friends who share my sense of humour.'

'Right,' said Hen, 'the sun is over the yardarm, snifter anybody?'

'My usual dear. I imagine Clara might want to celebrate after all the brouhaha.'

'Yes, indeed. Whatever you are having.'

Hen produced a bottle of homemade gin and poured three generous doubles, throwing in a dash of Indian tonic water and a thick wedge of lime. She took out a bottle of Captain Morgan in anticipation of her father's return.

'Cheers, here's to the good old boys and girls in blue, they got there in the end,' Hen raised her glass.

Clara savoured the startlingly good blend of juniper and rhubarb. 'To be fair the fires were stoked by Jo Burns-Whyte.'

Charles ambled into the kitchen carrying a box of freshly pulled rhubarb and a handful of tiny speckled eggs. 'Poor Gilly is practically naked she's lost so many feathers.' He poured himself a rum, 'I'm going to have to crochet a little jacket for her.'

'Oh dear, how did that happen?' asked Clara.

'Quail-on-quail I'm afraid. I've separated the bully.'

'And love Creation's final law, tho' nature, red in tooth and claw,' quoted Dolly.

'Which reminds me, my close encounter with death has focussed the mind somewhat. I've decided to do a PhD.' Saying it out loud somehow made it real. The vague idea that had lain on the back burner of her retirement had caught light.

'What a jolly good idea. Do you have a general topic in mind?'

She knew that she could rely on Hen to be unquestioningly upbeat. 'Yes, I've decided on the research area and I have a potential thesis title *The depiction of tortoises, rabbits and monkeys in medieval marginalia 1250-1400.* Now I just need to find a university and a supervisor.'

'Life is a long-time, one might as well make it entertaining,' said Hen, executing an impressive Hindu card shuffle.

'Marginalia did you say? What is that?' Charles poured out a bowl of twiglets.

She appreciated that none of the Cuviers feigned knowledge and were always willing to ask a straightforward question.

'They are the drawings in the margins of manuscripts. I'm

particularly interested in drolleries; humorous illustrations, they tend to feature outlandish creatures.'

'Are they jokes dear?' Asked Dolly looking up from her painting.

Well, they are comedic. Take rabbits for example, they're often depicted wielding clubs or axes. Many are revenge scenes, rabbits spit-roasting hunters for example.'

'Sounds utterly enchanting,' said Hen.

'Right,' said Charles, pulling up a chair. 'Deal me in.'

'So we have all got new projects on the go,' said Hen, taking a hearty swig of gin. 'Did you know the parents have started a branch of Extinction Rebellion in Marlow?

'That's fabulous. Well I'll join, I'm sure Phineas will too.'

'Excellent. I am the membership secretary so I will put you on my list,' said Hen.

Phineas returned from feeding the ducks. With his undercut hairstyle, Rainbow Warrior T-shirt and skinny black jeans he looked as if he had dropped from another world. Clara registered that he had regained a healthy BMI and lost his pallor. She watched him take in the scene: the room strewn with sleeping cats and dogs, the bottles of rum and gin, the poker game, Dolly dressed in a Peruvian shawl finishing her Extinction Rebellion banner. He looked amused. She felt proud of them and of him and of herself.

'This looks like some sort of alternative retreat for old reprobates,' he said with a grin.

'What a marvellous idea,' they said in unison.

41

Walking through the main doors of St Mangabey's as a free woman, even as a single, pregnant, unemployed, penniless one, lent Jo an air of authority. The bag of contraband stowed around her waist a sly delight. No one would dare to search a pregnant woman and anyway a mirror, sugar and a bottle of Malbec was hardly the crime of the century.

Returning to Primrose Ward as a visitor was less triumphant than she had imagined. Despite the visitor lanyard the ward manager treated her as if she had been Absent-With-Out-Leave, he double checked her details with the brusque enmity of US border control. She was told to take a seat outside the nurses' station. The same spot where she had waited on that first day when Eppendorf did not turn up, perhaps on the very chair she had wielded. The thought made her smile. The old lady in the urine-stained nightdress shuffled passed with no hint of recognition, Jo regretted that she did not know her name.

'Hey girl, you back with us?'

'Hi Daniel, great to see you,' it genuinely was. 'No, I'm just visiting Maz.'

'Oh yes, she's back in her old room. She was found mowing a neighbour's lawn at three in the morning. Police picked her up, they were going to charge her with possession of a bladed article but her solicitor argued that it was a robot so she didn't strictly have possession. She refused to give it up, lucky she's a white woman, I would have been tasered,' he let out a Frank Bruno laugh.

'Bless her, she's so thoughtful. She bought me a set of Sabatier steak knives.'

'She cleaned out her bank account in an online spree, bought me a plane ticket to Jamaica. It's a shame I'm detained, I don't have a passport and I don't fly no more; God's babies get seriously ionised up there.'

'Well it's the thought that counts. How's Terry, is he out of hospital?'

'He's good. Fractured his brain bone, what's it called again?'

'Cranium.'

'Yes, he's back here, happy as a lark, Tramadol on demand, he doesn't give me none though.'

Jo had missed Daniel's hearty chuckle.

'We saw you on *Loose Women,* we all cheered when you came on. But girl you're barking up the wrong tree with Clara Astrell.'

'You know her?'

'She sat and listened to me on a plane once. The best four hours of my life. I'll never forget her.'

Niki Sookun rounded the corner with a stack of files. 'Hi there, lovely to see you.'

'You too.'

'Looks like you've been busy,' Niki eyed her protruding abdomen.

Not wanting to raise suspicion, she mustered a coy expression. 'Think it might be twins,' she smiled.

'Well congratulations. Maz is waiting in the interview room. You know where it is.'

'Don't be a stranger,' called Daniel.

Maz looked radiant in mismatched florals, her unruly hair sprouting from a bright turban. They hugged under the watchful eye of an affectless nurse. The room was even bleaker than she had remembered, the clock had stopped at four-thirty.

'Hey, saw you on TV. You were fabulous.' There was a wildness in her eyes.

'Oh, thanks. It didn't turn out to be quite what I'd expected,' Jo took a seat, the Malbec resting awkwardly against her stomach.

'The presenters seem great fun.'

'Oh, they're not really my type, a bit shallow to be honest. I only did it to raise awareness of Andrea's case and now the whole 'body in the orchard thing' has been dropped apparently. Anyway, enough about moi, how have you been? I'm guessing not so great.'

'I should have listened to your advice mate. I did take a couple more doses but it crashed me to ground zero and I spent three days watching day-time TV until I lost the will to live. No offence.'

'None taken.'

A clatter of chairs from the day room, the alarm sounded, their sentinel disappeared. Jo took the opportunity to pass the goody bag under the table, Maz quickly secreted the items in her layers of clothing.

'Nurses respond to bells, like Pavlov's dogs,' said Maz.

Jo laughed out loud - something she had not done since their last meeting.

'So, how's it going with Game-boy?' Maz popped a sugar-cube into her mouth. 'Sorry I guess these are for Daniel.'

'They are. Things are a car-crash with Ludo, you were right to doubt him. Turns out that he's a drug dealer, a conman and an absolute total bastard.'

'Sorry mate, that's really rough.'

'Also, I'm pregnant.'

'Oh, Christ,' Maz crunched another sugar cube.

'He was extremely horrible about it, he even had the cheek to claim that the baby wasn't his.' As she spoke a hidden truth hit her.

'What is it mate? You've gone very pale.'

Jo ran her hands through her hair and spoke one word, 'Tim.'

42

One of the many things that Clara loved about the Cuviers was that they did not prevaricate. Once an idea had been deemed 'jolly good' there was no hesitation, no inexorable weighing up of costs and benefits, no wrestling with imagined dilemmas. They just did it. So it was that when she returned from walking the dogs the following Tuesday, the kitchen was full of old people wearing name badges.

'They're a lively bunch,' Phineas whispered. 'Charles did a warm-up, had them all singing *Enjoy Yourself It's Later Than You Think.*'

'We propose that this be a collective, there are no leaders, basically we do what we want,' said Dolly.

'Anarchy?' Asked a hollow-cheeked man in a tweed cap.

'Yes, Ralph anarchy,' said Hen decisively.

The audience nodded in approval. Clara pulled up a chair, she loved them already.

'We do have some initial ideas; mother if you would please?'

Dolly wheeled herself to the flip chart and revealed a large Extinction Rebellion symbol and the words Act Now. 'I propose that we have an activist wing with a focus on intergenerational responsibility.'

'What sort of activities?' Asked a woman from deep within a beanbag stroking Nosferatu, who had become uncharacteristically docile.

'Not activities, Mabel, activism: XR is a socio-political movement that uses civil disobedience and nonviolent resistance to protest against climate breakdown, biodiversity loss and the risk of social and ecological collapse.'

Clara marvelled that Dolly remained so astonishingly articulate at ninety years old.

'Oh, activism, yes count me in,' said Mabel.

'Is anyone else interested? We could organise transport to events and demonstrations, advertise boycotts, that sort of thing,' Hen replaced her monocle and scanned the room.

A sea of hands waved accompanied by a rousing cheer.

A woman wearing a chunky-knit cardigan, and an earnest expression, rose to her feet. 'I would like to propose craft workshops to make banners, eye-catching inflatables and such like to take with us on actions.'

'Excellent idea, like the Trump baby blimp but with an emphasis on climate change,' said Charles.

'Yes, I was thinking perhaps skeletal humans and animals, no offence comrade Clara.'

'None taken. I'd love to be involved; I could help to ensure anatomical correctness.'

'Jolly good idea,' said Hen, rising to the excitement. 'Might I request a placard depicting the head-burying amphibian *Dermophis donaldtrumpi* in remembrance of Andrea Gibbons from the RSPB. It is a perfect symbol for climate change denial.'

'I'm happy to attend protests but I do have concerns about being arrested,' boomed a large bearded man who Clara recalled ran Marlow's post office before it was converted into luxury apartments.

'Bollocks to that,' said the former vicar's wife from Tenbury Wells. 'I'm very happy to spend a night in the cells, can't be any worse than Lilac Springs.'

'Thank you Byron, thank you Cassie, all opinions are valid here, there is no pressure to do anything that one does not wish to do,' said Hen.

'Can we get a pet?' Asked Sylvia, a tiny well-spoken woman wearing several layers of clothing.

Clara gestured towards Betty, Morris, Nosferatu, Blue and the half-dozen cats now scattered around the kitchen. 'Take your pick.'

'How about this little chap?' Said Mabel gently placing Nosferatu on Sylvia's lap.

'Poor Mabel, lost her husband, had to move into Ogden Court,' whispered Dolly. Clara nodded.

'Just a query about the proposed croquet team,' said Byron. 'Will it be mixed gender or boys against girls?'

A chorus of tutting. Dolly cleared her throat, 'I propose that all activities, sporting or otherwise, are gender neutral. To clarify, that means open to male, female, transgender, those who do not subscribe to conventional gender distinctions, those who identify with neither, both or a combination of male and female genders.'

'Seconded,' said Phineas.

The proposal was warmly applauded, Byron looked suitably chastised.

'Right,' said Hen, 'The minibus back to Ogden Court via Lilac Springs will be here shortly. Perhaps we might decide what we should call ourselves. Any suggestions?' With swift agreement The Nearly Dead Club was born.

Tick-tock scoffed the worm from its fissure.

Following the public apology from Thames Valley Police the media cavalcade had moved on from Penns Lane so in theory Clara could return home and come over each day to attend to the wildfowl. But she felt a reluctance. After years of enjoying her own company and seeking solitude she now found herself so at home with the Cuviers that it would be a wrench to leave. Taking over the care of the ducks meant that Phineas could at last go to Dublin to visit Oisin. She had left him to pack, something about him stuffing rolled-up shirts into his rucksack had made her un-characteristically emotional. She told herself to get a grip.

As she filled the hoppers at Long Pond she realised that she was able to identify all fourteen species. She loved the way the Hooded Mergansers raised their crests, bobbing their heads in crazy conversation. There was Harry, a friendly Surf Scoter and Jonah, a Northern Shoveler, so tame she could feed them by hand. She recalled her first trip to the ponds, her inability to process the chaotic scene that now appeared so simple. So many things had changed in the last year. What was that ridiculous rating scale the practice manager had tried to introduce to screen 'ser-vice over-users' and refer them to counselling? The Holmes-Rahe Life Stress Inventory. She calculated her score: Retirement, major illness/nearly dying, death of close family member, unexpected travel, family changes. That list would put her in the high-risk group for stress-induced health problems, yet she felt the best she had been in years. She was content. She expected the worm to fire a mocking retort but it lay silent.

Back in the kitchen, Hen, Dolly, Charles and Phineas were discussing ideas for the first Nearly Dead Club comedy evening. Phineas suggested a 'Doctor, doctor' theme in honour of his mother's comedic double title once she had achieved her PhD. Dolly remembered one from circa 1965, 'Doctor, doctor, I sometimes feel that I'm invisible.'

'Next please,' everybody shouted.

The idea was promptly deemed excellent.

'Doctor doctor jokes actually date back to the third century,' said Clara, taking off her jacket.

'Perfect Reminiscence Therapy then,' said Hen, hooting with laughter. 'I have one; Doctor doctor, I have broken my foot in three places. Well don't go back to those places.'

Clara scrutinised Hen's cardigan, it appeared to have been knitted from Betty's fur. She saw Phineas glance at his watch. 'Are you sure I can't drive you to the airport Phin?'

'No Mum, I'll be fine.'

She sensed a slight tension in his voice and remembered.

'A hot beverage before you go?' asked Charles.

She gave Phineas an empathic look, she knew they were both thinking of his algorithm of the multiple factors that had led to Padraig's death. A brief delay in setting off for the airport, perhaps for one more cup of coffee. Somehow the shared knowledge made it bearable.

'Thank you, a coffee would be great,' he said.

Under the cover of the whistling kettle she whispered, 'Things will get better, or worse or stay the same.'

Phineas grinned and gave her a hug.

A hammering of the knocker set the dogs barking. Hen wheeled herself to the front door and returned with a handsome man holding a large leather bag.

'Clara dear-heart, you have a visitor, would you like to go through to the living room?'

'John, how lovely to see you, I'm happy to talk here if that's okay with you.'

'Certainly, if I'm not intruding.'

'Take a seat old chap,' said Charles, ejecting a fat cat from a chair.

'We're just about to have coffee.'

'May I introduce John Appleton, the officer I told you about who visited me in hospital.'

'Lovely to meet you all.' He stroked Blue who took an immediate liking to him.

The bag was drawing the attention of the animals, even Aunt Jobiska made a rare sortie into the kitchen to stare at the visitor and his strange cargo.

'Either they are picking up the scent of your dalmatian or you have something of mine.'

'Yes, I've come to return Ossy to your safe custody,' he nodded at the bag. 'Perhaps it would be safer to unpack him later.'

'It is kind of you to take the time to bring him yourself. It's ridiculous but I've been worried about him.'

'It's the least I could do. We would also be happy to cover the costs of re-committal.'

'Actually, I'd like to keep him where he'll be safer. He's somehow become part of the family.'

'I'm pleased you said that Mum, I feel the same way.'

'I'm so sorry for the whole debacle. In recompense Thames Valley Police are making a thousand-pound donation to a charity of your choice.'

'Excellent, let's split it between the tortoise sanctuary and Extinction Rebellion, I hope that won't cause any public embarrassment John?'

'Sounds good to me,' he grinned. 'Also, an officer has been allocated to help you should you wish to file a complaint for slander against Miss Burns-Whyte, just let me know.'

'Thanks, but that won't be necessary.'

'Piece of cake John?' Charles distributed his lemon drizzle and poured the coffee.

'Don't mind if I do.'

Charles turned to Phineas, 'Sorry to see you go dear boy, with whom am I going to play Black Jack?'

'You'll have to slum it with Mum and Hen's poker games; besides I'll be back next week.'

'I should really be going home once Hen is back on her feet,' said Clara to no one in particular.

'We've been talking about that in your absence old girl,' said

Charles. 'We have a proposition for you.'

Hen wheeled herself to the table. Clara noted that John, happily eating a second piece of cake, had been seamlessly absorbed into the family scene.

'You know I have always wanted to build a Passivhaus, my eco-pigsty comes close but to really hit the carbon neutral standard I will have to build from scratch. So, proposal: you sell your house, move in here while we build it, you officially become part of the Cuvier-Astrell estate. What do you say?'

Clara looked from Phineas, who held a 'not a bad idea' expression, to Dolly who was smiling encouragingly, to Charles who beamed and to Hen who was waiting expectantly.

'I say yes, what a marvellous idea.'

43

Detective Inspector Appleton met the gelid eyes of Ludo Mansfield across the interview table. He noted a flare of mutual recognition but could not quite place him. He wanted to do this strictly by the book, not least because DCI Wallace was watching from behind the one-way mirror.

'For the benefit of the tape the suspect has waived his right to legal representation at this stage. Please state your full name and date of birth.'

'Ludo Mansfield, twelfth August 1976. The glorious twelfth,' he added as if he were at a cocktail party.

'Constable Beech if you could just run the PNC for previous convictions and aliases.'

'Or you could just ask me,' said Ludo, removing his chewing gum and sticking it under the table. 'Although sure, get the rookie to verify my previous; court dates and disposals are not my strong suit.'

'Well, if you would care to enlighten us on your aliases?'

Ludo sat back in his chair and placed his hands behind his head, displaying his enlarged triceps. 'Let's see now: Hugo Grant, Terence de Caprio, Mateus Damon.'

'Really? What next Brad Pitt the Elder?'

'Mad isn't it? You won't believe the crap those women will swallow. To be honest it's a good screening device, if they buy that bullshit, they'll buy anything, lambs to the slaughter.'

Smug bastard, his glibness was grating. John felt the tug of the suspect attempting to take control. More ego-driven officers might have jerked the hook and reeled him back to the purpose of the interview but he preferred to let them run.

'It seems we have met before officer Dibble.'

'Appleton.'

'I expect you must remember me from the Tracey Taylor trial. A famous acquittal, some might say infamous,' he grinned. 'You lot were gutted.'

Oh God. It was him. His first week in the job, Reading Crown Court, 1998. His role had been to carry the bulging casefiles and the sandwiches and to act as gofer to the detectives giving evidence. The horrible murder of a defenceless young woman. The defendant as cool as a cucumber.

'Jason Loach.'

'The very same.'

Still it haunted him, that lupine whisper in his ear as they left the courtroom. He spoke it aloud, 'Bad girls make good victims.'

'You'd better believe it.'

John felt a pump of adrenaline, he imagined punching Jason hard in the face.

'We all knew you did it.'

'Ah, to feel the power of life and death pulsing through your own hand. Imagine what that would feel like?'

'Strange that I haven't had the pleasure of arresting you since.'

'Well, I don't soil my own patch. It's best to keep moving: London, Brighton, Home Counties, anywhere I can find easy pickings, juicy red apples,' he gave a slow wink.

John fought to remain calm. Heterosexual men could be so revoltingly crass, he pitied straight women.

Constable Beech entered with the PNC printout. John read it without comment allowing his hackles to smooth.

'Impressive huh?' said Ludo.

'Criminal versatility is not something of which I would be proud. For the benefit of the tape Constable Beech has now rejoined the interview.'

He waited for Bobby to take his seat before resuming questioning.

'Mr Mansfield, twenty-five kilograms of cocaine were found in the hold of the boat *Ariadne* moored at Henley-on-Thames. You were arrested this morning onboard that vessel along with a woman,' he consulted his notes, 'Miss Milena Horvat.'

'That is a statement of fact officer. Do you have a question?' Ludo lent further back letting the chair rock perilously on two legs.

'Perhaps you would care to offer an explanation?'

'Of course, Miss Horvat is a twenty-six-year-old show-dog handler from some god-awful hole in Eastern Europe. Willowy, nice arse, jaunty gait. She certainly fits my breed standard.'

His leer made John feel slightly sick. 'I was asking in relation to the drugs.'

Ludo let the chair fall back to the floor. He spoke with the authority of a prosecuting barrister. 'The thing is officer, I'm not the owner of *Ariadne* or of the cocaine. I just happened to be on board my friends' boat with a bit of totty. There is no crime in that,' he smiled.

'The route of the consignment has been traced so we are treating it as a trafficking offence. Fraudulent evasion of a prohibition by bringing into or taking out of the UK a controlled drug, Misuse of Drugs Act 1971 section 3. Class A, with your record you are looking at up to sixteen years.'

A long pause. Ludo picked at his nails. 'I'm sorry officer, did you have a question?'

'I see that your drug offence in 2000 attracted a custodial sentence. It was extended for an inmate assault.'

'The paedo in HMP Bullingdon,' he seemed to puff with pride. 'He ended up like one of those flat fish whose faces have all moved round to one side. A notoriety builder, everyone loves a nonce-beater, even the screws called me Picasso.'

'It seems that you are a dangerous man to know.'

'And I know plenty. It pays to have friends in high places. Knowledge is power.'

'*A plague upon it when thieves cannot be true to one another.* Are you familiar with Shakespeare Mr Mansfield?' He knew he should not play with the suspect but he could not help himself.

'He was a little before my time.'

'Falstaff, *Henry IV Part One*. It's a story about honour.'

Ludo's expression clouded, he exuded malice. 'Maybe honour is important where you come from mummy's boy,' he spat. 'When I was twelve years old I was earning ten pounds a time doing favours for the housemaster and his mates until I discovered less distasteful work. So, don't talk to me about honour.'

'Prison is a young man's game.'

A long pause. John let the tape roll.

'If you let me walk, I'll give you the bigger fish. That will help to keep boss-mummy happy. You might even get a promotion. Twenty years and still a DI, what a disappointment you must be.'

John imagined DCI Wallace concealed behind the screen with a faint smile on her lips. He wondered whether she could see that he had set up the chess pieces and how this creep was moving them as predicted.

'That decision is up to the CPS. It depends on the quality of your information.'

'Oh, you have no idea who I've got for you, he's a real plum. I'll need my whole slate wiped clean for this one.'

'I'll speak to CPS. Better make yourself at home, they never answer the phone between twelve and two,' he looked at his watch. 'Interviewed closed, twelve noon.' He turned off the tape and watched DCI Wallace's silhouette leave the viewing room.

'By the way Mr Mansfield, how did you know Andrea Gibbons?'

'Andrea Gibbons, rings a bell. No, can't place her.'

'You attended her funeral earlier this year.'

'Oh right, I attend a lot of funerals, they're a fertile hunting ground. Great places to meet vulnerable women in need of financial services, a manly shoulder or something a little lower if you get my drift,' he flashed his whitened teeth. 'Bereavement makes women needy and there I am ready and willing to help. The late Miss Andrea Gibbons: so young, so lovely, so many single friends.'

'Thanks Constable, you can take your break, I'll escort Mr Loach back to his cell.'

Beech nodded and hurriedly left the room, perhaps he too felt the contamination of malevolence seeping into his skin.

'And what service did you provide to Miss Gibbons?'

'Strictly financial as I remember. Had a tip off that she landed a nice redundancy settlement. I helped her with her investment portfolio.'

'The money seems to have gone astray.'

'Poor girl was clueless. But as I always say "If they sign on the line, there isn't a crime." I do like a good motto, don't you officer?'

'And Jo Burns-Whyte just another target?'

'Not so much a target, more low-hanging fruit. Turned out to be quite an eye-opener actually, shame she got herself up the duff, she was fun with a capital F. Although I'm guessing she's the bitch who grassed me up.' There was fury in his eyes.

'You really are a snake'

'I prefer to see myself as an entrepreneur, one has to create one's own opportunities,' he gave a disconcertingly mirthless laugh. 'Don't tell me you've never taken advantage of easy prey, all those strung out nurses in A and E desperate for some night-shift distraction. Bet they love a man in uniform.'

'What do you know about the wrecking of Jarrod Soames-Grayling's car? He's a friend I believe.'

'Maybe. I suspect one of his rent boys got a bit antsy. That's what happens when you bring bad boys into a neighbourhood; ram raiding and such like.'

'Thanks for the information.'

'Nothing is ever going to stick without me.'

'It's time we got you back to your cell Mr Loach.'

John dunked a digestive into his tea and reflected on the exchange. He had expected a 'no comment' interview but some cons just could not help themselves. He had met his type before: no conscience, zero empathy, basically the guy didn't give a rat's behind. So what he got was the truth. Maybe not the whole truth, slime like Jason Loach enjoyed conning people for sport but when their game was up they would sing like a canary. The interview and the drugs haul were sufficient evidence to secure a conviction. He would do his best to lock him up this time.

Poor Andrea. Poor Jo. He called her.

'I just wanted to let you know that Ludo Mansfield has been interviewed and remains in police custody, pending CPS decision.'

'Oh John, that's fantastic news. What's he been charged with, drug-dealing?'

'He hasn't been formally charged as yet but we're hoping to get a decision later on today.'

'Oh, I'd love to give you a big reward,' her tone flirtatious.

'I should let you know that police telephone calls are recorded.'

'Spoil-sport. I was meaning to come in and see you actually, I have some more intel that you might find interesting.'

'Not Clara Astrell again?'

'No. Ludo. He doesn't own the boat, he's been squatting.'

'A full investigation is in progress. I suspect there's quite a lot more to Ludo Mansfield than meets the eye, he's not the man he says he is, let's just say that he uses aliases.'

'The boat belongs to Jarrod Soames-Grayling, he's a front-bench MP, in the cabinet, Secretary of State for Justice.'

'I appreciate that you wish to be helpful Ms Burns-Whyte but it would be best to leave the investigation to us. We are well aware of the registered owner of the vessel.'

'I imagine that you are very thorough.'

'Listen, even if we do decide to prosecute, he's likely to get bail, I would strongly recommend that you apply for a restraining order. Given the situation you would certainly be granted a Section five prevention of harassment.'

'Restraining order! You don't know how funny that is given Ludo's proclivities. But no way, I don't need protection from that weasel, more like the other way around. I'm going to bleed him dry, starting with bloody child support.'

'He is a dangerous man Jo, you really need to keep your distance.'

'Perhaps we could meet for a celebratory drink once he's behind bars?'

'That wouldn't be appropriate Ms Burns-Whyte but I'll keep you updated on the case.'

'Bye-bye John,' she hung up.

44

As Clara drove to Penns Lane she ran through the belongings with which she could happily dispense and the necessities that she would collect today. Only three items made the cut: her photograph albums, her rocking chair and her Orwell collection. She parked in the driveway and looked at her house of thirty years.

A comfortable, solid house. She admired the Victorian carved latticework, the bright red front door that she had painted herself, the careful selection of flowering shrubs giving all year colour. The house to which she had bought two-day-old Phineas, the front steps where she had taken his photograph on his first day of school, and from which she had waved him goodbye when he left for Cambridge. The thousands of times she had gone to and returned from work. Yes, it had been a happy house. It had served its purpose. It was time to move on.

The door jammed unexpectedly, she bent to prise out the letters wedged beneath it and scoop up the handfuls of post strewn across the mat: some junk mail, Phineas's *BBC Wildlife Magazine*, dozens of colourful envelopes in various sizes. She carried a batch through to the living room and opened one at random. A card depicting a fluffy white dog running through a poppy field:

Dear Dr Astrell, sending our support and warmest regards at this difficult time. Mr and Mrs Thomas, Atwell Close. Who were they and how did they know that she had been ill? The next card was a sunset over the Dorset coast: *Dear Dr Astrell, you were so kind and helpful when my father was ill and when my daughter had that rash and I thought she had meningitis but it turned out it was only a nettle sting. I know you didn't do it and so do all your patients. Hope it's all over soon. Regards Mary Harrington.*

She looked again at the envelopes; most had been redirected from the surgery address. She opened and read each one, letting the tears run down her cheeks. She counted them, forty-seven cards, all wishing her well, all ex-patients. The majority were sent before she had been exonerated.

Clara knew absolutely that being a G.P. was what she had been destined to be, was all she could have been, a job that she had been good at, a job that she had really enjoyed. A working life well-spent. The worm recoiled. She knew it would not trouble her again.

Clara walked around her house and returned to the living room, she was ready to say goodbye, to start a new chapter. Raised voices from next door. Not the usual children squabbling, but adults. She had never heard Tim and Sally arguing, she suspected that he was a sulker and that she was adept at the cold silent treatment. But it was definitely Tim, she recognised his cadence. The woman was shrill, a pitch higher than Sally. Breaking crockery, then silence. She wondered whether that French-farce staple of holding a glass to the wall actually amplified sound. It did. A woman was crying, Tim's voice muffled, perhaps comforting. They were talking, she caught enough key words to understand the nature of the conflict: Baby, impossible, vasectomy. Oh dear. More crying. Then serious: Ludo Mansfield, Jarrod Soames-Grayling, *Ariadne* moored at Henley, Clara Astrell. Good grief what was going on? Then bizarrely, laughing and the words *Loose Women*. It was Jo Burns-Whyte, and she just knew that she would be wearing the same shade of scarlet lipstick that had adorned her aardvark coffee cup.

She struggled with a dilemma. Whilst deleting his backlog of emails, Phineas had discovered an old message from Andrea Gibbons. Thanks to the trio of exclamation marks in the subject line, it had lain unseen in his spam mail since Christmas. A brief and bizarre message bequeathing Darwin to her favourite pupil and disclosing that "an unforgivable act" was catching up with her.

Clara had wanted to tell Jo but John Appleton had advised her not to communicate in any way to avoid the risk of reigniting Miss Burns-Whyte's enmity towards her. Fuelled by the positivity that emanated from her good-will cards she felt a magnanimous wave of sympathy towards her. The woman clearly had Borderline Personality Disorder, occasionally tipping into acute psychosis, her best friend had committed suicide and now it appeared that she had become pregnant, the baby's paternity in question. Perhaps knowing the reason for Andrea's suicide and for her entrusting Darwin to Phineas would ease the burden. A coincidental meeting at the house of her next-door neighbour would not be breaching police advice. She put her coat on.

Clara knocked again. She could hear hushed conversation, urgent tones. She peered through the letterbox. Tim and Jo were standing in the hall looking startled and flustered.

'It's only me, Clara from next door,' she called through the slot.

'Sorry, I'm busy,' shouted Tim. 'Can you come back later?'

'I've got something I need to tell Jo. It's important. It's about Andrea.'

She watched Jo's swollen abdomen approach the door, her black-smudged eyes squinted through the letterbox.

'I thought your name was Abi,' said Tim.

Jo ignored him.

'Have you come to confess?' she snapped.

Clara could smell alcohol on her breath.

'I didn't kill Andrea for goodness sake, I promise you. I have proof.'

Beyond the layers of volumizing mascara Clara registered Jo's anger give way to doubt.

'Don't let her in, she's dangerous,' called Tim, his voice several octaves higher.

Clara wondered whether he was worried about her finding out about their affair or if he still believed that she had buried the body in the orchard. She chose to follow Jo's lead and to ignore him.

'It's okay Jo, I'm not here to cause trouble, I have something to tell you that might help.'

The door was flung wide, Clara stepped into the hallway.

Tim backed away as if she held a machete. He looked from Clara to Jo and back again. His expression total confusion. 'Do you know this woman from tap-dancing class?'

'What are you talking about? I've never been to a tap-dancing class,' Clara felt like she had stepped into an Alan Bennett play.

She saw his expression change to panic and followed his gaze; Sally and the children were walking up the drive. The little girl with a butterfly painted on her face, its pink and purple wings glittering across her cheeks, the boy wore the orange and black stripes of a tiger cub. Each held a helium balloon in the shape of a farm animal. The sight made Clara sad. Jo walked through to the living room, a strange look of glee in her eyes; it seemed that her need for revenge was not yet satisfied.

She had done her best, a rational conversation with Jo was now impossible, it would have to wait. She turned on her heel, greeted Sally and the children and went back home.

Clara greeted the attendees of the Nearly Dead Club comedy night in full skeleton costume, her old stethoscope around her neck. The living room had been transformed into an operating theatre. Hen - confined once again to her wheelchair following an unfortunate incident involving Nosferatu and a cinnamon teal - appeared dressed as a cuckoo complete with feathered hood, papier-mâché beak and nest. She was partnered by Dolly in starched uniform, as Nurse Ratched. Clara suspected that many who knew Hen from the RSPB, failed to appreciate the Ken Kesey reference and merely assumed that she had come in random fancy dress. Charles, in white coat and surgical gloves, was busy dispensing cocktails from a medication trolley. She studied his menu: Paralyzer, Bloody Mary, Death in the Afternoon, Ward Eight, Corpse Reviver, Painkiller. She opted for a Paralyzer. Clara presented her snacks to enthusiastic applause, she had prepared jars of 'thermometer' pretzel rods, jellybean 'antibiotics' and 'cotton swab' marshmallows. A large bowl of dusted truffles was passed around.

Mabel sat next to her, a Corpse Reviver in her hand and took a truffle, 'I was so looking forward to our demo in Marlow high street, what an awful shame.'

'Are you unable to come?' Asked Clara.

'Oh, have you not heard dear, that rat Soames-Grayling has banned such gatherings, says we are a terrorist organisation.'

'Good grief, well we'll see about that. I might just pay him a little visit.' Clara popped a truffle into her mouth, the bitter flowery taste of the coating contrasted perfectly with the sweetness of the chocolate.

A crash from the kitchen followed by raucous laughter.

'Enjoying the truffles ladies, they are proving very popular,' said Charles.

'What is the white powder? It's very unique.'

'Actually, I'm not too sure, I found a little packet in the annex, rather liked the floral scent.'

'Right, can anyone remember why we're here?' asked Hen, her cuckoo outfit shedding profusely.

'Evolution!' called Cassie, to cries of 'Truth' and 'Preach.'

'Forty-two!' shouted Ralph, eliciting hoots of laughter.

Several guests started up a round of *Always Look On The Bright Side Of Life,* rocking from side to side, their arms held out crucifixion style. Hen managed to steer them towards a round of doctor doctor jokes. As they finally petered out Hen opened the laptop perched on her cuckoo's nest and Phineas joined them from a bar in Dublin accompanied by the Guinness fuelled cheering of a room of happy strangers.

'Good evening from The Temple Bar, I heard that it was time for the best joke winner to be announced so I thought I'd better tell it first.'

A cascade of female laughter.

'Doctor doctor, I keep thinking that I'm a moth. You need a psychiatrist not a physician. I know but I was just passing and I saw your light on.'

An immediate show of hands heralded him as the winner.

Another face appeared on the screen. It took Clara's breath away; Padraig as he had been when they first met, green-eyed, curly hair, a rakish smile. Oisin.

'Hello there everybody,' he shouted in a beautiful Irish lilt. 'Now would you care to join us in a couple of songs?' The living room erupted in excited whoops that echoed those from Dublin. 'The Grafton Street Quitters welcome The Nearly Dead Club, come on and sing along now.'

The screen panned out to reveal a small band sitting in an alcove. Oisin raised his bodhran, his beat picked up by twin fiddlers and an elderly woman on a banjo. The living room rose to its feet, they all joined in a hearty rendition of *Dirty Old Town.* A huge ovation met the end of the song and greeted the start of *Tell Me*

Ma. Random pairs linked arms and leapt in small circles, some impressively jig stepping, others twirling wildly. Charles wheeled Dolly's Bath chair in reckless loops. Clara expertly manoeuvred Hen's chair on its back wheels, she caught a glimpse of Phineas dancing with a tattooed man who appeared to have no teeth. They danced and drank and danced again until the connection failed.

As the last stragglers hoisted themselves giggling into the minibus Clara answered her phone.

'Mum, I know it's very late and you are dressed as a skeleton, but I wanted to tell you something amazing,' Phineas was evidently drunk.

'Go on.'

'So, you know that Oisin said that there was something for me from dad, well turns out there are two things. They retrieved the present; it was in the glove compartment. Bloody amazing, it's a gold ring, inscribed inside with 'I am beside you'. It has the family crest, all of us sons have got one, you won't believe the symbol, you'll never guess,' a long pause, Clara wondered whether the question was not rhetorical. She could hear a hubbub of conversation and music starting up, must be a lock-in.

'Sorry about that, Oisin's just bought me another Guinness. He's great by the way, I've invited him over, or you could come over here, you'd love it, there's a great museum, it's got illuminated letters, lots of them in the shape of animals like that stuff you like, margins and stuff, drolleries.'

'Sounds excellent, I must visit,' Clara humoured him hoping that he might remember the family coat of arms.

'And we visited dad's grave. It was lovely, we put some flowers down, freesias because I know you like them. I took a photo so you can see it.'

'Thanks love, that's very thoughtful. By the way, what is the Devlin family crest?'

'Oh my God, you'll never guess. It's only a monkey riding on the back of a tortoise, I've no clue why, nor does Oisin, maybe it's a marginalia thing, wouldn't that be amazing, kind of full circle.'

'That really is amazing, that's made my night.'

'Oh yes, there's something else, the other gift. I've just inherited a hundred thousand pounds, well euros. We all got the same, his four children, we all got the same,' his voice cracked.

'Wow, that's fantastic, I'm so pleased for you,' Clara sensed Phineas' delight emanate from beyond the fiscal to what it really meant to him: belonging.

'I knew straight away what I'm going to do with it, it's something Peter and I have been talking about for ages, but we've never had the money. We want to have a baby, surrogacy,' he stumbled over the word. 'Surrogacy, so the baby would be biologically mine, it's the perfect legacy, that's my amazing news.'

Her eyes welled. 'It's the best possible news.'

45

John Appleton had enjoyed his day off; a picnic with Matt and the boys at the Oxford Arboretum followed by an excellent production of 'As You Like It' in Trinity college gardens. Matt had volunteered to drive so he had indulged in a bottle of Chenin Blanc, a decision he was now regretting. He waded through yesterday's emails, delete, delete, delete. One from the CPS marked urgent.

Shit. A reversal of the decision to prosecute Ludo Mansfield for possession with intent to supply, supplying a controlled drug and permitting premises to be used for supplying. It further instructed that the case be dropped with immediate effect and all documentation forwarded to the Ministry of Justice, care of the Secretary of State, the Right Honourable Jarrod Soames-Grayling. Unbelievable. An obsequious reply from DCI Wallace confirming that Ludo Mansfield had been released. That slime had been back on the streets for twenty-four hours.

The answerphone was flashing. One new message left yesterday, just before midnight.

'Hello, it's Jo.'

Well at least she was okay.

Her voice was crazed, 'I know it wasn't Clara who killed Andrea. I could see the truth in her eyes when I met them through the letterbox.'

He wondered whether she was drunk.

'I've worked out the riddle, by an exhaustive application of logic.'

As the message droned on he sat very still.

'It all fits into place, what you said about Ludo not being who he appears to be, the aliases. It got me thinking, he has monogrammed cufflinks, his initials in gold filigree, expensive, too expensive to replace, so of course he would choose the same initials, LM. Ludo Mansfield, Leon Maynard. Andrea's husband, remember I told you about him? He spent all her money. Boating accident my arse, no he came back to the UK and reinvented himself. He's constantly going to the Caribbean, he still has business interests there, and he was always so reluctant to talk about Andrea. It's him.'

He heard a shift in her voice, the crystallising atoms of hatred.

'He's got her name on his chest, Andi, the penny didn't drop at first, it must have been a pet name. And Andrea's clue, the bird book, it wasn't about the RSPB, it was pointing at him, to the bloody great bird tattooed on his chest.'

A silence, had she hung up? Then her last words, spoken in a detached voice.

'I am Ariadne, I have the ball of thread.'

The phone went dead. The woman was drunk, stoned or psychotic.

He dunked a digestive into his tea, his head was throbbing. He nudged open the window and took a paracetamol. The phone rang.

'DI John Appleton.'

'John, it's Clara Astrell,' concern in her voice.

'Is everything alright?'

'I'm down at Henley marina. I came down to talk to our MP.'

He could hear the wind blowing, the idling of an outboard motor.

'Anyway, the thing is, there's blood in the water, it's coming from a boat. I shouted but there's no reply, all the curtains are closed, no sign of life.'

'What's the name of the boat?'

Even as he asked, he knew the answer.

'*Ariadne*.'

He did not want to see her, what he must have done to her, for blood to stain the deep grey Thames, but he owed it to her to bear witness. He imagined her blood seeping through the fittings, inching down to the hold, pooling in the bilge before finding an escape. Blood in the water, billowing. He radioed the response cars, alerted the crime scene investigators, collected protective clothing and drove, slowly, down to the river.

Three officers were waiting for him on the deck, they had forced entry, surveyed the scene and retreated for air.

'It's pretty grim in there boss, you might want a mask.'

'Thanks guys, if you could seal off the tow-path, both directions.' He watched a young officer on the foredeck hanging over the bow ejecting his breakfast. 'And send him to get the coffees.'

The smell emanating from the cabin conjured an abattoir. DI Appleton pulled on his Tyvek suit and white boots. He took a deep breath of untainted air, fastened his mask and headed down into the galley. A wake of bloody footprints led from the sleeping quarters, stark on the white floor like a children's mystery trail. The blood-splattered door swung open revealing the body hunched in foetal position on the bed. He could just make out a dark plume patterning the bedroom carpet. Blood. The stench was overwhelming. He tightened his face mask and forced himself to enter.

He assumed that she had been shot, he could hardly believe the quantity of blood sprayed across the walls, the ceiling, the carpet wet with it. The blond hair blackened. Her face was unrecognisable. The hilt of a carving knife protruded from the throat, jammed with such force that it pinioned her neck to the mattress. As he grew accustomed to the gloom, he registered the sheets stained black, the muscular torso, the brawny forearms matted with blood, the chest heavily tattooed.

Ludo Mansfield. Jason Loach.

The pool of blood between the legs exposed a wound, he registered an absence, the penis had been severed, it lay discarded on the bedside cabinet like a bratwurst on a butchers' floor.

A woman's voice, 'Hello there, permission to come aboard?'

A cheery CSI officer joined him at the foot of the bed, her eyes drawn to the amputation. 'Someone's been a naughty boy,' she said.

DI Appleton felt a catch of bile in his throat. He watched as the officer took a flurry of photographs, the flash illuminating previously unseen details. The eagle covered his entire chest, the tattoo was obscured by cuts but some words could still be discerned: Andi, Tracey, Abi. A Sabatier steak knife protruded above his left hip like a full stop. He stood back as the cuts formed themselves into a pattern, in large letters, a name had been added. JO.

DI Appleton walked slowly around Jo's maisonette as the officers bagged up potential evidence. He had put out an APB but suspected that she would have fled the country by now. Or that her body would be snagged on the lock gates at Hambleden waiting to be discovered by an early morning dog walker and dragged white and bloated from the river. He hated the thoughts that arose, graphically illustrated, in his mind's eye. The job had hardened him, but still it had the power to shock him to his core. It was damaging, the relentless lack of decency, the mindless cruelty, the grating gallows humour. The reward of the occasional conviction was outweighed by the many deplorable criminals who simply walked. He had listened politely as Wallace hinted that a new DCI post would be becoming available and that his intel on the cocaine organised crime group and discretion over the Jarrod Soames-Grayling affair would be viewed very positively. Even as she spoke, he listened to his gut which spoke with clarity and assurance. He knew that he did not care. He did not want to be a copper anymore.

He looked through the living room window. An uninspiring view of new-build flats overshadowing the 1980s maisonettes, cars parked haphazardly, a spindly tree. Poor Jo. She would have basked in the glory of bringing down a MP, he guessed she was not interested in politics but it would have earned her another slot on *Loose Women*. It turned out that the Honourable Member for Henley-on-Thames had rarely visited his boat, it was purchased as a venue for meeting his tax-deductible rent boys and served as a putative constituency address to secure himself a second home in London. His links to Ludo Mansfield had been indelibly severed. At least with his press leak the bloated toad was going to have to resign.

In the kitchen a half-drunk cup of coffee sat on the counter, scarlet lipstick on the rim. On the window ledge, next to a yellowing cactus, stood a photograph of Jo with Andrea Gibbons in a sparkly top, both held up enormous cocktails and pouted for the camera. A block of Sabatier kitchen knives, two empty slots. She had gone prepared. He imagined her wrapping the knives in a clean tea-towel and placing them carefully in her couture hand-bag, she was smiling.

An officer appeared, a camera around his neck.

'Okay to start in here boss?'

'Yes, go ahead. Anything of interest?'

'You might want to read this.' He handed him a thin sheet of pink paper. 'It was still sealed, tucked inside a bird book.'

It seemed that Jo had missed the letter.

'And we found a list of countries on her bedside table. I did a stint in deportation; given the contents of the letter my guess is they are all places that don't have an extradition treaty with us, Turks and Caicos being a British territory.

John read with a sinking heart.

Dear Jo, I'm so sorry. I was going to start a new life in Venezuela. Who knows perhaps in time you could have come too. But it was all too much to bear. I lost my money. I lost my self-respect. Leon's sister keeps phoning, saying the police in Turks and Caicos have opened a murder investigation. The net is closing in. I could not cope with prison although it's what I deserve.

Live your best life,

Andrea xx

Ps can you finish my bird sightings? Only another ten to go, they are highlighted.

John sighed, it was all too sad. There had been no contact from Interpol, the sister must have failed to convince them, she was probably written off as a nutcase. He turned over Jo's Zen page-a-day calendar: *What you imagine, you create.*

46

Clara fastened her poinciana brooch and counted the Christmas table place settings; fourteen. Last year it was just her and her vacant mother in an over-priced Shrewsbury restaurant. She was enjoying the anticipation of the social gathering, she felt blessed, a new word to describe herself. You're going soft, you silly old coot.

A cacophony of barking and rusty-hinge squawking interrupted her table plan. She spied the culprits through the dining room window, Blue and Nosferatu chasing guinea fowl, several of whom were now perched complaining on the piggery roof. Blue had regained the exuberance of his puppyhood, it seemed that pack membership had rekindled his sense of mischief. George too had relinquished his clinginess, preferring to keep Aunt Jobiska company in the annex; they made a formidable couple. She watched Phineas piling logs into the wheelbarrow, Hen, now ambulant, directing operations as she roared with laughter. Clara guessed it was one of his duck jokes. What was the one he told this morning? A duck stood on the edge of the pavement looking both ways, a chicken walks passed and says, 'Don't do it mate, you'll never hear the end of it.' Hen had howled.

She smiled at Oisin and Dolly, an unlikely alliance, sitting by the wood-burner listening to the boys of King's College choir. Above them Ossy reclined on a high shelf safe from canine interest. Oisin picked up the solo for Once in Royal David's City, Dolly's eyes misting. He really was delightful. The minibus pulled up as a riot of tinsel, reindeer antlers and unfurling party horns announced the arrival of the Nearly Dead Club. Clara went to assist with disembarkation.

'I've just had a call from Cassie,' Dolly told her as they congregated in the kitchen. 'She sends her apologies; she remains detained at Her Majesty's pleasure. The poor lamb was due for release but she hung a banner from her cell window, alerted the press on a prohibited mobile phone and has had three days added to her sentence. She sounded very chirpy though, she asked us to watch in case it made the local news.'

'Christmas is traditionally a slow news time', said Oisin. 'Half the world is on holiday, so there's a good chance of media interest.'

Clara reflected that political wrangling and international hostilities might be considerably reduced if world leaders took more frequent vacations.

'The news is on directly after The Queen's speech,' said Hen. 'Let us start the festivities, I will set the cockerel.'

Peter was dressed in an outlandish gold Santa Claus outfit, complete with faux-fur trim and golden beard. Clara proudly introduced him to the NDC.

'This is Phineas' husband. He works for Greenpeace International, he's just starting a new job in Exeter.'

'That sounds wonderful, but onerous,' said Byron.

'The optimism of the action is better than the pessimism of the thought,' he replied.

Clara directed people to their seats as Charles wheeled through the medication-trolley laden with Secret Santa gifts. Hen appeared delighted with her duck print headscarf, Phineas with his beautifully embroidered cushion featuring a monkey riding a tortoise - the Devlin family crest - the tortoise recognisable as Darwin. He hugged Charles; the only person sufficiently skilled to produce such fine needlework. Clara noticed her son whispering to Peter who nodded in apparent assent. She opened her present, a framed print from the Dublin Book of Kells, the letter C described in ornate Celtic knots, a whippet head adorning each end.

'Oh, my goodness, this is absolutely perfect, I'll hang it with pride in my new house.'

'Any idea when it's likely to be ready Mum?'

'Should be next summer, the foundations are down, it will be fantastic.'

'Perfect, we should be moving into our apartment in January, did I tell you that we decided on the three-bed in the end? Looks like next year will be a major change for all of us.'

She had the distinct impression that he was leading up to something. 'Well yes, I'll be starting my PhD too, it's all very exciting, Dr Loris Madingley from Reading University has agreed to be my supervisor.'

'The strangest thing,' said Mabel. 'I was contacted by a solicitor. He sent me the deeds of a house. It seems that I've been gifted a maisonette by the nurse from Goredale, where my Stan died. She was struck off although I think the doctor was to blame.'

'Well that's lovely, communal living isn't for everybody,' said Ralph.

Phineas rose to his feet and tapped his wine glass. 'Dear friends, I just wanted to say thank you to our fantastic hosts, Hen, Dolly and Charles, for welcoming us all into their home and for this spectacular Christmas feast.'

A round of hear! hears! ricocheted around the table.

'I also wanted to make an announcement. Firstly, Darwin, our tortoise has laid a clutch of eggs and we have renamed her Darwini.'

He waited for the cheerful round of applause to subside. 'Some of you already know that Peter and I have been hoping to become parents. We are delighted to tell you that our dear friend and surrogate, Zahra is expecting our twins. They are due in the summer.'

Hearty congratulations filled the room.

'I do hope you will bring the babies for Christmas next year,' said Hen.

'We need to keep topping up the numbers, we've lost a few this year.'

'Honestly Charles, what a thing to say,' said Dolly.

'Only speaking the truth old stick. To absent friends,' he raised his glass.

'To absent friends,' they replied.

The first course was punctuated by toasts to the litany of those lost: Andrea, Gwam, Padraig, Ted, the list went on.

'If it wasn't for Clara and her Himmler manoeuvre, you'd be toasting me too,' said Charles, 'so here's to my favourite ex-doctor.'

'If Hen had not made me go to the hospital I would also be on the list, so thank you Hen for averting another near miss,' Clara raised her glass, everyone reciprocated.

'And Armands' daughter, cousin and father,' proposed Phineas.

'We danced with them in Madagascar earlier this year,' said

Clara.

'Oh my goodness, did they all die so recently?' asked Mable.

'Well, between 2014 and 2018.'

'Yes dear, very sad,' said Ralph, laying a comforting hand on Clara's arm, evidently accustomed to humouring the confused.

A discordant alarm sounded from the kitchen, Hen turned on the BBC news, the room hushed.

Brief mentions of routine global devastation; Australia was still burning; a deadly typhoon ravaged the Philippines. Then a photograph of Jo Burns-Whyte in combat jacket stared from the screen, her face orange and bloated. Clara and Hen exchanged glances.

'Police are appealing for information as they continue their search for a woman wanted in connection with the murder of Ludo Mansfield, a Berkshire businessman found dead on board a boat owned by former Secretary of State for Justice, Jarrod Soames-Grayling. They are warning that Miss Joanne Burns-Whyte is highly dangerous and should not be approached. Mr Soames-Grayling, who stepped down shortly after the discovery of the body in September, said in a statement from his lawyer that he had never met Mr Mansfield. It is understood that paranoid schizophrenic, Miss Joanne Burns-Whyte, was discharged from St. Mangabey's psychiatric hospital earlier this year, after only two weeks of evaluation and without a formal risk assessment. The BBC has learned that the lead psychiatrist Dr Germane Eppendorf, has resigned pending a full inquiry into the patient's care and treatment. A spokesperson for the Trust offered their sincere condolences to the dead man's family, they said that an internal investigation was already underway and that lessons would be learnt. Dr Eppendorf was unavailable for comment.'

'Is that the woman we apprehended trying to steal Darwin?' Asked Dolly.

'Yes, they seem to have used the police photograph from that very evening,' said Hen. 'Interesting that they did not report that she appeared on *Loose Women* making false allegations against dear Clara.'

Clara smiled to herself, she would not mention the postcard of a tortoise that she had received dated the day of her grim discovery, six words in a neat hand: Sorry, I was wrong about you.

'Good grief, that's the nurse!' said Mabel, somewhat delayed in her recognition.

'There's Cassie!' called Byron.

A photograph of a frail looking woman in a hand-knitted cardigan appeared on the screen to huge cheers.

'Eighty-six-year-old, Mrs Cassandra Fielding, is spending Christmas Day alone in a cell in HMP Eastwood Park, South Gloucestershire. The vicar's wife was arrested for criminal damage after daubing 'Tell the Truth' on the home of Jonah Villainous, Secretary of State for Environment. Mrs Fielding refused a community service disposal and was jailed for fourteen days, making her the oldest female prisoner in the UK. Our Home Affairs correspondent is at the prison. Nick, what can you tell us about her plight?'

The reporter in a camel coat and cashmere scarf, stood in front of Cassie's banner *Extinction Rebel for Life*, hung across the stark brickwork.

'Well Suzanne, this frail lady has been separated from her distraught family over the festive period, they are mounting a vigil outside the prison and have been joined by hundreds of Extinction Rebellion supporters.'

The camera panned out to reveal groups of people with placards, many dressed as reindeer, fluffy seal pups and elves.

'Despite the seriousness of Mrs Fielding's plight, the protest has taken on a carnival atmosphere. People have been arriving all day to offer their support.'

A gaggle of reporters desperate for a Christmas story, had gathered at the prison and were now warming their hands around glasses of mulled wine concocted by the protesters over a make-shift brazier.

'Charles, fire up the Landy! called Dolly. 'We can eat en route.'

The convoy was in high spirits, Clara navigating in the Land Rover, Oisin, Phineas and Peter in their battered mini, the Nearly Dead Club eating their Christmas dinner from Tupperware in the minibus. They briefly rendezvoused at the Northbound Gloucester services to discuss tactics and to change into their Extinction

Rebellion outfits. First worn at a rally against climate change in Hyde Park, the costumes were unexpectedly perfect for a Christmas protest.

The motorcade's arrival at the prison was timed to coincide with Channel Four News Live. They disembarked to cheers from the crowd that had now swelled to several hundred. Clara angled her placard to the camera: *In a time of deceit, telling the truth is a revolutionary act.* The reporter Jon Snow, festive in a Christmas tree jumper, held a fluffy microphone towards her.

'I see you are a fan of George Orwell, what is it that you hope to achieve by coming here today?'

'We've come to offer our support to comrade Fielding and her brave stand to promote the case for action against climate change.' Her voice was strong through her penguin beak.

'And who have you travelled with today?'

'We are a group of thirteen from Berkshire, our ages total over 800 years. We want our descendants to inherit a world as beautiful as the one into which we were born, with a re-balanced ecosystem, fuelled by renewable, clean energy and inhabited by a sustainable human population.'

Her speech was greeted by appreciative shouts and applause from the protestors before they resumed their mass choreographed rendition of *Staying Alive.*

'Would you like a slice of Christmas cake Mr Snow?' Asked Dolly wheeling herself over. She was dressed as a puffin.

'That's very kind of you,' he took a piece and continued. 'Do you think you will be successful in securing Ms Fielding's release?'

'No dear, we are here expecting to be arrested. I'm ninety-seven, I've been on protests all my life and I'm not giving up now.'

'Here, here,' said Hen, lumbering past in her polar bear costume brandishing her *Dermophis donaldtrumpi* placard.

Phineas and Peter set off flares as Oisin beat out a steady march to accompany the Nearly Dead Club as they moved towards the police line. Jon Snow's live commentary adding to the drama.

'A group of penguins, placards raised in Roman Centurion formation, are moving towards the prison like a giant tortoise. It looks as if they are going to try to blockade the gates. The police have been taken by surprise; they are overwhelmed by the number of protestors. Officers in full riot gear are attempting to disperse the penguins, who are refusing to move and have formed a huddle. Oh, my goodness a scuffle has broken out, it is carnage, a baby penguin has been pushed to the ground. The assorted wildlife are still singing and dancing. The arrests have started.'

As the cameras rolled Clara and Phineas climbed unresisting into the back of a police van and waved their flippers for the viewers.

She had never felt so happy.

47

Jo breathed in the crisp mountain air and watched the red sun drop like a stone. She knew that she was safe now, from herself and from others. No one knew where she was, maybe no one cared. The thought delivered an exhilarating freedom. The realisation that she had been engaged to Andreas's husband, that it was he who had killed her, had been too much to bear. She had suffered a derangement, been driven mad by rage and betrayal and a broiling desire for vengeance. It had been a temporary insanity, a moment of madness. Justified in nature if disproportionate in execution. Once she had started a frenzy took over, she could not stop.

She had no regrets, he got what he deserved. The queen was spent, she had felt the drones disperse as she walked away from Ariadne. So good riddance Ludo Mansfield, Leon Maynard, horrible vile maggot of a man, murderer, thief. Sometimes not getting what you want is an amazing stroke of luck. That is what the Dalai Lama said, or was it Sandra Bullock? Anyway, they were right, his death was the satisfying execution of the Law of Karma. In an equally karmic symmetry, she had ended up with the money that he had stolen. Andrea would have been pleased that her inheritance would be used to buy her best friend a condominium and she calculated, five years spending money.

Ecuador was turning out to be the perfect choice. She had known nothing about the place, geography was not a strong suit, but she had decided that a country that sheltered Julian Assange would be welcoming and not ask too many questions. She learnt that by serendipity the nearest islands were home to giant tortoises, some of which might have been seen by Charles Darwin, she felt that was a very good omen.

She ran her fingers through her short black hair, she was a new woman. Shedding the used and abused Jo Burns-Whyte had been a liberation. She had discovered something astonishing, an absolute revelation: life was better without a man, yes, they were dispensable! She had selected her surname from the Quito telephone directory, becoming bored after the first page of A listed surnames she had moved to the Bs and plumped for Banderas, it was easy to remember. Since her reinvention everything had fallen into place, she was learning Spanish, had made new friends and learnt that should the need arise, a British-trained nurse would be extremely employable.

Late evening, her favourite time, she carried her drink out onto the balcony. Although she longed for a glass of Ecuadorian Muscat, she virtuously sipped her orange juice and took in the vista. It was glorious. The twinkling lights of the city, the brightening moon illuminating the Andean foothills, she had never seen a view quite as breath-taking. Melodic laughter drifted up from the ramshackle streets, good natured exchanges punctuated by the tooting of mopeds and battered cars. She could smell her neighbour's cooking, a fragrant stew mingled with the sweet aroma of jasmine. She felt at home, she smiled; it seemed that she had had to travel six thousand miles to find a sense of community. Andrea would have loved it here, she realised with a start that it was a year to the day that she died; she raised her glass, 'To Andrea, friends forever.' There were so many birds, she had determined to learn their names and had even bought a bird book. From her vantage point she could see nightjars and hummingbirds and huge black condors. Andrea was close to her here.

Jo checked on her baby, she was sleeping peacefully swaddled in a soft pink shawl, the most beautiful baby in the world. Five days old. Andrea Epiphany Banderas.

ACKNOWLEDGEMENTS

Thank you to my son Jasper Williams and my sisters Claire Sayed and Bridget Rose for reading the early drafts and pointing out such things as Blue's unwitting change of gender. Thank you to Sarah Burton and Jem Poster for Madingley and more. Thank you to Rebecca Kelly and Patsy Westlake for friendship, encouragement and cake. To Carole Millin for discussions about the Oxford comma. Thank you to Lucie Brejsova and Eammon Ryall for our fabulously inspiring 'three mad writers' Zoom calls via England, France and Brazil. Special thanks to Herman, Paul Brodrick's tortoise.

Cover photograph by Melissa Keizer on Unsplash

CONTACT

Stay in touch:
Join my readers' club to ask a question, receive
news and updates

Visit my website:
https://emmawilliams.online

Leave an Amazon book review

Printed in Great Britain
by Amazon

72469706R00166